TIM PARKS

PAGE PUBLISHING, INC.
New York, NY

First originally published by Page Publishing, Inc. 2016

ISBN 978-1-68289-871-0 ((Paperback)
ISBN 978-1-68289-873-4 (Hard Cover)
ISBN 978-1-68289-872-7 (Digital)

Printed in the United States of America

This book is dedicated to my mom, Mary Parks, who along with Jeffrey Parish and Brett Card have been my biggest cheerleaders in life. Without them, I wouldn't have had the courage, strength and fortitude to have sat in front of a blank computer screen and created something out of nothing.

Chapter 1

For all intents and purposes, I am undead, not quite alive, not quite corpse. The life I have been living is disappearing with each passing mile, and the one I want to live remains a mystery before me.

My head is pressed against the window of the train; my breath, sharp and low, fogs the window, marking time with the sound of the wheels meeting the tracks. I am heading to a destination that is for now, in this moment, punctuated by small pinpoints of light stretching out before me as readily as the infinite blackness.

This seems to be a fitting analogy to my life.

The momentary fogginess of the window reminds me of the early morning mist that greeted me a million years ago this morning. I had awoken in the usual fashion, never suspecting that today would be the day that changed my life forever. Each mile that hurtles me into the dense unknown signifies the years away I feel from the confused sixteen-year-old that I was only a day ago.

I've always wondered where I fit into the scheme of things and why I have always been defined by my sexuality even when I wasn't subscribed to admit to myself that I was and am who I am. I could easily be identified as every gay, if I had ever suspected that I wasn't an island upon myself, always picked last for any sport yet chosen first for a rousing game of Smear the Queer, like so many of my contemporaries I hope to seek out.

Why had today been the cumulative effect of years of self-doubt, shame, and fear that fueled my life for as long as I could remember?

For some reason, *penance* is the word which keeps springing into my mind, a tiger lying in wait pouncing on a beleaguered victim. The full impact of its irony just about makes me laugh. There's a slight tickle in my throat, but the moment passes, and I feel tears well up in my eyes instead. The closest the Dodge family, of which I am the youngest member, ever came to being a religious family was when my grandmother would come to visit us, and church suddenly became a priority. Some of it must have rubbed off on me because I know I am paying for every wrong I have ever committed, and I can add lapsed Catholic guilt to my laundry list of wrongdoings.

I begin replaying an endless loop of how this came to be, me on the ten o'clock train to Los Angeles, a newly anointed runaway, trying to carefully document every instance that has led me here. I am having difficulty finding the thread that will link the beginning to how I ended up like this as I am stuck squarely in the middle of it all.

The conductor announces we are pulling into San Juan Capistrano, home of the famous swallows that return there year after year, while I am fleeing the only one I have ever known. The very thought of home threatens to loosen the levees that I am trying to fortify with nerves of steel. No tears come, though there is a 90 percent chance of rain forecasted for the unforeseeable future, a future that I could not even fathom predicting, which reiterates to me that the past is the key that will unlock the present.

My brain locks on to an image from ten years ago in 1975, when I was just six years old. That is where it had all started on this lazy afternoon, a head full of dreams, a heart full of fear that my secret, which I didn't quite grasp, would be discovered. I sat upon my beige beanbag chair thumbing nonchalantly through a J. C. Penney catalog; I would have to say that underwear models that adorned its men's section were my gateway drug. I could spend countless hours staring at them. And if any members of my family intruded upon my guilty pleasure, I had the toy section, with its offerings of Rock'em Sock'em Robots for the regular boys, earmarked with my index finger.

As I cozied up on my beanbag chair, deciding if I preferred boxers or briefs, a voice reverberated like one hundred claps of thunder. Mom!

"What are you dreaming about, Tiger?" she inquired.

My heart leaped, my index finger lost its place, and the J. C. Penney spilled to the floor face up. The teasing models, obviously happy with their underwear choices, lay face up, grinning ear to ear at my mother, a stark contrast to my terror-stricken face. My mind raced faster than the purported speed associated with a new pair of shoes.

"Oh no, she's on to me!" was what came flooding into my mind. But my mouth took control of the situation.

"GI Joe with kung fu grip," I answered back as calmly as possible.

"We'll see, maybe Santa will bring you one. Have you been a good boy?" she coyly asked.

"Oh yes, Mommy, real good." I answered, convinced that she knew better.

The smirking faces of the underwear models begged to differ. But my mother did not seem to notice. Why should she? I was a very grown-up six-year-old dreaming of the things that all little boys do, of wanting something to play with. I knew that what I had been doing wasn't what my brother would do, further solidifying my role as family pariah. As the youngest, I was the last piece in the family puzzle, and I didn't fit.

But I had gone on with my daydreaming nature, never mindful that the years of keeping secrets would eventually catch up to me in some strange fashion.

A small part of me wanted to lay blame on someone, anyone but me. The first place my mind allowed itself to go fleetingly was to an image of my parents, keepers of the rules, guardians of the misconceived.

"If they hadn't…"

My mind began down the perilous path of blame before feet of reality tripped that thought up.

I would not be lulled into a false sense of security by the slightly hypnotic train sounds when I had stepped on board firmly believing that this was all my doing. The events of the past few days had made that abundantly clear, but I was becoming more convinced by the minute that an impromptu history lesson was in order to help me sort it all out. Closing my eyes, I let the present melt into the past, a kaleidoscope effect of faces that are at first familiar then blur to an unrecognizable entity; the places they inhabit follow suit.

I had journeyed to my local library after school one day about five years ago, scooping up two books on drawing. One was designed for a fifth grade level; the other was a book on the male musculature, which beckoned to me with its promises that I too could learn to sketch torsos in just one month's time. I left the library putting the male torso sketchbook underneath what would be considered a normal boy's sketchbook with pleasant seascapes, cartoonish animals, and bowls of fruit adorning its cover.

I made my way up Arroyo Street, passing houses that looked like mine, save for the different colors; it was as if some architect had three different cookie-cutter shapes in which to create a suburban setting. Add a Spanish tile roof, Spanish street names and, voila, instant suburbia Southern California style.

But as I checked for the umpteenth time to make sure that an errant male nipple wasn't peeking out from under a turtle wearing a derby cap, I realized I was most likely living in a Gay Siberia. I knew from watching *Three's Company* that being gay was wrong, unless you really weren't and just wanted to live with two women and fool the wacky landlord.

Yet it was a crumb of gay sensibility that always left me hungering for more. Unlike my father and brother, in more ways than I could comprehend, I didn't laugh at Jack Tripper's faux gay act.

I knew all too well what it felt like to have to pretend to be something I really wasn't.

I had become all too aware of a group of schoolmates playing a rousing game of soccer on the side street adjacent to our family home that I now stood in front of. Their yelling and whooping echoed off the white stucco, catching in my ear, an anchor of masculinity.

Should I attempt to do what would make my father proud? Join in on a pickup game of soccer unforced? Visions of always being picked last at school for any team sport ran and then tripped through my head just like my athletic abilities.

Maybe I could happily coexist in the sea of Scotts, Steves, Kyles, and Mikes by making this attempt to prove my normalcy. Maybe this would be the make-or-break moment when I decided to conform, to join in. My life was a series of maybes, and I felt like the sidewalk in front of our house served as some sort of crossroads. I wasn't sure which fork to take.

I wanted to remain loyal to my secretive nature and start working on my new homoerotic homework that I had assigned myself. There was no extra credit expected but the unspoken joy it would bring me. So I turned away and made my way to our house, which never felt like ours but theirs.

I was hoping to pass under the radar of my mother, the home-maker, also known as she that waits at home, ready to ply me with chocolate chip cookies in order to find out the secrets of my day. At least she took an interest in me, whereas my father was just someone to point out my faults, never one to encourage any endeavors, save for my feeble stabs at what he saw as masculinity.

My role as the invisible citizen of the family was secured by my brother's belief that I fell out of the norm as standard-issue little brothers were concerned.

Tuning her radar-like hearing, able to detect the slightest vibration on a number of surfaces and situations, my mom called out one of twenty nicknames she had saddled me with since birth. I opened the front door, my Nikes sending out shockwaves onto the marble terrazzo before they were snuffed out in the lime green shag carpet.

"Is that you, Charlie Brown?" she queried as I steeled myself against the aroma of freshly baking cookies. Tasty morsels or torture devices, take your pick.

My voice was stuck in my throat and forever in my head.

Filled with a trepidation so powerful, I realized the one art book in particular I had procured was not tucked away in the safe confines of my notebook. My secret was on display for anyone, including my

9

mother, to see. But for that to happen, I would have to be noticed first.

Now, I know that I attached a lot of drama to the simple task of exploring a new hobby; but I felt for sure that the desire to draw, especially to draw what I clandestinely knew set me apart from any other boys, would only be looked upon as wrong. My world was always black and white, like the pencil shadings in my secret notebook, never affording me any shades of gray.

"Yeah, it's me," I managed to croak out, a dehydrated frog.

"Don't say, 'Yeah.' Say, 'Yes, Mom, it's me,'" she cheerfully called out. Apparently her afternoon coffee was kicking in.

With the meticulousness of any secret keeper, I stuck the "controversial for a ten-year-old male to have in his possession" sketchbook into the regular drawing at a fifth-grade-level art lesson book into my notebook. Had this occurred in a few years' time, I would have been securing the book in a Trapper Keeper of my dirty secret.

Although I knew that what I had hidden away could possibly push me further into the outsider role in the family, I could not deny the palpable feeling of relief when I didn't buckle under the most-likely scrutinizing look I had received from the librarian, her eyebrow arching above the cat's eye glasses that were popular the year I was born. I stood my ground by not giving into her silent baiting and treated the situation like I was checking out the latest Beverly Cleary book about Henry and Ribsy. I remained calm in the aged face of danger, facing up to who I was by denying it.

My mother was a different story. She had an all-seeing, all-knowing quality about her. I was convinced she had X-ray vision looking into the very essence of my being, so just hiding the book under another book would not do. I wished I had held on to my Ding Dong wrapper from lunch; perhaps the aluminum foil would have thwarted her attempts to look into my inner life, the way that Superman's vision was impervious to lead. If she managed a peek into my surreptitious book choice with her motherly superpowers, she would most likely see a hybrid of a kitten with very defined pecs transposed in her third eye's mind.

"You're a little late today." She waited a beat then went on. "Did you stop by the library?"

Her uncanny knack for unearthing the truth was only matched by her matriarchal poker face, which gave away nothing. Did the librarian call my mom and inquire as to why I might want to check out such an obvious homosexual behavior manifesto? Or was the fear of being found out radiating off me, red-hot waves of the sun setting on my inner most desires?

Kate Dodge lorded over a cooling cookie tray of chocolate chip confections as if to illustrate the point further, that it's not nice to fool Mother Nature. Her face, flanked by Miss Clairol blonde and bestowed with two of the bluest eyes God ever dared to create, remained unreadable, controlled, and beautiful.

As forceful as a quiet storm could muster, my mother's voice sliced like the blade of a butter knife through my silence.

"Henry Dodge, will you stop daydreaming long enough to answer my question?"

She knew I was a daydreamer. Within the realm of the imagined, the maybes, the should-have-beens, and might-never-bes, she and I were very much alike. I would often walk into any given room (usually it was the kitchen) and find her with a faraway look in her eyes. An inherently sad, unmistakable resolve that this was her life, taken with each deeply sighed breath inhaling vaporous ghosts of dreams and wishes gone and exhaling the solid reality of what her life had become. She would immediately perk up whenever she knew she'd been spotted in reverie, mentally infusing herself with the endless stream of caffeine she barraged her body with.

"Yes, I did," I finally spat out, not with venom, but with as much sugar as was poured into her "We have ways of making you talk" Toll House cookies.

"Did you get anything good, hon?" She reached out, not only with her mind, but for her afternoon cup of Joe, took a sip. She fixed those eyes on me, waiting for me to tell it true or dig my own grave by my omission.

"I got a book on drawing," I answered. My stomach was flip-flopping inside of me but feeling more like I was wearing it as a fashion statement on the outside.

There it was, simple, to the point, noncommittal. And apparently that was all I needed to say.

"Well, that sounds nice. It's good to have interests, a hobby."

Her eyes changed from steely blue inquisition probes to the welcoming waters I would swim in for support.

"Now go do your homework, sport," she recited in her best June Cleaver–esque voice. "And don't forget to take a cookie." Her beaming smile let it be known that she was sincere, either that or she needed to switch to decaf.

End scene, fade out on Henry Dodge, going upstairs to his room, solitary confinement, his corduroy OP shorts producing a *swish swish* sound, a little extra spring in his Nikes, his secret safe. Can I get a chorus of "Zip-a-Dee-Doo-Dah"? Amen.

With my hush-hush activities undetected, I felt invincible, as opposed to invisible, that I had faced up to a challenge somehow today. I was adamant to hold on to that victorious feeling, unfamiliar as it would be fleeting. The feeling would remain in my clutches only briefly though; life had other things on its mind.

Once at the top of the stairs, I took the necessary right to make my way to the sanctuary of my room. Unfortunately, I had to pass through the hallway lined with my brother John's sports photos, each one a monument to his achievements in normalcy and a further testament to my lack thereof. At age fifteen, John exuded a confidence that shone from behind the glass frames that captured his half smirk, a twinkle in his blue eyes that seemed that to say, "Oh yeah, I'm the shit."

There were a smattering of my pictures, mere afterthoughts of faux encouragement, all featuring different disdained looks of "why am I holding a baseball bat" or "what do they think I am going to do with this ball? I had obviously been forced into organized sports, and it showed in my nonexistent skills. One year of football had been more than sufficient to quell my father's desire to see me as a star quarterback; or as he had overheard another father proclaim, after my umpteenth dropping the ball debacle, "That Dodge kid couldn't catch a cold."

I feared my brother John, but not in the usual "older brother who can kick your ass" way. No, this ran deeper, providing a window into what my world was slowly becoming, his perceptions changed forever about his brother. The term *polar opposites* must have been coined the day of my birth, for it certainly encapsulated the ever-widening canyon of differences accruing between us. Looking at his picture versus mine made it painfully clear that we would never be playing on the same team, yet I wanted to keep him in my corner.

John and I did share one commonality, and that was a deep, abiding mistrust of our father's erratic moods. To John's credit, he did at least put forth an effort to bond with the old man. My brother and father were a team. They would fix our family car together, causing the profanity emitting from the garage to match the pollutants from the exhaust pipe of our "on its last legs" Kingswood station wagon being expelled into the California sky and beyond with their toxicity. Basically, they were two peas in a testosterone-filled pod.

The two held a vast interest in all things military and would even parlay that camaraderie into marathon sessions of playing Risk— even after an incident two years prior where my drunken father had upended the game when John had emerged victorious yet again.

In my father's defense, it probably wasn't easy to think properly about world domination when your blood consists mainly of Budweiser. And I do and don't give either one of them credit for not roping me into playing Risk when it was abundantly clear that I was strictly a Candyland kind of boy. Still it would have been nice to have been asked.

Being that our family was run by a dictator, there was a surprising amount of democracy that was allowed to prevail: votes on nonthreatening issues, such as McDonald's versus Jack in the Box for the dining out experience, or what TV show we'd watch together in a moment of rare family bonding, just four individuals all staring at an image that was as far removed from themselves as possible.

Seeing as El Capitan Dodge couldn't be trusted to operate heavy machinery or play nice when it came time to unleash his spirits, *Hollywood Squares* became a nonthreatening mode of togetherness. Every weeknight at seven thirty, we would collectively lobby our choice of true or false back at such stalwarts as Karen Valentine, Rich Little, and, of course, the incomparable Paul Lynde. He was by far my favorite square with his snarky replies and keen fashion sense. Who could blame a gay in waiting?

And I could relate to being discovered as a secret square, waiting for a blaring alarm to be raised, questions to be answered.

"His leisure suit is neat," I said on one occasion, unaware it was out loud.

In unison, two other Dodge heads swung away from the show in progress and looked at me until I got the sensation of being stared at; my father's focus remained on the game at hand. I felt my face turn one hundred sunsets worth of red before they turned their attentions back to the game-show antics. John broke the silence with an answer of true to some kind of geographic query that Peter Marshall asked of Karen Valentine, which of course was false.

"Jesus Christ, what are they teaching you in school?" Dad bellowed in perfect synchronicity with the next commercial break so as not to interrupt the flow of the game. Once the ads stopped, hocking Prell shampoo and its ilk, the only allowed talking was of the answering kind, only this time Dad didn't expect an answer from John that was a question for the San Diego School Board to be held accountable for and not his fifteen-year-old chip off the old block. If it had been me, I would have gotten the requisite, "Why are you so stupid?"

I needed a plan to counterbalance my unsolicited comment about Paul Lynde's fashions. I selected a tact hurriedly as the commercial break was almost over, and one lucky contestant would be vying for a brand-new Vega!

"That Karen Valentine is pretty," I said. "I bet she's not even wearing her tampons."

These were the noises as follows: a groan from John, who would be blamed for his little brother knowing about tampons in the first place; an audible gasp from Mom; and a "John, what have you been telling your little brother?" from Dad, who looked like he was vacillating between anger and laughter. His face flushed more than usual after a hard day's work for the government, finding relief within the steady supply of Budweiser at his disposal.

What I had meant to say was pantyhose, not tampons. For once I felt camaraderie with my father, if only in matters of being red-faced. The moment passed away into the ethers, assuring its place in the "I need to talk to you" post-TV-watching twilight.

I couldn't concentrate on cash and prizes secured by Fran, a housewife from Chicago. Perhaps my faux pas would finally bridge the gap of fatherly concern that my dad didn't bother to traverse in order to get to know the son I could be. But I didn't bother seeking him out either. His steely exterior, while softened by the effects alcohol held for him, didn't melt the icy regions that remained during the global warming of his rages. I looked away from the television set and fixed my attention on him.

At age forty-six, my father was older than most of my contemporaries parents. His black hair was starting to salt and pepper, the black glasses he wore hiding the only similarity between us, a pair of marble brown eyes. His nightly routine of "cocktail hour" was making its physical effects known. He was developing a beer gut, stretching one of his countless white T-shirts out; he would soon require a maternity lounging ensemble.

While he only stood 5' 10", he was an imposing figure due to his volatile nature. He had silent trip wires coming off him, and you never knew why they got set off. I'd been denied television privileges for one week for the time I thought it was okay to chew Grape Bubble Yum while we sat in our den, the television set bathing us in the rare light of togetherness.

He always knew how to hit you where it hurt, combining obscenities together with a "never treated for Tourette's syndrome" flourish; had they not sounded so out of control would have drawn laughter from John and myself.

But we knew better. We had years of hearing, "Go get me your belt," after something was broken or a command went unheeded. Ed Dodge was a former military man and still expected the troops to fall in line.

The *Hollywood Squares* bid their farewells to Peter Marshall, and Fran, an ecstatic brand-new Vega winner, as I began to say good-bye to my peace of mind. But my father did the unexpected; he silently rose from *his* leather chair and made his way to the bedroom he and my mother shared. He didn't even bother to look in my direction as he passed by.

It was a strange wave of relief that I felt, glad to not be getting chewed out but wondering why I wasn't even important enough to be dealt with. My father must have instinctively known what I would become. I was like a weeks-old kitten that is rejected; I had a different smell about me. Well, my father must have detected a gay smell coming off me that made his ignoring me justified in his mind.

In that respect of hightailing it to our rooms, my father and I were very similar.

I would while away the hours, not so much conferring with the flowers, just finding outlets to quash my loneliness. Much like the Scarecrow in *The Wizard of Oz*, I was awaiting someone, anyone, to happen along and rescue me; unlike him, I wished I didn't have a brain that wouldn't torment me with thoughts that left me questioning myself.

The upswing of this torment was that I could parlay the unspoken into a hobby. The reason I had picked up the book on drawing was to unleash the fantasy life that I kept trapped in my mind, a squirrel chasing itself endlessly until it could roam free on the outside.

I stood at my window, the outsider's poster boy, wishing that the compelling need that I had within me to forgo my homework in lieu of honing my sketching skills weren't pulling me asunder with its riptide intensity.

"I have to do it," I muttered to no one in particular, including myself. "I need to do it."

I knew that if I didn't get the drawing out of the way, I wouldn't be able to concentrate on the very uninteresting reality of math problems.

So I went about my ritualistic practices of preserving secrecy. While keeping an eagle eye on my notebook, I closed my bedroom door quietly so as not to attract unwarranted attention to the fact that I required privacy. I crossed the brown and yellow carpet to my tenth birthday present, a black and white Zenith TV, pulled the knob, and watched an image spring to life as I eased myself in to the beige beanbag chair that allowed me to remain almost unseen on the other side of the bunk beds.

Flanking me on either side were my bookshelves, guardians of the secret. For in a stack of movie-related magazines and comic books is where I literally kept my secret. Squired away from sight within an extra-large comic book edition of *Close Encounters of the Third Kind*, it beckoned to me while the movie's tagline, "We are not alone," held a comforting quality. I knew there were other people out there like me, but I'd never had a face-to-face sighting.

More often than not, the men I saw holding hands on the evening news elicited groans from my father and brother, their utterances of "Goddamn freaks" leaving me to stand in the cold shadows of indifference.

A rerun of *Batman* was playing itself out onscreen. Bruce Wayne, Dick Grayson, and I became comrades in concealing secret identities weekdays at 4:00 p.m.

My sketchbook was really nothing more than a small, ordinary notebook, but somehow the blue-hued cover seemed to shine, a beacon of release. I reached behind my head to retrieve the notebook and explore a new avenue of delight mixed with dread via drawing. But my hand froze as the belief that what I was doing equaled wrong flooded over me, a high tide of doubt that ebbed and flowed throughout my special time alone.

I should be out playing soccer or figuring out why if a train leaving Chicago at 2:00 p.m. and traveling a hundred miles an hour can arrive at a destination faster than train B from Los Angeles traveling at 150 miles.

Instead I wanted to buck the trends of everything I was being brought up to believe in, that I didn't agree with. If it was left up to me, train A would collide with train B, leaving a tangle of twisted metal and strewn bodies, and that gave me the answer I wanted, and I had known the answer all along. I was going to draw.

Gently placing the notebook onto the floor so as not to spill the contents of my true desires, I tried to focus on what Batman and Robin were doing and who today's special guest villain might be. As it turned out, the Caped Crusaders were up against Catwoman, as portrayed by the ultimate in feline dastardly Julie Newmar. It seemed that Robin had fallen into her clutches and was being used as bait to lure Batman into Catwoman's lair. Robin was always being captured, and I hated him for it. I was the one in need of saving, and I would switch places with him in a heartbeat. Besides, I would look really cute in his outfit.

I liked the dynamics of the Dynamic Duo: older man, preferably a wealthy one with a penchant for tights, and his youthful ward who needed a helping hand in being schooled in the fine art of true identities.

This thought, so tangible in my mind, elicited nothing short of a schoolgirl's sigh.

I always liked to do something normal when I drew for distractions sake, whether it was having the television tuned to the same Bat time, same Bat channel, or listening to one of my many Disney records. The current favorite was *Pete's Dragon*. I felt a kinship with Elliot the dragon, who could make himself invisible whenever dicey situations presented themselves. Besides, the soothing strains of Helen Reddy's "Candle on the Water," the movie's theme, helped me to get lost inside the inner world, where I so often liked to reside. In this world, anything was possible, dreams became obtainable, no questions were asked, and I liked Henry Dodge and his family.

There was still the real world to contend with as a kinetic stillness presented itself in my room. Ions, neurons, synapses all firing on full capacity, my brain desperately close to overload, "I shouldn't be doing this," my mind proclaimed. "It's wrong, it's not normal."

I could feel my heart steadily climb upwards, finding a nesting place in my throat. My eyes fixed upon my notebook, unwavering in their pursuit to not let it fall into enemy hands. I wish someone would take it away from me, banishing it forever, this thing that set me apart.

It was my conundrum, my solace, this ritual I put myself through each and every time I delved into the mysterious world that lay before me. In that fraction of confusion mixed with self-loathing, I would find the same end result.

Deciding I had spent enough time tap dancing around the subject at hand, I opened my notebook. The simple scraping of the cardboard-like material against the cover of my ill-gotten gain sounded the alarm that I was about to begin a new exploration, conquering the conflict within myself for actions being taken.

I removed *The Male Torso* from its hiding place, holding it close to my chest, feeling like a teenaged girl who'd just been asked to go steady. Then I held it out at arm's length, taking it all in. The beige cover held at least five different versions of the male form in various poses and really seemed to offset the chocolate façade of my closet door in the backdrop. The breath in my chest seemed to have been happy to just circulate in the upper regions of my lungs. I could not catch a deep breath. I took the plunge into its pages, finally coming up for air.

The sketches within the book made my crude attempts at recapturing the shirtless men I adored (James Franciscus in *Beneath the Planet of the Apes*; Brian Kelley, the dad on *Flipper*; and the penultimate Jan Michael Vincent, to name a few) look like stick figures. I opened up my sketchbook just to emphasize this fact.

Before I could get to the heart of my fantasies born from a fertile imagination and a number two pencil, I had to skip over the requisite pictures I had drawn of puppies, *Star Wars, The Wizard of Oz,* and monkeys so that if my sketchbook ever fell into enemy hands, they wouldn't get to my secret world right off the bat.

My mantra was Death Before Discovery. I would never hide the sketchbook in the same place. Sometimes it was hidden inside the paper sleeve of a Disney record or one of the discarded-by-my-mother *People* magazines that I liked to flip through hoping to catch a glimpse of a star.

I was reminded again of how easy things were for my brother. He had a cache of *Playboy* magazines stashed away in a game he no longer played with, and that my mother never made him get rid of. And if he had been found out with the proverbial shoe on the other foot, he would have no trouble explaining why he had a bevy of air-brushed beauties at his disposal. The reaction from my father would be something along the lines of "Boys will be boys," so would I get a "Boys will be girls" from my mother?

And speaking of John, was it not his unmistakable footfall, loud and hurried, that I heard nearing my bedroom door?

My heart was exploding, threatening to burst out of my chest. The seconds drew nearer to the sound of the bedroom door being opened, ushering in a new dawn, one that I wasn't prepared to deal with. Taking a cue from Batman, and not Robin in this scenario, I scooped up *The Male Torso* and my sketchbook, with all the agility I could manage with shaking hands. But where to put them? I questioned myself as the knob began to turn counterclockwise. Panic overrode fear of discovery, and my brain fired off an answer that coincided with another patented John expression, "Shove it!" And I did, right underneath my beanbag chair, and then sat back down as John made his interloping presence known.

"Hey, little dude, Mom wants you to take out the trash," he reported.

My mother did not have the corner on the dispensing of nicknames. John had her ability to cycle through any number of nicknames at will. Today I was Little Dude; tonight I might be Spaz. The possibilities were endless really.

Being saddled with my old-fashioned name, coupled with who I was, made it abundantly clear I was never going to be or would want to be known as Hank. The parade of nicknames that were trotted out by members of the Dodge clan, even my dad with his pet name of Creep and Twinkie the Kid, were a welcome relief from the constraints of Henry.

Upon delivering the news of my impending least-favorite chore, John vaporized from the doorway, the ghost of secrets kept.

My heart dwelling in my throat, I didn't even bother to respond, even if I could have conjured up any vocal ability. Instead, I sat perfectly still, a deer-in-the-headlights look planted on my face, transfixed by the close call. I exhaled the biggest sigh of relief ever known to man and sat on my secret for a few more minutes, suddenly not envious of Batman and Robin. Keeping a secret identity was a lot of work!

I collected my jangled nerves, happy suburban-boy thoughts, and dragged myself downstairs to the kitchen. Mom was busying herself at the kitchen sink, cleaning off the baking sheets from the cookies. She was just about to utilize them to full fish-stick potential.

I almost never asked, "What's for dinner?" It was too depressing of an answer.

The remnants of her cookie-baking passing of time were still residing on the cooling racks, having yet been transferred to their short-term housing in the R2-D2 cookie jar. Kate Dodge's chocolate chip cookies were a far cry from her interesting idea of what the great American dinner consisted of.

In a word, they were delicious.

And if I'd had my choice between the old Dodge family staple of everything tastes better with Velveeta cheese laid before me on our fine china or several cookies presented on a discarded soiled coffee filter, I'd opt for chocolate chip bliss every time.

"Henry, can you take out the trash?" she inquired of me as I silently obeyed the command.

As I removed the trash bag from the receptacle, a new thought lit up my head with neon intensity. I should rush upstairs and throw my sketchbook away. Then I may have a shot at normalcy and procure a place for being cared about in my father's heart. I could stop being the odd-shaped piece of the puzzle and complete the illusion of the perfect family.

The thought swirled around in my mind faster than Dorothy's farmhouse from *The Wizard of Oz*. I was stuck in the middle of a twister of indecision, waiting to land in the Technicolor dreamscape of Oz, far from the plainness of my own black and white Kansas existence. I wanted to escape from the world I was creating for myself and follow the Yellow Brick Road to different horizons than I was directing myself towards with my sub-rosa desires.

"I have to take out the trash in my room," I said, heading upstairs carrying the plastic coffin, a pallbearer at my secret's funeral.

"Oh, Henry," my mother called out sweetly, "you are such a good boy."

This time I was sure she was lacing her chocolate chip recipe with truth serum. Maybe my mother was brainwashing me into doing my sketchbook in. With one fell swoop, she got me to conform while doing the dreaded chore I was saddled with on top of it.

I hadn't even put up a struggle, taking a page from my mother's book on acceptance and resignation. The mental image of the farmhouse stopped spinning; it landed somewhere between highly and mighty suspicious, just shy of the border of insanity. But was wanting to be similar so crazy? Maybe I needed to stop feeling my stomach tied up in endless knots, providing a hangman's noose from which to swing if the secret got out.

I would deem this internal question with no concrete answer session as queer, if that wasn't a term that I already felt was derogatory. I now had it in my power to change my fate, altering destiny with nothing more than an "out of sight, out of mind" approach. If I didn't have the sketchbook to tempt me, I could be the son, brother, schoolmate that the world expected me to be. I left the kitchen intent on returning to it absolved of any crimes against normalcy.

The lime green shag carpet seemed to be made out of molasses. I could not get to my room fast enough, and it seemed that somebody had already beat me to the punch.

John was emerging from my bedroom. Now the shag carpeting became a tractor beam, the one on the Death Star in *Star Wars*, holding me in place and making escape futile. Help me, Obi-Wan Kenobi, you're my only hope!

Had he found my secret mere moments before I was going to banish it from my life forever? If I had known what irony was, I certainly would have applied the term to this twist in the plot of my life.

I stared intently at my brother. There was nothing in John's hands or in his eyes that said, "My little brother is a rotten little queer." But his mouth was about to spill forth some bit of information to me in this moment of truth.

"Your TV was on kinda loud, spaz," he reported. "I'm trying to do my homework."

With that said, he vanished into his room, none the wiser. I quickly traveled across the lime shag, crossing the border into yellow and brown no-man's-land. I mentally reclaimed the fortitude I needed in order to dispatch of secrets. I beelined it straight for my gayness and scooped up my beanbag chair. I forcefully grabbed the sketchbook so as to not let it escape, wrestled it into the garbage bag along with it all of the feelings of divergence I had ever felt.

Seeing as this was the only physical evidence, as they said on *Charlie's Angels*, I felt that my secret life would come to a quiet and uneventful demise. But I wouldn't be free until this particular corpse was six feet under. I was adamant that this is what I must do, that I must bury these feelings, laying them to rest in peace.

If I could do this, then it would be off to the library first thing tomorrow for *The Male Torso*. Maybe for tonight, I would just leave it under the beanbag chair. Right now I heard its siren's song calling out to me, and I was driven from my bedroom more assuredly than having a horde of demons on my tail.

Determination driving my every step, my Nikes carried me along at a faster clip than I would've imagined for someone not so sports inclined, as was evidenced by the smattering of my been-forced-to-play-sports photos versus John's myriad of being the family jock that adorned the hallway leading to the stairs.

I may have been paying too much attention to these capsules of difference, so much so that as I reached the second-to-last step on the stairs, I lost my footing. The garbage bag and its contents spilled all over the living room rug; a certain piece of garbage landed face up to a particular page featuring a specific scenario I had imagined when I was supposed to be studying my spelling words.

Oh there was a word for this fantasy. It was called a blow job.

It could only spell t-r-o-u-b-l-e for me as my mother was making her way out of the kitchen, drying her hands on her apron. As I had yet to finish my graceful landing, I made every possible attempt to alter my trajectory, landing on the offending piece of garbage that only a half an hour ago had seemed like salvation to me.

My mother called out, shock and dismay evident in the timber of her vocal range, her usually spotless living room strewn with the discarded remnants of Toll House Morsels bags and other assorted trash. But there was one item that had meant to be thrown away forever. I lay on top of it, hiding it in a different venue than I ever thought I would have to do. Kate Dodge surveyed the postapocalyptic *Sanford and Son* scenario that lay across the lime green wasteland before making her way over to me. I had affected a, surprisingly for me, perfect landing. No spasmodic flailing of limbs accompanied my mission to protect my secret at all costs.

Nadia Comineche had nothing on the perfectly synchronized routine I had just pulled off. I had landed a split second before my mother could have laid eyes on my sketchbook, unless her third eye had seen it. Much vigilance was still a necessity.

"Henry! What on earth?" she said with a mix of care and a hint of anger. "Are you all right?"

"I'm sorry, Mom," I said, channeling all of my energy and weight upon my sketchbook. "I'll clean it up. I tripped, that's all."

"Nice going, dork," John bellowed from the top of the stairs, always there in matters that needed a commentator. If he had been there a minute earlier, he would have been left with his mouth agape.

"Who's a dork, now?" I would have shouted that at the top of my lungs, if this wasn't such a clearly defined "keep it in check" moment. But it was what my mother said with her next breath that made me finally feel winded.

"Don't just stand there, John! Help your brother."

While John started in on the cons of enabling me at what was clearly a situation created by my lack of coordination, I lifted myself off the sketchbook, knowing that the outcome of my brother's pointless argument might prove that the third time for discovering my sketchbook could be the charm.

I seized the opportunity of the exchange between mother and son and their lack of focus on me to covertly slide the fortress of my deep-seated desires down my shorts. It scratched at my skin, but as I looked down at myself, I realized that my secret was tucked away underneath my shirt.

I silently began collecting the garbage so that by the time Mom and John had stopped the volley serve of their years-old tennis-match arguing abilities, my mother's case in point would be a moot one.

"John, why are you being so difficult?" my mother asked without the strong-arm tactics of her Toll House henchmen as backup. To which he swung back with an awesome verbal retort.

"Why are you being such a bitch?" he said with the abandon of any rebellious teenager.

Time stood still as John crossed the threshold from being Ed Dodge's understudy to his all-out twin. My father's combination of cuss words mixed with pinpoint accuracy acting as character assassins deadly quick with their jabs that left open wounds were mostly directed towards my mother. His belligerent disdain focused mainly on the woman he had married was fueled by the alcohol he consumed.

"You go to your room!" Kate Dodge bellowed, shattering the glass ceiling of her usual chipper demeanor.

Perhaps she felt she could lash back at John in a way that she couldn't with the formidable man she had promised to love, honor, and obey.

The stricken look on John's face said it all. He had taken on too much with my mother in his attempt to test the waters of how far he could push her. After watching our father do it for years, John must have been shocked by the wraithlike entity that had taken hold of Mom's being at that particular moment.

Without another word, not even a patented "Oh yeah," his standard answer to any given situation, John sulked off to his room, daring to slam the door, the calling card of pent-up emotions at 532 Arroyo Street.

Thank God I was almost done with the garbage detail I had assigned myself. I picked up the last piece, put it into the bag, and made my way out the door before my mother's concern turned into an unbridled attack on my lack of coordination. Or she unleashed the third eye to see what was making me walk so funny.

The sketchbook was pushing into the skin of my stomach, trying to make me digest the power it held over me. I saw fully what this book of the damned had wrought; it had me under a spell that

I must break for good. I was intent on tossing it out, taking a "good riddance to bad rubbish" stance as I drew nearer to the plastic trash barrels purchased at Sears.

First went the plastic bag; next came the removal of the sketchbook from out of my OP shorts. I felt weak in the knees, the precipice reached offering very little shelter should I fall, as the sketchbook became immensely heavy. So many blissful hours were spent drawing in it. Yet the tortured hours I spent worrying about its discovery weighed heavier in my decision-making process than it felt in my shaking hands. Even after witnessing the inadvertent way my secret had already caused a rip in the fabric of family relations, I was still on the fence.

My mother's nickname of Charlie Brown was very appropriate; right now I was being extremely wishy-washy.

The garbage bag awaited, its plastic-lined maw commanding me to make a decision as I stood in the now-or-never moment. My mind assailed me with endless questions, stirring up the waters of Lake Confusion with an approaching storm front. The ultimate question remained: was this something I could do? The catcalls of my schoolmate's soccer game reached my ears as I stood at the threshold of a welcoming world that adhering to a new approach offered.

A single tear formed itself, racing down the freckled plains of my young face, its final destination the garbage bag. I let that lone teardrop dictate what I was sure was my concrete answer, a harbinger.

Conflict gave way to loss, loss to suffering, suffering to freedom as I let the river current switch directions in the course of how my life could be. It was then that I had a very-astute-for-my-age realization: people are meant to live two lives. There's the life that you want for yourself and the one that others wanted you to lead. Seeing as I couldn't meld the two into one, I opted for the latter.

I let the sketchbook fall from my hands into the bag, watching its descent in slow motion, bracing myself against further downpours. The blue cover of the sketchbook shone iridescently through the cheaper-than-Hefty whiteness of the garbage bag. Its glow became heightened in my still not feeling relieved mind. Surely if my mother stumbled upon this garbage bag, the sketchbook would be visible. I reached into the bag, swirled my hand around in the garbage, and procured a shroud.

The Toll House chocolate chip bag was the perfect vessel for snuffing out the neon hues and bold marquee statement of "Henry Dodge is gay!"

Once enshrined in its mausoleum, I tied off the bag, making it harder for the living dead to walk the night and find its way into my room, a bogeyman of unsure fantasies now.

With the round light-green-colored trash can lid in my right hand held aloft like a shield fending off the tenebrous elements that were creeping into the rarely maligned Southern California day, I was ready to cap off my secret wellspring. I sealed its fate, placing the lid down extra hard against any potential staying power my secret may have accrued. I fervently hoped that it would reside in faded memories, until eventually it wasn't even a passing thought.

I walked away from the side of our suburban dwelling feeling like a new boy. Perhaps I would even run across the street and see if I could play soccer, a new sense of belonging propelling me along. Halfway down the driveway, before I could explore uncharted territories, the world stopped. I should retrieve my sketchbook and never look back, just realize that I would never find solace any other way.

I stood still hoping the influx of emotions would subside if I could just wait it out. I looked like a boy robot that had run out of juice to any onlookers that cared to pay attention, so I knew I was safe from the eyes of my family. I rebooted and headed back into the house.

Chapter 2

The conductor's voice announcing that Anaheim was the next stop broke my reverie. I could detect the miles falling away behind me slowly distancing the gap between what had been and what was. Since I was still grappling with what was, I once again settled on what had been.

A singular number, 1978, floated towards me in my mind's eye, and it felt appropriate as I made this great escape. It was the first time that I had ever stood defiant.

The Newmans had held court at 529 Arroyo Street for a little over five months before a job transfer had taken away my very best friend when I was nine. My mother had broken the news that we had new neighbors, and they had twins. I became more than curious than George, the literary monkey that got into mischief due to his appetite to find out why.

I had never known any twins, only Buffy and Jody, who I had spent many an afternoon with on reruns of *Family Affair*. Chris was the boy, slightly gangly with a mess of wiry brown hair and a very noticeable overbite. Kelley, on the other hand, was a demure girl and quite a striking opposite. It was Chris I was obviously supposed to play with, but on the day that my mother had told me to go over and introduce myself, he was off with his father.

Kelley stood in the doorway looking anxious, and I couldn't determine if she was waiting for me to go away or come in.

The next sentence she uttered formed the foundation of our fast friendship.

"Do you like Shaun Cassidy?" she inquired. "My mom just got me "Da Doo Ron Ron." You wanna listen to it?"

"I love that song!" I was trying to keep any telltale swooning to a minimum, certain she sensed something different about me. "Sure, that'd be cool."

I had channeled John Travolta in *Grease*, wanting to be the pantheon of cool. I did not bring forth the spirit of The Fonz. I thought he was a dork, and I already had enough help from myself in that arena.

I found it hard to suppress the shared enthusiasm that Kelley might have for Shaun Cassidy, which was acceptable in her case. Mine would have to be masked, and this was the lynchpin moment where I knew that I couldn't confide my secret to anyone.

Even though Kelley and my friendship took on a "Hardy Boys and the Case of the First Fag Hag" air, I kept mum on our sameness that constituted my difference, especially when I watched *The Hardy Boys* every Sunday night at the Newmans having an inner debate as to which boy was hardier than the other. I usually went with the public perception that Shaun Cassidy was the dreamboat so as not to ostracize the committee in my head. I wanted to be protected yet popular. But I knew that Parker Stevenson could solve the mystery of why I thought he was the cuter of the two any day.

Speaking of any day, that was when a special delivery was destined to arrive in the mail for a certain seen-*Grease*-four-times lad, even though most of the humor went over his head. I had been breathlessly anticipating the arrival of my black iron-on T-shirt with the T-Birds in the midst of performing "Greased Lightning," mouths forever frozen in a moment of song.

Of course, John had ridiculed my choice, asking me why I hadn't opted for a T-shirt emblazoned version of Olivia Newton-John all whored up as Sandy in her skintight black outfit.

But really, what was the lesser of two evils here?

What hoping to pass as heterosexual boy would actually pick a Grease T-shirt anyway? This is where my friendship with Kelley came in handy; she served as an outlet for me. I could skate—or even roller boogie—around subjects that I never dared to mention in front of family members. She was a confidant in all things disco.

If I were to divulge my love of ABBA, KC and the Sunshine Band, Donna Summer, and in particular, the Bee Gees, I would have received what is commonly known as an ass whoopin'. John considered them to be falsetto Antichrists ushering in a dawn of darkness that threatened his masculine musical preferences.

Each day that Kelley asked me if the shirt had arrived was extra painful when it hadn't. I wanted to have it to wear to her roller-disco-themed birthday party, which was fast approaching.

I had actually been extended the invitation by Chris. But by this point in time, the idea of his friendship was a courtesy at best, seeing as I was Kelley's friend. Mrs. Newman even joked that I was Kelley's "little boyfriend," when, in fact, I was nothing more than a girlfriend in sheep's clothing.

For appearance's sake, I did try to strike a balance of time between listening to "Shadow Dancing" over and over with Kelley to reenacting with Chris our favorite scenes from *Star Wars* with the Kenner action figures both of us coveted.

I just felt more comfortable around Kelley in her room, the smiling faces of *Teen Beat* hunk du jours like Leif Garrett silently chaperoning us as we tried our best to master the latest dance moves. With Kelley, our friendship took on a rhythm of its own, to the pulse of a disco beat, and allowed me to be the dancing queen that I knew lived inside of me.

Finally the day came—and with under a week to spare—when I came home from school one afternoon to find a package for Master Henry Dodge. I always thought the term *master* was strange for a young boy to belong to as it exuded power, and the only reference I had up to this point in time was from *I Dream of Jeannie*. Receiving anything in the mail held its own allure, showing me that I was not invisible and an actual like-it-or-not member of the Dodge household.

I tore into the plainly wrapped brown box that held my chance to dress to impress, to be seen wearing…an Andy Gibb shirt! That's right, I was sent the wrong shirt. All hopes were immediately dashed as I watched the sun set on my desire of being a standout partygoer, or would it?

Already the diabolical wheels were turning in my head. I could and would wear the shirt. What harm could there be in the wearing of the Gibb?

"You cannot wear that shirt!" my mother exclaimed as I showed her the mistake that had been made.

She looked as though I were clutching a shirt that was made out of rotten cheese; the pure stench of it was enough to cause the look of disdain evident on her face.

"Why not? I like Andy Gibb!" I gleefully exclaimed, opening my mini closet door a crack.

"Because little boys do not wear Andy Gibb T-shirts." She waited a beat before delivering the hammer-like blow of her next statement, which was phrased as a question, ironically putting my plans in jeopardy. "Why don't you give it to Kelley? Little girls love Andy Gibb." She emphasized the last part almost phonetically.

I felt pangs of regret, instantly sorry that I had revealed something I liked. My notions were quashed underneath the extra emphasis my mother was placing on the proper fashion choices and musical stylings that were gender appropriate, like a Mack truck running over a calf that was already leading itself to slaughter. Granted, my mother was not one to part easily with her four dollars and ninety-five cents. She seemed secretly relieved about the fact that I hadn't even received my *Grease* T-shirt. The next sentence she uttered, returning to the Chipperwa Valley of Kate Dodge, drove the nail into the coffin.

"Besides, we can't send it back. And if you can't wear it, then shouldn't your friend enjoy it? I know, you can give it to her for her birthday!" she said with a mixture of sugar and strychnine.

31

My mom already knew what the outcome of her query would be, as it always was: compliance on my part and a certain satisfaction on hers by having her voice heard for once.

"Yeah, I guess so," I said, trying to look like I wasn't going to cry.

In fact, I wasn't pulverized or compliant. Something in my head switched over at that moment to scheming of a way to make that shirt stay with its rightful owner, all judgments be damned!

"Good, I'm glad you understand," she said, clearly relieved about having successfully shadow danced away from the fact that I would have worn the toothsome visage with no reservations whatsoever.

With her lapse in judgment regarding the statements that iron-ons can truly make behind her, my mother went into the kitchen to scare up some dinner. The happy tune she was whistling faded away as she made her exit along with the need to further explain to the other male Dodges as to why I found it necessary to like something outside of the testosterone-driven norm.

For my mother, it was a closed subject; for me, it opened a door to my first outward act of defiance.

I stood on an island all alone, no one to understand me; only insolence kept me company in that moment until a brilliant retaliatory thought crept into my frontal lobe. There was going to be a showdown at the old roller disco corral, and Kelley, the one person that seemed to receive my wavelength loud and queer, was going to be minus one "I just want to be your everything" T-shirt come birthday time.

I would show everyone, including myself, that it was okay to be an individual—no matter what the cost. My mind reeled, thinking back on the plethora of afternoons I spent with families named Brady and Partridge or a certain scheming redhead named Lucy.

I was assured to come up with a sensational idea. I learned more from television families than I did my own, and television provided a much needed sanctuary from my everyday world that I had now gone from trying to survive in to wanting to conquer it.

Rather than wait until Saturday morning to see if *Dear Alex and Annie*, the Dear Abby of the *Super Friends* set, might on the off chance cover this ground, I hurried for the nearest TV set. The opening credits to *The Brady Bunch* had just ended, and I could tell by the tone of the musical score, which was dour compared to the usual upbeat intro, that this was an episode revolving around Jan.

I could always count on her for a good dose of preteen angst that was on par with what I might be struggling with. Somehow I doubted that Jan had been faced with this. But if she had, Mr. Brady would have been on hand with his infinite fatherly wisdom. Even though I knew he wasn't atypical of real fathers, Mike Brady's perfection resonated with me, especially when my own dad seemed to forget he had a youngest son. I severely doubted that his Cracker Jack parenting skills would be applicable to the knowledge that I was set apart because of who I more than suspected I was becoming.

I could pinpoint any *Brady Bunch* episode within seconds; this was the one where Jan buys the brunette wig to stand out from her blonde sisters. I perked my ears up, intently listening to see if any snatch of dialogue might clue me in to what I should do or say. There wasn't one singular thing that brought about any life-altering revelations. But I was instilled with a certain sense of understanding my dilemma just a little bit better. Although I suspected it would probably not be resolved in a half hour.

Being treated as an outcast is a double-edged sword at best. You yearn for the acceptance of being who you are; not finding it in the structure of family, you look for it elsewhere, wishing that you didn't have to.

The problem with Jan's plan was that she had alerted her family to the intention of donning a dark wig to her friend Lucy Winters's birthday party. I knew that I would have to keep the shirt out of Mom's sights as she was fond of telling John and me that she had a third eye on the back of her head. I would also have to be mindful to not alert the family Doublemint Twins, Tweedle Straight and Tweedle Straighter, that my love for Andy Gibb was higher than a mountain, thicker than water.

I could see the scenario of being discovered playing itself out in my imagination: me locked in my room, police cars rallied in front of our house after my father had called them because there was a suspected queer in the Dodge home. I would clutch Andy Gibb closer to my chest and whisper, "I've got you, Andy. And I won't let you go!"

At that precise moment, a canister of queer gas, which had the opposite effect of its name, shatters my bedroom window. It unleashes a deadly combination of Brute, Old Spice, and Paco Rabanne, making it difficult to breathe, trying to choke the gay out of me. I put Andy in my mouth. That is to say, I used the Andy Gibb shirt as a makeshift hazmat suit. I stand at the shattered window emblematic of the shattered dreams I held in my head. The outcropping glass stalactites catch the colors of the police siren, making rainbows on my ceiling. My father uses a megaphone, even though he was only ten feet down on our driveway and would only require his normal vocal range when he was truly upset.

"Put down the shirt and no one gets hurt! You have no choice!" he bellowed.

The queer gas makes its way to me and ferrets me out of my room, out of the window, and out of my head, where I had gotten my plan for squiring Andy Gibb away from a little girl.

The echoes of my father saying that I had no choice, when in fact I did, served as the catalyst for my plan of pulling the old switcheroo. It was time to make a stand, even one shrouded in a Catch-22 of damned if I do, damned if I don't.

This was my time to shine, to embrace my differences and not let anyone oppress me. I think my mom was right when she told my dad I was too young to watch *Roots*. Anyhoo, this would be easier said than done; there was my mother to contend with and the possible scorn I may be bringing to my own table. I could be the Man of Steel in my head, but the collision of reality versus fantasy often left me bewildered. I had such a clear-cut picture of how scenarios should play themselves out, but more often than not, things didn't go as planned.

But I felt determined that Operation Andy Gibb would be an exception to the rule of my young life as Saturday rolled around in a molasses of anticipation.

First I found a book I had ordered from school through Scholastic Books, one that didn't look too dog-eared. I had an affinity for movie-tie-in books but felt that the possible casualties of giving up *The Shaggy Dog* or *The Wizard of Oz* in my stance of personal freedom would prove too great a price to pay. I opted for a *Hardy Boys* knock-off called *The Mystery of the Green Mist*, seeing as Kelley and I had that in common. Besides, John had made fun of me for reading it.

"There's no mystery about why you stink! It's the Green Mist!" he said, adding a cackle-like laugh for emphasis. With a flourish of pure showmanship courtesy of his waving away the odor hand, he made that story vanish from my reading radar.

My mother had already wrapped the shirt up so that she need not be reminded that she had to diffuse the gay bomb ticking inside her little boy. I incorporated the skill I had acquired from John last Christmas, when it was discovered that my mother's packages were very easy to open and reseal undetected.

I took Andy out and in went the book surrounded by almost a whole roll of paper towels to adhere to the consistency of a shirt. I felt like *Hercules Unchained*, albeit not as muscular, with the mere act of one-upping my mother. She was thankfully off with my father at Sears, where America and the Dodges shop for value.

Deciding not to be too brazen in my wearing of the shirt, I took off my button-down Lightning Bolt shirt, exposing my less than Steve Reeves torso; putting on Andy, although he was a bit tight, was liberation. I hurriedly buttoned up, relishing in the look on my classmates faces when I did my nine-year-old version of Chippendale dancer.

Whether I was aware of it or not, I had enrolled myself in the Academy of the Dramatic Arts, assured to graduate with honors. I grabbed Kelley's present and headed out the door towards destiny, towards my shining moment 'neath the glimmering disco ball.

That spring Saturday held the promise of rebirth not only for flowers but for boys. There seemed to be an extra bounce in my step as I showed up at the Newmans' feeling like one myself.

Mrs. Newman answered the door, ushered me inside, looked frantically at her watch, and bellowed, "Y'all had better get a move on! We're gonna be late gettin' to the roller disco rink!"

She said this in all seriousness, as unaware as the rest of us that in ten years' time, that phrase would nary be uttered in any household in America. Mrs. Newman was at least a good five years younger than the woman who brought me into this world, but that wasn't the only difference.

She bellowed, and quite often, for one thing. She worked outside of the home at a doctor's office. Her most obvious trait was a twang to her voice, snapping each statement with rubber-band fluidity. Kelley had filled me in on its origin between trying to do the Hustle one afternoon not long after we had met.

"Mama grew up in Texas," Kelley reported. "But she and Daddy have lived all over. Me and Chris have lived in eight states so far." Then she preceded to name them off in a jump-rope, singsong voice, "Oregon, Washington, Arizona, New Mexico, New Jersey, Alabama, Colorado, California."

The last bit of information had dangled there, a harbinger of afternoons of me being alone in my room again, listening to the *Grease* soundtrack, mouthing the words to "Hopelessly Devoted to You" and thinking about Kelley.

But in the anxiety-filled spectrum of the here and now, I couldn't wait to see if I could pull this one off. There was also the added anticipation of being able to roller boogie down and strut our stuff that we practiced, sans skates, on many an afternoon. Soon enough, four Newmans and a Dodge piled into a Ford and raced the devil, as Mrs. Newman had put it, to get down to My Boogie Skates.

We arrived at the roller rink with its plain brown façade that belied that magical qualities that were inherent inside, where underneath the dancing lights, the outside world faded away. There were already several of the more popular kids from my class waiting for the Newmans plus their fifth wheel. Chris and Kelley were those kind of kids that breezed into town flaunting a specialty, in their case being fraternal twins, and were welcomed into the immediate fold of popularity. Well, at least Chris was; Kelley was more popular by proxy. And that explained why she had many a weekday after school free to hone and perfect our disco moves that we planned to wow the crowd at My Disco Skates with. Take that, Kristy and Jimmy McNichol!

I could see two of the three Scotts in my class talking to each other, probably wondering why I was there, no doubt. I suddenly wondered if my emergence as a Denny Terrio knockoff would go over so well. I switched the tide of my negative thinking, remembering that I was an uber young activist with a point to make: individuality is in. Mrs. Newman broke my train of thought with a point she'd already made several hundred times in the ten-minute trek to the land of getting down.

"See? I told y'all we'd be late," Mrs. Newman said under her breath, which had taken on the smell that I associated with my father's cocktail hours.

Mr. Newman was a beefy, mustached gent, the embodiment of macho; yet he was a trembling cat afraid of a sudden lightning storm that would emanate from his wife. The Newmans lived in a parallel universe compared to the familiar earthscape of home that I had grown accustomed to, where siblings got along and the father kowtowed to the mother's whims. I secretly wished that I could be adopted by them.

As they entered the birthday well-wishers circle, I stood on the outside of it, observing what it might be like to be popular. There seemed to be some kind of ritualistic behavior that involved high-fiving and speaking in tongues of a California tribe as the chorus of "Dude" sang out.

In the background, Alicia Bridges was extolling the virtues of loving the nightlife; was this my secret cue to unleash Operation Andy Gibb? I was still letting the self-conscious beast run amok in the jungles of my brain. Perhaps I could turn the tide on the way people saw me. No longer would I be the invisible boy who sought shelter within sitcom families and neighbors' homes. No, I could show them that I was capable of so much more, that hours of hard work and literal hustle would make me the envy of this birthday party and beyond! Andy Gibb would emerge from his slumber beneath my "all the other kids are wearing Lightning Bolt shirts this year so I will too" cocoon, allowing me to be the butterfly I had always imagined myself to be. Now that I had perfected the dancing techniques of the day and knew every nuance of the songs that would be played, I could become an unstoppable force to be reckoned with.

It was time to get those skates on. Kelley was sitting next to me, her other friend, Jamie, on her right. We looked just like *Charlie's Angels* in the roller derby episode minus the Farrah hair and the fact that one of the Angels was really a devil in disguise. My heart began to beat harder, keeping time with the music. This was it! While Kelley and Jamie were talking, I made my move, going after each wooden button on my white Lightning Bolt shirt with the tiki hut motif like a madman.

Off came the shackles of fitting in, letting Andy Gibb speak for me, telling this microcosm that I had arrived.

"Okay, Henry, you ready?" Kelley said, turning her attention away from Jamie and on to me.

Her jaw dropped, and my heart raced even faster. If Kelley disapproved or, worse yet, detected this was really her birthday present, I didn't know what I would do.

"Jamie, look at Henry!" she said, pointing at me, as my heart and my stomach started their own familiar choreographed dance routine.

"Wow, Henry, where did you get that?" Jamie inquired as my brain remained unable to process if this was a trap or not.

"Well," I began with a slightly trembling voice, "I ordered a Greased Lightning shirt, and this one came instead."

I left it at that, gauging reactions.

"It's really cool," Kelley exclaimed. "I wish I had one!"

"Well, you did up until an hour ago," I thought to myself, pleased that I had passed muster as Jamie's incessant nodding took on the quality of a bobblehead doll.

As if on cue, "Disco Inferno," my favorite disco song at the moment, came on. It was time to strut my collective stuff and show everyone what I was made of.

When I hit the circular floor, I had an instant realization that roller boogie may not be my forte. I fell twice in a row, unable to get my balance. If it was possible to die of embarrassment, I would have been six feet under. Kelley and Jamie skated away as my "Disco Inferno" was nothing more than a flameout.

I had taken what I thought was a stand, and it ended up being nothing more than a fall. This gave the two Scotts even more reason than usual to laugh and point as they passed me by. I watched in envy as Kelley flawlessly captured the moves that we had spent so much time practicing.

Once again my coordination did not match the lofty ambitions in my head, not to gloss over the fact that I had shame and embarrassment compacted by a sore butt and bruised ego.

I barely stood on the outskirts of the roller rink, watching the other kids and a smattering of adults whiz by me, trying to shuffle myself out of sight. I knew that being different was the way my life would play out no matter how hard I would try to be a part of things.

It was hard enough growing up and trying to fit in with my family, but there was also the world at large to worry about too. And here is the point where the canned laughter from a fake studio audience would interrupt my inner monologue about the cruelty of the life I had been chosen to live. I fell on my butt, laid low, and was unable to make myself get up as the swelling of emotions started their long and steady march inside of my head.

"Fag!" came hurling at me from the left, its hateful power holding me down even more effectively than the self-induced green kryptonite that was steadily invading my being. I couldn't tell who had said it, but I knew that it was definitely directed at me and by a Scott. I mean, come on, who else looked on the verge of tears as Andy Gibb smiled away, unaffected by the damage he had caused?

Of course, if I hadn't worn the shirt that was not strong enough for a little boy yet made for a little girl, nobody would have thrown out that hateful moniker at me. But someone did, and it hung in the air for a moment longer before a "Disco Inferno" snuffed out its life expectancy.

I didn't know what was hurting me more, my pride, my heart, or my butt. I gathered up whatever constituted for dignity in a nine-year-old wearing a pseudo Bee Gee shirt and picked myself up.

My mind was whirling at a faster clip than Kelley on her roller skates. Even though I was not the smash sensation I thought I was going to be, and as the bee sting of fag began to fade away, I felt oddly good for all the deceptions I had to go through today.

If I hadn't skated and fallen on this roller-disco road, I would not have received the lesson of keeping my secret to myself; the thought hit me as hard as my butt had struck the dance floor. I knew that I had to counter the assumption that I was a fag who wore a little girl's shirt and chalk it up to temporary insanity.

I would find a way into the secret society that coveted similarity. Of course, that deep-seated need left me feeling conflicted as the strains of "Get Down Tonight" by KC and the Sunshine Band danced out of the speakers.

A feeling of dread overcame me. This was My Boogie Skates's coveted spotlight dance, where one lucky skating pair was thrust into a literal spotlight and would showcase their signature moves. The spotlight encircled the round floor, searching out the persons that most embodied roller boogie.

I knew that my uncoordinated nature, which rendered me unfit to throw a baseball, catch a football, or to recreate disco moves practiced at length, had rendered me unqualified. The spotlight unsurprisingly glossed over me, but it added insult to my injury just the same.

It then swept past Kelley and one of the Scotts, and like something out of a German Gulag movie, swept back over the two, bathing them in the harshness of unexpected attention. The other skaters cleared the way for Kelley and Scott to perform the moves that I thought were patented by afternoon bonding sessions brought to you by the soundtrack to *Saturday Night Fever*.

As Kelley and Scott wowed the attendees of My Boogie Skates with their preteen showmanship, I watched enrapt for other reasons. This was supposed to be my moment to shine, but instead I had fizzled. Not only had Kelley gone on without me, but she picked up the mantle of popularity by getting down midafternoon with Scott Rainowsky, most likely the one who had spoken the word that I most associated with my feelings about the same sex.

The slap of this betrayal left me to seek out the comfort zone of the shadows. From these murky depths sprang a montage of movie monsters, my fellows in the misunderstood. I was a preteen Frankenstein with roller skates bolted to my feet, an anomaly sought out to be destroyed from the torch-wielding villagers, who could only shuffle away. I wanted to stop barely moving and explain myself to them, plead for an understanding I hadn't begun to fully comprehend myself. As I saw the hate radiating stronger than heat from the torches they held, I knew it wasn't a good idea, and I resumed trying to get away. Before I could do this, they were on me, tearing me apart; my very essence crushed by indifference with my soul now lay bare.

This image reinforced my seesawing commitment to keep my true feelings inside. I was feeling very Olivia Newton-John during the *National Bandstand* scene in *Grease*, when John Travolta threw her aside to win the dance off with Cha Cha. She had been passed over for a more popular choice too.

Well, I didn't need a perm-induced epiphany to know that I needed to change some things about the way the world at large viewed Henry Dodge. Today hadn't exactly helped, but all I could do was try, try again, as the famous saying about not succeeding went.

As "Get Down Tonight" faded into "You Should Be Dancing," I plunked down on a wooden bench, semi-defeated, ultimately hopeful, and slightly less confident that one day I could fit in. My Lightning Bolt shirt sat waiting for me to reclaim it, and I was ready to do just that. I had effectively monitored my male classmates' dress codes in a futile attempt to conform, and this year, Lightning Bolt shirts, corduroy OP shorts, and Nike tennis shoes were all the rage among the popular. Making sure that no one was looking, and I wasn't really expecting anyone to be, I peeled Andy Gibb off my body. If this had been the real deal, I don't know that I would have been so keen to have him removed from my skin.

The trash can off to my right apiece practically begged me to feed it sustenance, and with an unexpected flourish born out of my newfound resolve to fit in, I scored a two-pointer, swish indeed.

As I was remembering Andy Gibb all wadded up in the garbage and my sketchbook buried alive in our trash can, the act of burying secrets brought my trip down roller boogie lane full circle. Six months had now passed since Kelley and Chris's birthday party, and the lingering memory of it still stung a tad.

Kelley and I were never really the same, and inevitably the pair had moved on to yet another state that she could add to her jump rope song, "Alabama!" Yet I remained the same. I tried my best to be included at school; it was as if the image of Andy Gibb across my young boy's chest had left a permanent mark, labeling me a freak, which made most classmates actively avoid me. Their whispers may as well been screams in my ears, their silence towards me deafening, both speaking volumes with their effectiveness.

About a month after the Newmans headed off to the South, the For Sale sign came down in their front yard, and my hopes went up that the new denizens could be the answer to my prayers.

It would definitely turn out to be a case of be careful what you wish for.

Chapter 3

A singular word, a name actually, floated up on ethereal wings: Danny.

I should have known Danny Woodson was trouble the first time I laid eyes on him. The teenager who had moved in with his parents to the Newmans' old house was tall, athletic, and good-looking to a fault. Yet there was something beneath his winsome smile, a hunger that I couldn't quite put my finger on. He was the ideal candidate to awaken the lust I was trying to suppress, if not vanquish, but the tidal pull of his surfer-boy dazzle proved inescapable. I will always remember the first words he said in my general direction.

"Dude, Miss February is giving me a boner!" he exclaimed. "Man, I would give it to her so good."

And from the looks of things, Miss February would have been busy for a few leap years, at least, because Danny was hard-pressed to get his manhood crammed into his tight white shorts that he wore to perfect effect. The contrast of the white shorts highlighting his sun-kissed muscular legs gave me images of the tan line heaven that was hidden underneath.

My eyes traveled over the bulge that was beginning to stretch the fabric in his cotton-covered crotch to its limits. And just like that, the world's youngest size queen was born. I wish I had the X-ray abilities of Superman or Mom; then my racing mind could answer the question of "What does it look like?" The singular and persistent thought bouncing around in the confines of my mind would stop on its one track. Or maybe he'd be willing to show it to a certain excitable blond-haired, freckle-faced young man with an old man's name. Although I was only twelve, I would have been ready to partake had a situation arose, so to speak.

Therein lay my frustration as it began to bubble far below the surface in the guise of red-hot molten-lava lust, which I could not act on for any number of reasons. I mean, who would want to get a blow job from a twelve-year-old? Certainly not the caliber of Leigh McCloskey look-alikes that I wanted to seek out. No, in all likelihood, if a sexual scenario presented itself to me now, it would most likely come from the stranger-danger male that they warned us about in school who would want me to help him find his puppy.

The time that I spent in my brother's green and blue den of masculinity, the Rolling Stones mildly blaring from the speakers, his sports trophies adorning his made-in-woodshop shelf, was interloping at its finest.

I was a sexual spy of sorts, finding out what my brother's friend wanted as a means of pleasure, storing it all away in some mental filing cabinet.

Those times also served as an object lesson in the fine art of disguising my true feelings in order to be a part of while adopting the mannerisms of those I surveyed so as to further build the barrier around my gayness. I protected who I was becoming on the inside so that no one could hurt me. And they included me in their world, taking me out of mine, if only for a while, until I would find myself casting too many sideways glances at Danny. When that moment occurred, both exciting and terrifying, I extracted myself from the room with some feeble excuse.

Once in my room, I would set the caged bird free and fly into the realm of fantasy. However, on this particular day, my mind took a different flight plan into its travel itinerary. Danny had moved into the house across the street, which had been previously occupied by the one and only true friend I had ever had, Kelley Newman. She and I bonded over endless hours of perfecting our disco moves to the strains of the Bee Gees and KC and the Sunshine Band.

Somehow I felt the only dancing I would be doing with Danny would be akin to a two-step with me doing all of the footwork, so as not to be found out by the epitome of the proverbial boy next door or across the street in this case, if one happened to live in close proximity to Mount Olympus, that is.

As it was, I was most likely closer to the seventh layer of hell as my mother delivered a not-so-shocking bit of news one Thursday morning following a Wednesday night that saw John and myself daring to sass Big Ed because we wanted to watch *Real People* and he didn't. The one-sided discussion ended with both of us calling him a dick in unison very far under our breath. But he had been in his usual stupor and well into his cans, so what was dared to even be whispered seemed to register before he threw the TV remote in our general vicinity and stumbled upstairs.

"You will both have to help your father work on the car this weekend." She issued the statement as if she were in a dreamlike state.

I looked dead-on at Big Ed, not remembering if the night before I had confronted a lion or a bear and what the protocol was on making direct eye contact with either animal. His smirk remained unchanged throughout my mother's announcement, and it denoted that he was indeed a puppet master of epic proportions.

In helping Big Ed fix the car, there was an abundance of cussing, deciphering, and hunting down metric sockets as opposed to regular ones and also included the added bonus of pop quizzes on the differences between regular and needle-nosed pliers.

A normal Saturday and Sunday could whiz by me at top speed when I was in the free and clear. But helping out with the car meant a lot of waiting and degradation, all of it unfolding in slow motion so as not to miss any of the subtle nuances of the finer art of automobile repair. Every time I had to run to the Craftsman toolbox, which smelled vaguely like vomit, I would panic, buckling under the pressure of the mental time clock my father had instilled in me to find the nine-sixteenths wrench in both a correct and timely fashion.

I could understand why John had to help him; he was actually adept at being mechanically inclined. And I'm sure he figured a couple days of hard labor on the Kingswood station wagon was enough motivation to turn me into the young man I should be. In actuality, all it did was fuel my desire even further to ferret out my adoption papers.

"And there will be no television for either of you tonight!" My father spoke of this latest wrinkle in the punishment front as if it were the ultimate sacrifice we could possibly make. Well, it kind of was actually.

And from the pained expression on John's face, it looked like he would think twice before rising against the machine again, especially when it meant no Friday night out with friends. For me, it meant I would miss the debut episode of *Pink Lady and Jeff*.

So that night I scoured my bookshelf for something else to occupy my mind. *Then Again, Maybe I Won't* by Judy Blume seemed an appropriate title that encapsulated my topsy-turvy brain. I had already burned through her other books and felt a special kinship with another of her titles, *Tales of a Fourth Grade Nothing*.

As I settled onto my beanbag chair, I became entranced by the book, only pausing every once and again to check the clock or to listen out for the footfalls of approaching parents. The standout portion of the book is when the main character, Tony, has what are commonly known as wet dreams. I knew about scary dreams, seeing as my daytime life often crept into dreamland, where I was always running away from some element of my existence. I got the gist of what a wet dream entailed but wondered why I had never had one. I ended up finishing the book around midnight, just as I was ready for bed and slightly hopeful for what the next day might bring, which of course meant my mom would have to change my sheets.

What the next day brought was school and the quietest breakfast I'd ever had as the fallout from yesterday settled into the soil, waiting to be dug up at some later date; its taint would lay dormant.

The kitchen walls seemed extra white today. Sunlight dazzling in its brilliance poured in through the windows, offering us a clearer view of ourselves. Outside had all of the earmarks of an atypical Southern California day; inside a dark stain ran a silent perimeter check.

Our kitchen, our whole house really, was an analogy for the lives we led with very little change. Sure, Mom every once and again rearranged some knickknack that adorned the shelves above our heads. But it would only be a slight variance of what had already been established, and soon enough, it would be back in the place where it had resided previously. Mom sat at the far end of the kitchen table, coffee mug firmly in hand, the living embodiment of her décor; it could have been any day ending in *y*.

"You know, I've been thinking," Mom began, "what would you boys think if we painted the kitchen? Maybe"—she looked around the room, mentally deliberating the perfect color choice—"maybe a nice yellow. Yes, that certainly would spruce things up, now wouldn't it?"

Neither John nor myself answered; this was Mom's version of rhetorical questions 101. We had learned from early ages that both parents were fond of questions to which no answers were necessary. With only one day and counting until I had to play junior mechanic, I also wondered if I was to become the Michelangelo of Arroyo Street, but not in the manner to which I had wanted to explore my artistic endeavors.

Brother John tensely ate his breakfast, avoiding eye contact with Mom. His anxiety was twofold, heightened by the fact that he had a big test in his history class today. I watched him clench his jaw in between bites of his cereal. School didn't fill me with dread as it did for John, at least on an academic front. I was good in every subject except for math and socializing with the other denizens of Ocean Shore Grammar School. I did have two semifriends, Mike and Kevin, who were also in Mrs. Harris's class and on the same level that I felt I was on in concern to where we fell off the social ladder. We always hung out at recess and lunches, figuring that there was strength in odd numbers.

Tetherball was always a time-honored tradition, seeing as it couldn't get out of hand, like the touch football games that were played by the cool kids with their Nerf footballs. Today would prove to be the exception to the rule as far as the dangers of tetherball were concerned.

The usually abandoned area that kept the three of us entertained at recess saw an influx of activity; a crowd was gathered on the asphalt around the tetherball pole. Figuring some other kid was getting beat up, and that shifted the odds in our favor that we wouldn't, the three of us went to see what was happening.

Of course, it was about Scott R., he of the effortless charm and hateful epitaphs, who had his arm in a cast. Apparently he had been the victim of a skateboard stunt gone awry. The way everyone was fussing over him, you would have thought that he had missed jumping over Snake Canyon on his rocket-powered skateboard by a fraction of an inch.

"Did it hurt?"

"How long do you have to wear that?"

"Can I sign it?"

These questions were voiced in unison and in extreme volume by Loni, Julie, and Stephanie. They were vying for the kind of undivided attention that Scott R. was able to muster.

Like a celebrity of the sixth grade set, Scott R. simply raised his uninjured right arm to silence the masses and to take on their questions one at a time at his own personal press junket. He would simply point to a person from this point on, and they would ask him a question. He would respond in kind, moving on to the next kid— even if they didn't have a question but would then feel compelled to ask one—until he came to my group.

I knew that none of us really had anything to ask him unless it pertained to the secrets of being such a popular and already handsome twelve-year-old. Call it kismet, fate, or just impeccable timing, but the bell rang, ending Scott's question-and-answer session. I knew I would not have been brave enough to ask him what I wanted to know: if he had been the one who called me a fag at Kelley's birthday.

As we all filed back into the classroom, cattle in pursuit of a higher education, I got another brainstorm. I always knew when I got a good idea; you could almost hear the click go off in my head. It always reminded me of Melody's ears wiggling on *Josie and the Pussycats* whenever trouble was afoot.

For once Scott had inspired me, not leaving me filled with revulsion at his seamless dexterity of knowing he was a much-sought-after commodity. If my arm was broken like his, not only would I get out of Big Ed's auto shop, but I might have my time in the spotlight too. And I knew the where and how that my painful attention-getter would take place, right at the spot where Scott had held court at the now-abandoned tetherball pole.

I approached Mrs. Harris's desk mentally prepped to turn my poetic justice into an extra credit assignment.

"Mrs. Harris, I need to use the bathroom," I said, trying to look anxious, like my back teeth were floating. "It's an emergency!"

I added this for good measure; endless days in school had taught me that teachers could not deny a child of a bathroom emergency.

"Henry, you should have gone at recess." She sighed. "But I'll make an exception this time."

Mrs. Harris was an early thirties hippie type who let students be teacher for the day, picking out an arts and crafts project or to choose a story for the class to write. She was probably the sole reason that I had continued drawing after the days of my secret sketchbook had passed as she was always very encouraging about pursuing our passions. But I wondered how encouraging she would have been if she knew the extent of my artistic endeavors of the past.

One of which involved a crudely drawn version of her husband, who would drop by school from time to time, always looking dashing and never exposing the imagined tree-trunk-sized penis that I had drawn behind the barrier of my bunk beds.

I always hoped that having a third eye was not a female trait and that Mrs. Harris didn't notice that I instantly perked up, as if mainlining caffeine, whenever Mr. Harris stopped by. He had a penchant for dressing in tight slacks. He resembled Mark Spitz, all dark good looks, and he sported the ultimate fashion accessory, the mustache, which graced his boyishly handsome face. What I wouldn't give for a sneak peek at him in Speedos; he would win the gold medal for sure in my eyes.

I had to severely chastise myself for wanting to think of Mr. Harris, or other men, in that capacity. Hopefully, Mrs. Harris was seeing the strained look on my face, linked to the inner conflict, as a bigger indicator of a twelve-year-old's regular kind of emergency. She didn't ever seem to be any the wiser to my adulterous intents as I hid behind being a recent Standout Citizen Award winner.

It seemed that Mrs. Harris and other adults always took my mild-mannered façade at face value, like the freckles that lined my face spelled out *trustworthy*. Today did not prove to be any exception to the unwritten rule that Henry Dodge was such a nice boy. Mrs. Harris motioned with her hand for me to go to the boys' room, innocently scooting me off to carry out my latest plan as harmlessly as she would shoo a fly.

The halls were empty; dead silence prevailed where noise reigned supreme at recess and lunchtime. I went in full-out invisible mode, striding confidently over to the tetherball pole. My cry for help attempting to garner attention not only utilized my copycat skills but my high pain threshold from years of feeling the sting of the belt.

I got into the mind-set, conjuring up instances of hurt to counterbalance the physical pain I would be putting myself through. The most readily available image was my father blowing his top. With each one of his cuss words directed towards me, I redirected their route and let them push me forward, smashing my left arm as hard as I could against the cool steel of the tetherball pole. My arm was starting to smart almost as much as the memories that were dancing in my head, like the tetherball would do on each strike of my attack. Back and forth the memories went, to and fro the tetherball swung, until on the fifth assault, and on the mental heels of "You stupid fucking kid!" I reached a snapping point.

My arm was throbbing when I finally made myself stop attacking the pole like some demented parakeet that pecks at its image in a mirror. I had not broken my arm. There was no bone protrusion, but it would need medical attention. I felt somewhat deflated that I couldn't even do this right as I went into the boys' bathroom with its always noxious smell, a combination of rancid meat and disinfectant, to double-check my arm in the mirror.

I needed a cover story for my arm just as I needed one for my life.

Obviously, the truth would hurt me more than the aching that was beginning to rise in greater volume in my arm, which I was cradling like a newborn baby. The overbearing smell of the bathroom, the white tile with little black flecks in its pattern, and the shiny chrome of the urinals handle all collided as I slipped in a puddle of water. It had remained previously undetected as I had tried to think, think, think about what I was going to say. I hit the floor with a thud and conveniently landed on my left arm, problem solved. As I got up, a new dilemma had arisen; the front of my shirt was soaking wet. The pool of water I had slipped in was from an overflowed toilet.

"Oh nifty," I said, using my latest Henry Dodge catchphrase.

Just then Mike came into the bathroom; he had been sent by Mrs. Harris to find out what was keeping me so long. If this had been a true bathroom emergency, and if Mrs. Harris had ever come over for a Dodge family dinner, then she would have known why I might have been gone for as long as I had.

"Henry, are you okay?" Mike asked with general concern, not taking the obvious route to make fun of my soaked from toilet water shirt.

"I need to go to the nurse," I said, affecting my most pathetic of inflections and cradling my arm for added effect.

Mike nodded, held the door open for me, not closing it at the last minute. I was lucky to have a friend like Mike. Hell, I felt lucky to have any friends at all. But our friendship rarely ventured outside of school into the realms of homelife, especially mine.

The outcome of my attention-getting scheme was not all it was cracked up to be. First off, I had only sprained my left arm. Therefore, there'll be no clamoring over who would get to sign my cast first. I had to wear a sling on my arm, which meant I'd still have to act as tool gofer over the weekend. I had planned on going back to school on Monday, wanting to get the lion's share of attention away from Scott, but that hope went right out the window or, rather, down the toilet. What kind of tale could I tell?

"Well, I really thought the tetherball pole would get the best of me," I would start only to cut myself off, realizing this was not in conjunction with the lie I had spun.

"Well, an alligator came out of the toilet. He thought he would get the best of me, but…"

Too bad Sears didn't sell kid-sized alligator boots; dammit, that really would have made my story come alive, much like I had in wanting to be a "real boy!"

Alas, all I wanted again was some peace of mind. And that was not to be had as Saturday rolled around.

I leapt out of bed, humming, smiling from ear to ear. Why, I was the happiest boy in all of the land! Or I pulled the sheets up over my head, hoping not to be discovered and dragged down to the bowels of our garage, unable to protest about child labor laws since I had never heard of any such thing.

"Boys, come on!" my father bellowed from the bottom of the stairs. He may as well have been shouting into my ear. The volume of his woofer and tweeters were set on stun. I tried to imagine that he had only called out the singular *boy*, as in John, and not the plural *boys*, as in me and John.

Big Ed almost never addressed me by name; more often than not I was Little Creep or "Hey you." Sometimes a name was not needed as there was the ultra effective whistle that he could perform to seek John and I out wherever we may be.

Once when I was visiting my aunt in North Hollywood, I could have sworn that I heard the whistle, but it turned out to be a jet breaking the sound barrier, just like the whistle was now doing to my eardrums: threatening to split my head in two. That was fine by me, I had hoped this would be a nine-sixteenths-free Saturday, as I was nursing a sprained arm and now bleeding eardrums.

Big Ed's whistle was akin to a foghorn on a higher-pitched frequency, but rather than guide his ships to a safe port of call, the whistle instantly sent shivers down the spine, and not heeding it destined you for rough seas ahead.

It was a signal, a countdown to a temper flaring if it went unheeded or was not responded to in a timely fashion. Big Ed was all about internal deadlines; he was like some demonic boss rather than a father. And the thought of forgoing the *Super Friends* and their Saturday-morning ilk in favor of scrounging through a Craftsman toolbox seemed a mighty unfair punishment. It would be made ten times worse if I didn't hustle, Big Ed's favorite word for me getting a move on, all of its disco connotations lost on him.

No, Big Ed was an Elvis man, followed in short order by Fats Domino, Tommy Dorsey, Hank Williams, Johnny Cash, Marty Robbins, Roger Miller, and strangely enough, Judy Garland. But his favorite Sunday-morning musical salute/motivator against staying in bed too late was to blast the "1812 Overture" loud enough to match the whistle.

I wondered, as I got my work clothes on, if it was too late to get Big Ed into *The Guinness Book of World Records*. Last night had seen him break the pattern of cocktail hour in the first time, well, since I could ever remember. He seemed even edgier than usual at dinner, until he finally uttered, "I'll have my dinner upstairs."

Since John and I weren't in on his promise to try to curtail his alcohol consumption and to be more understanding with us, my mother simply asked for us to be nicer to our father as he was going through a rough time. I was hoping our lives would turn into a case of instant karma, leaving Big Ed thoughtful and minding his p's and q's for once.

It was only halfway through our adventures in auto repair before he proclaimed it was time for a break. He made his way stealthily to the refrigerator we had in the garage, which was used to keep the one in our house from overflowing with cases of beer. It's eleven in the morning. Now comes Miller time!

I sat down on the grass of our front lawn underneath the pepper tree, with its branches that grew every which way, and started daydreaming. I opted for the relaxed route as opposed to only watching a snippet of one of my favorite Saturday morning staples, which would make it near to impossible to want to return to the tasks at hand. At least with my imagination, I could be coaxed back into reality a little bit easier and with no threats of the belt.

My sprained left arm remained in the locked and semiupright position as I lay back on the grass and let the patches of sunlight lull me into a semicatatonic state.

I'm not sure how long I lay there before a shadow crossed over me. I immediately thought it was Big Ed, belt in hand, ready to knock some metric socket sense into me. I let my eyes flutter, trying to be the picture-perfect "Oh, I must have dozed off" little angel that I knew I could look like.

I ended up seeing a sight that sent this angel to heaven while immediately laying me at the devil's doorstep.

With both legs firmly planted on either side of me stood a mightier oak than the tree I lay underneath. I followed the tanned-leg highway until I got to the overpass of Danny's crotch. From my vantage point, I could now end my burning question of "What did it look like?" in relation to Danny's privates being seen in public. This isn't to say that he was standing over me, wagging it around, trying to hit me with it to wake me up, because from what I could see, one hit from that and I would be knocked out cold.

I could see that Danny was a free baller and also that congratulations should be going out to him and his impressive member. This was the first time I had ever seen what another male's manhood, aside from my own of course, and I felt that I could literally never measure up to his behemoth. But next to Danny, I was a nine-year- old in thirty-degree water, a Shrinky Dink that didn't need baking.

"Then again, maybe I would," I thought as I restrained my hand from snaking its way up the golden stretch of California highway heading towards Hungsville. Temptation was nothing new to me. I had been inclined to pinch an extra chocolate chip cookie here and there; but this was an exercise in pure torture. Danny's cock was the proverbial serpent, calling me forth to a Garden of Eden as I wrestled internally between the pearly gates and the seventh layer. The voice of God broke the spell.

"Hey, little bro, what did you do to your arm?" As God spoke from the heavens, a patch of sunlight backlit Danny to full supreme-being effect. I remained silent, struggling in my purgatory.

Taking my silence as a sign that I hadn't heard him, Danny knelt down beside me, my eyes catching his descent's every nuance. I wanted to leap up, run for cover, go shouting into the house that the mailman had arrived with a big package, and I wasn't sure how to handle it. Who would listen? I was still in the belief of the road not taken, but as Danny knelt and the landscape of his body redirected itself, I was finding that road a harder one to trudge along.

In his current position, he could have been Michelangelo's *David*, except for the fact that he wasn't nude, and Michelangelo would've had to use the entire ceiling of the Sistine Chapel to truly capture the magnificence and glory of Danny Woodson's gargantuan member, which had now popped out ever so slightly.

Danny remained unaware, as if it were his lot in life to have this happen, so much so that he had grown numb to the times when he might be exposing himself.

"Fell. Sprained. Ouch." I managed monosyllabic answers that must have come from my father's side of the family.

My mouth was so dry, which surprised me. I thought that I had been salivating at the sight of my first cock. I had wished there would have been some sort of divine intervention to what transpired next, a televangelist to lay his hands down upon my very overactive imagination, pulling the demons right out of my head.

Speaking of head, that's what my right hand "accidentally" brushed against when Danny asked where John was, and I went to point to the garage with my good arm. There was an immediate sensation that my whole body was a towering inferno lit by the fuse that Danny provided. It was brief, it lasted seconds, and it was heaven on earth. I was so rattled that I couldn't even remind me of the hell it could put me through.

Danny did not remain oblivious to the fact that his cock had been poking out now. He reeled it back into his shorts, like the errant dog that runs out of the yard and its master says, "Oh, did you get out again?" My mind wanted to shriek, "Here, puppy. Come here, boy! That's a good fella." But Danny's Great Dane was now leashed behind the fence of his shorts. Danny was different than John's other friends. I couldn't put my finger on it, aside from the one that had touched his man flesh. He hadn't sprained my other arm and had just accepted the fleeting moment as an accident and was moving on towards our garage to seek out my brother.

"Does your little brother have any more pain pills?" I heard Danny ask John. And he was free to ask it above a stage whisper. Big Ed was foraging through the fridge for another beer, oblivious to anything but reenacting his impression of a bear hibernating for the winter and stocking up on supplies.

He emerged from the fridge with three beers on a plastic ring, which acted as a divining rod back to the work at hand, forsaking his promise to my mother in lieu of fixing the years-old problem with our station wagon with a buzz in his head, a thousand killer bees, stingers poised. Yet he could not seem to muster the strength to take a nine-sixteenths to his own alcoholism. I could never understand how my father could let something get so out of hand.

When I was a child, I often vowed never to let anything like that happen to me, to be so out of control that nothing else would seem to matter. As I grew older, I would see that my father and I shared more than eye color, that I was in fact his son, his son who was now grappling with his own forsaken promise, albeit an inner one, to not like men in the capacity that I did. I was feeling the torment creep back at a slow flood then become tidal-wave proportioned, knocking the ocean liner of my resolve upside down surely to send me on my own *Poseidon Adventure*.

"Boys, let's hustle!" Big Ed bellowed, breaking the spell that Danny's man flesh was holding over my vacillating mind.

He pulled the tab off the beer, threw it to the ground, leaving it for junior ace mechanic 2 to pick up later when there were no tools to go scurrying about for. Speaking of scurrying, that's what Danny was doing. The monster in his pants started doing a pendulum dance, which was right on the money of where my mind-set was.

I was swinging back and forth too as to where I might end up in the world of straight and gay.

Even though Danny and John had been friends for a short time, he knew the time-honored rule of no outsiders being allowed in the garage during the Mr. Fix-it and Sons show.

So why was I here, aside from being a gofer and being so bored I would smear extra amounts of grease (it's the word) on my shirt to look like I was hard at work? There was no amount of imagination that could offer an escape as these projects were laced with tedium. All the while, I lived in terror of not deciphering the delicate intricacies of a flatheaded versus a Phillips screwdriver; this was more like the Mr. Fix-It and Son show. John and Big Ed really bonded over the many attempts to resurrect our family car. They were like Dr. Frankenstein and Igor, both speaking the same language, most of it destined for the gutter, before Dr. Frankenstein would utter, "It's alive! Alive!"

There was something different about John's demeanor today; he seemed agitated and high-strung. I also detected a great amount of more-so-than-usual tension originating from underneath the car too. The empty beer cans now stood at two, sobriety, zero, as my father cracked open another cool one. John was grinding his teeth in time to the music that my father listened to on his portable radio. KPOP featured many of Big Ed's favorites from the forties, fifties, sixties, but none of the hits from today.

So I was glad about the no one outside our family rule being able to hear "Sentimental Journey" when my friends' parents were learning how to do the latest disco dances. Big Ed was more subscribed to remember the good old days when he and my mother did The Stroll. But his musical interludes made me a force to be reckoned with on music trivia. I would always best my classmates and our music teacher, Gary, a stocky German man with sweating issues, when we would play our own version of *Name That Tune*.

And now it seemed that Big Ed was going to be a force to be reckoned with. His seasons were changing from winter's sleepy grace to the dog days of August in the drop of a hat—or in the drop of a wrench in this case. Seems that Big Ed must have been on a sentimental journey of his own as he began to drift off into some nether region of remembrances past. Well, the wrench that was raised above his face came crashing down into his glasses, smashing them.

"Jesus Christ! Motherfuckersonofawhore!" he bellowed.

The sheer volume, velocity, and magnitude of his vocal earthquake would have been enough to shatter his glasses, had they not been so already. To make matters worse, in his flailing around beneath the car, his shirt became snagged on some pipe, exhaust hose or some equally confusing car part.

So now Big Ed was temporarily blinded, having to keep his eyes shut from the glass shards he could feel on his eyelids. John and I dared a peak at him to see what may have transpired. What we saw both horrified and amused us to no end. Big Ed looked like the shark in *Jaws* fiercely shaking his head back and forth, trying to rid himself of the broken glasses, while futilely trying to unhook his customary white T-shirt with his right hand. On top of his multitasking, he was hurling more obscenities.

Watching my father right then brought a perverse sort of smile to John's and my face. We had our own Otis, the town drunk from Mayberry. He was here in the flesh to fix our station wagon, and now look at the wacky shenanigans that have ensued! The mouth muscles in John's face looked as though he had been hooked by an invisible fisherman's line, opening and closing, opening and closing.

Had I known that Danny had stopped by to give John some speed, I may not have found it so funny. But it brought the first laugh, which my father thought was aimed at him, much like his Concerto for the Blasphemous, which was conducted in F major and was really playing for a crowd of two, when in fact it was being played solely for the benefit of the conductor. Big Ed was so infuriated now that he began to take his up until now lame left hand and hurled tools; he had a greater problem with accuracy than his words would often impact with.

An errant nine-sixteenths started off the fracas; it knocked over the three beer cans, "Stee-rike," as my father's doppelganger, Mr. Frederick Flintstone, was apt to yell out on his bowling night. John and I backed away from the car, laughing as tools were being thrown about. It was like our station wagon was rejecting donated organs that would benefit its speedy recovery. But this was not to be, nor was my father's solar flare-up to be his last. What transpired was we ended up getting a 1978 Dodge Ram van; my father eventually tired and freed himself, sustaining no damage to himself and miraculously inflicting none on us.

So he kept a half promise and brought John and I together in a bonding moment that was better than watching *Hollywood Squares*. Our laughter wasn't forced at something witty Wally Cox had said. No, it was born of the realization that we were in cahoots now when it came to our father. John had really thought long and hard about the path he was choosing in becoming Little Ed. Not too long before *The Empire Strikes Back* rolled into movie theaters that summer, we both got a lesson in the "Luke, I am your father" arena.

Sometimes you can change your fate; it might take a moment, sometimes years. The trick was to see beyond situations at hand, but this lesson would not be unveiled to me for a stretch of time yet.

In this moment of shifting landscapes, brotherly bonding, failed attempts at garnering attention, and flying tools, I began to slowly open my closet door ever so slightly so as not to let anyone hear the squeak of my door. In the dead hours of the pitch-black night, a fraction of light was shining through.

Chapter 4

Early on I formatted the pattern in my life of setting myself up for pain and heartache. When situations did not take on the glossy hue of a vibrant sunset, pink merged with orange in a disarming way that always left me breathless; I could always proclaim retreat and live inside of my head for prolonged periods of time. But like anything, it was knowing the precise moment of when to do so that could prove a challenge. And while Big Ed was yammering on was not the time to be doing so, even if it felt wholly warranted. As his meaty hand smacked the back of my head, causing me to stumble and snapped me out of Henry Dodge's inner world, I realized that wasn't the only misstep I had taken in bringing me back to reality.

"You aren't even listening to me, you little shit!" he growled in grizzly intonations.

Here we were in a public venue on a sandy beach underneath the unflinching Southern California sun, on display for anyone who cared enough to put a halt to his abuse, but all the bodies that peopled this paradise found were more likely to be wondering if they should be putting on more baby oil rather than derail the actions of something that was none of their business.

Here again was a perfect example of television failing me. On the *ABC Afterschool Special*, this is where the music would dramatically swell as some unlikely hero put an end to my father's rage.

But I suspected I had that one coming to me, that I deserved it. So I held back the tears. Because if I let them go now, the sorrow that was inherent within me would cause the oceans to rise as a flood of unexpressed emotions mixed with the sands of time seeping into the wounds that lay deep within me.

"Sorry," I mumbled, no hint of sarcasm this time.

Big Ed didn't answer me, but his forlorn expression told me that I would be extremely sorry for not paying attention to him on our way back from the bathroom. We arrived at the spot where John and his new girlfriend, Jeannie, were soaking up the sun and still dripping wet from a recent romp in the ocean. I wondered if they had born witness to the touching display of fatherly love. If John had seen it, he might not act upon it right now for fear of scaring away his latest female acquisition.

John had become a walking powder keg, but unlike my father, his flare-ups were mostly directed at people outside of our family unit. He certainly did not exclude membership to Big Ed when times called for an invite to a verbal foxtrot. In fact, John could hold his own when it came to a shouting match with Big Ed. Whereas I still liked the sparring to take place inside of my head, each bob and weave was followed by a well-placed punch, leveling Goliath.

"Let's pack it up and head on home," Big Ed exclaimed with as much enthusiasm as he could muster. He sounded akin to a pioneer father rounding up his family into the covered wagon instead of our tan and brown van.

I collected my items quietly, always the observer, watching John and Jeannie sneak in a kiss, while my father gathered up his cooler. Thankfully, he put his shirt back on, as Baby Budweiser looked like it was about to be born any day now since my father's beer gut had expanded and dropped into its current fleshy position. My father had a penchant for baring his flesh like some out-of-work male stripper who didn't realize his beefcake physique had been left out in the rain. It was embarrassing but never as mortifying as one of his verbal lashings in front of outsiders could be—or as trite as his overruling on radio station choices while piloting the family vehicle, each click of the odometer signaling some semblance of control.

KPOP was blaring as much as our van's tinny sounding radio would permit. The Mills Brothers were encouraging the glow worm to shine and glimmer, glimmer. As my father began to tune in, I began to tune out, again shutting off the world around me. I thought of the divide that music provided between father and child, how the generation gap was more like a generation chasm in my family life.

My musical tastes were now running away from the taint that disco and all its aftereffects of confessing to liking it entailed. This was 1981, and disco sucked. So never one to want to rock the boat (oops, disco reference), I jumped on the burgeoning New Wave bandwagon. For my twelfth birthday, John had given me Devo's *Are We Not Men? We Are Devo*. I always wondered if John knew that I whispered this question over and over in my head, never getting the answer of d-e-v-o but always h-o-m-o.

I loved that record so much that I saved up my measly allowance to buy *Freedom of Choice*. Mike, Kevin, and myself would listen intently to "Whip It" to see if they were really singing the word *testes*, as that year in sixth grade had been our introduction to sex education.

I always felt that I had a jump on that department, thanks to John and company. I knew what was supposed to go where and so on. Somehow, I never thought that the conventional sex education program applied to me. I thought they should have gathered up all the suspected gay kids and shown us what it would be like for us.

I felt a lot of stigma attached to looking at drawings of the penis in a class full of contemporaries and supposing none of the other boys were thinking the thoughts that were dancing as fast as they could through my mind.

I had a heapin' spoonful of shame thrown in for extra measure always where my sexuality was concerned. I wanted to be invincible against all the slings and arrows I aimed at myself and always rushed to shoot them first, so that others wouldn't get the chance to penetrate the fragile castle walls of my self-perceptions.

I wished I could be like John, so fearless in the face of a challenge the way he carried himself around the world at large, instead of the way I wanted to carry the weight of the world, forever subscribed to the victim role.

He was seemingly indestructible, while I was always poised to crumble. He was the gladiator due to fight; I was the ruins of the Roman Coliseum. His resilience belied his own secrets that he harbored and seemed to mask with a sturdy disposition. John was in the throes of drug addiction. He had developed a speed habit, but you wouldn't know it from his outward appearance.

At seventeen, my brother had the bronzed-god qualities that I hoped to aspire to one day once all was said and done with puberty. Danny had become not only his best friend, but his supplier as well, and it seemed that the fuels of speed and friendship were forming a lasting bond. If I had known that John spent many a sleepless night underneath the trophies that he had racked up, crying himself into a sleep that wouldn't come, I am sure I would have wanted to emulate him even still. We both hated it when Big Ed was drunk and took it out on us, so John kept his addiction to himself, and he struggled, fighting the not-so-good fight of being in those trenches.

Still, my father would promise to stop drinking or curtail it and end up being more miserable to deal with on a daily basis. If I had understood the intricacies of addiction at twelve, I may have had more sympathy for my father. But since he was more than willing to lay blame on others at every turn, each slip on the precarious black ice that lined his path away from sobriety had helped to widen the line between love and hate for me.

My mother had thrown herself into avoidance mode. Her own escape was now mired in watching others' lives be torn asunder daily on ABC's powerhouse soap opera lineup. I would make it home in time to catch *General Hospital* with her, and I became entrenched in the characters too. I was so willing to form another mutual bond through avoidance with Mom that I stayed home "sick" the day that Luke and Laura got married. Apparently I had a raging case of gay.

My mother had a faraway look in her eye that day, and from our vantage point on the couch in our den, we could both see the silver-framed photograph of her as a young bride so full of hope.

Except hope in our family was something that was dreamed about and always felt far out of reach. We all had our escape routes planned; finding our footing towards the doors that lay ahead, whether they remained closed or not, was the bigger question that needed answering. Each step we took was a little bit further away from the people we imagined ourselves to be. The shoes we wore were so comfortable, ragged with shoelaces always dangling, threatening to trip us up, that we couldn't imagine life without the dramas that laced together our everyday living.

So as my mother and I sat on the couch that day, watching "our story," I wondered what hers was and how she had gotten to this place in her life in a dead marriage with a pickled cadaver. My mother was willing to give sparse details if I innocently asked her, and I readily listened to what she had to say.

Kate O'Donnell had been set up on a blind date with Edward Dodge, and her first impression of him was that he was stuck-up. But they dated for five years before launching into the "marriage and having children" routine. Perhaps twenty-eight years of marriage mixed with being held underneath Big Ed's thumb had done little to change my mother's initial perception.

Her inability to walk away from a man that treated her with little or no respect always saddened me a little bit and left me curious as to why she put up with my father's inconsistent behavior. If I had wanted to dwell in the school of thought that came from too much information, I would have learned that my parents' sex life was the one vital link that made up for all of the love-lost moments my mother faced.

I was so immersed in thought that I hadn't noticed that we had pulled into the driveway and that everyone else was filing out while I remained behind. The reverie was broken by my father exiting the van, giving the door its familiar slamming. They had all left me. I began to wonder if I really mattered at all. If I just stayed out here in the stillness, listening to the engine cool and tick, would I be reported as AWOL? Could I find the solitude to quiet my always questioning mind? I knew that the sooner I snapped out of this thought process, the better off I would be. So I unsnapped my seat belt, gathered up my belongings, and made my way into the house after washing the sand off my feet, adhering to house protocol. I began the long countdown to seven thirty so that my secret nightlife could ease my troubles while building up my forearms.

There was not only a lot on my mind during that summer of '81; there was a lot of time spent with my right hand.

In addition, tools of all sorts were being pulled out of real and imagined toolboxes. And morning was not the only variety of wood I was working. There was also actual lumber purchased at the local lumberyard sitting idly in the backyard after Big Ed's announcement of what it would be transformed into.

I was a little anxious about that for myself too. Junior high was only two months away, and I was already dreading it; putting a negative spin on a situation that had yet to present itself was my forte. I was also dreading the next Dodge family project. Big Ed had decided that a greenhouse, which encased a Jacuzzi, was just the thing to soak away life's troubles when the soaking of his brain in alcohol wasn't working for him as it once had. He needed to up the ante on his relaxation skills as it was—surprise, surprise, surprise—discovered on his last doctor's visit that he suffered from high blood pressure.

So I spent the remainder of the summer as a gofer of tools while John and Big Ed did the hard physical labor. The bright side of this, I figured, was that at least I'd have a legitimate excuse for crawling into bed at seven thirty.

My mother seemed to be the only one who was the least bit suspicious of my sleeping patterns. She thought we could all benefit from a healthier diet (i.e. keeping the breaded confections down to once or twice a week now would do just the trick to keep her boys in tip-top condition). In their place had come a bounty of all things Crock-Potted and a new least-favorite dish for me—pepper steak with alfalfa sprouts or blond worms, as they became not-so-affectionately known as by the Dodge brothers. Branching out in the culinary world seemed to bring peace to my mother, giving her a sense of place in a family of men.

Although our family was embarking into the second year of the 1980s, we could have easily been cast from the mold of *Leave It to Beaver*. A breadwinner father, stay-at-home mother, jock older brother, and Henry Dodge as the Beaver. But somehow, knowing the other connotation that *beaver* held made me realize that the show would have to be changed to *Leave It to Woodpecker*. I knew that there could have been a plethora of very special episodes that could deal with the secrets my family held.

The building of the greenhouse was a perfect analogy for our family's life: "Let's cover over the things that soothe us, dipping our toes in the waters of life, putting up a pretty façade, and let the undercurrents of what was really troubling us float around in endless circles."

My family structure held no floor plan like the one that Big Ed had drawn up for the greenhouse, just a vague idea, a notion of how things could be versus how things really were. I always felt like I was the only one that could see things clearly but got caught in the family trap of never uttering my observances for fear of repercussion.

"Henry, eat your waffle," Kate Dodge said with conviction. "You look tired."

And there it was. The Dodge family golden rule: "Let's fish for answers instead of just asking something point-blank."

"I'm fine, Mom," I responded as programmed, a robot boy, emotionless, not caring.

I went back to the task of eating my waffle when I stumbled onto something. No, it wasn't some grand perception of why my family didn't communicate to the fullest extent possible. It was something brown and crispy that was housed inside my waffle. For a second I thought that my mother had cleverly found a way to combine breakfast and dinner in one nimble leap. The dweller in my waffle was not of a breaded nature; it was almost unrecognizable as bacon, but I did determine that's what it indeed was. My mother caught me staring at my plate. I hope the mortification wasn't too clearly evident.

"I put some bacon in your waffle. It's like a little treasure." She smiled, obviously pleased with her subscription to *Ladies' Home Journal* or whatever had prompted this breakfast experiment.

I shuddered at the thought of my parents sex life growing stale.

"I've got some bacon, Big Ed. Feel like a treasure hunt?"

And that about did it for breakfast and me that morning just as Big Ed's whistle signaled it was time to get to work. Soon this set the pattern for the rest of my twelfth summer: get up, gofer, go to bed, get off, get up.

While it was not the idyllic scenario to how I wanted to spend my summer vacation, I did get to see how applying yourself and hard work could really pay off. Besides, there were some fringe benefits to slave labor every once in a while, Danny would take part in the construction chores. If I had the balls to admit to the public at large that I still liked disco, Danny definitely would have fulfilled the construction worker from the Village People fantasy.

The way the sweat would escape from every pore, leaving him awash with a gleam, gave me a boner each and every time and also left me wanting to ask him if I could towel him off with my tongue. Seeing as I was dwelling in the house of all things are better left unsaid, I never did. I could swear that Danny didn't mind me silently worshipping his godlike veneer. In fact, if I was not mistaken, I swear I caught him winking at me a time or two.

"Henry, can you hand me that hammer?" Danny had asked one especially hot afternoon.

"Sure," I said, always trying to hide the excitement of him talking to me with a cool nonchalance.

I was never sure if the force field guarding my pounding heart couldn't be penetrated, so I'd throw in some testosterone cliché for good measure.

"Here you go, dude," I said in my already deepening voice that would only reach minimum deepness when puberty was a distant memory.

"Thanks, big guy," Danny lobbed his own attempt at bridging the hetero gap back at me while giving me a wink, a smile, and something to think about in the dead of a summer night that would make me feel alive.

From my vantage point, standing above where Danny was kneeling, I could see the outline of his fully erect penis. The throbbing seemed to be keeping time with my own accelerated heartbeat; that wasn't the only throbbing that was happening beneath sheet of clothing. I too was getting a tad bit excited.

Danny locked eyes with me, adding a heat to the already blistering day. We were shielded from view by the backside of the greenhouse. It seemed like he wanted something to happen; of course, I would have been more than willing. Suddenly his eyes withdrew their focus from me and returned to the other task at hand of hammering roofing nails into wood. I slipped away, and I chalked it up to the heat of the summer making me envision this mirage or the fact my brain was spun out on the super sweet concoction known as Tropical Punch Kool-Aid.

Unlike my father or mother, I had not developed a knack for caffeine. Every morning before we got started on our summer project, it was my duty as a gofer to fetch coffee for Big Ed in his favorite mug emblazoned with an owl on it. It was as if the ceramic owl was echoing my inner question of "Who, who, who was Henry Dodge?"

Sooner than I knew it, the summer had flown by, the greenhouse was erected, and so was I on a nightly basis. The night following a day of Danny and his quest for tools had transpired was an especially hot evening, and I'm not just talking about the temperature. I actually counted seven orgasms that night, all of them inspired by different imaginings of Danny and me in a variety of situations that required us to be naked and going at it hot and heavy. If I had heard of Tennessee Williams at this point in my life, I would have seen that this was my long, hot, and hard summer complete with a hunky lust interest and family doings all under the not-so-watchful eye of Big Ed.

Miraculously, our central father figure had amazingly few flare-ups as the dog days of summer were leashed to the fall. Hell, he had even broken standard Dodge protocol by allowing Danny to help out on the construction project that was now near completion. I had a very Shake 'n Bake feeling whenever I looked at the structure that was taking up a better portion of our backyard, and I helped.

Three nights before the summer of '81 was to be all but a memory, a calendar page ready to be turned, we held the first inaugural soak. Like many best-laid plans that encapsulated life at home, my father made one fatal error in judgment. He had decided that the spa would be solar powered, which meant that you could get a hot soak only when warm weather prevailed.

So on an eighty-something-degree day in an eighty-something year, John, Danny, and myself all slipped into the spa, wincing at the heat, preparing to be parboiled. But it was worth the heat. The pulsating jets not only could help ease strained muscles, but their bubbling effect also hid those nasty and embarrassing instant hard-ons that had been plaguing me as of late. John and Danny were very talkative, like two parrots jabbering back and forth in a nonsensical fashion.

"Dude, let's go to the arcade after this. I gotta play Pac-Man, Puc-Man?" Danny said.

"No, no, no, no, no, no, no, nobody can do the boogaloo like I do. It's Pac-Man," John explained.

I sat back literally soaking it all in. It was like the twosome was holding private auditions for a guest spot on *Mork & Mindy* and were perfecting their manic Robin Williams speak to a captive audience of one. But I wasn't only captivated by their 78 rpm conversational skills; I was sitting directly across from Danny, taking in every glorious view that his being half naked was providing me. I would always stockpile images from my day so that I had plenty to draw upon later at night. And that night would be all about Danny emerging from the spa dripping wet in white see-through shorts that left nothing to the imagination. It was funny, but Danny never ventured forward with sideways glances and the like whenever John was present. The more I tried to dissect Danny's behavior under the microscope, the more I began to realize that I was looking into a mirror. I tried my best to keep my secret longings and behaviors under wraps, so must

Danny, I realized. He was even more fascinating to me now because I felt like I had someone I could finally look up to, learn from, and hopefully, when the time was right, experiment with. As Heckle and Jeckle, the hyperbolic talking magpies, walked across the wooden floors and out the door, I gave myself the first of many self-given hand jobs in the spa.

Once the bubbles of the jets stopped and I had cooled my own, I noticed something floating in the water. It looked like... Oh no, it was! The remnants of my autoerotic manipulations or, in layman's terms, a healthy batch of baby batter! It looked like a man-o'-war, its sticky tendrils pulsating back and forth, the now one-man spa giving it an open ocean in which to swim. I was just about to scoop it up in my hands, but not in the manner which had produced it, when I heard footfalls on the wooden floor.

There before me was not the vision I wanted. I was hoping it was Danny, that he had forgotten something or had something to show me. But it was both my parents, ready for their own soak time.

"Time's up, little creep," Big Ed announced.

"Henry, look at your hands!" Mom chided. "You're starting to prune."

I didn't think from his vantage point that they could see me trying to capture the elusive flotsam and jetsam produced from my own body and an active imagination. I was just about to scoop it up when the bubbles sprang to life again, causing it to be ripped from sight underneath the rolling seas. I was as sunk as that spunk, and I also knew that my parents wanted to soak away their problems as I started emerging from the spa, letting mine soak in.

I was going to get busted for sure, probably never able to use our spa again unless it was under a watchful eye. It was a clear-cut case again for me wishing I was like other kids on my block. I was certain none of them would be facing this dilemma. Just as my left leg was propelling itself out of the spa, something slapped against it; my prodigal son had come home. And it was sticking to the just-sprouting forest of hair on my leg. I reached down, acting like I had been bitten by a mosquito, and reclaimed my errant jism. All of this went unnoticed by Big Ed and Mom. They were passing me by on the wooden steps leading into the spa, blissfully unaware that they had been moments away from taking a very special soak.

Again sighting my penchant for being the invisible boy, along with the qualities of properly securing secret behavior, I skulked out of the spa, a handful of homemade dippity-doo in my right hand. I felt like Indiana Jones redux. I had reclaimed my prize before it fell into or onto or smacked against the hands, legs, torso of the enemy. Whistling the *Raiders of the Lost Ark* theme, I made a beeline into our den bathroom.

It was adorned with very tacky wallpaper, and I am not talking about the glue that was used to adhere said wallpaper to the bathroom wall. Every time I used this bathroom, I was assaulted with images of turn-of-the-century French magazine covers. My mother had won the battle on this front, but she had always picked and chosen her battles with Big Ed in a more sedate way. It seemed as though she had relegated herself to a wallpaper-like existence: you were aware of her presence, could see her, but were never sure what was being covered over. She almost always had a faraway look in her eyes; her demeanor and body language suggested defeat, instant surrender.

We still lost ourselves in the corridors of *General Hospital* each afternoon at two. But with the onset of junior high creeping slowly like a snail coupled with the ferociousness of some otherworldly creature intent on making my life even more miserable, soon our story-watching afternoons would fade into the distance, a long ago memory.

I would be getting out of school at two thirty, so by the time I got home, Luke, Laura, and especially, Dr. Noah Drake would be ending their broadcasting day. Rick Springfield would have defi-nitely been a poster on the wall, overlooking Kelley and my attempts at eighties dancing, had she still lived nearby. More than likely we would have got our groove on with "Jessie's Girl," which was all over my radio station of choice, the Mighty 690.

Although I was starting to embrace New Wave, Top 40 still held its magical saccharin spell over me, spinning its fine, cottony web, all but cocooning me and forcing me to listen to endless rounds of "Bette Davis Eyes," "Celebration," "I Love a Rainy Night." More often than not, I found myself relating with the lyrics from the theme from *The Greatest American Hero*, "Look at what's happened to me, I can't believe it myself." This was humming through my head as I dispatched my interloper. If only all of life's little messes could be so easily solved by flushing them away.

In the upstairs bathroom I shared with John, I took a shower to rinse off the chlorine. As always, I was unable to wash away the feelings of sin that shrouded my secret life. I stopped the shower, grabbed a towel, listened to the nothingness, and I took a swipe at the mirror to rub some of the fog off it. My image was at one moment crystal clear, the next overtaken by the fog, and the juxtaposition of the two images I saw was not at all lost on me. I was spectral, not yet complete. I couldn't wait for the day when I could proclaim my freedom; until then I would bide my time and try to strike a delicate balance between fantasy and reality. I wrapped a towel around my waist and headed for my bedroom.

While I put on my pre-out-and-proud ensemble of shorts and a tank top, I switched on my latest hand-me-down acquisition, John's old transistor radio. Its red housing slightly faded to a more appropriate shade that leaned towards pink. I was hoping to hear Blondie's "The Tide Is High."

A knock at the door overpowered the poor radio reception, interrupting Reo Speedwagon's journey down the highway of heartbreak. Even though I was at present not involved in any kind of criminal act of self-abuse, the volume and consistency of the knock caused my heart to skip a few beats. I crossed my room, which had remained semi-intact to the way I was used to it growing up, except the bunk beds were now Laura and Rob Petrie-like in their side by side proximity. The far left bed was the one I slept on, and still allowed a certain degree of privacy, when the desire to draw was so strong in me.

And as I opened the door, I stood face-to-face with Danny, the embodiment of many sketches come to life. He was no longer dripping wet or wearing a see-through white bathing suit, but his mere presence was breathtaking. The brown of his skin matched the deep marble brown of his eyes. His hair was sun-kissed blond, and an athleticism structured from a daily ritual of surfing helped build his chest and arms. The hairs on his arms were light, almost translucent, as was the dazzling brilliance of his teeth. Yes, Danny was definitely going to be in a "stranded on a tropical island sans clothes" kind of scenario tonight. But he had other thoughts there in the trembling moment of reality.

"Hey, little dude, we're going to the arcade then the drive-in. Wanna come?" He asked this last question so pointedly that I was sure he had somehow been witness to my escapade in the greenhouse.

"Sure," I instantly fired off, not even pausing to think if Big Ed or Mom would find this a reasonable evening suited for a twelve-year-old. Then realizing the hurriedness in which I had answered, I threw in a "Dude" to soften the anxiousness that was eating me alive.

He smiled and beckoned for me to follow him. I would have gladly walked across hot coals just to be in closer proximity with him as the fires of my desire matched the searing coals intensity with each and every step towards him. Puppylike I followed his lead, taking in every nuance, the way his musculature rippled underneath his clothes begging to be released from their cotton prison, just as I had my hopes pinned on Danny being the one to set me free. I was completely oblivious to anything else—like the fact that my radio was now playing "The Tide Is High." And I did indeed feel the waves of lust crashing all around me, seeking out the foreign shore of Danny's reciprocation.

John was already outside in Danny's vehicle, a VW microbus, the ultimate in California surferitude. While Danny had seemed to have calmed down, mellowing like a fine wine, John was a caged animal, letting his feet and other extremities do the pacing. If I had been privy to see into the past, I would have seen Danny smoking a hash-laced joint and John refusing to partake. This was three years prior to Nancy Reagan's plea of "Just Say No;" to which John would've added in the present, "To drugs that will slow me down."

"If the van's a-rockin', then don't come a-knockin'," Danny said upon seeing John's hyped-up mannerisms. He chuckled under his breath and unleashed one of his killer smiles, equal in precision and magnitude to the nuclear bombs that Russia could drop on the

United States at any given moment. The fallout from that smile did not have me running for cover; it melted my insides instantly, giving me a radiated glow from the essence of my being.

"Whatever. I don't care. Where are we going? Let's play us some Pac-Man then Donkey Kong. Man, that game is bitchin'." John had strung together three separate thoughts into one sentence that was spewed forth in rapid succession.

I piled into the backseat, sitting behind John, so that I could steal sideways glances at Danny, who, if it were at all possible, looked even sexier when he was driving. I envied the road as it was the target of Danny's undivided attention. Danny popped in an eight track of Devo, and "Jocko Homo" came blaring out of the speakers.

"Devo rules!" Danny yelled above the din of music, catching my eye in the rearview mirror and giving me a semblance of a knowing smile. I wanted to broadly smile back, grin from ear to ear in such a way that it would look like I was all teeth or an Osmond. I was willing to push my brother out of the van, take his shotgun position and drive off with Danny, and let the highways of life take us where they may. It wouldn't matter because I felt that he got me, and I really wanted him to have me.

But for right now, I would have to be content on him taking me. Well, not taking me in the biblical sense, but we were arriving at the arcade, then after that it was the drive-in—all destination spots that were happening because Danny had thought enough of me to invite me along.

Somewhere in my schoolgirl-crush mind, a world of furtive glances, blushes, and misconceived notions, I thought that a strapping specimen of a seventeen-year-old was the one I wanted to be with for the rest of my life—a life that had yet to start, as far as I was concerned.

We made our way out of the surfboard-wax-smelling environs of Danny's vehicle to the more noise-encrusted sparkling gem of another burgeoning obsession—the arcade. It seemed as though the bells, whistles, and assorted beeps were programmed in such a way that they hypnotized the youth of America to part with their hard-earned cash. All I knew was that this arcade, which required quarters to keep the game play alive, felt like an extension of myself. All I wanted was for someone to push my buttons and grab my joystick.

After about an hour's worth of Pac-Man, Galaga, Tempest, and my personal favorite, Donkey Kong, we hopped back into the microbus. I had watched fascinated as both John and Danny had displayed their individual styles to game play. John was manic, all over the arcade, hopping from one machine to the next, displaying some sort of newfound ADD (arcade deficit disorder). Every once and again he would let a curse word fly out of his mouth as quickly as the quarters were coming out of his pockets. Danny, on the other hand, was a sly and understated player. He would pose just so at the machine in a semi-hunchback position so that the proper g-force was being applied to his rippling musculature. He was all about the seduction, whereas I knew what I liked and just wanted to play.

I had no idea how this boys' night out would pan out. We left the arcade, my head full of notions until we took a detour. I was more than completely devastated to learn two of the boys were on a double date, and like so much of my life, I was the odd man out. The microbus sat idling, but it was my mental engine that was revved up, threatening to overheat. I felt like I had been tricked, brought along to be shown the rituals of heterosexual courtship, as Jeannie, John's first real serious girlfriend, and another girl piled into the van.

"Hi, guys, this is my cousin Deannie from Seattle," Jeannie spoke this turn of phrase entirely oblivious that I was already sizing up my competition and was not coming up with any pluses for her.

Deannie was sixteen, had mouse-turd brown hair, small boobs, and a mouth full of teeth that would have done Mister Ed proud. She was obviously not on par in the tanning department with her California Dreamin' cousin with the similar name, save for one letter. Creativity must have run long and deep in the Carson family.

Already at a young age I was equipped with a catalog of cut downs, but I had culled them from other kids' perceptions about me. While I didn't want to wound someone intentionally, somehow it seemed warranted in this scenario, and I thought I'd have to make a big exception in Deannie's case.

"Geez! What stinks?" I questioned no one in particular and one person in general.

If there was anything I knew how to do, it was the time-honored Dodge family tradition of the "make you question your self-worth" undercut. I knew Deannie would be fair game. I had ferreted out her obvious weakness in no time flat. She was awkward, probably felt subpar next to her stunning cousin, and was feeling as nervous around Danny as I was. So I tapped into that, being all too familiar with that well-walked pathway to self-loathing lined with stones that were worn to the nub. I let the directness of my stare alert everyone that I already had a culprit in mind.

Albeit it was not a case of a silent-but-deadly air strike, but that was the prevailing and lingering aftereffect I was striving for. Sensing that all eyes were now indeed on her, Deannie, if it was possible, turned two more shades of white, fading into the off-white interior of the microbus. She very visibly swallowed, mustering up the strength to give some form of an answer.

"Oh it must be my perfume. It's Charlie. Do you like it?" She nervously smiled and asked me a point-blank question; to which I gave a point-blank answer.

"No, not really. I'm allergic to perfume, especially the cheap kind," I replied tersely.

I could see her eyes seeking me out, trying to detect the similarity she must be sensing. But I was too busy being in tune with turning my inner bitch into an outer one to return a look that said, "I am just like you." This was the first instance where I would use my snappy comebacks for self-preservation, a preemptive strike on the enemy. I could also sense Danny, John, and Jeannie looking at me, a mixture of confusion and awe prevalent on each face, but none of them uttered one word to me.

Then I returned my attentions back to the crestfallen expression that Deannie was wearing. My empty gaze gave her nothing to grasp. No "Just kidding" was thrown out, a rope to hoist her up from the canyon floor, as the walls around her began to crumble and collapse.

The silence was deafening until Deannie uttered a squeak of "Oh" and took a seat next to her cousin in the backseat, where they belonged. I was really upset that the female interlopers, or just Deannie really, were going to be adding estrogen to what was supposed to be a testosterone-only evening.

The double bill at the drive-in was *An American Werewolf in London* and *Porky's*. I heard this information being discussed as I hid underneath a blanket in the area behind the backseat. Since we men had all spent more than anticipated at the arcade, this money-saving measure was necessary. It was also reasonable since I didn't think that John could pass as my legal guardian. All the same, I felt it should have been Deannie that was forced to hide. Then again, it was something I excelled at and gave my mind free range to work unencumbered to calculate a defensive attack.

We got in without any problems. I am sure that the microbus full of teens looked like the average make-out mobile and maybe eerily like the Mystery Machine on *Scooby-Doo*. Danny was Fred, Jeannie was Daphne, John was Shaggy, but I wasn't sure if Deannie had the emotional range to portray both Velma and Scooby.

And then there was me, hiding out, a ghoul ready to strike, as was clearly illustrated by my earlier unleashing of the beast with sharp claws. Just like the titular beast of *An American Werewolf in London*, I was sniffing out the weaker prey. There were two werewolf movies playing that summer, the aforementioned *American Werewolf* and *The Howling*; out of the two, I really wanted to see *The Howling*.

I wasn't sure how up to snuff Dr. Pepper pitchman David Naughton's acting abilities would be. All I had to go on was his stint as Dr. Pepper's pitchman, which entailed him singing/dancing/encouraging me to be a Pepper. As it turned out, *American Werewolf* held my attention, especially when David Naughton was naked. I am surprised that I didn't spear the popcorn box with my ever-growing erection.

"Hey, I didn't order mayonnaise on this!"

Someone was apt to utter that cry if the movie showed me any more Dr. Pepper man flesh. But as it turns out, no one else would have noticed. I was alone sitting in the shotgun seat, noisily munching popcorn, jumping at the scary parts, fully immersed in the cinematic experience.

Meanwhile, in another part of the microbus, John and Jeannie were partaking in a heavy petting session on the blanket that had hidden me from view. While Danny was sitting side by side with Deannie, making idle chit chat. If the silence between them took on too long of a span of time, I would double-check the rearview mirror, making sure they weren't making out. If they had been, the best line of defense I could come up with was to jump up and scream at the horrors on and off the screen.

So far so good, as the awkwardness between them was as evident as the fact that I had ordered butter on my popcorn, which I was still munching on despite the images of carnage that were transpiring on the screen and the screams that were elicited out of the two speakers that dangled precariously on the inside of Danny's windows.

And speaking of the windows, it seemed that John and Jeannie were trying to reenact another horror movie with the waves of heat their bodies were emanating. *The Fog* came rolling in from the back of the van, creeping slowly but surely, and was bent on obscuring the viewing of other cinematic scare fests.

"Geez, you guys, take a breather!" Danny half-mockingly chided. "There are people who are actually watching the movie."

He turned and gave Deannie a smirk and a half shrug, and that was all the provocation she needed to lunge; guess ol' Deannie had also learned a trick or two from *An American Werewolf.*

Wherever her brazenness had sprung from, she was more than willing to ride it out literally. She had straddled Danny, who looked as though he were drowning in a sea of girl. His arms were flailing, eyes wide, couldn't catch his breath. Yup, that was pretty much what I thought kissing a girl would be like. I was torn between the show on the big screen in front and the one I was catching in the rearview mirror. I decided to let it play itself out.

Both were fascinating examples of the nature of horror, and at that moment I felt very disconnected, like there was something taking hold of me so tightly that all of my emotional components were being squeezed out.

Although I really wanted to coldcock Deannie, I knew it was she that was going to be the one dealing with the heartbreak of rejection and not me. I just had to bide my time. I suddenly got why I was so enthralled by that night's viewing pleasure. I was a teenaged American werewolf! I was going through changes, granted they didn't involve me writhing around in pain on all fours (well, not yet anyway), but I was like the main character in other ways. He had a secret to hide and could only act on it when the time was right, albeit mine didn't have to be based on a lunar cycle.

I remained lost in thought for a moment then decided to return to the more exciting show of the two. Just as an American werewolf was shot and killed, so were Deannie's chances of scoring with Danny. He had finally managed to remove her body from his; there was a faint hue of red underneath his always tanned face. He was breathing like he had just run a marathon, and perhaps he had.

Well, in his favor, Deannie was not the typical girl that Danny could have. Besides, Danny and Deannie was probably the most annoying couple's name I could think of. But what did I know? I was just an impartial observer.

The next movie, *Porky's*, had a few things going for it, even more male nudity for one, and Danny was now in the captain's seat while I was more than happy to play his copilot. Even though the popcorn was at least an hour's worth of gone, I still held the empty bucket steadfastly on my lap.

The dreaded boner was making lots of appearances tonight. Although I would not have minded Danny giving it a tug, I did not want to be in the public eye when this happened. Then again, covertness did not run in my family. Brother John was still going to town, so much so that Danny had to turn on the defrost just so we could see the movie. Deannie was fast asleep, whether from exhaustion from her unsolicited attack on Danny or the joint the four teens had passed around earlier and always by me.

I remembered thinking, "I am never going to do drugs." Well, if my world was lived in hindsight, there would have been a lot of *nevers* that would eventually be known as *always*.

"This movie is pretty good, huh?" Danny asked me at one point, where I had to tear myself away from the abundance of male ass shots onscreen. He had a dreamy look in his eyes and a huge bulge in his shorts. God, I wanted to unzip his pants, unleash his beast, and show him the newly found skill I had acquired over the summer. But I knew I couldn't, even though that's just what he might want me to do. The conflict over having the things in life that you want and having the things that you need was firmly cemented that night.

"Uh-huh," I muttered and returned my attention to the movie; wanting to live in fantasy rather than reality did have its saving graces.

Porky's ended, John and Jeannie emerged from their own private sauna, Deannie remained asleep, Danny was the captain, and as his copilot, I was willing to traverse the new worlds which lay ahead. And there were new moons surrounding each and every one of them.

Chapter 5

I laid my head back against the headrest, the steady rhythm of the train on the tracks lulling me into a false sense of security while I fast-forwarded my tape past "Like a Virgin" to "Over and Over." It seemed an apropos anthem for this leg of my journey with LA looming not too far off now.

I rewound my mind again, going back to one year prior.

Some years are geared towards being stellar, seminal, if you will, and 1984 proved to be no exception to the rule. There was no big brother watching over me; John had upped and joined the Navy in hopes of seeing more than the world at home could allow him. His decision made complete sense to me in a lot of different respects, no more Big Ed is one plus that immediately jumped to mind. The other one is that John had probably seen and made me watch every John Wayne movie dealing with war. *The Fighting Seabees* and *The Green Berets* were probably his two favorites.

So it only seemed logical that once his inner war had ended, he needed a safe haven after having gotten away from the path that drugs had been taking him down for the last few years. John had found the proper footing after nearly ruining his chances of graduating from high school. I had helped him with his homework, usually anything that had to do with English, history, science, and biology. Anything that did not entail utilizing my basic math skills was always a welcome relief.

In some ways, our roles were reversed. I became the protector, helping him out in my own small way, repaying back the loan that the services that his shielding had provided. It left me feeling good about myself, which was not the feeling that encompassed me on the inside.

I was still trying on skins at age fifteen, not sure what I wanted people to see me as, unsure of how I saw myself still. Was I a surfer type? No, I just liked to dress like they did and could utter the word *dude* at the drop of a hat. Was I a jock? Well, if a jock is someone who likes to watch the other guys in the showers during PE but hates the physicality of playing sports, well, let's just say that I'd never be Heisman Trophy material. Was I a brain? To a degree, I had started utilizing my endless amounts of free time to study. Was I heavy metal? Um, I liked Def Leppard, Van Halen, the Scorpions, and Quiet Riot. Was I New Wave? More so than being a headbanger, although I still delved secretly in the world of Top 40 overlorded by Casey Kasem. Was I gay? Was I straight?

On these latter questions I could say that I was sliced down the middle, a cattle taken to the slaughterhouse. I desperately wanted to fit in, to be considered cool, or at the very least, to be a part of something.

I didn't want to be singled out as different, so I did not act on my burgeoning sexuality for fear of reprisals. I wanted to be the James Dean of San Dieguito High, a rebel with a cause who would be a giant east of Eden, west of the sun. High school life does not lend itself to proclaiming, "This is me, this is who I am," as was clearly illustrated by the TV show *Square Pegs* and movies like *Sixteen Candles*.

I had been pulling double duty on hiding out, awaiting discovery of my true self to be ferreted out by others, so I retreated further into myself. Oingo Boingo had a song out that year as I began my freshman days in high school. It was so indicative of my everyday existence. "Who Do You Want to Be?" could have been the national anthem for my state of confusion.

Since I was unsure of which side of the fence to jump, leap, or skip over, I decided that I should at least attempt to have it look like I liked the grass in the girls' pasture.

There was a girl in school, name of Sue, whom I had known since the heady days of junior high, when we were both in the same art class. I figured she was nice and probably would leap at the chance to go out with me since she was pigeon-toed. There was a crispness in the air that was counterbalancing the sweat I could feel forming on that night of the homecoming dance.

I didn't know what the protocol called for me to do. Wasn't it enough that I was making an attempt? Should I try to "score" even though our team wasn't? My hands felt way too clammy to even attempt holding hands. My mind raced, and I felt that all eyes were not on the field but on us or, rather, me. A slow and steady chant of "Go, go, go!" started out as a bee's whisper and ended up a lion's roar in my ears.

I turned my head and looked at her; she was completely engrossed in the game. I started to make my move, pressing in closer for a kiss. Just as I reached a close proximity of her arm, she leapt to her feet, her elbow knocking me hard in the nose, popcorn raining down on my head.

She sat back down, face flushed with excitement—our team had just scored, even though I knew there would be no chance for me doing the same. There was a steady trickle of blood leaking from my nose. I tried to innocuously wipe it with my sleeve, but Sue caught me. She fished a tissue out of her purse without saying a word; the disgusted look that rested upon her face spoke volumes. She had thought I was just another crude teenaged boy.

Even though I was feeling deflated and a bit perturbed, I also knew I had nothing vested in Sue, so what did it matter? Along with some blood, I had swallowed some pride and a cold, hard fact. I knew at that moment I was not cut out for the chase. Maybe the homecoming dance wasn't the perfect venue for walking the straight and narrow with a pigeon-toed girl, but it did accomplish something.

It pretty much cemented that I was not herding the right cattle by being a ranch hand at the Gay Is Not Okay corral. The dance itself proved to be interesting as we danced with a group of her friends from the school band to countless one-hit wonders that the eighties seemed to produce.

One of them, Tommy, was dancing directly across from me during "Wake Me Up Before You Go-Go." He had a very inviting smile, twinkling eyes, and now that I think back on this, I should have asked Tommy to go to the homecoming dance with me. Sue was no Kelley when it came to getting down. Tommy, who was appropriately a drummer, marched to his own tune of above-par white-boy dancing. This was also the case for me. I had turned my disco-days moves into New Wave smoothness as that evening truly was a homecoming to eking out my existence as to what I wanted to be.

My love of all things escapism had reached almost a fever pitch that year. There was so much going on inside of my mind that when I wanted to tune it out, I could watch the endless streams of videos on MTV. But even the simple task of watching TV could become overwrought with my teen angst that was on red alert.

If that was the case, there was always the arcade, eating up the funds that I got for doing Big Ed's bidding or the quarters that my mom left in the piggy bank that adorned our kitchen counter. Yes, it seemed as though Mom had discovered new avenues of collecting as there was also a pig cookie jar to match its smaller quarter-coveting doppelganger.

Kate Dodge, wife, homemaker, mother of two, set out on a voyage across Formica seas on an endless quest for things to fill her time. She was on a search for things to make her forget that her husband was a cold, sometimes cruel man. She was a doormat for him to wipe the residue of his stress-filled work life onto, his actions all but burying the welcome message that had once been there, clean and hopeful, now covered in years of mud.

But she pressed on, navigating from the pages of *Ladies' Home Journal* in hopes that she could avoid rocky shores and claim newfound lands in the name of all bored, frustrated housewives. Each new discovery bolstered her confidence, but not enough for her to claim a land for just herself.

My mother must have bought every Betty Crocker cookbook that was for sale at the Crown Books where Jeannie (still John's girlfriend) worked. She knew that the old adage "The way to a man's heart is through his stomach" must hold true for Big Ed.

He truly loved her cooking, but she knew that this did not necessarily mean that he loved her as much as her pork roast with crispy potatoes. And just like the characters on *General Hospital*, she would formulate, calculate, and hatch a scheme to make Big Ed happy. So it was off to Crown Books yet again.

While she perused the aisles in search of the perfect recipe to remedy a nearly loveless marriage, I made my way over to the magazines. I pretended to be intrigued by the harmless offerings of *People* magazine and its ilk. But reality and an equal dose of hormonal drive shifted my eyes to the top shelf, where the eighteen-and-over section held the latest copies of skin mags. I eyed the top tier carefully, working my eyes from left to right, just in case someone happened by and saw me blatantly giving a visual clue to my proclivities. *Playboy* led the charge. I stifled a yawn, boring. *Penthouse* was next on the roster, a little better, but only because of some of the "Dear Penthouse" forum letters had related some sparse same-sex experiences. Then it was the penultimate, *Playgirl*. Cha-ching, jackpot!

There was a mirror above the magazine section, assuredly to keep the likes of my same-age counterparts from lifting Miss October in her glossy glory and taking a sneaky peek at her, ahem, spread. But I wasn't just interested in a momentary fluttering of my stomach as I gazed meditatively at a staple-stomached god. No, I wanted to be able to have the immobile image in my possession, to be at my beck and call whenever I dared to take a risk and more than a preview. But was I willing to steal more than a glance?

I checked the mirror and my surroundings like I was crossing an unknown street. I looked left, right, then up into the mirror until all systems were go. The coast seemed clear. I stretched my hand up like I was giving Jane Fonda a run for her aerobicized money. And one, two, stretch it out, feel the burn. My hand neared the soon-to-be ill-gotten booty; as it clutched the magazine, I imagined me experiencing the burn of an eternity in hell. Instead, my throat decided to do its best impression of a desert, and my stomach followed it with its rendition of "Strike up the Band."

Now I had common thief on top of secret homosexual to add to my list of "accomplishments." I also had a magazine that, if I was caught with it, would certainly signal the death knell to both being an ancient Chinese secret.

A flush of shame overcame me, tidal in volume, followed in short succession by fear. For a nanosecond, I imagined I could just put *Playgirl* behind the copy of *Sports Illustrated* I should be interested in, no harm, no foul. A lyric from Marvin Gaye's "Sexual Healing" bounced into my head, "I can't hold it much longer," a perfect summation of the current climate. I needed to make up my mind and quickly. I opted for hiding it down my pants, covering over my dead giveaway with my T-shirt. As always, I was covering over my desires.

Now I had to figure out what to do with my child born out of wedlock of the norm. I spied an aisle way devoid of any patrons, including my mother, still blissfully unaware of what I was up to. She was debating which recipe was destined to spice up her marriage. I casually strolled into the aisle that housed travel books, as I myself was on a journey of sorts. I was testing my resolve to see how far I would go in the pursuit of harboring a fugitive, namely naked photos of men.

Before, it had been my sketchbook that had added the spark to the forest fire of curiosity about members of the same sex. Now, in the visual age of MTV, I needed better eye candy than I could draw, even though I was a perfect example of the adage "Practice makes perfect."

I laid the *Playgirl* on the middle shelf, cover down, and I was flipping through it backwards like a Japanese text book. It was more like an Evelyn Wood speed-reading course designed to seek and tear out the pictorials as fast as humanly possible. Each rip, each tear dripped with volume. With another cursory glance and still no one in my sight line, I took the pages and stuck them down my pants and stashed the remnants of the *Playgirl* behind a large photography book illustrating the tropical bliss of Hawaii. I tried my best to appear nonchalant. Unfortunately, the pages were digging into my inner thigh, making the casual gig near to impossible. I was just about to readjust when Mom's always surprisingly cheery voice laced with kittens, lollipops, and all things associated with joy startled me.

"Oh hi, hon, did you find anything interesting?" she said from directly behind me, meaning she was in the travel aisle. Looks like I was going to be saying aloha to my covert operations. Had she spied on me? Was my mom just waiting for the perfect opportunity to draw a conclusion to the endless hours I spent out in the Jacuzzi? Did she always suspect that her son was a chronic masturbator that needed a little male-enhanced jump start to keep things lively? I expected the next words out of her mouth would be "Aha!"

"Did you hurt your leg? You're limping a little!" she asked.

Concern was emanating from her in such a way that I knew she was none the wiser, but I knew she could also be fishing for the truth that she didn't really want to know. Her face was a blank canvas, giving away nothing, and I could only wonder if she had connected the dots to get a clearer picture.

"Yeah, guess I pulled a muscle in gym class or something," I answered this in an unwavering tone, knowing full well there was only one muscle I would be pulling when we got home. "I'll just soak it out in the Jacuzzi."

"What a great idea. That should help," she said, gazing down upon her soon-to-be- purchases, satisfied with my answer. "I found so many good recipes. I just don't know which book to get. What do you think?"

She had bought it, not knowing what I had stolen, which seemed to be an oxymoron of sorts. I knew she would have never had asked John this question, for he could have cared less about the questions my mother directed towards him. But I liked to take the time to pay attention to my mother, clearly another fuchsia flag that went ignored.

I looked at the spines of the books and tapped a few quickly, taking great pains not to bend forward too much. But I must have gone a tad too far. I clearly heard the sound of paper or, in this case, the naked men in my pants crinkle. I did my best to cover it with a cough. But no matter, Mom was busy rearranging the books that I had haphazardly selected as perfect, remaining none the wiser.

We made our way to the cash register that Jeannie was commanding; there was nothing on her face that said, "My boyfriend's little brother is a dirty queer." Imagined slights were also a source of killing time for me. I overemphasized what people must think of me since I still did not know how I felt about myself. I was just counting the minutes, the internal clock keeping time with my elevated heart rate, until I was in the clear.

I strayed from the register in case Jeannie had some sort of intuition that I was guilty as sin. I looked at the latest cache of bestsellers, hoping that there was something I could sink my teeth into. Devouring a steady diet of books still provided a salve to the wounds that loneliness opened.

"Hi, Mrs. Dodge, Henry, how are you?" she asked with a suspicion-free tone.

"Oh yeah? What's that supposed to mean?" my criminal mind rallied.

Instead of voicing the thought, I gave a cursory nod, indicating I was fine and certainly did not have any absconded pornographic material in my ownership. Since John's sojourn into the military, the only time our family saw Jeannie was while she was slaving for the man. I couldn't fathom her just stopping by for a visit, especially if Big Ed was into his cups. My mom asked her if she had indeed chosen wisely. I felt a quick jab of scorn that was more irksome than the pages digging into my leg. Wasn't my opinion good enough?

"These are all good choices. My mom swears by this one," she said, indicating a particular pasta book with an orange cover. "Henry helped me pick them out. He's so...thoughtful." She chose the last word with extra care, peppering her sentence just so as she would one of the dishes that she would concoct.

Jeannie looked in my general direction. I felt as though I should accidentally knock over some books to diffuse any unwarranted attention.

"Isn't that nice! Oh, I almost forgot," she started, fishing out a plastic bag before proceeding.

"Uh-oh," my mind raced, "the jig is up!"

"I got a letter from John today. I can't believe he's only been gone for two weeks. It seems like forever."

"He'll be back sooner than you know it."

Even though I was facing away from her, I was sure she had mustered up her most reassuring of smiles.

"Henry, we'd better scoot. I want to try out one of these recipes tonight. Won't your father be surprised."

Just about as surprised to find me with my non-subscription to *Playgirl*. Big Ed was a creature of habit; any deviance from the norm was liable to set him off, even something as mundane as a new culinary creation. You just never knew with that man. Too bad he didn't come equip with an emotional Doppler so as to forecast his emotional state, "There's a slight chance of thunderstorms tonight."

I put all thoughts out of my mind save for one: getting the hell out of there. A new recipe from Mom was not completely out of the norm. Ever since she had also discovered the joys of cooking chicken, it had been a Dodge dinner staple. We ate poultry so often that we started naming the chickens Henrietta. I never thought of it as a slur on my manhood, or lack thereof, but now that I think about it, maybe Henrietta chicken was the giveaway that my mom knew all about me. Yet she never had the brass to say anything to my face. But why should she go against the grain of the Dodge family creed of avoidance? "Quiet, there be no reason to speak the truth," could have been on our coat of arms.

While she busied herself in the kitchen with the task at hand, so did I in the Jacuzzi. There were several different variations of men to focus my attention on. Of course, it was the one closest in proximity to looking like Danny that brought about an end result. I had been soaking my sports injury for close to an hour, according to the run of afternoon shows that had gone by on the television I was using solely as camouflage. Yup, nothing happening out in the Jacuzzi except soaking and watchin' the tube. The smiley face thermometer on the wall above the Jacuzzi seemed to be laughing at that equation, but I always had to have a good cover story. The thermometer also indicated that I had increased the heat quotient by a good ten degrees since my arrival. All of the windows may have been shut, the blinds drawn, but I thought it had to do with my own greenhouse effect. My solitude came to an abrupt end when I heard the whistle louder than a chainsaw cutting through the locked greenhouse door.

I couldn't risk being caught by my father, who would be expecting my immediate departure from the no-fly zone I had established. I looked furtively around the greenhouse, its wood-paneled walls holding not a single hiding space. Time was both moving too fast and too slow, a convergence of the frenzied with just a dollop of molasses. I needed to remedy this panic and quickly. Then like most things in my life, the answer was straight ahead of me and right in front of my face. I had been kneeling on the wooden floor a foot away from the stairs that led into the healing waters. Between the floor and the stairs was a space no more than two feet high and maybe three feet wide at best. Beyond it, the wood from the floor provided a shelf, a perfect hiding space.

Dropping to a crawling position, a lifetime of doubt and an hour's worth of pleasure clutched in my hand, I scuttled into darkness. The smell of wet wood and earth greeted me as I wedged myself deeper, and in my panic, the space seemed endless. In fact, it took me no more than ten seconds tops to perform this task, reverse course, attempt to stand up on legs that had nearly fallen asleep from being in the same position, throw on my wet bathing suit, grab the towel, and make my way into the house. My cramped legs added validity to my extralong soak session. As I started up the three stairs that led from the den to the living room, I could see Big Ed sitting in his chair, arms folded.

"What took you so long? Dinner's in five. Go get ready," he questioned and ordered as only Big Ed could.

Without a word, I ascended the stairs as fast as I possibly could. With thirty seconds to spare, I descended them, joining the table in the nick of time. Mom had already scooped out what appeared to be an offshoot of every other pasta dish we had ever eaten, the infamous Velveeta being the glue that held the familiarity and newness in place. There was a slightly fishy smell to it. Big Ed wrinkled his nose, downed some ever-ready Budweiser, and spoke.

"What do you call this one, Kate, tuna gunk?" he maliciously asked, knowing that my mother's new cookbook was still out on the counter.

"That's as good of a name as any," she said with a tight smile, picked up her fork, and stabbed a helping of said gunk.

Big Ed grunted, laughed, drank some more beer, and proceeded to polish off his dinner in no time, immediately leaving the table to catch the evening news. I tried to make up for my father's cold behavior by tempering it with a proclamation that it was great after every mouthful. It was to no avail, the damage had been done, and it wasn't up to me to offer my condolences to her dead marriage. My mom pushed the food around on her plate, a watery glaze covering her usually sparkling eyes. I wondered what those eyes saw in the man she had married.

A false sense of security was always prevalent in this house. She could be standing upright one moment and, without warning, be lying on the floor with a verbal rug pulled out from under her feet by my father. All of the pain she felt was kept under that rug when she placed it back; dust bunnies that must have been the size of Texas resided there, always welcoming more insult into the dark enclave.

At present, Big Ed was so far off the wagon that it was tilting from all the weight being applied to just the one side. On the plus side of my father's alcoholism, he would usually pass out cold early, leaving my mother and me to practice freedom of choice in the area of television viewing. Since we both enjoyed the daytime soaps so much, we found that the world of nighttime soaps also fit us like a glove. *Dallas*, *Dynasty*, *Falcon Crest*, and *Knot's Landing* were all thriving in the prime-time spectrum.

I loved *Dallas* in particular and had even started watching the reruns they would show every night at seven o' clock just so I could see J.R. be as bastardly as he wanted to be. I thought he was the coolest, and I really studied him. He was so quick to cut people down to size and got away with murder where his wife, my favorite character, the longsuffering Sue Ellen, was concerned. The fact that I didn't discern any parallels between the Ewings' and Dodges' marriages went unnoticed for a long time. It's ironic that I was captivated with J.R.'s evildoings while my own father's not-so-random acts of cruel and unusual were not a TV show I wanted to tune into. Or maybe I was so fascinated with J.R. because I thought Larry Hagman was cute when he was on *I Dream of Jeannie*. Whatever the case was, I used *Dallas* to fill the empty space of socializing with my peers on a Friday night.

To shut out either the dead quiet or the bluster of my drunk father, I could also play one of the cassettes that I enjoyed while sitting down to draw. I still considered it a passion, as I did with one of my new favorite singers, Madonna. There was something so raw, so uninhibited about the lyrics on her self-titled debut album. Songs like "Burning Up," "Physical Attraction," and "Think of Me" always made me pine for Danny. He had since left town, moving to LA, where he had gotten some gigs modeling and was even trying out for a role on *General Hospital*. The news of him being a part of Port Charles's landscape was thrilling; the pangs that I felt whenever I thought of him explained to my heart why they call it a crush. I hated being fifteen, I hated being young, and I wanted to live like an adult and skip all of the bullshit and melodrama that go along with being a teenager. Pat Benatar had put it very well in "Love Is a Battlefield," "We are young, heartache to heartache."

I suspected that's where some of my teen angst was coming from, but I also knew that the other part of that equation was that I could not tell anybody, well, anything about who I really was. I knew what I wanted to be, a fully realized version of the Henry Dodge that resided inside of my head, and not the boy who found solace in the shadows. It was like some key ingredient was missing to make me complete. I needed to find my inner Velveeta and quick.

But as always, I was at a crossroads as to where I could seek out others of my own kind. I kept a vigilant eye out when out on excursions to the nursery with my mom or when she dragged me happily along to the mall to do some shopping. All I had to go on were the images I had seen on TV, so unless someone resembling Billy Crystal on *Soap* happened along, I was sunk.

Big Ed's paltry concept of allowance earned versus the work entailed to achieve it usually found me penniless in no time flat. Since I had multimedia needs to feed, it was time to get a job. I was actually excited about the prospect because I figured it was one step closer to being a man. As always, I didn't know the half of it.

Lavar's BBQ was famous around town for its great homemade sauces, fun work environment, and an unspoken parade of young busboys that would quit in a relatively short time. When I spied the Help Wanted sign on the window, I had a gut feeling that not only would I get the job, but that it would be a great experience for me. I applied, interviewed with Lavar's son, Steve, and was hired that day. And that really boosted my self-esteem, and I excitedly rode my yellow Schwinn ten-speed home to tell the parentals the good news.

Big Ed greeted my news with the usual nonchalance and popped my helium-inflated balloon of self-esteem. Was he worried that I would slip out from under his thumb by branching out and doing something on my own?

"Well, don't think you can use this as an excuse not to do your chores," he slurred.

Didn't I know it! Ever since John's absence by surgically removing himself from the availability of helping out around the house, I had become a very secondary choice in that area. I was now expected to cut the grass, take out the trash, and all for a very paltry sum of cash.

Another benefit to my father's return to excessive drinking was that he wasn't as apt to start up any home-improvement projects. The downside of all of this was that his temper had returned, not quite full force, but still baffling in its intent. The first time I mowed the lawn, I knocked an orange off one of two fruit trees that gave our backyard the feel of being in some slipshod orchard. Well, this just sent Big Ed over the edge, and I was grounded. Even when I tried to argue that the branches of the tree bearing the fruit was an inch off the ground, Big Ed didn't care. And that left me with the feeling that he really didn't give a shit about anything I said or did.

It was like he was invisibly knocking the fruit off his own tree, trying to create a distance from the branches of the family tree to its roots with every swipe. But there was my mother to gather the fruit up, checking it for bruises.

"Oh, hon, that's wonderful!" she exclaimed, surprisingly not clapping and hopping up and down.

As she spoke, I could actually hear the exclamation points inherent in her praise. I am sure she could sense the open wound that I became whenever Big Ed was less than receptive to my bearing news of any sort. He probably thought that every time I started a sentence with, "Mom, Dad, I have something to tell you," that this was the moment he had been secretly dreading, that the remaining part of the sentence would finish out with, "I'm gay."

If I had known that the actions I had taken today would actually be steering me towards that destiny, maybe I would start clapping, whooping, and jumping for joy. How was I to know that on the horizon there was a sky full of possibilities and one that would forever change the way I saw myself and the world at large?

For me, working at a barbeque restaurant is a clear-cut example of Freudian longings: all that meat, especially the sausages. How was I to know a Saturday night that featured Lavar's famous spicy ribs was going to end up being just as spicy?

Eric had called in sick. So I was stuck pulling double duty of bussing tables and doing the dishes. Had Eric been there that night, would it have been his fate that was forever altered? As it was written in the stars and in conjunction with the full moon, I was about to experience my first big bang. As the last customer left, Steve locked the door, and I got down to the enviable task of scraping the cast-offs of uneaten meals into the garbage.

But there are other memories of working at Lavar's that far outweigh washing dishes and the like. The October night was crisp, refreshing in its contrast to the Indian summer we had been experiencing in Southern California during daytime hours. The night was ripe with contrasts. Right was wrong, and wrong was right; there were no shades of gray in the illuminated world I was about to enter.

"I noticed that you've been lifting the bus trays wrong all night," Steve said as I gathered up the last one that was filled to medium capacity and waited for him to chastise me about it.

I must have looked puzzled, but in actuality, I was always nervous around Steve. He always seemed to be scrutinizing me in a way that I couldn't explain. He took my silence for wanting a lesson in proper bus-tray-lifting etiquette, showing me how to bend at the knees.

"Your back is probably hurting," Steve said, his face just a profile before turning and giving me his full attention. "Would you like a massage?"

"Sure," I said this neither too quickly nor too slowly; although my body was now starting to tingle in anticipation of a man's touch. I followed him into a hallway that housed the bathrooms off to the left and the food storage pantry straight ahead. The smell of meats slowly roasted over days hung lazily in the air, never able to escape. Steve switched on the hallway light, but I could already sense a charge of electricity. It was sparking from me, and I was doing my best to keep it in check.

"Lie down on your stomach. It will work much better if you take your shirt off," he said nonchalantly.

This is where I felt my first pang of trepidation. I was a skinny kid with no muscle tone, and by October I was definitely showing my Irish heritage of being a white, white boy, as opposed to Steve, who was the chocolate to my peanut butter and had a tight, firm musculature hidden beneath his casual waiter's attire of a maroon Le Tigre shirt and tan cords. Still, I had to know if another man would find me attractive, or else I would be doomed to taking girls I had no interest in to the homecoming game. So I soaked in the moment of now or never, removed my shirt, and lay on my stomach.

His hands were surprisingly soft for someone who practiced jujitsu, and there was an air of expertise to his gentle touch that caressed my skin. I was lit up like a fireworks display; each and every fuse on my bottle rocket was attempting lift off.

But I was still nervous, afraid that this would come to pass at a misguided launch of some kind of cruel joke. I guess that's what I got for watching *Carrie* every time it was on TV. At least I did not think the evening would end with me in a blood-soaked prom dress. From the feel of things in my underwear, it was more than likely that

I would have to chisel them off. As the touching continued, so did the amount of precum happily spilling forth from its source.

"I need to get your lower back and legs. Can you take off your pants?" he murmured halfway between a whisper and a demand.

Not feeling an answer was needed vocally, I let my pants do the talking as I took them off hurriedly but not in a manner that suggested that I was expecting anything but a massage. The radio station switchboard operator in my head kept accepting calls from a longtime listener, first-time caller who went by the name of Lust Puppet—and he wanted it all. I got back onto the floor. The carpet was leaving marks on my stomach. I was pressed so hard against the floor, feeling exhilarated and scared.

My breathing was shallow, not able to keep up with a heartbeat that was set to 78 rpm. I tried finding a focal point in the hallway; my eyes kept drifting up and over to my left, fixating on the sign that read Men on the door leading to the bathroom.

"Just relax," Steve cooed as if he too had a third eye that was now probing my mind as assuredly as his hands were gliding down my back. Suddenly my lower back became a region known as my ass. Steve was kneading me like unbaked dough, and I wanted to laugh like Poppin' Fresh, the Pillsbury Doughboy, just to do a litmus test that I hadn't gone crazy and that this was in fact happening. He lingered on my ass longer than he had on any other portion of my body, so I decided from his vantage point, things couldn't look all that bad. But then he moved on to my legs, giving them a perfunctory massage light, before he asked me to turn over so he could do the front.

Well, there was no getting around the fact that I was hard as a rock or that my stomach had dropped down to my knees. This was it, make or break time. I didn't think it would pose a problem for Steve, but then he spoke.

"Oh are you aroused?" he queried.

"Uh-huh," I managed to get through the overbearing cottonmouth I was experiencing.

"Looks like you're secreting quite a bit."

When he used the term *secreting*, I was suddenly transported to Mr. Manning's fifth-period biology class writing down the terminology for secretion, never thinking that it would be used in relation to my deflowering.

I snapped back to attention as Steve uttered this musical refrain, "I wonder what it tastes like?"

My underwear came off, guess I didn't need a chisel after all, just a man ten years older than me that wanted a taste.

And with no qualms whatsoever, Steve began to answer his own question. The warmth of his mouth surprised me as he began working up and down on me; I let the unfamiliar overtake me, first in an auditory way. There were slurping sounds punctuated by soft murmurs that were as far removed from a cold Popsicle on a summer day as they could get. Visually, I looked straight on at Steve. He was so engrossed in what he was doing that he did not make eye contact. I decided to lie back, shut my eyes, and hang on for the ride I had always been itching to take.

Getting my first blow job was such a weird sensation. I was somewhere near ecstasy yet somewhere adjacent to it as well. My mind wouldn't shut up long enough for me to just enjoy what was transpiring. It had to plague me with the fears that had already penetrated it a thousandfold before that I was as good as a marked man now, Meaning that everyone was going to know what I had been up to tonight, from my parents to the kids at school, to my two and only friends, Mike and Kevin. Perhaps the worst thought that traveled like wildfire spread by a carelessly discarded cigarette on a dry, hot Santa Ana day was that whenever someone at school called me faggot that it was now going to be true.

Steve didn't seem to be harboring any reservations about it as he greedily licked, slurped, and sucked to his heart's content. Why was I so worried about the outcome? This was a defining moment I had been waiting for, well, it seemed like, forever! I gave my brain a rest and let my body respond to Steve, even daring to roam my hands over the still-clothed reaches of his tight body. As if some hidden signal had been initiated by my touch, Steve stopped long enough to remove every stitch of clothing in about twenty seconds flat.

His body was amazing, not one ounce of fat; every muscle looked to be carved from the finest mahogany. If I had any doubts that he was not really into me, his penis dispelled any such rumor with the sheer volume of its hardness. I took a good long look because I could; there'd be no shy-eyed looking away now. The time had come for me to practice what I secretly preached. My destiny was within an arm's reach and was shaped like the banana seat on my old Huffy bicycle that I rode around on in third grade; it curved upward and was definitely not a kiddie ride as it was, in a word, huge.

I reached out and began stroking him with the nuanced subtleties that only a chronic masturbator could know. Hours spent practicing on myself had given me keen insights as to the proper grip and how to best utilize that on another.

Steve closed his eyes and tilted his head back. Either he was enjoying it or was having an epileptic seizure because his body had started to twitch. As for my own body, I felt like I was not a part of it. I was an impartial third person, a voyeur who had stumbled onto this scene. The thought was still running through my head, "I can't believe this is happening." But it was. The moment had finally arrived; all of the scenarios I envisioned on sheets of paper could actually happen now. I had unlocked the rusty gate that held back the doubts and fears that I wasn't good enough and set them free while ushering in a whole new set of them, silent interlopers that had been waiting on the other side.

Acting on unsure instinct, I decided that a firm grip was all well and good, but I wanted to try giving a blow job a whirl. Steve was more than willing to be a good sport about it. Again, not sure if the kind of convulsing his body was doing was natural and seeing that I was the one getting the tongue-depressor treatment, I just mimicked what Steve had done to me moments before. I am sure that a blow job from a virgin is not at all about technique. But I do have to say that I took to it faster than I did learning how to swim at the YMCA when I was seven. I never did learn how to dive, but I effortlessly parted the crystal blue waters of pent-up desires, pinned hopes of Danny being the first I would do this with, and every crush I had developed up until this frozen moment in time.

Steve's shucking and jiving was increasing in frequency; he was trying to fit every inch of his banana seat in my mouth. And being the novice that I was, I couldn't handle all that man!

My jaw felt like it was going to cramp; the cottonmouth I had was an obvious hindrance in this situation. I was about to take the bull by the horns and remove him from my mouth when an explosion of warmth flooded my mouth and slid down my throat. It reminded me of the time I had swallowed too much saltwater at the beach. The moan that emanated from Steve was guttural, animalistic. He pulled away instantly. In my focus on what I was doing, I hadn't noticed that I had manipulated myself into an orgasm. Or maybe Steve's saltwater treat was so massive in force and sheer amount that it had forced my own juices to overflow. Whatever the case was, I had now had my first encounter of the fag kind.

I got up off my knees, licking Steve's sweat-glistening body as I stood up. When I got to his mouth, he turned his head, a fussy baby that doesn't want its mother to feed it stewed carrots. Apparently kissing was not on the agenda.

He drove me home that night. There was a little chitchat, but never about what we had done. As Steve's Honda CRX pulled onto Arroyo Street, it was the same as it had always been, but somehow it looked different because I was different. The streetlights seemed to burn extra bright. I felt that I was burning brighter too.

Although Steve was not ideal boyfriend material, at least he was showing me the ropes so that when I did land a man, I would know what to do with him. He used me; I used him. Weren't relationships supposed to be about give and take? We had our little Saturday night dates off and on for the nine months that I worked at Lavar's, which saw me be a semi–pitch hitter when Steve's girlfriend wasn't putting out and I gladly would.

My favorite date night featured a mutual tug-of-war involving Wesson oil as a proper lubricant to all of the frantic pulling that ensued. But even the randomness took on a specific rhythm. He would ask if I needed a ride home, which of course meant that his girlfriend was not giving it up. Now that I was an easy mark to him, he always took it for granted that I would need a ride, which entailed a pit stop to check and make sure all of the fluids were topped off.

Towards the end of my tenure at Lavar's, Steve's siblings, Craig and Yvonne, came to work on the weekends, as Eric was long gone. Yvonne and Craig were both younger than Steve, and Craig was a junior at my high school. I could count on one hand the number of black students at San Dieguito, so having only a scant knowledge of commonalities with Craig from watching *Good Times*, I asked him atypical white suburban youth questions.

"So do you like Prince or Michael Jackson better?" I inquired, not at all thinking that what I asked could be construed as ignorant.

"Do you like Hall and Oates or Air Supply better?" he said this as he was heating up cornbread in the microwave, his back to me. "Actually, I like Oingo Boingo and the English Beat."

I hadn't meant to offend him whatsoever and didn't want there to be any bad feelings between us, seeing as I was his brother's bitch and all.

"Cool, me too." I paused. "I love 'Nothing Bad Ever Happens to Me' and 'I Confess.'"

"Rad, those are bitchin' songs." He turned and smiled. "Do you like to read?"

"Yeah," I said in a perky tone, "Stephen King mostly."

"Dude, *The Stand* is my favorite book. Have you read it?"

"I read it this summer," I answered, not filling in the blanks of you know before I started working here and having sex with your brother. "Great book, but I think I liked *The Shining* better."

And with that news, he removed the cornbread from the microwave. The steam coming off it reminded me of the heat that Steve and I created but that had started to cool off with the addition of his family working on the weekends.

"Cool, that's my second favorite. I gotta go, but I will talk to you later."

There was something about Craig that I couldn't put my finger on. I got a vibe from him, smaller in frequency than the one his brother had emitted, but it was there nonetheless. Craig and I actually struck up a very comfortable friendship.

Yvonne was in college and was always bringing around a new boyfriend every other week to the restaurant; usually they were white guys with pseudo Flock of Seagulls haircuts. These guys never seemed to faze Lavar or Luanne, owners/parents, who were very nice to work for, but it was Steve that I worked under mostly, so to speak.

Ultimately, I wanted to experience more than a "pseudo hetero bordering on pedophile" relationship could offer, so I moved on. I quit Lavar's, much to Steve's disappointment that seemed to border on paranoia that I would spill the beans on our nights.

I would hang out with Craig, and he would share his Stephen King knockoff stories that he had written. In turn, I would show him the artwork that was fit for public consumption. One afternoon, he produced a joint that he had stolen from his parents. I had never done drugs before that springtime afternoon, not wanting to make the same mistakes I saw my dad and John making with their poisons. Well, I have to admit that I liked the effect the pot had on me. It took me further out of myself than any entertainment-geared distraction could. It let the guards that were constantly standing at their predetermined posts in my brain down just a little bit. I was glad to have them relieved of their twenty-four-hours-a-day sentry duties.

I wanted to fly, to explore, and to seek out life forms that were not indigenous to Encinitas. I wanted to find full-fledged gay men who would take me under their wings and show me what life could be like. I was ready for that man to be Danny, as it should have been all along.

I made an escape plan drawn from the blueprint that countless runaway teens in the big-city movies (most notably *Dawn: Portrait of a Teenage Runaway*) had shown me over the years. I knew that I had to hop a bus or train, but I knew that unlike the hapless television teens, I needed a foolproof plan, and if I waited for just the right moment, it would present itself. Or patience be damned, I would make that instant happen as I saw fit, and the time was drawing near. I could feel it in my soul.

Chapter 6

If 1984 was the year that things became clear to me, then 1985 was the year that they went hazy. It was shrouded in a thick air of deeper mysteries. By the time I turned sixteen, I had given up any such illusions that I could walk along the highway of life, thumb out, hoping for just the right ride to take me where I needed to be, on a path predetermined by others.

I became outwardly rebellious, unleashing the uberbitch Henry Dodge that had taken Deannie to task on her choice of perfume and ratcheted it up to a new level. It became increasingly difficult to mask my true identity to anyone, except myself. I knew what I was, what I had always been, which was a source of ridicule. So I chose to start skipping school, first in small increments then for extended periods of time. Sometimes I would hightail it to the local mall and use my lunch money to feed my video game hunger. Other times, I could persuade Mike or Kevin to join me.

On a nondescript atypical Southern California day, as Kevin and I sat huddled in a dugout buzzed from the joint I had procured from Craig, a crack opened up in my wall, setting its longest dweller free.

I was looking with glassy eyes at the baseball diamond, and they must have reflected the swell of emotions I was feeling. I had been made to conform on this field. Big Ed had thought it best to make me play Little League, even after it was abundantly clear I would never be any good; ghosts of old hurts, the residue of a thousand dropped balls, and strikeouts only fortified the feeling of separateness that traveled with me at all times.

"Hey," Kevin asked gently in a creaky voice, "you okay?"

"Not as much as I'd like to be."

Eyes still glued to the field rotated in my skull and began to fixate on Kevin. He had it easy; his life was streamlined, never any huge bumps in the road for him. How I envied that, the effortless grace that surrounded some people in life wrapping them in a security blanket of confidence. Somehow, I instinctively knew I would never be that kind of person.

"Have you ever wanted to be something that you're not?" I asked.

"I don't know. What do you mean? Like..." His thought process slowed by the joint, he fumbled, waiting for me to clue him in as to what I meant.

I had been unconsciously making lazy circles in the dugout dirt with a long stick I had picked up on our walk from school. I couldn't tell him what I meant. I'd barely begun admitting it to myself. Whatever part of the brain, be it the left or right side, that controls impulses must have been asleep on the job. Before I stopped myself from writing the last letter in the sand to follow "GA," I could see the look on Kevin's face change dramatically.

So I stopped myself one letter shy of the truth. Who was I kidding? What else could I have been spelling besides *gay*? The awkward silence now drowned out any birdsong or passing car. I erased the letters in the dirt hoping that I hadn't irrevocably altered our friendship. Then it hit me, harder and with more dexterity than I ever could connect a ball with a baseball bat—Kevin might just think I was coming on to him.

"Listen," I said, not knowing what else I could say, so I didn't.

"Hey, if we head out now, we can make it for fifth period," he said, completely skirting the issue, making it sound like we had to trudge across an icy tundra rather than walk back a few blocks to school.

"I think I'm just going to hang out," I said, already feeling a sense of disconnection on Kevin's part.

"That's cool. I'll see ya later," he said this like he meant it and was gone in two seconds flat.

In a moment of weakness, I had only been left feeling more alone than ever. Whoever said the truth shall set you free really had it wrong. At least I could depend on my ever-trusty sidekick, the Walkman. I slipped on the headphones and out of my worried frame of mind, letting Billy Idol sing directly into my ears about "Eyes Without A Face". There was a line in the song that always intrigued me, "Steal a car and go to Las Vegas, ooh, gigolo food." At least that's what it sounded like.

It planted images into my mind about running off and finding a world I could call my own in the fertile soil of my imagination. By the time my buzz had worn off, the sun was becoming dogged in its pursuit for the horizon. I was hoping I could just chalk this one up to (a) a hallucination or (b) a hallucination. I knew there was going to have to be some backpedaling involved or a "Just kidding" thrown onto my next conversation with Kevin.

Preemptive was the way for me to strike, before my silence equaled death about letting anyone else in on my secret.

I got inside the house just minutes before Big Ed and with ten minutes to spare until dinner was served. I retreated immediately to my room, sat down on my bed, and waited until I screwed up enough courage to both eat dinner and then call Kevin.

Once dinner was finished, I resumed fretting, spying the telephone in my room with a wary eye, like I expected the cord to slip around my neck and strangle me. Then I slipped into how the phone call could go.

"Hey, Kevin, it's Henry. Funny thing about pot, huh?"

"What's up, dude? Huh? Oh that! Nah, I was just pullin' your leg."

Instead of supposing, I needed to be focused on reality, such a time-honored tradition, really, that I held in the highest of regards. With palms sweating, a full field of cotton sprouting up in my mouth instantaneously, I reached for the phone as my nerves took hold, like I was calling Kevin to ask him out.

Oh shit, I couldn't let him think that! That was the last thought that crossed into my stream of consciousness, wading in the ankle deep water, treading very carefully as what the best approach was to take. The dial tone was the only prevailing sound as I began dialing Kevin's number by rote. One ring, the Callahan clan might be eating dinner. Second ring, I should probably hang up and try my call again. I mentally replayed the voice of the operator when a number is disconnected. On the third ring, someone picked up the phone.

"Hello?" Mrs. Callahan said, sounding a little wary as to who might be calling around the dinner hour.

"Hello?" she asked again, sounding more like the Mrs. Callahan I was familiar with, who was very defiant.

Oh who was I kidding? She was a harpy—a loud-squawking woman who stood 5' 10" and had opinions on everything and then some. She could turn an innocent comment into a tirade that you'd have to endure. I always did my best to stay extra guarded around her.

"Oh hey, Mrs. Callahan, it's Henry." I tried my best to remain stoic, to not give anything away. Just making a regular phone call. There's nothing to see here, move along.

"Hello"—her voice was clipped free of its every once-and-again traces of pleasantries—"I suppose you want to speak to Kevin."

"Yes, if I could." I was about to go further, but her shrill calling of her firstborn's name cut me off. Kevin had inherited her brown hair and eyes, but certainly not her vocal range or her subtlety.

"Kevin, Mr. Homo is on the phone!" she squelched.

Did she say what I think she said? Why in the hell would Kevin actually tell that to the jackal who had stumbled upon a human baby at some point and claimed it as her own?

Great! If he told her, I was good as sunk because that meant he had no reservations whatsoever on who to disseminate information to. Why did I have to be so weak? There was nothing I could possibly say that would sway Kevin into believing what had transpired today was untrue.

All of these thoughts entered into my brain in a machine-gun-firing succession. Rat-a-tat-tat, I was fucked. Another round was in the chamber, ready to go after whatever semblance of hope I had, when Kevin got on the phone.

"Hey," he said.

That was it, nothing else.

"Hey," I parroted back, hoping that he would still buy into the "I am as normal as you are" scenario. But as the seconds started ticking and the awkward gaps of a normal conversation widened to the size of the Grand Canyon, I decided I didn't want to play that game either. I hung up the phone without another word. We had been friends for so long, and now I was in the same league as something to be avoided, like white after Labor Day; I really didn't have anything left to say to him.

The gravity of there being nothing I could say anyway was still weighing down on the very essence of my being. I sat down at my drafting table that acted as a makeshift desk and started writing out a note. I concentrated on getting just the right tone across and the best possible way to convey sorrow. Upon completion, I poured over the less than a paragraph masterpiece I had created.

> To Whom It May Concern,
>
> Please excuse my son Henry from school this week. We have had a death in the family and need to travel back East for the funeral.
>
> Sincerely,
> Kate Dodge

The next morning I headed out to school extra early and stuck the note under the door of the administration office. I felt no qualms about what I had to do to preserve myself. It was a good plan. I had mimicked my mother's handwriting perfectly and had made it so she would be unreachable. The week passed without incident or raised suspicions; I avoided school, always on my own. I always switched up the locale of where I ditched to. But I could never return to the dugout; it had lost any luster it didn't have in the first place.

When the next Monday rolled around, I decided to bite the bullet rather than dodge it.

School had the usual tedious rhythm except the usually stagnant air seemed to crackle around me, alive with the knowledge that some people were whispering as I walked by. I tried to pass it off as concern that I had lost a loved one.

But that only lasted until the next day, when it seemed even more prevalent. In the locker room to change up for PE, you could have renamed me Moses because I parted a Red Sea of boys upon my entrance. Nobody would look me directly in the eye, and the term "actively avoiding someone" went to a whole new level. The locker room cleared out in a matter of seconds, leaving me all alone, which was heightened by being forced to participate in baseball. We rotated through different sports, and this week would have to be the one I was extra bad at.

To make matters worse, this was the one class that I shared with Kevin. I saw him sitting on the bench with one of the four Scotts that were strewn throughout the game and the one I had the most history with, Scott Rainowsky, he of the hurled epitaph. I took my turn at bat. Each time I swung and missed, they both started laughing; and on my third strike, not only was I out, I was pissed.

I threw the bat down against the chain-link fence that separated open humiliation from closed defiance. I briefly caught the clanking sound followed by a rattle it made upon striking the fence; the overriding auditory sense was being swallowed up by the sound of blood roaring, the distant call to an unfamiliar shore. Then there was silence, save for one remark from Scott.

"Struck out again, Dodge? Well, what you can expect from a faggot!"

Exhibiting speed and precision that I never thought myself capable of, I was around that fence in no time at all, standing nose to nose with Scott. I caught just enough of a whiff of his breath to know that he had eaten a tuna fish sandwich for lunch, and a good part of it must be stuck in his braces. I also detected a slightly fright-ened look in his eyes while his face held the crooked smirk that had earmarked his confidence since grade school.

"What did you say?" I asked him point-blank, no patented Dodge beating around the bush on this one.

"You heard me, faggot," he said, the sun glinting off his braces as he turned to look at Kevin with a full-blown sneer.

And that's when it happened; something in me just snapped. I lunged at the off-guard Scott, pulled him by the shirt collar to the ground, and started taking out my frustration on him.

My primary target was his face, and I kept hitting him until his upper lip started bleeding where his braces were cutting into it. Nobody came to his aid, and he had zero reaction time to retaliate. The field was hushed by actions nobody thought I would take, least of all myself. Kevin backed away from Scott and out of my proximity too. He started yelling for our coach, who had snuck around the back of the gymnasium to partake in a "health break." I caught sight of him running, cigarette in hand, and I started my private tryout for track and field.

But not before I said this to Scott, "Always remember, you got beat up by a fag."

I hightailed it back to the locker room propelled along by vin-dication, fear, and a sense of retribution paid in full. I changed as quickly as I could and was out of there. Where did I go from here? I couldn't go to any more classes for fear of reprisal from any number of Scott's popularity goons. I didn't want to go back anyway. I just wanted to move forward; there was only so far I could go without running into obstacles. I had inadvertently set up a huge roadblock back on the ball field. There was no way that my parents wouldn't be hearing about this from both the school and Scott's angry parents.

A grounding or worse was definitely in my future, and I felt ill prepared to make the escape I had so often dreamt about. Like a row of dominoes, feelings set into motion actions, tumbled by anger's lingering push and I had the distinct feeling there was no turning back now. I had a reserve of untapped anger; it was the fuel that was driving me towards home and uncertainty.

A lot of my anger stemmed from being shown only a portion of the things that I wanted to do sexually. Steve had acted as some kind of second-rate pusher, had given me a taste of a horse of another color, then sent me out on the mean streets craving more and not knowing where I could score. The more time that I had away from Lavar's, the more I began to see that what Steve had done to me was wrong. Sure, it was consensual, but I was nowhere near to being an adult. I knew that I had the upper hand in the situation, and fueled by a strong resolve to get to Los Angeles by any means possible, I did what any J. R. Ewing–loving wannabe would have done. I set out to blackmail him.

I formulated this plan on the long walk home. Fortunately for me, it was well before my usual getting home from school time. So Dad was still at work, and Mom appeared to have gone shopping. There was a light blinking on our answering machine. I pressed down on it, and the voice of the school's vice principal informed my parents that I had "attacked" Scott in an "unbridled fashion" and that Scott was currently in the emergency room to stitch up his lip. There was more about an immediate meeting to discuss disciplinary actions, but with the touch of a finger on the erase button, there was nothing for them to know—just like Steve, who would not see me coming, so to speak.

"You need to give me all the money in your bank account," I said this with an unwavering gaze just to prove that I was serious before I continued, "And if you don't, well, we both don't need to think about that, now do we?"

I was practicing the little speech that I was going to use on Steve in the mirror. I was holed up in the bathroom, playing to an audience of one; the only fan present was the noisy one I was using to disguise my monologue as a precautionary measure.

I had gleaned the language from J. R. Ewing, but my delivery made it sound more Alexis Carrington Colby Dexterish. I could feel my nerves of steel melt away into nerves of aluminum about a face-to-face meeting with Steve. But time was of the essence, and it had to work, said the steel side of me. There was also the fact that Steve knew jujitsu, that his brother was now my friend. Plus, I knew from past experiences, my best-laid plans weren't always that, causing the aluminum side to chime in.

I stared into the mirror like a vampire that finally catches its reflection even though, as dictated by horror movie lore, it is not supposed to. I wondered if I was brave enough to start this journey.

But I had to do this. I wanted to get away from home, from school, from the knowledge that I was different while at the same time understanding that I did fit somewhere; that was my conundrum. If I had needed a catalyst to further illustrate why I hated high school and saw it as a daily exercise in torture, then Scott's one word of true slander was enough motivation for me to get away. I had always wanted to stand up for myself, to yell in the face of my aggressor and lash out.

Now I had, and I wasn't sure how I felt. I had enough anger stored up to detonate a small nuclear war, not quite the Big Ed–style cold war free-for-all, but something with enough firepower to decimate the wasteland where I now resided.

I knew that the war raging inside of me must have been a fragment of the cinder that lit the fires within my father when he was younger. And I'd be damned if I was going to turn out like him. If it took running away from home to try to get a better sight line on the Henry I was becoming, then so be it. But would I end up using it as an excuse to run away from myself when, in fact, I thought I was running toward my destiny? I was sixteen, afraid of the person I could become, knew the person I wanted to be, but somewhere in between, the two collided in an intense explosion, leaving much carnage as to which idea was right.

Things would have been clearer to me as to which path to take, but I was starting to partake in the daily ritual of smoking pot with Craig. The smoke that I greedily inhaled deep inside my lungs and held on to for the proper effect was causing a haze over my ability to think straight.

Then again, thinking straight had never been my forte.

I was using the pot to cover over the fact that I was feeling actual physical pain; it was as if my head and my heart were becoming detached after the whole Steve thing. And being friends with

Craig was an exercise in restraint. I felt I could trust him, that he might understand me, but ultimately knew I couldn't tell him what had occurred with his brother.

The essence of which had changed me, was making me come out of my shell, while still using it to protect myself from slings and arrows with little effect. My life was not only full of teen angst, but I was starting to latch on to very powerful adult feelings. My life was such a Catch-22, and I just wanted to find the answers that would unchain me. In effect, I had been seeking emancipation from myself through the television shows I adored or from certain refrains of an especially poignant piece of lyricism in the music I listened to.

I felt other changes occurring in me too. The awkward portion of my teenage years was starting to come to a close. Maybe it was brought on by the sexual encounters with Steve that had left me feeling that I had more of a purpose than before. As the months went by, I began to feel a heat building up inside, an intensity that passed with every waking hour. I wanted more.

And as the seasons started to give way from spring renewal to early summer malaise, I felt that the time was right to do what I was planning to do. Now all I needed was to tap into the furnace that was starting to rage inside of me—that and a viewing or two of *Dallas* wouldn't hurt.

So this is me, sitting in front of a mirror, figuring out the best tact in which to blackmail a man ten years older than me, a man that I had sex with, a man that could snap me in two with his pinky if I am not careful. Sure, this was just another typical after-school activity. Then again, today hadn't been fraught with normalcy.

There were certain things that I could count on. A new *Friday the 13th* movie every year, even after *The Final Chapter* gave birth to *A New Beginning*, was in its own way a comfort with the air of familiarity it provided. Stepping into the unknown always left my stomach flip-flopping, but I knew how to quash the dance with an "actions speaks louder than words" approach to situations.

Of course, this was easier said than done. The curse of the artistic is the imagination. I could serve up any number of situations that could unfold by trying to blackmail Steve; the worst of which saw him reacting by kung fu fighting me. The best saw me in LA, poolside with Danny, taking turns rubbing each other down with the ultimate tan getter, baby oil.

The only way I would be able to do this was by doing it, I told myself in a very Yoda-like voice.

I took one final look into the mirror at the boy I was, straining to see the man I could be. I was starting to come into my own, yet I was cast from the mold of looks that my classmates effected before me. I was a hybrid.

The preppy side of me loved Le Tigre shirts and topsiders, hold the socks. The "still wanted to be like the surfers" past stole from their hairstyles and choice of shorts. I couldn't imagine myself striking out, making a bold fashion statement, like one of my contemporary heroes, Boy George, had done. He was somebody I greatly admired, yet if anyone were to ask me if I liked Culture Club, I would have said no. So deep was my paranoia that I didn't even want to be guilty by association by kissing to be clever. I needed so desperately to set my ideas of being gay versus straight by seeking out my own kind.

And I knew that LA was just the place to do it. Before John had left on his West Pac, he and I and Jeannie had paid a visit to Danny, who, if it was at all possible, had become even more beautiful to me. We only stayed for a few hours, and John seemed noticeably uncomfortable, even with his steady, Jeannie, by his side. I'm sure that the waters that John had once swam against the currents in with Danny were nothing but a painful reminder of how close he had been to letting his life slip into the undercurrents.

On our way home, we drove down the Sunset Strip, ironically enough, listening to Huey Lewis and the News sing about how the heart of rock n' roll was still beating and how the Sunset Strip is really something everyone should see.

"Sunset Boulevard is for the girls, and Santa Monica Boulevard is for the boys," John said as we spied our first hooker selling her wares to any passerby that would shell out the cash.

The woman on the corner looked like she applied her makeup with a cement trough; it was applied layers thick and bore no resemblance to Eve Plumb's or Donna Wilkes's from the movie *Angel*. I remember the movie's tagline: "High school student by day, Hollywood hooker by night." The duality of it really hit home for me: high school student by day, gay by night.

Well, of course, I wanted to see where the boys were! While our travels didn't take us to Santa Monica Boulevard, I did discern that it was just a block down from Sunset. I duly noted it on my mental notepad and filed it away in the accompanying mental filing cabinet under Future Reference.

The future was now. I was ready to spread my wings and try to fly far away. This thought built up my confidence as I picked up the phone and dialed the number to Lavar's. I mentally put a ten-gallon hat upon my blond head even though cowboy hats were so five years ago.

"Good afternoon, Lavar's." The voice was instantly recognizable to me; it was the same voice that had told me on many occasions that what I was doing to its owner felt good.

"Hi, Steve."

I paused, hoping that I also had an unforgettable voice.

"Who is this?" he inquired.

Obviously this was not the case and answered my question while raising my ire. How could Steve not remember my voice after nine months of employment and sexual gratification? I had always felt like I was a mild distraction to him as it was; now I wished I had held out for Danny.

Never again would I have a first experience, although technically I was like a virgin, I had racked up some learning lessons under my boy toy belt. Steve and I had a rhythm to our playtime; we never kissed or did anything more than oral favors for one another because that would be too gay for him. He'd ask if I wanted a ride, get me off, drop me off, and probably put the whole experience in a locked room—whereas my enjoyment of the experiences were brightly lit in a showroom. The situation was always controlled by Steve. If the question of needing a ride or not was not posed, then I knew better than to ask for fear of seeming too clingy or whatnot. I was starting to see Steve as less of a savior and more or less the devil incarnate.

"This is Henry Dodge. I need to talk to you right now. Are you at the restaurant alone?" All of this came out of my mouth before my brain had a chance to stop its course and without an ounce of hesitation to halt it. There was no edge to my question, and I'm sure that Steve thought we were going to be preheating the oven prior to the dinner rush.

"Hey, Henry, sure, come on by." His voice had a musical quality to it; the symphony of lust was conducting his orchestra.

"Great, I will see you shortly," I said this with an air of professionalism that I did not know I harbored.

As I rode my yellow Schwinn with the handlebars turned upwards, I began to think of how it might feel to actually get what I wanted. I had so many examples of wishing for things only to have them not be at all what I expected: GI Joe with kung fu grip, roller boogie disasters, and even Steve, especially Steve. After all of the years that I had spent dreaming of all the imagined scenarios that could ensue from sexual encounters, Steve had shown me how repetitive they could be. It was sad to think that I may never encounter my lazy naked afternoons with a Christopher Atkins knockoff. But should I really gauge all that sex could be on a closet case like Steve? Hell no, Steve had robbed me, and now he was going to pay. These thoughts turned over and over in my head as the spokes on the bike's tires made their endless loops.

I wanted to be a sexual provocateur, the male Madonna, and discover something more than my life was offering me. Somehow, I thought that using sexual means was the answer to all of my life's problems.

For the first time in my life, I hadn't felt under the radar, and that was because someone had sat up and taken notice of me. I wasn't hideous, someone to be pitied or despised. I could be someone that was—gulp—desirable, and I was bound and determined to make that point known repeatedly. I was also hopeful that Steve would get the point too. He'd better, as he was poised to be the soul benefactor to my little voyage of self-discovery.

As I pulled up in front of Lavar's, I tried to keep the anger present and accounted for. I dismounted my bike and walked to the front door with an overwhelming sense of purpose knowing that I was about to change my destiny. The restaurant was two hours away from being open, so I had to knock on the glass front door. I had thought this a better way to go than to go through the back door, which led to the kitchen that housed all types of sharp instruments. I guess I had taken away something from all of the horror movies I watched after all: don't give the enemy any additional weapons.

Steve came to the front door, and the smile he cracked upon seeing me told me all I needed to know about why he thought I was here. But there would be no illicit afternoon delight to be had. In fact, there was nothing from me that he could ever have, take, or use ever again. He would only serve one purpose to me now, just as I had only served one purpose for him. He turned the lock, but I held the key.

"Come on in, Henry." His voice resonated a very "spider to the fly" quality. Yet I was the one spinning the web. "It's so awesome to see you. You look great." He eyed me up and down, taking in the changes in my appearance since last we had performed the hallway tango.

"Thanks. But I'm here to talk to you."

I heavily emphasized the word *talk* so that he would get the hint that there was to be no funny business.

I brusquely continued, "Can we sit down?"

"Ummm, sure." He looked a little taken aback. I had the element of surprise and fully intended to go through with my plan, no matter how much my stomach threatened to uproot and supplant my throat. I just envisioned J.R. grinning underneath his size-of-Texas ten-gallon hat quashing any minute flashes of Joan Collins. "Must stay strong" repeated in a mantra formation, marching on the fields of my cerebellum. The restaurant was just as I remembered it, except warmer.

Oh wait, I had clothes on now; therein laid the difference.

I had to halt all thoughts of what Steve and I used to do in the hallway almost every Saturday night for nine months. Nine months that he had used me, now it was my turn to return the favor. I had

paid with the price of having my first sexual encounter be with someone who didn't care a thing about me; now I would be compensated.

"What's up?" he asked, trying to appear nonchalant. But I could
sense that he was feeling very aware of the fact that a sixteen-year-old
boy that needed to talk to him after they had a sexual relationship
could only spell trouble.

It was the last thought I seized upon before I let him know what
was indeed up.

"Well, Steve, I need some money."

When I saw him reach under the table, I thought I may have
miscalculated where all the cutlery could be stored. But he came up
with his wallet. Damn, that was easy! There had to be a catch; there
always was.

"How much? Twenty dollars?" he inquired, not catching my eye
but rummaging through his wallet to avoid looking at me.

"Not exactly. How much do you have in your bank account?"

This was definitely an attention-getter. I remained outwardly
poised while inside the gymnastics my stomach was doing were prepping to go for the gold in '88. I couldn't believe I had said it; the
wheels were definitely in motion now.

"Excuse me?" he asked, although he knew what I had said.

"Well, Steve, let me put it this way." I paused for dramatic effect
to heighten the tension for him. "I am a minor, you are not. We
had sex, I need money. So you need to give me what's in your bank
account—unless you want the police involved in this."

I wanted to add on a *darlin'*, just like J.R. would've done, but
refrained from doing so.

I didn't know if it was possible for Steve to look pale, but somehow he did; he looked almost ashen. As for me, I was feeling incredible. For someone who was terrible at sports, I had really hit this one
way out of left field.

"Excuse me?" he asked again, but this time it was much more of
a mouse's squeak than a lion's roar.

"Oh you're excused, Steve. Don't be a broken record. You will
leave the money in an envelope in my mailbox. It is to be there no
later than nine o'clock. I'm sure you remember where I live. Didn't

you give me a ride home every Saturday night for, oh, about nine months? Don't be late, and I won't have to call the cops."

I felt more James Bond than J.R. Ewing. As I spoke these words, I felt empowered and still a little nauseated. Seeing the blank look on Steve's face begin to turn into a recognition of what had just been said to him signaled to me that this conversation was now over.

I got up from the table and made it to the front door in record time, leaving Steve wondering what the hell had just happened. What the hell had just happened was that I was incredible and had pulled off the impossible. Never being one to believe in himself, I had strange feelings washing over me. Self-like was replacing self-loathing. But before the transfer of emotional states could be completed, a hand fell onto my shoulder. I froze, glued to the spot in front of my ten-speed, sure that the blade of a butcher knife was about to pierce my flesh. It just figured that the moment I started to believe that I was possible was the moment that I would be taken away from life.

After a few prolonged seconds with no knife gutting me like a jack-o'-lantern, I managed to catch a glimpse of the hand that was clamped down on my left shoulder. It was indeed the hand of a black man, but it did not belong to Steve. It belonged to Craig, who had come in early to help out his brother. It belonged to Craig, who had been listening at the kitchen door as I told his brother the language of cause and effect. It belonged to Craig, who had also had sex with Steve.

The story unfolded over Big Macs and was almost as hard for me to swallow as the meal itself. I knew about incest, I had seen *Something About Amelia*, but that was on television. And this was not some made-for-TV-movie; this had happened to a friend of mine. He recanted his tale with hushed tones. I felt like a priest listening to a confession. I didn't know what to say. I just nodded a lot. There were tears swimming in the dark marble lakes of Craig's eyes, giving them an oil-and-water effect. It was as if the weight of keeping his secret was being lifted, but at the same time he was reliving it too.

We made our way out of McDonald's and snuck around to the back alley to smoke a joint. The harshness of the smoke burning my lungs was starting to underscore the information I had just taken in.

"I knew I could tell you, Henry," Craig said, eyes diverting to something on the ground. A lucky penny perhaps? A bug that could be squashed at the slightest provocation by an inadvertent action caused by something bigger than itself?

Whatever was keeping his eyes from me had nothing to do with anything on the ground but obviously everything on his mind. I think he was waiting for me to dismiss him, to see him as nothing more than damaged goods. What I saw was someone that had been in the same boat; although we had traveled two entirely different rivers.

"You know you can trust me." As I spoke this, even I was unsure of the validity, if any, that it contained.

How could Craig be expected to trust me when he couldn't even trust his own brother? Maybe it was that the pot seemed extra mind-numbing after all of the information I had taken in or that this was not familiar ground that I was treading upon. I felt like I was making up my life. I was a television character, and nothing was as it seemed. The world was a fake veneer, a soundstage with painted backdrops to make the outside look pretty to cover over the insides. I had spent my entire life, which at sixteen seemed like a lot longer, looking for someone to get me. I needed to let Craig in on something, but I think in reality, I was forcing the spotlight and the focus back over to me. After all, I was the star of the show, and Craig was just a secondary character.

"I'm pretty sure I would still be gay even if Steve and I hadn't, well, you know."

I let the thought trail off, not wanting to conjure up images for Craig. I couldn't believe what I had just said. I had, out loud, no less, referred to myself as gay. I was shocked, as was Craig apparently.

"What happened does not make me a faggot!" he said in a very loud voice, breaking the mantra of the whisper-toned stoner.

Before I could chide him with a "Use your outside voice," he was running down the alley. His shadow trailed a distant second as it elongated and shrunk down, finally disappearing. I was still holding the joint, dumbstruck by Craig. The smoke from the joint danced in front of my eyes and suddenly took on a red, then blue hue.

I thought I must have been really out of it until I realized that the red and blue light show was not something born out of a Laserium show sans Pink Floyd musical accompaniment, nor was it produced from my ever-fertile imagination. Nope, it was coming from the cop car that had spotted me with a joint in an alleyway behind McDonald's. I was pretty sure this was an episode of *The Courtship of Eddie's Father* that I had missed.

Somehow I knew that the first time that I dared to utter to the outside world what I had been keeping in secret pockets all this time that I would certainly be arrested. I was awaiting a SWAT team to drop down from helicopters, but their moniker no longer stood for special weapons and tactics; no, they had brought in another branch for cases like me. Straight, white, and totally not gay would haul me in for a thorough brainwashing. I would be left without a trace of gay, a career fixing mufflers, and a wife and kids.

So naturally I started to run, maybe not so much like the wind, but I wouldn't stop until I was truly free. I could hear the surprise in the cops' voices echoing down the alleyway at me, catching up with my shadows. No doubt they would give chase, whether it was on foot or in their car. But neither one was the case. They probably figured that chasing me down was to no avail. Or they were blocking my exit at the end of the alley. Too bad I wasn't Super Gay, able to leap hetero cops in a single bound, taking flight into the night sky, up, up, and a gay! My mind effortlessly came up with pop culture conjectures that would catch me like a safety net every time.

"Hold it right there!" a very beefy baritone-voiced cop ordered.

What choice did I have? There wasn't anything I could do but comply with what they wanted, just as I had done my whole life with authority figures. Speaking of authority figures, I knew that Big Ed would have a new home-improvement project, one that involved shitting bricks, when he found out about this. Of course, my mother would think it was all some big mistake, even when the evidence was right there in front of her.

I stopped dead in my tracks; my little game of cops and stoners came to an end when the other cop, blond and tanned, placed me in handcuffs. Again, had I seen gay porn at this time in my life, then I would have seen the scenario as this: alleyways equal gay sex and a little two-on-one action from the cops.

As it turned out, I chose my right to remain silent, even after Big Ed came to pick me up and started in with his diatribe about how fucking stupid I was. His idea of tough love just repelled me and drove the idea even further into my head that what I needed could not be found at home.

"You are grounded, you stupid fuck! No beach, no friends." He looked at me dead-on as we were stopped in the van at a stoplight, the red light holding me hostage to his ranting and was reflecting off his glasses, showcasing his heightened state of anger even further.

"Well, the no-friends part isn't really a concern, is it, Henry? I mean, what the fuck is wrong with you? Do you know what this is going to do to your mother? Do you know how goddamned embarrassed I am by you?" He eased up as the light turned green, signaling that I needed to make my escape a go.

I knew that I could halt him in his tracks just as surely as any red light could with just two words: I'm gay. But I felt that this would result in shock treatments or some other 1950s mind-set as to how best to deal with a child's homosexual leanings. I just let him rave, a lunatic madman shackled to a marriage and family he didn't want anymore but didn't know how to escape from except via the bottle. Well, cans was more the case for Big Ed. I was numb, not from the pot, but from the obvious truth that my father really didn't want anything to do with me and felt saddled with a lame horse ready to be sent out to the glue factory. Well, I already knew that he wouldn't have to worry about me, not that he seemed to anyway. I was just someone else to kick around, to try to control, when in fact, he couldn't even control himself. Looking at him go on and on, I actually felt pity for him.

At sixteen, I felt like I was going on forty, and it was from instances like this that grew me up in a heartbeat. I was developing a wiser-beyond-my-years mentality, adding it to the protective layer that surrounded my fragile ego, cocooning the truth.

We arrived at Casa Dodge, made our way inside. I had tuned out Big Ed's rant about what a useless son I was. If only he had known what I had accomplished today, then he might think differently about me. I shuddered at the prospect of picking up garbage on the side of the road all summer at the behest of the police. But that seemed mild compared to what Big Ed would probably have in store for me.

However, I had plans of my own.

And they didn't include the lunatic who didn't feel a need to get at the heart of the matter, who only wanted to bellow his familiar gibberish. I didn't need any added ammunition to propel myself out of the barrel of the gun. I was already faster than a speeding bullet with the actions I had taken on today to get away from home. Sure, I'd be just another teenaged runaway, but somehow I felt that my plan would make it better. Steve had better show up, then I would have money and a place to stay with Danny. Life would be better than I ever imagined. It couldn't get any worse than it was at this moment as Big Ed knocked me to the ground with a slight of backhand.

"You'd better start listening to me, you little motherfucker!" His emphasis on the last three words were brimming with hatred and, as if on cue, brought my mother out of the room they shared to see what new commotion had been wrought.

"Ed, leave him alone!" she pleaded. "Tonight's been hard enough on him as it is!"

"Hard on him? Hard on him?" he thundered, focusing the storm away from me and onto my mother. "What he did was wrong, Kate! I don't want a drug addict for a son." He said all of this as if I wasn't even present to hear it, like I was the proverbial fly on the wall.

But I was here, present and accounted for, tired of the invisible-boy treatment, ready for action, and manning my own flyswatter.

"How about having a son that's gay?" I mustered with all of the courage I had and not even thinking twice about letting my question hang in the dead silence of now or never.

Images of Linda Blair's head spinning around in *The Exorcist* come to mind when I think of Big Ed's reaction. His eyes seemed to take me in, sizing me up, doing some final tally in his head as to why his youngest son acted so out of the norm. Even when I had presented him with the answer, he still seemed to be confused.

I had let the wind out of his sails with what he had suspected all along but didn't want to know about. He looked me up and down, like he was looking at something that hid under the bed in a Stephen King novel. His repulsion of me was even more evident when he turned away, dashed upstairs, slammed the door without nary a stinging slap from closed-minded words or his open-ended palm.

My mother had taken the news sitting down; she was staring at me from her perch at the top of the stairs. Surprisingly, Big Ed's vapor trail from his supersonic speed exit had not knocked her down the stairs. She started crying silently, her body heaving up and down, taking the news in as though I had told her I had killed somebody.

Maybe I was guilty of murder; perhaps I had finally killed the invisible boy who lived in the silence and shadows, afraid of both, who never had the strength to change his situation. I did feel oddly empowered by my confession, yet I was still looking out the living-room window to see if any more cop cars would be making their presence known at my impromptu press conference. Whether I was ready or not to accept questions on the subject was about to be answered as my mother spoke. "Yes, you in the housecoat," the reporter inside me signaled that question-and-answer time was indeed in progress.

"You're just going through a phase," she said.

"No, I'm not. I've known this about myself for a long time."

"It's a very lonely life."

"It doesn't have to be."

"I don't want you to get AIDS!"

"I'll be careful."

And that was the best I could do and hope for as I came out in the era that coined the phrase *safe sex*. I also knew that I could not stay here, didn't have to, didn't want to, and wasn't going to.

My mother just sat catatonically on the top stair as I moved towards her, not to give her a hug, but to finalize my escape. I went up to my room, still shit brown and piss yellow, never changing since I was a child, much like my life had always felt, like I was stuck. Well, not anymore. There were some signs that I had evolved past listening to Disney records and keeping secrets—a Billy Idol poster hung on one wall. My mother always remarked that it looked like he didn't have any pants on. Guess she might see that in an altogether new respect now. I knew both parents would see me a lot differently, but that would be the trick, seeing me at all.

I took a harder look around. Everything seemed miniaturized. Nothing seemed to fit me anymore—not the BMW mirror with the No Wimps sticker that John had given me or the Police sticker that I had put on it to show I was a cool kid. It was a mirror I could look into with little resistance now that I was seeing myself so clearly. I peered into it, expecting some great transformation to have occurred from finally letting loose the demons that had guarded my private hell.

I still looked the same, exactly as I always had, and that angered me, as did the concept of no wimps and the painful reminder of my own encounters with the police today, minus Sting, Andy Sumner, and Stewart Copeland. I knocked the mirror from the wall, and it smashed to pieces on the drafting table I used as a desk. Glass shards peppered the latest drawing I was frustrated with. I took the biggest piece I could find and went to work on ripping to shreds one of the many dreams that resided inside my head—that someday, I would be known for my art. Fuck that!

My mind roared, scaring me ever so slightly and invigorating me in the same instance. I carved a word in scratchy letters, Freedom, onto the drafting table itself. I wanted to overturn everything in the room, but did not want the noise to draw attention to my actions. My digital clock informed me that it was after nine o'clock and time to get the fuck out of Dodge!

I packed up my overnight bag with the essentials, shorts and tank tops, as summer was fast approaching, Walkman, cassettes of Tears for Fears, Bryan Adams, Madonna, Phil Collins, General Public, and other stalwarts like Duran Duran. I waited till I knew that my mother wasn't on the top step anymore, took a look around the room that had housed as many secrets as it had a bad paint job, and made my way to the great big world that lay in store for me in the summer of '85. The last thing I focused on before I closed the door behind me was the word Freedom, a sliver of moonlight capturing it, but it was mine for the taking.

Chapter 7

Even though it was only ten o' clock at night, it felt later. Even though I was only sixteen, I felt like the events of the day had given me a final growth spurt and I was now a man. Even though I was excited about the prospects that life now held for me, I was filled with trepidation. All of these thoughts played on an endless loop as I awaited the Amtrak train that would take me into a world I was ready to explore.

I had decided on a train ride because taking the bus into Hollywood seemed very clichéd and somehow more naïve to me. I was a grown-up now, able to successfully procure three hundred dollars from Steve. There was a moment of dread when I had left the house, my life packed up in my bags, feeling my way around inside the darkened mailbox, playing blind man's bluff with the envelope of money that Steve had stuck all the way at the back of a makeshift safety deposit box.

Although I wasn't sure if three hundred dollars was all that Steve had in his bank account, I did feel it was adequate for services rendered, and it seemed like a small fortune to me. I had taken the wad of twenties out of the envelope while I was in the bathroom at the train station and found it a new home in the pockets of one of my pairs of shorts.

I felt very much like Janet Leigh in *Psycho* after she steals the money her boss wanted her to deposit in the bank but instead takes for herself to start life anew. Considering her demise in the shower at the Bates Motel, perhaps Janet Leigh's doomed Marion Crane wasn't the movie character I should be thinking of. Upping my gay card, I thought of Judy Garland as Dorothy in *The Wizard of Oz,*. I knew that LA would be akin to the Technicolor splendor of Oz for me. Everything would have a different hue to it than the black and white constraints that I resided in at home. I knew that all of the huffing and puffing my father did by blowing his verbal tornadoes at me would surely contain enough power to keep me somewhere over the rainbow for a long time.

The train arrived with no fanfare except the usual horn blowing. Perhaps I was expecting a contingency of fellow queers to be riding the rails in anticipation of accepting a newly out member. I boarded the train, leaving behind the boy I was, yet, unknowingly had him stored away in the invisible baggage that I carried.

Taking the train to Los Angeles was nothing new to me. I had gone on several occasions to visit my aunt in North Hollywood; yet there was a live wire of excitement that traveled from my heart to my head. I had done it! I had gotten away from home. I was free. I was free to be you and me. I was free to be anything I wanted. I was free to be whoever I wanted.

That thought stopped me dead in my tracks as the train rolled along its own. I should take what I had learned from *Grease* right before Olivia Newton-John's big transformation: take a deep breath and sigh and say goodbye to Henry D. Just in case anyone came looking for me, I could deny who I was—just as I had done for so many years of my life. I wanted a fresh start, and a new name was a step in the right direction.

With the Walkman's spongy orange orbs providing musical interludes, I began going over my choices for ditching Henry Dodge in lieu of something more modern. Maybe Trey? Realizing that I had found the source of inspiration from glancing forward at the seat in front of me with its tray in the locked and upright position, I opted on a big N-O.

My mix tape featured many songs that truly reflected the depth of pain that I felt before I had emancipated myself. After Spandau Ballet's "True" ended, Phil Collins's "Don't You Lose My Number" came on, and the tale of wayward Billy got a big eureka in my mind.

"They didn't know him, and they didn't understand. They never asked him why. Get out of my way! They heard him shout..."

As these lyrics made their way through my ears and into my brain, I felt as if Phil Collins was singing directly to and about me. I decided that my new Los Angeles name was to be Billy Collins. I knew that Danny would finally be the only person to truly know Henry Dodge. But I needed a backup plan just in case.

As the miles click-clacked away underneath me like a woman's high heels on linoleum, I began to physically feel freer. My body was becoming lighter, my head less convoluted. I felt exhausted from the day's adventures and began to nod off, assured that all would now be right in my world and that the truth truly does set you free.

As I let the lyrics of Tears for Fears's "Shout" drift into my unconsciousness, I knew that I had performed the right actions that day. In violent times, you shouldn't have to sell your soul. In black and white, they really, really ought to know. These were the last words to reach my waking thoughts, until the conductor woke me up with a "Hey, kid, we're in LA." It took me a moment to take in the validity of what he had said to me. I was here. I had made it. I had arrived.

I had taken the last train out of nowhere to arrive as somebody. And now that I was standing at the front door of my life, I was still feeling scared to knock, afraid as to who or what might answer the door. It was well past midnight; the dawning of a new day was upon me.

Before I gathered up my bag, I opened it up to make sure the three hundred dollars were still residing in their compartment. I had a moment of panic that someone might have absconded my newly acquired illicitly gained life savings. And that's just what the money represented to me; it had saved me from a life that I couldn't bear to exist as I had in anymore. But as one of the books I had done my last book report on stated, that was then, this is now.

I boarded the train as Henry Dodge, and I was exiting as Billy Collins, who was a good two years older than Henry and was kicked out of his house for being gay.

This was sure to garner more sympathy in a town without pity or remorse, where it was all about what was on the outside that counted. My heart was beating faster as it was beating for two now. I walked through the nearly empty train station, resplendent in its old fashioned architecture, not feeling drained anymore from the day that I had.

I was full of life, a new life that was waiting to be had. All it was going to take to get me started was one of the taxis that I spied awaiting me through the main doors, idling as I had done for so long.

I stepped out into the mild late-spring night and approached the taxi stand. I picked the least-scary-looking and "possibly would steal my money and sodomize me after he killed me" taxi driver. I picked the one that might want to have a sixteen-year-old posing as an eighteen-year-old to give him a hand job in lieu of payment.

He was scruffy looking but in a "he'd clean up nicely" kind of way. I wasn't sure if he was gay or not, but I did see his eyes look me up and down when I informed him my destination was Santa Monica Boulevard. But seeing as my gaydar was not yet modified with the proper detection software, it was always a crapshoot to figure out who might want to play with my hard drive, not that I had really gone seeking out a bevy of men after Steve. He had answered some of my longings regarding what sex could be like but had brought up more relevant questions. For instance, since he and I had only ever performed oral sex on each other, what was it going to be like to kiss a guy or have a guy inside me or vice versa?

I felt like a fledgling. I had only taken partial flight; now it was time to fully spread my wings—and most likely my legs. My heart was beating in my chest like a sparrow's; I hoped that whatever electricity flowed between the conduits of Danny and myself was still there, waiting to provide enough juice to light up the entire West

Coast. That was my dream; my dread was that he would send me home on the next and fastest mode of transportation.

I practiced what I would say to him, opening up a line of mental dialogue plucked out of any number of bad B movies filed under the category of drama.

"I had to leave, there was nothing for me there," I would say. "No one to understand me, no one like you."

"You know that I will take care of you. The big bad world is a scary place, especially for those of us who are, well, different."

He would sweep me up in his arms and carry me off into the sunset. Cut. Print. That's a wrap.

Either I had been mouthing the words to the dialogue in my mind's eye or the taxi driver was checking me out for other reasons, I caught him on three separate occasions staring at me in the rearview mirror.

Utilizing my newfound confidence by overriding the old-record fear-based reality of Henry Dodge, I decided to find out if my gaydar was starting to be up and functional. I also wanted to see what type of sexual allure I may have in the City of Angels. Were my surfer-boy good looks enough to help those in doubt about their own sexuality turn the corner? I wanted to help. I wanted to give, to give back what I had not so freely given myself by finally saying what was on my mind.

I started to rub my crotch through my Stussy shorts just enough so that if I was wrong about the taxi driver, I could play it off like I had jock itch. I could tell by the way that his eyes lit up with delight, a thousand-watt lightbulb, that I was right on the mark instead of being way off target. At first I thought that the reflection of light that caught my eye was provided by his unbridled lust; it was a streetlight reflecting off his wedding ring.

There was a smattering of cars on the road, surprisingly few considering that this was Los Angeles, yet not so unfathomable considering it was a Wednesday night. Correction, it was a very early version of Thursday that saw me in the backseat of a taxi using my innocence and a heapin' dash of raw sexuality to make the taxi driver have difficulty in keeping his eyes on the road.

When I removed my penis from the confines of its cotton underpants prison through the escape route the right side of my shorts provided, I thought he might swerve off the road. But my eyes were darting between looking at my engorged penis in my hands and then looking in the rearview mirror to gauge what type of reaction I was eliciting.

When he took the next off-ramp and found an out-of-the-way alley, I knew I was garnering bravado raves. But he didn't jump into the backseat offering to ride shotgun while we played a special kind of tug-of-war with each other. No, he was subscribed to watch what I was doing while he took care of himself. Guess this way he could absolve himself of connecting what he was doing with cheating on his wife, who was most likely awaiting his return at home. Either that or she was shacking up with the biker that lived next door to them in some shitty apartment complex to complement their shitty life together.

I knew I had the upper hand. Hell, I had the lower hand too. I heard the taxi driver moan ever so slightly, his eyes never wavering from the point where my penis was poking out. I could tell that he had climaxed because the cab was filled with a guttural, animalistic sound, like from an animal that was snared in a trap. Perhaps he was; the wedding ring was like a bear trap for him, snapping its steel jaws down on his finger, ever reminding him that he was not being true to himself. I was glad that I was able to know myself better than a twenty-something cabbie voyeur. I let all of the thoughts spill from my mind at the exact moment I released my first of many orgasms in LA.

We never uttered a word; I didn't get his name. This ride in the taxi signified my first foray into the world of anonymous sex. It also cemented a fact for me that I could escape the shackles of not being good enough by feeding my sexual appetites.

I was beginning to like Billy Collins much more than Henry Dodge; he was freer, more in charge of who he was. Maybe it was Billy who had instigated all of the doings back home. I knew I was just playing a big game of "Let's pretend." But I still wanted to underscore how brave I had been in the steps that I had taken. The duality that was present within had transformed fantasy into reality for me.

Back in the moment, the cab driver turned the defrost on high, and the fog that had clouded the windows faded into the ethers along with the experience. He was pulling a stunt I was more than used to by then, the silent treatment, which was fine by me. What did I really have to ask him about himself that I couldn't already concoct in my imagination? Once the windows were safe for driving, he pulled out of the alley, reinserted himself back onto the freeway, and we arrived at Santa Monica Boulevard in no time flat.

He waved away my hand with his that sported the wedding ring when I tried to pay him for the cab ride. Perhaps this was his act of absolution. He could free himself of the act by not taking the money; therefore, the act never occurred if there hadn't been a fare. It was a little too steeped in Catholic-church guilt for me, but I was just happy to not shell out the money.

He drove off looking at me from his rearview mirror the whole time, and I swear I caught sight of a lone teardrop. It refracted a spectacular array of colors, almost like a rainbow. Maybe Santa Monica Boulevard was my somewhere over the rainbow? I was just hoping I could remember exactly where Danny lived. In the happenstance of the day's events, I was hoping to go by memory and that hopefully it would not steer me in the opposite direction of my intended paramour. Danny, where for art thou, Danny?

But wouldn't you know it, all of the side streets were blending together. I wasn't even sure I was at the right part of Santa Monica Boulevard. It didn't seem chic, fabulous, or remotely gay; it was starting to seem downright dirty and more than a bit scary for a boy used to the suburbs. The urban jungle lay before me. I was a great explorer now seeking out a tribe to call my own that would accept me for who I was. After a homeless person asked me for money, I decided to use my personal shutting-out armor. I strapped the Walkman to my ears and was serenaded by Bryan Adams. "Run to You" seemed very apropos of my current situation. It was funny, but I didn't feel like I was running away; I felt that I was going towards something.

Finally I started to feel a little safer in my environment yet still a bit out of my element. Oh who was I kidding? I was scared shitless; the bravery was just another mask that I chose to wear, like when I was six and would play alone in my room, Fisher Price people my only friends as I wore any number of the plastic Halloween masks that my mother had stockpiled. Breathing through a small slit, my eyes tunneled vision to just see what the task at hand was, rubber bands providing a security that no amount of words of kindness ever could made me feel somewhat invincible, even if it was only momentary.

Well, I had ripped off the mask tonight, snapping the rubber bands, allowing myself to fully see and to be able to breathe. I was still feeling that everything that had happened was surreal, yet if I really looked at it, life before that moment was surreal. I was a real live gay boy.

I was a little fish in the big pond now, a pond that was murky and was hopefully going to be not as stagnant as the one I had just swam away from. But I didn't know. Although I was now in the land where box-office deals were made, I had no one scripting my life; I was just doing what I felt was right. Suddenly I felt very vulnerable, an easy mark. Maybe I should have waited and taken the train in the morning. Even though I was walking forward, trudging on, I felt that mentally I was standing still.

Bryan Adams was rasping poetic about heaven while I was pondering the very real possibility that I was in hell. I was looking for an angel, yet the fires were licking at my feet, propelling me along. I was waiting at a crosswalk for a light to turn green, signaling that I should move forward, when I had my first confirmed sighting. There were three youths gathered on the opposite corner, not engaging in what I would term hetero horseplay. No, they seemed to be taking their cues from *My Pretty Pony*.

They were grabbing their crotches as cars slowed down to check them out, putting forth such a sexual vibe that could possibly rival Madonna's writhing in her videos that I felt like I was being sucked into a vortex. I may have avoided them altogether, but I felt as though my feet were not of my body. Fortunately, I was not going against the light as the little green man assured me that it was indeed okay to proceed. I turned down the volume on my Walkman, not sure yet if I was here to observe or to partake.

I knew these boys were hookers, hustlers, street meat. One late night, before we had purchased our VCR, I had stayed up to catch the sequel to *Dawn: Portrait of a Teenaged Runaway*. It was called *Alexander: The Other Side of Dawn*, and the primary focus was on Leigh McCloskey, so I knew instantly that I would like the movie. The movie was all about him being a male prostitute falling for an older ex-football player. I dozed off before it was over, so I was not sure if Alexander was giving a Hollywood happy ending or a grim finality courtesy of real life. Well, whatever the case was, I now found myself standing next to these boys of the night, who had probably gotten a little too much meaning out of Pat Benatar's "Love Is a Battlefield" video.

"Keep on truckin', motherfucker!" a Latino with bad skin huffed as a potential "date" drove off. "You could be so lucky!"

And just to add a visual exclamation point, he mooned the driver so fast that I wasn't sure if what I was seeing was real or not. He caught my gaze, and as if the three of them were on some psychic hooker wavelength, they turned in unison to stare in my direction.

Suddenly, I felt like a zebra that had stumbled into the lion's den. I wondered if they could sniff out the fear I was starting to feel. It seemed they were threatened by my new meat quality coupled with the innocence that was missing from their street-hardened lives. All three of them, very aware of my presence, began to circle around me, taking me in, looking me up and down, spitting out critiques.

"Ooooh, it's Goldilocks! I got something that's just right for you!" little Mr. Poster Boy for Clearasil said, grabbing his crotch just in case I didn't get the gist of what he was trying to convey.

I took in the other two hookers: one was faux blond from a lot of time spent with a peroxide bottle, and the other was another Latino who was much cuter than the self-described leader of the pack. They all seemed to be dressed in the haute couture for street hustlers, very tight shorts and very tight tank tops. I looked down at my aqua green Le Tigre shirt and Stussy shorts and thought I was not too far removed from them.

I slid the Walkman's headphones off my ears, catching each of their eyes with my best Arnold Schwarzenegger glare in *The Terminator*.

"How are you guys tonight?" It was the best I could manage, and I have to admit, it was much better than "Lovely weather we're having."

Blank stares from vacant eyes that saw the world as a cold and cruel place answered my question. Each of them looked like they ate, but there was a hunger about them. Perhaps they were zombies in a fabulous all-singing, all-dancing extravaganza of *The Night of the Living Dead*. They craved human flesh in order to survive; they feasted on it and needed more and more to keep their lives together, lives held in place by Scotch tape.

"Oh we're fine," the leader of the pack spoke with a peacock strut and a snapping of his fingers. "Question is, how are you? Who are you?" Then he eyed me up and down. "And more importantly, what are you? You lost, Valley boy? Well, this ain't no information desk, all right? So you better get your ass home before someone files a missing person's report on you."

He said this all in one breath. It sounded very well-rehearsed, and I could see a spark of life inherent in his eyes when he was all fired up and giving his speech. My guess was he was once a boy who had dreams of making it big in showbiz; when it didn't happen, this is the off-ramp his life had taken.

He had to be in his early twenties, starting down the slopes towards over the hill in his current occupation. Therefore, he had to be very territorial when it came to fresh meat coming into town. Hookers are like lightbulbs: the old ones get burned out, then a new one replaces them, all full of light and ready to shine.

Instead of running into the night, I extended my hand, looked him square in the eyes, and said, "I'm Billy."

It was the first time I had uttered my new moniker out loud. I was surprised at how effortless it seemed to flow, an uninterrupted river. He stared at me while the other two members of the Supremes awaited a cue from Ms. Ross, the boss. I stood my ground, realizing my insights were serving me well.

The leader was afraid of the new-meat aspect, unscathed, untarnished, that I provided, all but sure that I was going to be stealing his thunder. Truth be told, I wasn't looking to make ends meet as a hooker, but I was obviously fascinated by them. Well, maybe I could give hooking an old college try. They were like a TV movie playing out in front of me. Maybe I could learn something from them, if they were willing to teach.

"I'm Angel, this is Pollo, and that's Rocky," he said this with a switchblade smile that told me he admired my balls but was not one to trust someone right off the bat.

Angel also presented each of his cohorts with a flourish of hand that would make Vanna White scurry out of town. I supposed if I had laughed that his name was Angel (Santa Monica Boulevard hustler by day, well, Santa Monica Boulevard hustler by night too), it wouldn't have been the best of decisions.

I also knew that Pollo meant chicken, but I did not realize the gay connotation that it held. I was not heavily immersed enough into gay culture to know that everything could be a double entendre or have other meanings. Steve was in many ways the wrong person to induct me into gaydom. He had given me the necessary skills, albeit oral ones, but there was so much more to learn. I was really latching on to the idea that these three were just the ones to help me along, to give me the proper inflections of dialogue, to steer me in a queerer direction.

"Nice to meet you," I said in all my naivety and decided to throw a punch verbally. "Do you guys have a joint? It's been one shitty day. My parents kicked me out of the house, you believe that?" I threw it in for good measure to score a sympathy joint and used it as a gauge of my credibility.

I thought that drug use must be rampant to mask the pain of their lives. I knew that it worked for me, that I could soar above the pain to a place where nobody could touch me.

"You're not a cop, are you?" Rocky asked point-blank and with a straight face.

Obviously Rocky was not the bright one of the bunch. Maybe the peroxide that he bleached his hair with had seeped into his brain.

But I could see the appeal of him; he was very C. Thomas Howell as Pony Boy in *The Outsiders*. Stay gold, Rocky, stay gold.

"Do I look like vice?" I asked, very aware that I must have lifted that line from some cop show.

"Well, ah, no, I guess not," he stammered.

"You can never be too sure out here," Angel said, a forlorn look of weariness crossed over his face, the moon experiencing a partial eclipse.

"Yeah," Pollo confirmed; his voice was light and musical.

I could tell that Pollo, who was around my fake age, was the low man on the totem pole. He had a taut appearance that didn't make him look severe but innocent, a man-child. He didn't seem threatened by me; he seemed relieved, like I was an ally. Maybe I could be. Maybe I could try what they were doing. I didn't want to go to Danny as a novice, I wanted to be all things to him, and I wanted to be there in every way for him.

"Well, it just so happens that my shift is up," Angel proclaimed like he was working retail instead of the streets. He stood with his arms akimbo, a pantheon of stereotypes I had seen portrayed on my television screen over the years. "And I do think I can help you out."

A slight smile revealed why he had probably not been going after his SAG card. He had very crooked teeth of the ones that were still remaining in his mouth. Coupling that with a face that only Clearasil could love, it was understandable why his marquee dreams had been dashed. Perhaps the crash and burn of dreams unrealized had given him the edge that was apparent in his mannerisms and speech.

I felt a momentary sadness for all that I may be missing out on by the choices I was making right now. How were they going to affect my future? What were my dreams? I still liked to dabble in drawing, but other than that, what did I have to offer the world at large? I wanted to fit in, yet I was hell-bent on rebellion. Here among society's outcasts, I felt like I could actually have found a place for me.

Angel pulled me out of my reverie with his barbwire bantering skills.

"Let's move it, Mary. None of us is getting any younger."

Well, as a matter of fact, some of us were claiming to be two years older than we were. I was Billy Collins now, and he had a keener sense of adventure than Henry Dodge ever did. He strode into the night with his sashaying tour guide, looking for ways to forget while trying to find ways to discover.

We took a taxi to our destination, this one not ending with any type of sexual gratification. Our conversation was sparse, but during the span of it, I did learn some pertinent facts, like where it was that we were going.

"King George always has the best stuff," Angel stage-whispered to me, thinking that the fiftyish Middle Eastern taxi driver was at all concerned with us.

"King George?" I asked. Suddenly feeling very sleepy, I stifled a yawn.

"That's what we call him. He looks after us, those of us in his kingdom. And he can help you if you're sleepy."

I conjured up images of a nude bodybuilder-type man sitting upon his throne, overseeing his minions, providing them with whatever they desired. I was filled with an overwhelming excitement that quashed the sleepiness I had been starting to drift into. I wanted to bow down before the king.

We arrived at his "palace," an innocuous apartment complex in Studio City. Even though it was nearing two o'clock, there was a light blazing in his window; a low volume version of "One Night in Bangkok" was seeping through the door. I expected Angel to use a three quick rapped secret knock on the door. Instead he produced a key, and we entered into an empty living room, the stereo playing to a nonexistent audience.

Black leather sofas, glass and chrome tables, Patrick Nagel prints, faux flowers made out of a silky material all told me we had not entered into the fifteenth century but rather the lair of an eighties man. Angel made his way to a closed-door room to retrieve his majesty.

I stood in place admiring the Nagel prints—I loved his work— and silently wondered if Duran Duran would ever want to use my artwork on their album covers. I had been the number one student in my art class, amazing the teacher with my advanced skills. Now there would be no more classrooms, only the lessons the school of life had to teach me. I wished I could see the syllabus that was outlined for me.

I heard the door open down the hall and turned around to present myself to the king, almost tripping over my bag when I caught sight of him. He was no Adonis but rather a mild-mannered midforties man who had latched on to Henry VIII's eating habits. He didn't sport a crown nor a robe made out of the finest furs in all of the land. Instead he emerged in his underpants, the waistband barely able to manage the task of keeping his expanded waist in place. He looked very alert for that time of night and was sniffing a lot, like he was an allergy sufferer. He laid his eyes on me, but I already knew that wasn't all he wanted to lay on me.

"Well, well, who do we have here?" I was expecting a James Earl Jones voice to emerge from his vocal chords; instead I got Richard Simmons ratcheted up a notch or two.

He was eyeing me like I was an all-you-could-eat buffet. I supposed if I were to experiment in the realm of hookerdom, this would be the kind of person that I would be catering to.

"I'm Billy. It's very nice to meet you," I said in my best manners-for-company voice. It was like addressing a long-lost uncle, yet I would learn later that it was more or less saying hello to Daddy. Again, I was shocked at how easily, and at such a late hour, I was able to not stumble over my newfound identity.

"Well, we're quite the gentleman," the underpants-clad Saint Nick wannabe said, laying a finger on a side of his nose. "And quite the looker."

He walked around me, looking me up and down. I felt like I was being inducted into the army. He turned his focus away from me and on to Angel.

"Oh yesss, he'll do very nicely, very nicely indeed," he said this without regard to my presence in the room; although I knew he was more than well aware of it, if the beginnings of his hard-on were any indication.

"I did good then?" Angel queried, all of a sudden soft-spoken, puppy eyed, and in desperate need of affection.

"Yesss indeed."

The yes had so many attached *s*'s that it seemed as though the king's tire-like belly had sprung a leak.

"Go get what you need in my bedroom, and I'll make our guessst more comfortable in the den," sssaid the ssspider to the fly.

I had more than a sneaking suspicion of two things. One, Angel just pimped me out, literally, for drugs. Two, and even more shockingly, I was going to have to become one of Santa's very special helpers in order to get mine. It didn't seem quite fair that Angel only had to give lip service that did not include sexually satisfying Jabba the Hutt's second cousin twice removed.

Well, this was going to be my litmus test to see what I could endure if the body before me wasn't chiseled out of black mahogany like Steve's. But Steve was a part of Henry Dodge's past. King George looked to be in Billy Collins's immediate future, and he escorted me off to the den.

"Ssso you just get into town?" said the king, spying my bag and utilizing his sleuth-like abilities.

"Yeah, my parents kicked me out." I let the thought dangle there, feeling that I didn't have to say "Because I told them I'm gay," that it was a natural assumption the king would make on his own given our current very close proximity on the couch.

"That'sss a ssshame," he pronounced with an appropriate modicum of concern then was grappling with his hands that began searching out my body. He began by lifting up my shirt and made lazy circles around my nipples.

I had to admit, if I shut my eyes, it could be anyone doing it to me. But upon opening them, I realized it was the king, breaking all illusions. He was quickly undoing the button on my shorts and started to work the zipper. I knew that it was now-or-never time, that if I could do it with the king, then I could give hooking a try. Besides, isn't life a series of compromises? So what were a few compromising positions when it boils right down to it?

I was sure that the king would only reconfirm for me that sex didn't put this big wonderful spin on everything. It hadn't been that way with Steve. I had expected everything to be different, the world to look fresh and anew. Maybe at first it was a little bit, but then Steve's behavior towards me dictated otherwise, leaving me feeling even more alone than before I had the experience under my belt. It was like many things in my life; the inner world I shone in far and away put the real world to shame.

As the king peeled back my underpants, I realized that it could be different with different men. Maybe there could be one to truly satisfy me. And in my heart I hoped that it would be Danny. But for right now, his substitute was starting to go to work on me, licking me sloppily. I was wondering if he was imagining that he was going to town on a bucket of KFC. Well, whatever his motivation was, I was starting to get lost in how good it felt. It felt so good that I just let all of my inhibitions literally go. Hope this extra crispy dinner came with wet naps because I had some gravy spilling onto my thighs. The king must've been reading my mind; he produced a tissue lightning fast and watched as I dabbed away pleasure's evidence. I pulled my pants up, wondering if he was expecting me to do the same to him.

"Ssso, you're ssafe, right?" the King inquired.

I was a little bit confused to say the least. Safe? Safe from what? I was safe in knowing I had made the right choice by leaving home. I was safe from nuclear fallout, at least for now. I guess the only way to find out was to ask the king. But before I could, he asked another question.

"You've been tested, right?" He was looking at me point-blank, gauging my face for even the slightest hint of a lie.

I was still in the mind-set of having been a high school student as of last week, so I was starting to wonder if he was asking about school. Did he mean safe from harm of the cruelty that classmates can inflict? Did I take my SATs? I began to wonder if I was somehow going to be duped into joining some offshoot version of Jehovah's Witness. They heralded the second coming of staying in school and went pounding on doors, their *Watchtower* replaced by a Scantron and a number two pencil.

"I'm not sure I know what you mean," I admitted.

"AIDSSS, you've heard of it, right?" he asked somewhat smarmily with just the right inflection to remind me that he was near my father's age.

Of course I had heard of AIDS, it was 1985, for chrissakes! Hell, my mother even knew about it. But since Steve and the voyeuristic cabbie were my only two dalliances into the world of gay sex, I didn't know about getting tested for it.

"Ummm, yeah," I said with my by now-perfected smart-ass retort, "I know about AIDS. I haven't been tested yet. You're only the third guy I've been with."

I thought about embellishing the number to make myself sound cooler, but given the king's admonished state, I thought it was best to tell the truth. Then a thought hit me: who gave him the nickname King? It sounded a little too self-important and manly for him.

"So why do they call you King George?" I asked in all earnestness and happy to be onto another topic.

"Because Queen George was already taken," he said without missing a beat, awaiting peals of laughter to spill from me as easily as my orgasm had.

I must have been looking at him like he had been on fire or something. Well, I guess he was flaming. But you see, I did not have the reference points to know that a queen flames. Much like my childhood had been, it seemed that my fast-living teen years were going to be about finding it out on my own.

"Oh dear, you are green," he declared. "Who'sss been ssshamefully negligent in teaching you the prosss and consss?"

"Well," I began because I was able to discern what the gist of his question was, "there was one guy I slept with for about nine months. But he wasn't gay. He had a girlfriend."

It was so weird to be able to say the word *gay* out loud and not have to fear any repercussions.

"Oh pleassse! Did he sssuck your cock? I hate the ones that hide behind the ssshield of 'I have a girlfriend.' Sssorry," he said eyeing me, looking for me to become wraithlike and come to Steve's defense.

Well, I think blackmailing him was a very telling sign of the direction my opinion of him had traveled. So I just shrugged, treading water lightly.

"Ssso, Billy, ready for that joint?" I could tell he was trying to read me, to tell what kind of guy I was. But if I didn't really know, then how could he?

Although I was already tired out, I thought the joint would provide the perfect cap off to the day that had been had. I nodded a yes; he produced a pipe already packed with the green stuff. See, I knew Hollywood was the place for me to be. Sex twice in one day, pipes all ready to be smoked, someone to explain things to me—what more could a sixteen-year-old masquerading as an eighteen-year-old want out of life?

"So"—I let the thought trail off as I took a hit of the pipe and held it in for the proper length of time before I finished my train of thought—"what's a queen?"

And with that began the question-and-answer portion of my introductory course to All Things Gay 101.

Chapter 8

A few days later, George and I sat on the patio at the French Quarter Restaurant in West Hollywood. I was having trouble concentrating on the menu and what to get for brunch on a particularly sunny Sunday afternoon. Everywhere I looked there was a legion of gay men in all shapes and sizes. After the waiter approached our table for a third time and then left with no order from me and a heavy-handed sigh, George snapped me out of my reverie.

"Ssso what looksss good?" he asked one side shy of annoyed and on the fringe of sounding jealous. "Apparently, it'sss not sssomething on the menu."

"I'm sorry. It's just, well..." I tried my best to explain why I was feeling broadsided by being among so many gay men at once. "I guess it's just that I always felt so alone, know what I mean? I never realized it could be like this. And everyone is so different."

"It'sss not like it isss on television," he answered, cutting to the quick. I had revealed that weakness too early in the game. I had to practically beg him to watch the *Dynasty* season finale as he detested soap operas in any way, shape, or form. A sign at a floral shop across the street caught my attention and let me know that I was not alone in my love of drama-filled cliffhangers, "Guess who lives and who survives the Moldavian massacre and win!"

Two men approached the restaurant holding hands as if it were the most natural thing in the world. To them it was, and I could only hope that someday it would be for me. I hated that word *someday*; it's a word that people use when they were unsure of themselves. I wanted to be in the know. I saw the waiter approaching again, quickly decided on pancakes and sausage, and watched him maneuver among the landscape of men. Just as quickly he was swallowed whole, evaporating back into the chaos of patrons that undoubtedly knew what they wanted more than I did.

"Well then, pop quiz time," George announced, surprisingly not clapping his hands. He loved to spring these quizzes on me whenever we took a sojourn into West Hollywood in the hopes of fine-tuning my barely there gaydar and terminologies.

"Him," he said, pointing nonchalantly at a burly man sporting a white T-shirt and leather vest.

"A bear," I answered.

"And?" he pressed.

"A daddy," I said, not realizing that we had ventured into multiple choice.

"Very good," George said in a way that my father never had.

George became like a surrogate father to me. In and of itself, the whole world now looked like a page out of a Richard Scarry book; each man had a label attached to him: butch, nelly, queen, top, bottom. My perceptions, having been limited before, were now becoming finely tuned to determine who might be a sister, as George called our ilk.

Even though I was thrust gratefully into a world I wanted to learn more about, I still needed my escapism fixes. So far I had spent my severance paycheck from Steve on movies, music, and a few trips to the arcade. The rest of my living expenses were covered under the umbrella of being George's boy. I wasn't expected to cook or clean while George was away at his office crunching numbers as an accountant. No, that was Angel's job, as he was George's houseboy.

I never expected Angel to clean up after me, and I tried to engage him in conversations to no avail. He felt like he was now getting the short end of George's stick, resigned to staying in the servant's quarters of the spare bedroom adjacent to the den. He did the dishes; I did George, as I was expected to be more than ready, willing, and able to help him relieve the stress of his job with some quality naked time.

It wasn't like I was blindsided to the fact that George was using me for my body because I was using him too. Pumping him for information in every literal sense of the meaning so that I could show Danny that I wasn't some naïve small-town boy made me feel at turns exhilarated, yet, somewhat guilty.

I knew in some respects I was getting a free ride but that there are other ways of paying.

I also felt that people on the outside looking in would immediately think that I was just some twink. Well, I may look like one, but my insides were not made out of some type of whipped-cream-like substance, all fluff with no substance. I was still feeling different, even within the community I was seeking out.

George was like a practice boyfriend. I would learn what I could from him until the time came to ride without training wheels, hobbling from side to side until I got it just right. And with the trajectory I had within me, there weren't enough miles of roads or stretches of highways to slow me down.

The king also served as my first lesson in the true meaning of how a person could prove to be a juxtaposition. I thought that with his speech patterns and flair for decorating that he fell into the category of typical queer, as seen on television.

But George was a man of many surprises. I learned that he had fought in Vietnam and had been in close enough proximity to an exploding booby trap that had hurled him into the air. It was one of the few times in his overweight life that George had realized his dream of being lighter than air. Unfortunately, the consequence of this flight that was not so fancy was that he had landed face down on a rock and knocked all of his teeth out.

So the slow leak his speech patterns took on were a direct result of ill-fitting dentures that he now sported.

I was also amazed to learn that he had been married at one time and had a grown son named Troy. I was even more nonplussed to learn that his son would soon be joining the already-full house that was George's apartment.

Sure, George was like the aforementioned surrogate father to me, and in all respects, I was young enough to be his son.

But the idea of seeing him interact with his real life flesh and blood was a little unsettling. I had a barrage of questions for him. Out of the several that I asked, George opted to answer the only two he felt were pertinent.

"Does your son know you're gay? How long will he be here?" These were the two he chose to address.

"Yesss, he knowsss. He always staysss with me in the sssummer," he said as we sat side by side on the couch in the den, deciding what rerun to watch or to see what was on HBO. I knew from his clipped tone that was the end of the conversation.

The remote that I controlled happened upon the opening credits of *What's Happening?*

"Wow, check out the booty on Duane!" I said this with a new-found confidence, yet I felt as though I should pull out the aptly named *Webster's New World Dictionary* just to make sure I had said the right thing.

The smile on George's face told me that I had done well in my verbalizing skills; the longer he stared at me, told me that I was about to see if my oral abilities were still passing with high marks.

Just as George began to unzip his work pants, the doorbell rang. I suddenly felt that I was being saved by the bell. He harrumphed and got up to answer it, since Angel had begun his shift down on the boulevard.

I often wondered during my ample free time if I was being primed to replace Angel. Would I end up on the streets, slinging my hash for cash? Or would I fit more into a houseboy mold? I had overheard Angel and George discussing the possibilities of me working the streets while I faux slept on the couch as George prepared his world-famous Steak Diane a few nights ago. His culinary skills were that of a master chef, explaining the extra flesh encompassing the bones on his body, and put my mother's attempts at all things Velveeta to shame.

"We could make a lot off him, you know?" Angel said in a stage whisper, his unrealized dreams of stardom still prevalent in the way he could project his voice.

"I know that," George said tersely and, dare I say, a bit protectively. "I just think he'sss too green right now. Hell, he didn't even know what a top wasss. Let'sss jussst sssay, he'sss in training right now. When the time'sss right, I will let you know."

"Well, he's gonna have to start helpin' me out around here then," Angel said as though my week there was far overstaying my welcome by a good six days. "When are you going to tell him about…"

He let the thought trail off like the smoke of a jet plane, there one minute, the next a hint of what it once was. Tell me about what?

"Jussst give him sssome time. The kid'sss been through a lot."

"Fine, we'll just wait for the little *mijo* to become a man."

Although my eyes were closed, I am sure he said this with a sneer residing on his broken-out face.

I wanted to like Angel, but he made it so hard to do. He felt threatened by my presence; of that I was certain. I had to win him over somehow.

"Precisssely. Now get me the musssshroomsss." When the king said this, I immediately thought that he was referring to the hallucinogenic type.

It seemed that the king's apartment could have served as a makeshift pharmacy. He had all sorts of drugs, which he would send off with Angel when he began punching his time card on the corners of Santa Monica Boulevard and a dead-end street.

The king was like an overseer of Angel, Rocky, and Pollo, but I couldn't quite determine if he was their pimp or not. He was very covert in his dealings with Angel and the boulevard set. I knew he packed Angel's lunch for a hard day at work; a white powdery substance they both called Tina replaced the usual snack packs of pudding.

George had tried to get me to try Tina, but I liked the way that pot slowed things down. And from what I could determine when George was snorting what looked like cocaine (if my watching *Miami Vice* had taught me anything) and the way he talked a mile a minute afterwards, a symphony of *s*'s gone awry, there would be nothing mellow about it.

George returned to the room as I returned to the present. By his side was Nick, his forty-something contemporary, who was always showing what he did for work as he sported paint-spattered clothes. Nick and George could've have passed for brothers, and for all intents and purposes, they were. They both sported the same body type and seemed to love the younger set.

"George, how 'bout a couple of brewskis? Hiya, kid," Nick said with a breezy nonchalance that belied the way that I saw him staring at me as he entered the den that was going to be of iniquity before his arrival had halted any such plans.

"Hey, Nick," I said with feigned interest in his presence.

"Whatcha watchin'?" Without bothering for an answer, he seized the remote, sat down in close proximity to me. He smelled of turpentine and had stale cigarette breath. I looked at him, taking in his profile, and was immediately reminded of the silhouette of Alfred Hitchcock at the beginning of his TV show—well, Alfred Hitchcock minus the English accent, droll sense of humor. Just add the hair that he wore down to his T-shirt collar and, voila, you had his white-trash American cousin! A few stations down the line was Ricky Schroeder in *Silver Spoons*.

"Damn, he is one fine lookin' lad!" Nick said as though he were eyeing a sugary confection trapped behind the window of a sweets shop.

I guess for all intents and purposes he was. I felt slightly anti-quary in comparison to the younger Schroeder and more than a bit repulsed by the elder Nick. I kept waiting for Nick to twirl the end of his almost walrus-like mustache, ala any number of cartoon villains. What he did next, I didn't expect.

"He's not as fine lookin' as you though," he said under his breath and copped a feel before he heard George arriving with good times in a can. He returned his focus to the television, playing it off like we were deeply in search of something of quality to watch.

I was feeling confused; his touch hadn't repulsed me in the slightest. I had actually gotten quite a tingling sensation in my nether regions from it; although it was quick and to the point. Was it possible that I could end up as the cover model on his warped version of *Teen Beat*? Win a dream date with Henry/Billy and find out what kind of girl he likes. Well, a girl without breasts and had other dangling glands would be more up this cover boy's alley.

Yet I shouldn't have been so surprised, I guess. I always spent a good portion of my day pawing through George's massive porno magazine collection that he kept in a box in his bedroom closet. Then I would spend a better portion of the day pawing myself, usually maxing out after five go-rounds and still ready for George when he came home. Ah, the joys of being sixteen! My autobiography could have been entitled "Raging Hormone."

So even the slightest provocation, the mere nearness of another man's touch, regardless of whose, was enough to get my motor racing. I was starting to feel the Indianapolis 500 racers revving their engines; the checkered flag was dropping, signaling it was time to burn rubber.

"Let's fuck," I whispered in George's ear before he was even all the way sitting down next to me. Catching him midair and off guard didn't deter the playful urgency that he must have sensed in my voice. He stood fully erect in a moment's notice, took me by the hand, and led me into the bedroom.

"We'll be back in a while," George called over his shoulder at Nick, not catching a slightly smoldering look aimed in my vicinity.

He was hoping to rub two sticks together with me, build a fire, and play Boy Scout and den master. But this scout was off with another troop leader, ready to go for his merit badge.

Maybe I let myself be excited by Nick's touch because it had three nights ago that Angel had eluded to the fact there was something George needed to tell me, which he still hadn't spilled the beans on. So a little groping session with his friend may just have to be in order to even out the odds. I was silently mad at George. I didn't feel

I could say anything since I had been eavesdropping. I was still none the wiser, but as soon as that bedroom door closed, all of the other thoughts that cluttered my mind were eliminated. I only had one thought, and that was, "I'm gonna get me some!" It was the most important facet right that second in relation to how George could ease my mind.

It was funny, but for all of George's rhetoric about the importance of safety first in all matters concerning the bedroom, he and I never used condoms. He just assured me he was safe, and I trusted him completely. He had taken me under his wing, the fragile bird that had flown the nest before it knew how high it could fly.

Hell, George had even taught me how to shave properly. No, I am not referring to trimming the bushes. I mean the hair that sprouted on my face. He was fulfilling his surrogate father role out perfectly with the perfect measure of care and understanding. He was opening my eyes to a world my own father would be disgusted by. At the thought of Big Ed, I almost had a pang that reeked of homesickness, but it was quickly undercut by the lust factor. In the card game I was playing, a hard-on always beats an emotion.

We went at it for two hours that night. Maybe it was me trying to soften him up to tell me what he needed to say by keeping him hard as a rock. The only thing that he spilled was his seed all over his barrel-shaped torso at one point. That was the other thing about George: not only was he a fountain of knowledge in all things gay, but his mantra could have been, "Why sssay it when you can ssspray it?"

We took a shower together in silence; George had no idea that mine wasn't due to the sexual marathon we had just partaken in. I felt like a kid on Christmas Eve, impatient and wanting to know what was inside of all the packages that lay underneath the tree. What was he keeping from me?

The sun set; the heat from our passion play slipped underneath the horizon also. I listened as George began to snore softly. I was a little nonplussed that my plan had not worked. What did those big-haired bitches on *Dallas* and *Dynasty* have that I didn't except for a huge Aqua Net bill? George was tougher to crack than I thought, but maybe those he surrounded himself with would prove to be his Achilles's heel.

I knew that my sexual wiles would work on Nick; that was a no-brainer. So I silently got out of bed, threw on just a pair of shorts, and made my way to the den.

Not bothering to knock on the closed door—I lived here after all—I found Nick sitting on the couch almost exactly as I left him. The only watermark that time had passed was the number of beer cans that had cropped up on the coffee table in front of him.

He looked up, not surprised, not affronted that I had just walked into the room when he could have been doing God knows what. Somehow I think it would've been masturbating to a rerun of *The Little Rascals*. No, he was watching *Firestarter* that George had taped off cable.

It was on the same tape that captured two more celluloid classics, *Porky's* and *Rhinestone*, starring Dolly Parton and the incomparable, or just plain incomprehensible, Sly Stallone. How did I know what tape was playing? Well, let's just say that George had a penchant for repetition. Although I didn't mind watching *Firestarter* and was happy for the good memories *Porky's* elicited, *Rhinestone* on a fourth viewing was like Chinese water torture with a Brooklyn accent. Even though I knew the answer, I still wanted to act the innocent.

"Oh you're watching *Firestarter*. Do you mind if I watch it too?" I detected a feigned lightness in my voice and hoped that Nick wouldn't.

"Not at all," Nick said this straight-faced, so there was a more than probable chance that this snow job would turn into a blow job. Hopefully he knew George's secret.

Nick even patted the black leather couch cushion next to him for added emphasis that he did not mind at all. I think he might have been just a tad drunk, but his four empty beer cans and two in preparation to be consumed were no litmus—not when I thought of how this would've been Big Ed's practice run.

I stopped the thought cold. This was the second time today that I had found myself thinking about the oppressive place I used to call home. I didn't want to think about the person I had once been, scared and confused, maybe a little unloved, but never unlovable.

And why in the hell did my mind keep turning to Big Ed? Simple deduction, my dear Watson! All of these older gentlemen, in fulfilling the requirements of surrogate fatherhood, made my own father's distance towards me all the more confusing. Was I that bad of a son? No, he was just a bad father. I just wanted to know why he was like that. Deep inside I still wanted his approval, not his reprimands. I put a padlock on the Henry Dodge cavalcade of father issues, sponsored in part by Velveeta and Budweiser.

I still had never had a beer, what with all of the emotional damage that my father's drinking had caused my life.

"Go to your corner, you're getting a time out!" I shrieked at the confines of my brain, which kept forcing Henry Dodge's issues on Billy Collins.

Without asking, I picked up one of the remaining two beers, popped the top, and took too big of a sip all in one fell swoop. I thought the beer was going to come shooting out my nose, like one of the many times at the dinner table when John had made me laugh with a mouthful of milk. He was notorious for that. But I managed to keep the beer down while suppressing further memories of my family. The beer was all right, I polished it off with no problem, but I was still a pot smoker at heart.

I dipped into my stash I kept in a nearby drawer and that George allotted me throughout the week. I took out a big bud, stuffing it into my marble-like pipe as I did not have the hand-eye coordination to roll my own joint. No one had taught me how to do that; just like a lot of things in my life, I was winging it.

All the while, Nick watched me dip into my addictive behavior patterns in silence, hoping that the "willing to try anything" aspect that came along with it would manifest itself onto his crotch. I offered him a hit of the pipe as Drew Barrymore's *Firestarter* started blowing away the enemies with her incendiary prowess. Nick shook his head, confirming he was strictly an altogether different kind of bud man.

Every time someone got blown up on screen, I took a hit off the pipe. Pretty soon the body count was as high as I was. The movie ended. I was feeling very good, able to perpetuate my out-of-body experience better when I was not in the right frame of mind. Nick put down the can of Budweiser that he had a death grip on, picked up his pack of Marlboro Lights, tapped it out, lit one, took a deep breath, exhaled, and eyed me. All of this was viewed in a haze, like he was being shot through Cybill Shepherd's *Moonlighting* lens.

Or maybe it was all of the combined smoke that was being expelled into the room. I stood up to open the window a little further, lest Angel came home and thought we were sending out smoke signals. As I stood up, the effects of mostly the pot and not the unfinished can of beer made me swoon. I quickly sat back down, miscalculating where I had been sitting previously, ending up on Nick's lap.

That was all of the justification he needed to start pawing at me. His touch seemed somewhat electrified as it sent little shock waves over my bare flesh—either that or he still hadn't put his cigarette down. But from my vantage point on Santa's lap, I could see that it was snubbed out in the ashtray. I grabbed hold of his package, unafraid to tell Santa what I really wanted. Nick was probably a few years younger than George, in my estimation, but he was already huffing and puffing like a man twice their combined ages.

"Whoa!" He wheezed harder than a Pinto in need of a tune-up. "I need to take a breather."

Either he was embarrassed by his heavy-breathing crank call sans phone or he was really finding it that difficult to breath. His face was turning tomato red, so I got off him instead of getting him off. Was this the universe's way of telling me one of two things: be direct and ask for what information you need from the source, or never give the people, especially pseudo pedophiles, what they want?

Whatever the lesson to be learned here was, I was pretty sure that I should go get George. Nick was clutching at his chest; I started thinking he was having a heart attack. But then he started pawing at his shorts, leaving me to think that even in near death, this guy was good to go.

He seized my hand hard and started drawing it near his crotch, taking a last-minute detour to his right pocket. There was an outline that I hadn't noticed before by sitting on his left-hand side. It was at too odd of a bent angle to be his dick, but this early on in the game, how was I to know?

Nick began to anxiously point to the sheathed item; in his panic at what was happening, he couldn't make his body work as fast as mine could. Reaching into his pocket, I found something that wasn't fleshy but plastic. Oh great, Nick is a cyborg from the future assembled by Kmart and sent back in time to find mankind's last hope, Ricky Schroeder.

All at once, I became clearheaded enough to realize that this was an inhaler. Nick had asthma. The coupling of smoking and weight-lifting me had started up an attack. But as I reached into his pocket and withdrew his breath of life, my hand did manage to give his dick a graze, kind of like a comforting along the lines of, "Don't worry, when you can breathe, we can still do it."

I handed him the inhaler; he took three quick shots in succession. I realized then what I must have looked like toking off my pipe. It probably seemed that I needed my pipe to breathe as well.

For the first time in a long while, I felt like crying. Maybe it was Nick, maybe I was starting to doubt if I had chosen wisely at the crossroads of life. I turned away as a few teardrops made a hasty escape down my face, destined to be wiped away undetected. I wanted to feel like I was above the emotional waterworks.

But the more I thought about the fact that at sixteen I had told the truth only to live a lie elsewhere, the harder the tears fell, staining my skin with their heavy descent.

Nick regained his natural color as I tried to do the same with my composure. I felt a hand caressing my back, and that single act of tenderness let loose further torrents. I was crying for all that I never had, all that I wanted, and everything I was still unsure of. Nick pulled me backward; I was caught in the tractor beam of his meaty arms. As he held me, I was careful not to squeeze him too much for fear of causing him another attack or letting my guard down more.

I took in the smell of turpentine and was instantly transported back to the time when my family and Danny had built the green-house. I was in charge of painting a lot of it, but only an arm's reach above my head. So the paint job was very sparse looking. Danny would come around, and we'd be painting side by side, sometimes chatting away until Big Ed would come over and proclaim social hour was over. After a hard day's work of painting, stealing glances, connecting with a member of the same sex more so than I ever did with the girls I was supposed to, Danny and I would exfoliate the skin with a healthy dose of turpentine.

That sense memory racked my body with more sobs. Why wasn't I with Danny now? How did I end up here, trying to find out what George was keeping from me, having animosity thrown at me by Angel, and being nothing more than a sex puppet with George holding the strings?

"Shhhh, everything's fine," Nick said, his cigarette-rasped voice that was usually loud and abrasive now taking on the soothing strains of a parent comforting a child.

I looked up at him with my tear-soaked face. He wiped away the final tears that had streamed from my eyes that were looking for a way out, knowing where they emanated from, a place of pain that was always tangible.

"I think George has been keeping something from me," I sob-choked.

"Really?" Nick queried, and immediately I was struck by the sincerity tinged with concern in his single-word question.

"But I don't know what it is," I said, just a hair under whining. "Can you help me find out?"

Nick's answer came in the form of a "swallow you whole" kiss. I had to keep from laughing; his mustache was tickling me. I also had to keep from getting him to stop long enough for a breath mint as his combination kissing an ashtray soaked in beer was overtaking my mouth almost as much as his probing tongue was. I knew that I was probably no breath of fresh air either, having smoked enough pot to give me a proper alibi should George awaken from his slumber.

Nick pulled his tongue out of my mouth with an audible pop, but there was still something on my tongue. They were medium-sized and Chiclet shaped, and I tried not to swallow whatever it was. I spat the interlopers out into my hand and put them on the coffee table next to the plethora of discarded beer cans. It seemed that Nick had not applied his Dentugrip very thoroughly that day as his faux front teeth had been seeking out new housing in my mouth.

"Thorry about that," he said, giving me the impression even more so that he and George could be born of the same cloth.

I wondered how Nick lost his teeth. But before I could ask him, he had popped two more top teeth and four bottoms. I was too shocked to say anything, which was just as well, as Nick began to pull off my shorts; I knew I had swayed his loyalty in the brotherhood of man on man.

As Nick went down on me, my mind went elsewhere. If Nick didn't know anything and I was too afraid to admit to George that I had overhead him and Angel, where did that leave me? Only in a precarious position with my benefactor's best friend. I was supposing that my punishment for eavesdropping and breaking trust would be exile from King George's castle of black leather couches and faux orchids in clear vases adorned by a smattering of clear and black marbles.

So what would the king say if he saw his best friend going down on his new boy on one of three black leather couches?

Nick made a noise like he had telepathically heard my question and was trying to answer. Apparently his mother hadn't been a stickler on the "Don't talk with your mouth full" page of parenting or, in this case, "Don't suck with your mouth full."

"You are tho hot," he said as he came up for air.

My answer was a smile that was either meant to convey I know I am or that I appreciated him saying that. I left it up for him to decide on my "not quite yet a man of mystery" allure.

He went back to the task at hand, well, at mouth really. I do have to say this; it was the best blow job I had ever gotten thus far. In all my imaginings of scenarios that could be and then put to paper in my secret notebook, I hadn't really figured on this one. I think that was a common theme in my life, expect the unexpected.

Well, that and the best laid plans usually go awry. I was also starting to see how I could use sex to get what I wanted. And that was another great escape to take me away from the world at large.

The world that loomed beyond my grasp could now be reined in by utilizing my sexual prowess.

I tried to focus on what Nick was trying to accomplish, but the foothold in my mind was overriding the pleasures that my body was experiencing. If Nick had proved useless in terms of information he could provide, then perhaps I needed to get closer to the source without really going to the source.

It was time to try my wiles on Angel. And I knew the best time to strike would be tomorrow, when we were both alone in the palace. Seduction would probably cut into my watching the heavy rotation of videos on MTV. The soundtrack to the summer of '85 had taught me a few things: Things can only get better, everything she wants is everything she sees, everybody wants to rule the world, and *Goonies* are good enough.

I pulled back my thoughts as I pulled out of Nick's mouth. His brown mustache became snow white thanks to me; I almost wanted to say bless you.

"There, all better?" he inquired as he reached for one of George's ever-convenient tissue boxes and wiped me off his mustache.

He extended his arms out to me and smiled. The missing teeth may have felt good, but they were not a pretty sight. I kept expecting him to tell me I had a purty mouth. Unfortunately, I could not return the compliment.

I would allow him that rare instance of intimacy. I was used to "You're done, clean up, get dressed, get going." I mashed myself against his teddy bear–like frame and let him smooth my hair and run his hands all over me.

I didn't know why, but I felt that I could trust Nick. Maybe it was for the simple fact that I felt I couldn't feel that with George and that too much watching of daytime and nighttime soaps had made me realize I could pit them against each other.

"Thee, ith okay. I'm here for you," Nick said this without a doubt in my mind that he didn't mean it. "It'h okay, Billy."

"Henry," I said before I knew it was escaping from my mouth, "my name's Henry."

Chapter 9

It hung there in the air like the smoke that had been filling the room earlier, only this time I didn't open a window. I had let my real name out because I felt I could trust Nick, and I wanted to let someone see the real me. I had spent so much of my life already living a lie as to who I was and who I wanted to be that I didn't feel the great, compelling need to hide in the shadows that grew steadily darker outside the window—darker like the interior of my heart was becoming in matters concerning George. I knew that if Nick was on my side, I was bound to find out what George was keeping from me.

I had already learned the power of persuasion that sex had afforded me, like some offshoot bastard child of my mother's chocolate cookies. I wondered how my mom was doing, stuck all alone with no one but Big Ed to deal with; the silence between them was so palatable that if they were even keeping up appearances to break it, a chainsaw would be needed.

It was almost June. I had been a guest at the palace for almost three weeks now. I am sure my mother thought I was lying dead in a ditch somewhere. My father probably didn't give me a second thought, glad to be rid of the little faggot who was steadily trying to find out from another father how to be a big fag.

Little did they know, and little did I care, I tried to convince myself. But it had wounded me as surely as the final climb to freedom over the barbed wire of their preconceived notions of all that being gay entailed.

As surely as I was free, it was now my longsuffering mother who was the prisoner. And for that, I felt a pang of regret that I had left her there. I didn't understand her mind-set; it wasn't like Big Ed was the catch of all time or something. He was an abusive alcoholic whose treatment of her was subpar to how you would treat a three-legged dog.

The truth was, I had no idea if Kate Dodge was still holding down the fort or not. Maybe Big Ed was all by himself, drinking himself into the inevitable oblivion that came with his mass consumption of alcohol. Perhaps my mother had redesigned her life. Maybe she was out looking for me right now. Or she was glad I was gone, out of her hair. Of this I couldn't be sure, unless I went to the source. I guess I could have applied this lesson of just asking up front to George. But then how could I test out my newfound powers? I was treading into the land of unknown, charting a destiny for myself that I had no idea was right or wrong but I knew was necessary.

"Tho why did you tell uth your name ith Billy?" Nick said, now that his dropped jaw had realigned, enabling him to speak.

He sank back into the black leather backdrop, an anxious playgoer ready to find out who done it. I realized that by revealing my secrets that I could stand before the world naked. But somehow I knew that if I told my tale to Nick in the altogether, then he would not be focusing on what was being said. I found my shorts on the floor, pulled them on, giving Nick a brief backside view, before turning around to face him again, this time as Henry.

"Well," I started, pausing not for added suspense but trying to decide where to begin.

"Are you in trouble with the law?" he asked in all seriousness, yet the twinkle in his eyes told me I had a captive audience that was thirsting for some drama.

"No, it's not that," I replied, just shy of being offended.

As I spoke these words, I wondered if they carried any validity. I mean, I had taken off from home the night that I was arrested for smoking that joint. I was supposed to be cleaning up garbage at the beach all summer. But that hadn't happened, now had it? I wasn't planning on a homecoming anytime soon, or ever, if I had my way. I had a feeling Nick wouldn't rat me out to my parents after I told him my next bit of news. In fact, I had a sneaking suspicion that another blow job would probably be heading my way.

"I'm only sixteen. I ran away from home because I told my parents I was gay, and they didn't understand."

The light in his eye was now at supernova level. It was as though he was taking me in for the first time, and in a way, he was. He was seeing Henry Dodge, age sixteen, teenaged runaway, not Billy Collins, age eighteen, teenaged runaway. The two-year age difference between my selves apparently was not that big of a deal to Nick nor was the fact that I had lied.

Sooner than I knew it, Nick had pounced, a zaftig jungle cat who had grown accustomed to trapping smaller animals that wandered into his domain. His hands were all over me, and the frenzy of their activity would tend to dictate that he was a sex-starved individual.

But I knew for a fact that he was not; he just needed to show me his acceptance of me only being sixteen. Then he did something, which I hadn't asked George why gay men do it. When did the ear, and more specifically sticking your tongue into somebody's ear, become an erogenous zone, and why didn't I get the memo on it? Nick was going to town on my ear, acting as though he were my own personal Q-tip. Maybe he had dropped some teeth down there or had started looking for Jimmy Hoffa. Whatever the case was, it was not exciting me in the down belows.

When Nick's right hand realized this was the case, he took his tongue out of my ear long enough so as best to utilize it for his conversational prowess.

"How many timeth have you cum today?" he inquired; the look on his face was both serious and devilish.

"A few," I answered while mentally trying to do the math in my head. I came up with—no pun intended—lucky number seven.

"Well, maybe we can find something to get you going." As he said this, he got up and opened one of the smaller doors on the entertainment center, and he began to ferret through some of the multitude of videotapes that George had.

"Thith oughta do the trick," he cooed.

The always-present leer in his eyes basically told me it was up his highway and not my way, which would've been to call it a night if my secret was to remain intact. There were so many upper hands being dealt, all of them non verbally, that my drug-addled brain was having a hard time keeping up with the distinction between fact and fantasy.

I suppose it was just my projecting he had ulterior motives instead of the fact that I had gotten off and he hadn't. Adding an element of self-imposed drama to my life had carried over into my other existence as Billy. But now Nick knew I was really Henry. I guess I could relax and enjoy the ride.

The innocuous videotape began. There were bad voice-overs, and it had the production value of a home movie, and of course, there was the penultimate of porn—the bad soundtrack complete with its catcalls of bow-chicka-bow bow.

The movie was from the golden era of porn, which in layman's terms meant pre-condom. Speaking of which, Nick had done some more rooting and produced the thin sheet of latex that could mean the difference between life and death along with its partner in crime, Elbow Grease lube, from behind the plethora of porn. Had I known this stash existed (I do have to give myself credit, I didn't go snooping as to not incur the wrath of Angel or break that area of trust with George), I would have been going to the city, and not to town, on a daily basis.

So far this movie wasn't really doing all that much for me. Realizing there were still credits on the screen and the real thrust of the plotline had yet to materialize, I tried to turn my mind off long enough to enjoy the fact that Nick was stripping me out of my shorts. His gumming of my nether regions was strangely exhilarating and a little bit creepy, like having Grandpa pop out his dentures and offer you a hummer.

I looked at the action that was transpiring up on the screen. Two youths were walking down an alleyway when from behind some metal trash cans sprang two "ruffians," and from the back, the one tall guy with a blue tank top looked eerily like Danny. Maybe it was the pot playing tricks on me, but I could swear it was him. And when he took out his huge cock, I knew it had to be him! I mean, I had never seen it, but I had certainly committed to memory the size and shape of it. And those ten inches filled the entire nineteen-inch screen.

When the camera panned away from the cock that conquered California, my fantasy became reality. It was Danny; of this I was more than 100 percent sure. There was no mistaking his slightly older handsomeness. I mean, if I was going on voice identification alone, then the badly dubbed commands he was barking out in muted non–lip synching would not have led me to the conclusion that this was my dream man, my dream man who was supposed to be getting work in the legitimate theater of daytime soaps, where I doubt he ever had to audition by reading a line like "Don't bite it, just suck it" or "You like that, don't you, bitch?"

My heart began to race, and for once I just let the blood ride to where it wanted to, the other head that was doing most of my thinking lately.

I was more excited by what was happening on the screen than what Nick was doing on his knees. But he didn't know that was the case. He thought I was really into what he was probably considering the best blow job in the world, considering how strong and throbbing my own manhood was. But it wasn't the Hoover hummer he was giving me; I was in another vacuum of sorts, lost among the dust bunnies of hazy memories that were becoming clearer by the second.

He stopped what he was doing long enough to add his own improv line to the porn happenings.

"I want you inthide of me," he said just a hair shy of pleading.

Without a word spoken and still catching the action on the screen, I heard him unwrap the condom, put it on me, and lube both he and myself up for proper effect. I didn't have as much giving as I had receiving experience, but "A good top remembers what it's like to be a bottom" had become my instant philosophy, given the situation.

So it wasn't all into the school of hard knocks, at first anyway. I had Nick positioned over the coffee table so that I could still watch my first noncelebrity crush project a screen presence that even the poor quality of the film could not damper. The boy that was struggling to take Danny inside of him and not look like he was being fitted with a flagpole did bear an uncanny resemblance to someone else—me.

It became very easy for me to imagine that I was him, that it should have always been Danny and me. I now had people's exhibit G (for *gay*) playing out in front of my eyes. Danny was gay, I was gay, and it seemed like a natural equation until you subtracted sixteen years. Would Danny care about that if I sought him out like I had initially planned? Would he just focus on the fact that I seemed older? The only way to find out for sure was to talk to him face-to-face.

I was matching Danny's rhythm on the screen, and when he and I climaxed at the same exact moment, it sealed the fate I knew we were destined to be together. Nick was about a minute too late on his orgasm, and his aim left something to be desired too. He had stood up and managed to get his jism in my stash; my stash is in your jism. While I wasn't sure that these two tastes would taste great together, I wasn't about to cry over spilled seed or spunk weed, as the case was.

I was very literally spent and very excited about the prospect of knowing that Danny was gay and not a bit remorseful that I had just sodomized George's best friend. Everything felt muddled. I knew I had my best intentions at heart, but my actions were starting to cause a bit of conflict on my conscience. I had learned that I could counterbalance these moments by latching on to certain feelings and then detach myself sexually. I could tap into instances from my past as readily as I could tap into what George may be keeping from me.

What really hurt about that was that George obviously didn't see me as someone who mattered. Who knew? I could have been just one of many in the long line of successors to the thrones of black leather, and I was just like the other cast offs. Didn't he see that there was something different about me? As quickly as the thought came to me, I realized that he couldn't possibly. I was lying to him from the start, using him, and now I had tried to find out what I needed by seducing his best friend.

I was the one putting up walls that would've been wholly approved of in China. It was time for an intervention and quick; somebody needed to put me into the Larry Hagman Clinic and try to detox the soap opera plotlines and mannerisms that resided in my head.

I opted for bed instead as a wave of tiredness began to take me to the sea of dreams. It looked as though Nick would be reprising his recurring role as the best friend that spends the night. His eyes were as droopy as his mustache. He and I were adamant in our silence; neither one wanted to solidify the moment by speaking. He exited the room first, putting on his paint-spattered attire so as not to raise any suspicions, and made his way to the guest bathroom to take a shower. I sat for an extra moment, taking in what I could before sleep enveloped me completely.

The door to the den swung open silently. Thinking it was Nick, I didn't go to any great lengths to disguise the fact that porn was still playing on the TV or that there was an empty condom wrapper and lube in plain sight. I could hear the shower start running, thinking that Nick had forgotten to take something into the bathroom with him, like two of his errant teeth that were left behind on the coffee table, which had become a catchall for deceit.

"Don't tell me you're ready for more?" I said this nonchalantly, staring at the TV to further illustrate my disinterest in another go-round.

"Well, from the looks of things, haven't you gotten enough?" said the voice that didn't belong to Nick but rather to this gun-for-hire Angel.

I looked up, feeling more exposed than my uncovered kibbles and bits, which were in need of a much warranted break.

"Ummm," I stammered, feeling the effects of being overly tired kick into overdrive as I feebly tried to think of something to say that would dissuade Angel from telling George, "it's not what you think."

Even as I said it, I knew that it was clichéd, the grimace I could feel spreading across my face, a blight of the knowledge that I had not been so quick in the "thinking on my feet" department.

"Really? 'Cuz I have a very good imagination. That's why I am such a popular date. Oh what do we have here?"

As he said this, he made a beeline inside and over to the coffee table; a look of smug satisfaction was present and accounted for on both his face and in his actions.

"Looks like Nick gave you one of his famous gum jobs," he said, eyeing the teeth that Nick had left behind.

"He had an asthma attack, he almost choked on them." I mentally checked the air for straws because I knew that I was grasping at them.

"I'll bet that's not all he choked on." The smugness was replaced by something else, a look of longing, distinct yet far away, and Angel looked as though he was grappling internally.

I used this moment to seize the underhand—I mean upper hand. I wanted to strike before the look of reproach came back and, at the same time, put him in the same category as Nick, who would hopefully be taking a long shower.

I sat up a bit more alert than I had previously felt. I reached for the remote and shut off Danny's stunning film debut, not wanting his celluloid image to be privy to my manipulative side anymore.

I wished my life could be as easy to control, that there was some sort of button I could push that would rewind, pause, or stop the actions that I took. But there wasn't, so I proceeded as unplanned.

Although my cock was beginning to feel just a tad raw, I gave it a playful tug. Immediately, I could tell that Angel was intrigued. I am not saying that I was all-powerful or irresistible. I just figured after servicing AARP card recipients all night, I must have been a sight for sore eyes.

I realized that Angel and I weren't so different, really; mine was a more subtle form of whoring. We used these older men as a means to get by, thinking there was no other way to do it than trading in on our youth, letting them use our bodies to feel young again while we used them like emotional vampires, draining their life force and disappearing into the night before the sun came up and we could see what it was we were doing.

Again, I got the smallest inkling I had chosen unwisely, that I was setting myself for failure in the future. But I managed to get a grip on the present, just as surely as I was going to get a grip on Angel in no time flat.

I shifted into my "I don't care" mode, mentally teasing my hair within an inch of its blond life and affixing shoulder pads to balance me out so that I wouldn't tip the scales into the debate between right and wrong.

I could see that Angel's daisy dukes were beginning to expand, so I thought about going over and removing them. I stopped myself. I wanted him to make the first move. If he did, anything he could say to George about me would sound like heresy; like in a school-yard fight, I could say, "He started it!" I felt more contained and in control now that I was becoming fully awake as well as engorged.

Without saying a word, I sent out the telepathic message that he should come over and pick up a little overtime. And it appeared we were on the same wavelength. Angel came over to let bygones be bygones.

Up close and personal, his face resembled a moonscape, craggy with the rough terrain made worse by his forays of seeing his secret mistress, Tina. His body was very nice, so I focused on that, mentally cutting off his head.

Deciding that instead of putting up our dukes, he dropped his, and right before my eyes was something I had yet to experience in my limited world of penises. His seemed to have been chilly because it had pulled the hood up on its sweatshirt. It resembled a worm, or rather a small snake in his case. I was a little nonplussed, a tad grossed out, but infinitely curious.

I went to work, exploring with my tongue, checking under his hood, and discovered there was nothing wrong with his engine at all. It was funny, just this morning Angel had gone off on me for listening to his "Into the Groove / Angel" twelve-inch dance mix and not putting it back into its proper place. Now, it was all about making nice with him via the unspoken word and a warm mouth.

Although I was fully awake down below, Angel didn't make any attempts to reach out and touch someone, namely me. Perhaps it was because he instinctively knew it needed a rest, lest the skin shed itself like a snake would. Maybe it was because I had just had my way with Nick.

Speaking of Nick, I realized that I did not hear the shower running. I bent Angel's penis at an angle to afford myself a better view of the door. It remained closed, so I went back to doing what would keep Angel from telling George. He must have liked what I was doing because he was starting to moan and thrash about like a great white shark latching on to its prey.

In fact, he was so noisy that neither one of us heard the door open. Our symphony of deceit reached its crescendo as Angel turned my face into a commercial for Pillsbury Toaster Strudel resplendent with its white drizzled icing. I was just about to wipe it off when a voice broke the silence.

"Well, well, well," said the voice that belonged to the master of the house, "looksss like sssomething'sss going on behind my back, right in front of my face."

I peeked out from behind Angel's groin region, hoping to explain my way out of this one. Not only did I have egg on my face, I also had a side of hollandaise sauce for me turning Benedict Arnold. Angel remained statue still, like we had been playing a very adult version of freeze tag.

All of the anger I had at George for keeping me in the dark turned immediately to fear as I saw the look of rage on his face. You never want to piss off a queen! I was at a loss for words, especially when Nick came bounding out of the bathroom, whistling through his missing teeth. He cut his song short upon the sighting of George, who was taking in the evidence that lay across the coffee table, clues that a blind detective could have put together as an act of treachery.

"Nick, Angel, will you pleassse excussse me and Billy?" he literally hissed. "We need to have a little chat."

Without a word, the two of them did George's bidding, each one throwing a distinctly reproachful look over their shoulder as George closed the door behind them.

Chapter 10

There was no way out of this one, I had been caught red-handed—well, white faced was more apropos. The evidence was strewn about the table like some haphazard people's exhibit A, B, and C of how to cheat on the man who took you in. I didn't know what George was going to do or say to me but figured the longer I stayed silent, the better my chances were for not pissing him off.

I had to wonder myself where it all went wrong.

Well, for starters, George was not being very upfront with me. The secret he was keeping from me was a more excruciating kind of being kept in the dark, far greater than not knowing what packages under the Christmas tree would contain.

I had to know, yet suspected that I shouldn't ask, that George needed a moment to collect his thoughts. We were both sitting side by side on the couch, glorious in our silence. I was not used to a father, be it surrogate or otherwise, who didn't shout at me when things went astray. I expected the table to be upended, spilling teeth, lube, and pot with a little something extra. But all he had done was to ask me to put my shorts on and take a seat. He was acting as though he was a receptionist at a doctor's office rather than the man I had scorned twice over in one night.

"Well, what do you have to sssay for yoursssself?" This was said with a calm reserved for a wayward kitten that is brought in, taken off the streets, given a home, and then decides it's time to show it's feral, revealing its true nature.

I knew the first thing out of my mouth could make or break my time in the palace. Usually, I would have just gone straight for the putting something in my mouth to quash any worries. I suspected that I had played out that deck of cards; all of my aces had turned into jokers.

"I don't know." I opted for the typical teenage response, not sure if what I wanted to say could necessarily be articulated. I wanted to confront George but felt any more slurs against my made-up character of who Billy Collins was would only damage my case.

"Well then, I have a few questionsss for you and a few thingsss you had better lisssten to," he said very curtly.

George's lisp never underscored the directness prevalent within his nature, which made the fact that he was keeping something from me all the more frustrating. And the fact that he seemed so nice seemed like some sort of veneer, a mirage in the desert that turns out to be waves of heat coming off the sand when you had thought it to be cool, healing waters. This oasis that I had fallen into was a far cry to the stifling heat of repression that prevailed at the Dodge homestead.

Somehow I felt that my time here was drawing to an end. Maybe I could make it up to George and promise to never even look at another man while in his vicinity. While all of my cards on the table revealed nothing but the laughing faces of jokers silently mocking me, there was still the wild card that Danny provided. I wanted to find him. I needed to find him.

"Okay," George began speaking, and I braced for the diatribe, "you have been a guesssst in my home for, what, almost a month now, correct?" He didn't even look in my direction to see me nodding. He stared out the window into the canyon with its eucalyptus trees that gave me allergies, looking out into the darkness like I was looking inward and seeing only the darkness of uncertainty.

I stared into the black nothingness of where my life was going. I was only sixteen, for God's sake, but I already felt like I had carried the brunt of the world's weight. While everyone else my age was worrying about prepping for their SATs, I was awaiting my fate to be determined by my lover who was thirty years older. Maybe he was waiting for a verbal confirmation before he went on.

"Umm, yes." As I said this, I was all of six years old, trying to explain rationally to my father why I had thought that putting a *Planet of the Apes* sticker on the television screen had seemed like a good idea.

Ideas are what got me into trouble; I would get a notion into my head and would not be able to resist its charms until I acted on it. My imagination, whenever it was fueled, was like an out-of-control rocket traveling through space, awaiting its crash and burn on some desolated planet. The question always remained: would it be a safe landing? Could I emerge unscathed only to let seeds be planted again and again in the young soil of my mind until I learned how to weed out the good from the bad? I never had anybody to show me how to do some of the most rudimentary things, and standing with his back to me, deciding my fate, was the man who had taken the time to do so.

And how did I thank him? Well, having sex with a man's houseguests may not be a Hallmark card in waiting.

"Roses are red, violets are blue, fucked your best friend and gave your houseboy a hummer too."

"What are you trying to accomplisssh here?" he inquired. "I have been nothing but nice to you, and my thanks isss thisss?"

Right at that moment I realized that George must be a good parent; he had the giving of a guilt trip down pat. I knew I should be groveling, begging forgiveness, feeling nothing but overwhelming guilt and shame. Instead, I felt the wave of how dare you crest over me. I only did what I did because George was keeping something from me, something that I was bound and determined to find out right then and there. I shifted into soap mode.

"What I am trying to accomplish," I began, trying my best not to imitate hisss leaking-tire ssspeech pattern and trying to tap into my inner Big Ed, "or, rather, what I am trying to find out is something I should have asked you about. But I've been too scared to find out. So I've been tiptoeing around subjects rather than ask you face-to-face. So, George, what is the big secret you are keeping from me?"

He turned from the window and stared at me puzzled, like he was seeing me for the first time.

"What are you talking about?" he asked earnestly.

"Well, I overheard you and Angel discussing something when I was just waking up from a nap, something about how I am in 'training' right now, and when the time was right, you would tell me. What is it you want to tell me, George?"

Now he was starting to look almost happy, or maybe it was relief; I could not differentiate between what was showing on his face and what was going through his mind.

"Oh that." Now I could clearly detect a smirk, signaling that George thought that the ball was back in his court.

He opened his mouth to tell me; the words were forming, ready to release the secret that had in its small way been driving me to distraction as of late. This was it, curiosity would not kill my cat, or in my instance, curiosity would not make me sleep with any more of George's friends. The smirk still plainly present, the first word escaped from its hiding place.

"Well," he began and was silenced by a knock at the door.

Nick did not wait for a response; he popped his head in, followed in short succession by the rest of him.

"Umm, sorry, I'm heading out, and I needed…" he trailed off, but his gaze was focused on the coffee table.

George said nothing, obviously irked at the interruption but was probably glad to have another moment to see me twist in the wind from the hangman's noose that I had hung myself with.

I had to remember that I didn't care, that George had brought this upon himself. I could feel the shields being raised, much like when I was a child and needed an escape and would be drawn towards happy family television shows or would let my imagination take flight. I needed to fortify my armor with a tougher, stronger casing so that what George may have to tell me would just slide right off. I needed a Teflon heart.

Nick grabbed his teeth, catching my eye before he made his hasty retreat, mouthing the words, "It will be fine." The gaping holes in his mouth where he needed to get a Denta Grip were distracting me, much like his entrance had proved a mild one for George, who winked at Nick as he left.

Maybe it wasn't a wink; maybe George had been fighting back the tears at my deception? Well, when one door closes, another one opens, as I was soon to find out from George.

"So you want to know what you are in training for."

I understood this must be a rhetorical question, so I just tried to think what way I could sit that would remind him I was a hot commodity. I opted to lay back, legs slightly spread, so I gave off the illusion of not caring with just a hint of sexuality. But I had my hands thrust into my shorts pockets, and they were balled up. Hopefully George did not think I had chosen an inopportune time to play pocket pool.

"Why do you think Angel brought you to me?" George asked this directly, but I was still assuming it was part of his monologue. When he remained silent for a moment and started glaring at me, I knew better.

"I thought he felt bad for me because my parents kicked me out," I said this with an earnestness that threatened to let down my guard. I mentally thought of Joan Collins taking the male-domi-nated business world by the balls as Alexis. I needed to bolster the feeling that I was the only rat left on a sinking ship.

"Well, that does play into it. You sssee, Billy, I take in straysss like yourself and try to elevate their sssituation in life. Ssshow them a little bit how the proper guidance can lead to better thingsss," he explained as if to a slow child. "I mean, look around you, I have everything that I could possibly desire and maybe even some things I don't."

When he said his last bit, he looked directly at me, before he continued. And try as I might, I felt my heart sink.

"Here'sss the deal, Billy. You have violated my trussst, and that is not sssomething I take lightly. Now I do feel for you, being kicked out, feeling like you have nowhere to go, no one to turn to. I want you to know that you can ssstill turn to me."

As he said this, I could feel the tears begin to well up, but his next speech stopped them dead in their tracks.

"But there's sssomething you have to do for me. Angel usssed to be just like you, ssslept in my bed, ate my food, and he never paid a cent towardsss any of it. Then one day, I came home early from work and found him in a compromisssing position with Nick," he detailed in a surprisingly calm manner. "Well, Nick is my oldessst and dearessst friend, and I would and will forgive him of anything ssshort of murder. But you sssee, boysss like you and Angel are a dime a dozen, ssso common in your purest notionsss of getting ahead by giving head. Ssso when Angel did this, when he violated my trussst as you have tonight, I told him he could ssstay here under certain conditions. He had to get a job and pay his way around here, keep the place clean, and I would be glad to look after him. But there would no longer be a place for him in my bed. Are you sssseeing any parallels? Any of this sssinking in there, Billy?"

"Yes," I said, mentally wondering if I should add "Mommie Dearest" to help break the moment with levity.

But it probably would have reminded George that I had been sitting around his apartment, watching movies he had taped off cable, and had enough time to see *Mommie Dearest* at least a dozen times so far. I knew that Joan Crawford was one of those gay icons, but I was confused as to how beating one's child with a wire hanger made for entertainment value. The first viewing of the movie had actually frightened me a bit, thinking that Mommie and Big Ed would have made one hell of a "scare the bejesus out of the kids" tag team.

But something compelled me to face my fears and watch it again and again and again until I realized that this movie had been mismarketed as a drama when, in fact, it should have been a comedy. I felt my attention span was drifting away from George, who was waiting for a response. I added an obligatory "sir" to the end of my sentence; I was doing it so I wouldn't have to tender my resignation at the palace. I knew I could get a job, maybe at the movie theater down the street, where I would while away some afternoons in lovely but albeit boring Studio City.

"Good, I am glad we are on the sssame page," George replied.

"I'll go out tomorrow and find a job. I'm sorry I hurt you, George," I said it with so much sincerity that I actually felt like I meant it wholeheartedly.

Something didn't add up. I was in training to get a minimum-wage job to give George money for food and rent when it was obvious he didn't need any help in that department. That didn't make sense, and it must have showed.

"Oh there's no need to look for a job. I have one lined up for you. You will go to work under Angel. I am sssure that won't be sssomething you aren't used to," he said, akin to a cobra spitting out so much venom. "You will ssstart on Friday, which will give you two daysss to get into my good gracesss again. If by that time you are unwilling to comply with my wishesss, you will no longer be welcomed here. In the meantime and until my son arrives tomorrow, you can sssleep on the couch in here. Then you can bunk with Angel. Won't that be fun?"

He was telling me the secret as to why I was really there, all of it said to me like I was a child that would be going away to camp for the summer.

But I wasn't going to be going away to Camp Snoopy. The camp I would be attending would be more on par with Camp Crystal Lake from the *Friday the 13th* movies, where danger lurked in the shadows. I was being sent out on the streets. I was being sent out to become a prostitute. No other words were spoken. George did not wait for a response and left the room as quietly as he had entered.

My mind was reeling. I had believed that George had truly cared about me, that he was the next best thing to having a father that loved me. But he didn't and he wasn't. I sunk even further down on the couch, the squeaking of the leather measuring how low I had gone.

I decided I had to outweigh my options here, to rise above, to prove victorious, and to formulate some kind of plan. The first thought that crossed my mind was to go home. Maybe denying who you are was better than selling myself short. Servitude on Santa Monica Boulevard seemed a more viable option than to return to the place I had so desperately wanted to escape from for so long.

There was always my not so dark but hung like a horse in the running, Danny. I had to at least try to contact him, to see if there was any chance that he would want to see me. I had two days to do it in. Part of me thought it would be no problem whatsoever to parlay my exuberant sex drive into cash. But since some of that cash would be going to George, and he was now feeling less like a father figure and more like a mother hen, I was feeling conflicted.

These were the times when I wondered where my life was taking me when I was so focused on the youth that I was and not so concerned with the man I would become. Maybe I should just collect my things and leave. I was sure there were a dozen, hell, hundreds, of men like George, minus his propensity for sending kids off to work on the street. Before I could hatch a cohesive plan, sleep overtook me, carrying me out of the deep end into the shallows of a new day.

I awoke to find the sun streaming into the room, and the day was already announcing that it would be a scorcher. My mental alarm clock reminded me that I could not hit the sleep button as far as coming up with some viable options on what I was going to be doing. I needed to set the plan into motion. I couldn't afford to waste time and take for granted that George might change his mind about me.

I peeled myself off the black leather. Little lines ran up and down my body on the right side; perhaps they were a secret map that had detailed how I could plan yet another escape route.

Wishful thinking was already being replaced by common sense in my sleep-addled attempts to just motivate myself all of the way off the couch. I swung both feet over the edge and planted them firmly on the ground and sat up as straight as an arrow. Someone had been in the room while I slept!

There weren't any traces of last night's debacle of love thy neighbor and thy other neighbor anywhere to be seen. The coffee table was wiped clean, and all of the accessories to the crime had been placed back into their respective places. Maybe last night hadn't really happened. Maybe I had just dreamt the whole thing asleep next to George's resonating chainsaw snores—maybe, but not bloody likely.

In their place was a folded-up piece of note paper with the word Billy scrawled across the front. I didn't even need to open the note to know that it was written on palace stationery with a friendly neighborhood real estate agent substituting for a royal coat of arms.

I was compelled to read it, but there was another pressing matter at hand: the morning emptying of the bladder. I guess motivation to get on your feet and start your day can come in many guises.

As I was taking care of business, I began to imagine what the note had to say to me. It was either an immediate kiss-off, rescinding the two days to get on board or get out right now, or it was an apology, the two clearest choices I could come to with a mind full of cotton, or at least that's how I was feeling after a night filled with sex and drugs but fell short on the rock 'n roll portions. Of course, the only way to find out for sure was to, obviously, read it with me own peepers.

I emerged from the bathroom and was headed back to the den to read the note that could hold my future in its black-inked monologue. A thought struck me like a bolt of lightning, something that hadn't seemed all that clear in the pot smoke and suds of beer last night. George had told me what I had already suspected was the case, that I was being primed to be pimped out. There was still something he was holding back. Angel had trailed off those many weeks ago with a "Tell him about…"

I was going over the possibility of things that it could be. I knew about his son who was arriving today, so that wasn't it. I sat down on my makeshift bed and reached for the note, pondering the fact that it could contain the information that I was feeling excluded from.

Billy,

I know that there is a lot going through your mind right now. I want to talk to you, but not

here. Meet me today at two at Oki Dog on Santa
Monica Boulevard. You can look up the address
in the phone book.

Angel

So it was Angel that had straightened up the room while I slumbered. Well, it made sense, I couldn't really see George doing that, not if he was ready to sell me off. I knew that at two o'clock today, the mystery would be solved, that my decision to stay or go was in Angel's hands.

It was so easy for me to give myself to men sexually; it seemed even easier to give myself over wholeheartedly, to let them control my destiny, charting courses that I was not adept to take on at present.

I was still finding my way. I didn't have the kind of role models that my straight counterparts did. I didn't have acceptance. I had already geared my life up so that I could see it queered up. I knew what it was like to be different. I thought that when I came to the city of men, that all of my problems would be solved. Now I found myself steeped in dilemma. I could only hope that Angel would prove to live up to his name because I did not know how to make it on my own.

The phone book was located in the kitchen, above the fridge that held a multitude of culinary concoctions for George to whip up. Thinking I could read through the white pages while I chowed down on the less-conspicuous bowl of cereal in lieu of George whipping up one of his world-famous omelets, since I didn't see that happening anytime in the immediate future.

George was off at the salt mines, as he called them, and yet he was willing to send me off to the coal mines of Santa Monica Boulevard without so much as a canary to gauge danger with.

My head was dancing around the pros and cons of punching the cock rather than the clock. My guidance counselor had said to do what I love, but I am not quite sure she had envisioned me strutting down the boulevard in daisy dukes. Of course, I had long been fascinated by the whole concept of prostitution, but it was purely from an entertainment standpoint. I was sure that once the gloss of the manufactured Hollywood version was wiped clean, things wouldn't look as pretty.

I took out the breakfast accoutrements, bowl, spoon, cereal. I opened the refrigerator door and was assaulted with the inventor of the Post-its wet dream. Every food item in the fridge had a Post-it stuck to its front, giving me its retail value. I felt like a contestant on *Price Is Right* and knew this was George's way of saying, "Come on down."

I closed the door, dazed until I saw that I had completely missed the note that bore my pseudonym and was stuck on the fridge with a Barbra Streisand in *Funny Girl* magnet.

I must have been blindsided before in my quest for nourishment that I hadn't seen it before, but now it was as clear as the nose on Bab's face. The handwriting on this note was different from the note in the den, so I knew it wasn't from Angel; although it was on the same stationery. The real estate agent known as Susie Ann Perkins and her 175-watt smile belied that the note would contain some happy news. But it didn't.

> Billy,
>
> Since this is no longer a free ride and you are going to be paying your share, I thought a little visualization of how generous I have been was in order. Everything in the refrigerator is marked with a price as well as everything in the cabinets. If you would like anything to eat, you will know how much you will now owe me.
>
> George

Not only was all of the food marked at price, but so was I.

My free ride, which I had mistakenly thought was one person helping another one out, was officially over. Last night's festivities had shown George just what kind of houseguest I could be. I was the kind that would steal the little seashell soaps when you weren't looking. I checked the cabinets; George had indeed labeled every item. He must have been up at the crack of dawn, if he had slept at all. I was starting to feel bad that he felt so compelled to express his anger through innocent yellow sticky paper and didn't feel he could talk to me about it.

I felt bad about it until I thought his little demonstration of how he was going from boyfriend to pimp had been predetermined the moment I walked into the palace. I was hungry, but not enough so to take out the box of Fruit Loops that now had a $2.25 Post-it adhered to it.

George had purchased it for me earlier in the week; now he was going to sell me, if I let him. And with my minimal math skills, I was trying to figure out how many Fruit Loops plus a dash of milk would run me. Figuring it might cost me more to give into George's pettiness, I would grab something in the neighborhood this morning. I still had money from Steve, albeit a lot of it had gone to feeding the entertainment beast that resided within me. I figured I had probably gone through at least half of what had afforded me this predicament.

I knew that my instincts were telling me to run away, to grab my things and go—those were my Henry Dodge instincts. Billy Collins was curious to see how all of this might play itself out. While the two grappled with each other, I pulled down the Yellow Pages first followed by the White Pages; both made a healthy thump as they hit the marble countertop. I was surprised that there wasn't a Post-it alerting me that there was a perusal fee.

First, I looked up the address for Oki Dog, listed under restaurants in the Yellow Pages. I wrote it down on one of Susie Ann Perkins's "confident that this will make you buy a house from me" notepads. Then I tossed aside the yellow sister for her white counterpart with as much thought as George must've had in his dealings with me.

I started closer to the back, seeking out W, as in Woodson, as in Danny. I passed through Wagner (unfortunately not Lindsay's home number), Weir, Woodcock, but there was no Woodson at all. Maybe he was using his porn name. Pseudonyms and boys from Encinitas using them didn't seem too far of a stretch. I hadn't been paying attention to the credits that much, so I guessed I could, oh, I don't know, maybe flip on *Up Your Alley* just for research's sake.

I closed the phone book and saw why I might not have found Danny under his born identity. The White Pages were only for Studio City and other valley regions. Danny had resided in Hollywood the last time I had seen him. Just in case, I took a pad of paper and pen with me to write down all of the names on screen.

Back in the den again, the place that made turnabout fair game, I found the tape still in the VCR. Although yesterday was a red-letter day in the stamina department and I should be giving it a rest, something stirred in me at the thought of Danny.

I pressed rewind, warmed up the TV, and dropped my shorts all in the span of fifteen seconds. I tried to remember that I needed to do some serious thinking that I couldn't just go about my normal day (i.e., spanking the monkey for innumerable hours).

The tape stopped and so did my eyes on the "somewhere near one hundred" videocassettes that were practically overflowing in the sheer volume of porn that had been at my fingertips but had remained previously undetected. Damn, I could have been rubbing myself raw to these instead of using my imagination over pictures and scenarios in the magazines that George had and harkened me back to my sketchbook days.

The thought of my sketchbook made me realize how far I had drifted away, not only from the boy with the secret, but the boy that would take the world by storm with his vision. How did I get myself into the mess I was in? The answer came to me swiftly with the ferocity of a boxer's one-two knockout punch.

I had opted for an entirely different sort of education, an education of gathering life experiences and sorting through them. I was seeking out what it was like to be gay from other people, just like I had sought out any crumb of gay sensibility on television to help me identify with.

I suspected that by embracing the stereotypes I didn't know any better about, if I latched on to the commonality of knowing who Joan Crawford was -would this make me a full-fledged gay? I had put my trust in George, a man that left me a terse note adhered to the refrigerator with a Barbra Streisand magnet. I wasn't sure if I hated George or the diva that was supposed to be one of my icons if I were to adhere to the rulebook. By having George be the one to show me what gay was, I had made a terrible mistake, and now I would have to pay for that mistake in some fashion.

Being gay was starting to feel like a revved-up version of high school with its cliques and the pressure to fit in. I just wanted to be happy, to be me, and here I was, staying with a man thirty years older than me under an assumed name, getting ready to revisit a childhood crush that was symbiotically living under false pretenses.

Funny that I had this epiphany just on the outskirts of the town that ballyhooed the joys of being beautiful, of being glamorous, of being fake. I was still hungry to find out what it was I could make of my lifelong same-sex attractions. I felt that I had put a tainted spin on what it could be like right off the bat. Deception, blackmail, and their ilk were all well and good for soap operas, but my pattering behavior after them was in no way helping me make it through the wilderness.

I needed to take what I had learned, the terminologies, and reapply them in a fresh environment, one that I hadn't left my signature of fucking up on like a dog marking its territory.

But where would I go, and what would I do?

Well, I had proven it to myself before that if I didn't like my living situation, I had it in me to just up and leave. If I wasn't being appreciated and downright oppressed within the confines of my newfound freedom, then I didn't have to stay. A part of me felt that I owed something to George that wasn't written down on a Post-it and stuck to a food item. I had hurt him and felt a desire to make amends for letting him down, for being a disappointment.

In a lot of respects, George was just the perfect man to act as a surrogate father to me. He could turn his back on me, an icy breeze pushing him away. Maybe George and Big Ed were right in not embracing what I had to offer each of them on entirely different fronts. Maybe I was just not the lovable scamp that I saw myself as, the little boy that could turn the world on with his smile. I was just unsure of whom I was going to be in this world and needed a helping hand to guide me, and the two men that had been assigned that task didn't seem like the right ones.

The world was probably full of guardian angels assigned to give me guidance, and when one didn't work out, I could just as easily gather up my belongings as surely as I could gather up what I needed to learn. I wanted to do that now, but I also wanted to see how some things were going to play themselves out.

Realizing that I had been lost in my reverie and was still kneeling in front of Dr. Caligari's porn cabinet, I rose to my feet. My shorts were still down around my ankles, anchoring me to the spot. I was reaching down to pull them up when a porn title caught my eye. It was called *Chicken Hawk*. I went back over my mental crib sheet. A chicken was an underage boy; therefore a chicken hawk was someone over legal age that preyed on the younger set.

The VCR stopped rewinding *Up Your Alley* at that moment and, with a hiccup then a burp, ejected it from its maw. I was curious about this other movie; something was compelling me to put it in the VCR. I laid Danny's movie to the side; there was time enough for a private screening before I needed to head out.

I put *Chicken Hawk* in, and it picked up where the last person to watch it had left off. Sure enough, a young man was the star attraction, making sure the-I-supposed-he-was-older-man-because-all-I-could-see-was-his-cock, very happy.

He was moaning up quite a storm. The camera began to pull back, and at just that moment, I heard the front door unlock. I would plainly be caught with my pants down, so I began to pull them up and was trying to seek out the remote to silence the action on the screen. Just as my scramble was about to be overtaken by panic and as the footfalls were drawing nigh, I heard something that stopped me cold. It wasn't the encroaching footsteps; it was a snatch of dialogue from the movie.

"I want you inthide of me."

Chapter 11

I heard the voice, ethereal, a ghost from my not-so-distant past. I heard the footsteps impending, faster now, bringing themselves and whoever was attached to them into my present.

I couldn't find the remote; either Angel had really tidied up or I had fallen asleep with it in my hand and it had rolled underneath the couch. I somehow did not think that *Chicken Hawk* was for my eyes at all, but they did manage to recognize a sense memory that a familiar-looking penis did hold. Realizing a split second before the entity in the hallway would burst through the doorframe that I could simply shut off the entire television with the push of a button, I saved myself from the shame of being caught.

The pseudo shame I would have felt if Angel or even George were at one with the footsteps that had stopped dead in their tracks just outside of the door was nothing compared to the fleeting moment of shock when I saw who the feet belonged to.

It was Danny!

The blond hair, the height, they all equaled him when taken in at a momentary glance. But when studied or, more aptly, stared at, my mouth agape, for more than five seconds, they revealed his twin must be none other than George's son, Troy.

It was truly eerie for a moment, like having a premonition of an impending death. More than likely I could chalk it up to a huge dosage of wishful thinking on my part to think that Danny had actually found me when nobody knew where to look—if they were bothered with looking at all.

The stillness and silence all but threatened to encase us, shrouding us in frozen synergism as we stood motionless staring at each other.

"Who the hell are you?"

When he asked me this, there was no question that he was George's son; direct and to the point must have been that family's creed.

Although it was an innocent enough question with just an undertone of venom, I wasn't sure how to answer. "I'm a friend of your father's" sounded both false and lame at the same time. "Just a guest" seemed like an understatement. "New bitch on the block" seemed a tad premature. So I opted for simplicity.

"I'm Billy," I said this without stumbling over my false identity; it was now tripping off my tongue as though it were my real name. "You must be Troy. It's nice to meet you."

I said this all like I meant it. Troy didn't know what the circumstances around the palace had been like in the last twelve hours. If he went looking for a snack, he would surely find out that the climate had been bracing for a cold front in the middle of the swelter of a July day. I saw a look of distrust emerge on his face, unmistakable and as severe as his father's.

"How old are you?" he fired away.

"Eighteen," I volleyed back.

"What year were you born in?" His arms were folded across a worked-out looking chest; it was uncanny the way that he resembled Danny. He didn't have the surfer-dude motif going for him; he seemed more of a corn-fed version.

"Oh great," I thought, "he's using my archenemy, math skills, to try to catch me in a lie. Well, I'll show him. I'll just add a two to my existing birth date and wait for him to ask me my rank and serial number next."

I may have paused a minute too long or had a strained look on my face, like I was trying to figure it out, which was the case. Troy let out a huge sigh, like he was finally going to find out the meaning of life, and then God had answered another phone call, putting him on hold.

I wasn't sure why I felt a compelling need to jump to attention for Troy; it was probably some sort of guilt complex over his father, I was sure. I was always hoping that people would like me, that I try to remain faultless. But in the palace, everyone knew differently.

Hell, I'll bet Angel snickered when he did my laundry and found the strange-looking greenish skid marks that I had been invading my underwear as of late. I didn't know why they would look different from the ones that had cropped up from time to time in my life. I just attributed it to my system getting used to George's culinary prowess. I just wanted people to like me so that I had a sense of belonging. Troy had now started tapping his foot, the ultimate in unspoken expressions of impatience.

"1967. When were you born?" I decided to fight fire with fire and not with a flame.

"Geez, they're getting younger and younger all the time," he said this to no one in particular; it was as if his thought was readable, like a cartoon character's word bubble.

Then he took the snarling tiger look and turned it into a soft, fluffy kitten. His face when relaxed became very good-looking without all of the bitterness attached to him. The barnacles of past situations were waiting to be scraped off and dropped to the ocean floor, burying themselves underneath the sands of time.

"I'm sorry. It's not you. I had a long-ass drive and I'm a little bit tired." As he said this, he made his way into the den, dropped his bag, eyed my bed last night, sans sheets and a pillow.

I hoped he didn't sit down in a puddle of drool produced by a deep sleep as I could feel one beginning to form in my mouth in my waking moments. I didn't think Troy was gay, but he could have been the poster boy for all things West Hollywood from what I had seen on the scant excursions into wonderland.

His hair was just right, gelled to perfection, teeming with the flaxen shadow so closely associated with everything So Cal. He was maybe a shade or two off on his skin tone to really hoodwink people into believing he wasn't the goods, a bona fide native. Well, this native was getting restless just looking at him.

That's when I realized, I was standing next to the television with a pad of paper and pen, hoping to jot down Danny's porn name, before Troy had made his entrance. I probably looked like a makeshift waiter awaiting final confirmation on the verdict of medium or well-done. I put both of my hands behind my back, symbolizing the hands-tied feeling I was having lately. Troy didn't utter a word. He was magnificent in his silence; that is until he opened his mouth.

"Do you mind? I'd like to take a nap. Now quit staring and close the door behind you," he snapped this time, wholly unapologetic, and the tiger's ferocity transformed his face again.

I could feel mine turned a shade of red underneath the healthy tan I had achieved by braising myself with baby oil. I exited the room quickly, so fast, in fact, that I almost didn't remember that *Chicken Hawk* was playing on the VCR. So if Troy turned on the television, he would be assaulted with the exploits of "younger man, older man" encounters. However, from the lambasting he had given me about my age, I suspected this would be nothing new for Troy's blue green eyes.

I determined that I needed to get myself motivated if I was to meet Angel at the appointed time. On top of that, I needed to find a phone book that would, hopefully, contain Danny's real moniker.

The things that I sought out always seemed to be contained within the pages of a book—whether it was idealist wishes sketched out in the notebook that saw its fate doomed to the trash can or the White Pages, Hollywood division, that might bring me face-to-face with Danny again.

Talk about reaching out and touching someone.

I made my way into the bathroom that served as both Angel's/ guests' pit stop. I spied my bag on Angel's bed and knew I fell into that category of guest now, albeit a temporary moniker I imagined. The door to George's room was closed, shut off to whatever feelings he may have had for me, if there were ever any at all.

I was still clutching the pen with a death grip in my right hand and was applying the same pressure to its neighbor, the pad of paper in my left hand. With only two days to decide my fate, I could relate with the feeling of pressure the pen was undergoing. I knew there was something afoot if Angel wanted to meet me outside the palace. Perhaps a changing of the guard might be in the works?

In a few short hours I would know, but I wasn't feeling geared towards being patient. I wanted the immediacy, the rush that was analogous to having an orgasm. There was so much pent-up frustration that I felt at the choices I was making that I just wanted to feel the bliss, the afterglow, to be on the knowing side of things.

I closed the door behind me as an unforeseen shower began on its own. A surge of tears pushed passed the tough front I was trying to keep up. I sat down on the lid-down toilet seat and had myself a good old-fashioned boohoo.

This type of release was much more warranted than dropping to my knees for an emotional distraction. I was always glossing over how I felt in lieu of external pleasures. I had a thought that most teenagers will have in their young existence. I couldn't believe that this was my life. This thought was directly responsible for starting a whole new dirge of feelings of self-loathing, which lent themselves in perfect harmony to the tears, creating a symphony of discord.

All I had ever been seeking was a place to belong, to flourish like the stunted flower that doesn't have the likelihood of succeeding and is always just shy of getting ripped from the garden forever. I wanted to blossom underneath cloudless skies, happy to just be, but my head would never allow it.

Now a storm front was causing flash flooding warnings that sprang from my eyes and would more than likely signal an early frost for my heart. I wanted to be tough, to brush things aside constantly, to be a man. I was nothing more than a lost little boy calling out for anyone who might heed my cries of help.

I had set myself up to be some kind of lone wolf, only able to depend on itself, not needing the world at large in order to survive. I felt like such a walking contradiction of terms, independent enough to come out and run away from home yet still hopeful that some stranger, any stranger, would show me something about myself that would make me realize that I was special.

I had been playing a prolonged game of hide-and-go-seek, but the game grows tiring when no one comes to find you and all you can do is hide behind things, finding it difficult to shout out, "Here I am." I had a faint idea, an outline, of how I wanted my life to be, but I wasn't bothering to shade it in.

This last thought brought my focus onto the pen and paper still in the death grip even after the waterworks had been turned on. I ripped a piece of paper from its resting place and flipped it over, exposing the solid white underbelly.

I released my grip a bit on the pen so that I could draw for the first time since I had left the world of mandatory academia behind. A ballpoint pen wasn't my instrument of choice, but it would suffice.

I drew an outline, an impression of a man, in a succession of quick strokes and shaded in the surrounding white space to give it more depth. I silently wished life were this easy to fill in as the tears renounced their existence; the only traces that they had been around were a telltale red face and a sniffling nose.

I set the paper and pen at the counter, disgusted with my feeble attempt to recapture my love of drawing; I crumpled the lone make-shift canvas up, throwing it in the trash. It seemed like a long-ago passion that had been stifled and suppressed to the point of blinking itself out of existence, once a supernova that now was a dwindling, soon-to-be-dead star. Even when it was burning bright in my art classes and I would receive praise for the work I did, I was always skeptical of its staying power.

I didn't want to believe that people could see good in something I did as I was the eternal fuck up, least likely to succeed.

Ironically, I was having this epiphany there was nowhere to go but down while sitting on a toilet. That's where my life seemed to be heading, and it was all because I had bucked the norm and struck out on my own at such a hypersensitive time in life.

I looked into the mirror and didn't see youthful exuberance. I saw defeat and doubt prevalent on my tear-stained face. I should be worrying about what electives to take for the fall semester, not if I should stay on George's good side as he took full advantage of my youth. If I kept on this trajectory, I would just watch it go by the wayside, leaving me at some juncture to ask, "Where did it all go?" All washed up at sixteen, to borrow the subtitle from the theme song for *Flashdance*, what a feeling!

Angel had a ghetto blaster on the back of the toilet, not caring what song came out of its speakers; I just wanted to quiet the tempest of self-defeat raging inside my mind. I pressed play, and the opening strains to "Into the Groove," immediately bringing solace to my besieged mind. And you can dance for inspiration. So far in my progression into the gay world, Madonna was the one musical entity that was providing the soundtrack that I could relate with. I let the song take me out of my negative reverie until I heard a shout from the den of, "What the fuck?"

I suspected that the musical interlude had woken Troy up or was preventing him from falling asleep. And just like his father, rather than come to me directly, he was taking the roundabout route.

His curse-filled shout gave me a chill, making me realize how much of my life I had been doing the eggshell shuffle—whether it was around my father, my talents, my desires, or now Troy.

I had always been carrying the flag that bore the snake and the slogan that read Don't Tread on Me. I remembered seeing that flag with Big Ed and John on our mandatory pilgrimage to the aircraft carriers, my male Dodge counterparts' idea of a great way to pass away a Sunday afternoon.

I liked the concept of being confined at sea with a ship full of men but had already learned from my father what being screamed at because I hadn't made up my bed was like.

Right now, Brother John was navigating towards home as the six-month West Pac almost completed. I wondered if my parents had told him about me. I wondered if he would still like me or be my brother. Then I remembered that I had a steely resolve to never set foot on Arroyo Street again. Then why had I been trespassing on private property lately? Was I homesick?

"Billy, get out here!" Troy's bellow cut my thought right off.

I was immediately cowed by the fury intrinsic in Troy's vocal intonation. I turned off the tape player and emerged from the bathroom and almost walked right into Troy's fist, which was about mid-knock and/or pound.

He uttered nary a word and clamped his hand down hard on my wrist and practically pulled my arm out of my socket as he dragged me into the den. Not too surprisingly, the television was on, but I didn't know why he was having this violent reaction to the man-on-boy action on the screen.

"Where did you find this?" he said this, and a vein ran down the surface of his forehead, a ripple in what could be a normally placid lake.

He released my wrist; there was a red mark from the short trip from the bathroom to the den. I looked at the screen. Nick was still only a featured penis player, but as the more discerning viewer that had encountered a true close-up, I wasn't sure that Troy would know the difference. He seemed to be staring at the young man that was going for Oscar gold with his subtle performance.

"It was in the cabinet. Why?" I asked this last question with an air of trepidation, not wanting to set him off on another jag.

"That's my best friend from home! What the fuck?" he repeated this last statement, which had been the harbinger to my unexpected return to the den. "He came out here with me about five years ago. I brought him because he seemed really cool with the whole 'My dad's a fag' thing. I didn't know he was this comfortable."

He switched off the television, vacillating between disgust and anger. He stared at me dead-on, like I was the one behind the camera yelling, "Action."

I didn't know if my role was supposed to be that of informant or confidant. I was unsure as to why he thought I had some special insight into why his buddy from the sticks had made an amateur skin flick with his father's best friend, no less.

I just said nothing. He turned away in a huff, opened the cabinet, and started foraging through the porn like a kid in, well, like a kid in a porn store with carte blanche. I had a feeling though that he wasn't really looking to see if his father had collected all of the titles available from Falcon Studios or had *The Young and the Hung Part 3* in 3-D. He was pulling out the endless stockpile of homemade escapades of young lust, West Hollywood style.

He took out all of the titles pertaining to chicken; one was even called *Finger Lickin' Good*. I was surprised there wasn't a title called *Shake 'N Bake, and I Helped*. I couldn't believe that George was also dabbling in the semikiddie porn pool; he was an equal-opportunity exploiter.

"He told me that he would stop. He promised me!"

Troy knew I was in the room, he had dragged me there, but he was not addressing me.

I didn't think I was providing any moral support, or he just needed me to bear witness to what he started doing next to give it extra validity. He took a rather ornate-looking paperweight that resided on one of the shelves and began destroying his father's wrongdoings. He put his muscle into it until there was nothing more than broken videotape casings, spilling their guts, so that no other eye could ever see the sins of his father.

I began to back out of the room, afraid that he would somehow transfer his rage for his father indirectly at me. As I was just about out of the line of fire, I saw a tattered title affixed to a broken tape that brought it all into sharp focus, *Chicken Hawk 2: Nick and Troy*.

I had hoped it wasn't *Up Your Alley*, but Troy had seemed pretty methodical at the titles he was after. I don't know if I was more dumbstruck by the fact that George had either taped or let Nick tape a sexual encounter with his son or that he was as clueless as to write down the titles as he had. If he ever got busted by the cops, there wouldn't be a wide berth around what the subject matter of the tapes were.

I knew despicable characters when I saw them, thanks to my viewings of soap operas. George made J. R. Ewing and Alexis Colby seem like rank amateurs. I was also realizing that I had chosen unwisely as to the company in which to introduce myself to what it was to be gay.

George was like a poster child for any Anita Bryant type of antihomosexual beliefs. What he had done went beyond the border of being gay; it was nestled into the state known as insanity. I knew that there had to be a world at large that was very far removed from the doings at the palace or from what I had experienced with Steve.

I knew that there had to be good people that weren't looking to utilize my youth for their own ill-gotten gains. I knew that the gay world I was clamoring to find wasn't all, well, it wasn't all rainbows and fairies, that there could be darkness as I headed for the light, that despite sexual orientation, we were all under the umbrella of the human race.

I managed to get back behind the sanctity of the bathroom door without raising Troy's ire. Unfortunately, there was no lock on the door. I was doubtful that he even knew I was gone. I had taken on so many conflicting emotions surrounding George in the last twelve hours that I felt ill prepared to deal with the scope of what was happening.

I was about to submerge into the icy waters of ambiguity; the submarine that was preparing to dive was covered with window screening so that everything was coming in at once. This was either sink-or-swim time, and I wanted to stay afloat, to be above all of the madness that was encased within the walls of the palace.

George had proved a most unsuitable candidate to show me what gay life could be. Maybe he had been there to show me how not to be, much like my own father. I didn't have the kind of role models in my life that made me want to be like them; quite the opposite was true. This must have been how I needed to have been shown in order to become someone that I considered necessary and wanted to be.

What I had just witnessed in the den must be what Angel wanted to talk to me about as I fervently hoped he did not bear news that would prove to be the nadir of my breaking point; for I truly did not know how much more I could withstand.

I started the shower, deciding that music may not calm the savage beast and that I needed to just wash and go, Pert Plus. I set the pulsating showerhead to high, closed my eyes, hoping that the drama of the past day would somehow be magically washed down the drain.

Before that hope could become a reality, I heard the shower door open. Expecting Norman Bates dressed as his mother wielding a butcher knife would have been a less shocking sight than what my eyes were seeing.

Troy was climbing into the shower, and he definitely could have passed for gay now. He had a Speedo tan line and was sporting an erection larger than his father's. I was feeling a lot of things, and whatever conflict that had been subletting rental space in my head was immediately vanquished.

Neither one of us spoke, seemingly pulled by an electromagnetic force until we were standing face-to-face. I doubted that Troy and I were ever going to see eye to eye. He was the closest guy so far that had even remotely resembled my ideal. I closed my eyes; the water was pulsating on the top of my head, creating surging rivers that ran down my back. When I opened them again, I was alone, as I felt this was the manner in which my life was subscribed to. There was no Troy in the shower; he had never been in there standing in front of me, awaiting gratification. My mind had conjured him up in this setting, testing myself to see if I had the fortifying resolve to resist him should that particular scenario come into play.

So much had happened in a short amount of time that my mind found its happy place, and of course, that always included a blond.

There was so much fear built around the outcome of the next few days with more and more threads of the tapestry unraveling at every corner and wrapping me up in their cocoon. Of course, I went to the most natural of places for me now that I had staked my claim to the land of gay sex.

I knew that I had a deeper longing than the propinquity of these fleeting situations provided. I rushed through my shower, primped and preened, snuck off to my new bedroom, got dressed at a very fast clip, and headed out the door to meet Angel.

As I walked out the palace doors in what seemed like an eternity, I dared to glance behind me to see if I could catch any movement from Troy. But as always, I should have been looking into the future and not the past.

Troy was walking down the cement-floored hallway, a towel draped over his right shoulder, a bottle of baby oil in his left hand, and my psychic flash that he was a wearer of Speedos was right on the money. The black Speedo clung to his ass perfectly, as if preventing two of the ripest melons from escaping the produce bin.

He turned as he heard the door shut behind me. He was showcasing his angelic side once again; there was no sign of illegal entry from his dark side. I just kept waiting for him to fade away, to disappear into a vapor. This time he was really in front of me and actually smiled at me before speaking.

"Hey, Billy, sorry about before. I was kinda upset. I hope you don't think I'm some sort of monster. I just get…frustrated. Anyway, what are you up to? Going out?"

I just nodded, not feeling compelled to do any more than what was required. It was intriguing how people present themselves in certain settings: completely freak out and then act as though they were competing for Miss America. From where I was standing, Troy definitely had the swimsuit competition sewed up. However, Miss Congeniality, that was a crapshoot at best.

"I'm headed up to the roof to work on my tan. Wanna come?" he said this with just a trace of innuendo.

Well, there was no reason that I couldn't look up Danny's name after I met with Angel; it wasn't like I wanted to be hanging around the palace when George got home.

"Sure," I answered, simple, understated, and all I could manage to get out at the prospect of lying side by side with Troy or getting to oil him up.

We made our way up to the impromptu beach on the roof of the apartment complex; there was a sparse arrangement of beach chairs and one table. The day was blazing. There were no stiff breezes coming off the canyons that held trees and no residencies.

For an urban dwelling, George had picked a prime spot in which to proceed with his illegal endeavors. Those that dwelled in the apartment complex only did so at night when their jobs had been kind enough to allow them the time to come home and recoup from a hard day's work. I saw the deadened look in their eyes and remembered they looked similar to Big Ed when he got back from the rat race.

I had only seen a few of the neighbors, and they all seemed like the nose to the grindstone variety, only uttering a grunting of a hello if I said it first. Maybe they just figured I was another disposable friend of George's, that in no time flat, I would be gone.

Well, that was tomorrow's dilemma. I wanted to concentrate on the moment, for once, as Troy laid down his towel, the muscles in his arms flexing just so, highlighting his biceps and triceps.

Whenever I saw a worked-out gym body, I always felt like I was just a scrawny kid, an anorexic piece of chicken, next to a potential side of beef. When I thought about chicken, I thought about Troy and Nick and wondered how the hell that had all come about. Troy didn't seem like the kind of guy that would've allowed such an act to happen, much less have it be taped.

I hadn't noticed that Troy had snuck some contraband out of his father's bedroom. I guess I was still naive. Troy obviously didn't feel restricted as his father had violated his trust. There was a baggie of pot, rolling papers, and a lighter sitting in the middle of the towel.

He straddled the towel, falling out of the sight line of the eucalyptus trees and was perpendicular with my crotch. I thought he might reach up and give me a little grope; instead he dove into the baggie of pot and rolled up a joint in only seconds flat, no fuss, no muss.

I was strictly a pipe man myself; it seemed to be one of those offshoots from lack of coordination, or it was that the pipe provided instant relief, smoky gratification. He lit the joint, and I sat down on one of the stray chairs that made up the haphazard beach off to his right. We smoked in silence; wheels were turning slower in our minds by the end of the session. I sat next to him, sneaking those furtive glances that would have gotten me beat up in school, taking in the vista of his well-defined body. I wondered where his treasure trail led to when he finally broke the silence.

"Hey, we need some music. Go get Angel's ghetto blaster." He had a lopsided grin, more of a smirk, really, like he was sitting on some big secret, waiting for the exact moment to best utilize its shock value.

"Yeah, cool," I responded dreamily.

Whenever I smoked pot, these two staples of vocabulary prowess could answer a question, ask a question, "Yeah? Cool?" or even punctuate any given conversation, "Yeah! Cool!"

I was not one of those intellectual types that felt the compelling need to fill the room or what have you with as much vocal smoke as was filling up the area with the real deal. I liked the fact that pot had a deadening effect on me, especially in light of the last twenty-four hours. I scurried off, nearly tripping down the stairs, not from lack of dexterity, but in a big attempt to please Troy. When he was purring like a kitten and not roaring like a tiger, Troy was adorable.

Once I set foot in the palace, I was confronted with reality. The reality was I shouldn't be up on the rooftop with George's son smoking George's pot. The reality was I needed to find Danny so that I could get away from the petty tyrannies of the palace. The reality was I had a sudden and compelling need to call my mom and make sure she was okay.

I now knew what it was like to have to do the wifey shuffle, and I had a huge pang of remorse that my mother was stuck by herself with only my father to consort with. I went to the kitchen phone. The answering machine sat stealthily, its red eye not blinking, signaling no one had bothered to leave a message at the beep for George.

My hands instantly began to tremble, the subtle cotton mouth I had been experiencing was replaced with its stronger twin. I resisted the urge to forage in the fridge for any juice. God knew that I couldn't pull off any sort of mathematical equating at that particular instant. My hand almost had a firm grasp on the phone as it raised its alarm that there was an incoming call.

I jerked my hand back like I had been scalded. I decided to let the answering machine field this call as it would be skirting palace protocol to answer it myself. After two rings, the machine clicked over, and a familiar voice spoke as if he was in the room.

"Troy? It'sss Dad. Are you there? Jussst called to make sssure you got in okay. Give me a call at work when you get thisss. Make yoursssself at home. There'sss plenty in the fridge."

George's message seemed more than parental concern; it seemed like a feeble attempt to get under my skin. I was momentarily deterred, unsure if I should call my mom; I didn't want to make Troy upset if he was left waiting too long. Before I knew it, I was picking up the phone and dialing the phone number that my mother made me memorize in a singsong rhyme before my first day of school.

The phone was on its third ring and I was just about to hang up when I heard my mother, and apparently she was out of breath.

"Hello? Hello?" she spoke. I remained silent. "Henry, is it you?"

"Yes," I replied, and as I did, I realized the pot made it seem stranger to be called by my given name, like I was now a shadow of my former self.

"Oh, hon!" she exclaimed with exuberance usually reserved for getting a "buy one get one free" coupon in the Sunday paper for Gorton's fish sticks. "Are you all right? Where are you? When are you coming home?"

She fired off her lightning-round questions, not pausing long enough in between to let me get an answer or word in edgewise. I wanted to fire off my own stoned brand of answers: "Lost my legs in Nam. Ecuador. How's the twelfth of never work for you?"

But that wasn't the reason I had called. I wanted to know that I was missed, that somebody worried about me. I didn't know that most nights before she went to bed and didn't sleep much, she would stand in my room, look out the window, and wonder where I was as tears ran down her face.

"I'm okay." I decided to plead the fifth on the other two questions.

"Your brother, John, is coming home tomorrow. I don't know what to tell him about you, about what's happened."

And there it was. She made my being gay sound like I had been diagnosed with terminal cancer or I was in prison on murder charges. I tapped into the unbridled anger I felt at being treated like the family leper.

"Just tell him the truth, Mother." There was a very discernible edge to my voice now.

I never called her Mother unless she was riding me too much about something as trivial as doing my homework. But now I was upset that she hadn't seen the error of her ways by letting me go out into the big world without warning me to look both ways as I crossed the street. For if she truly cared about me, being gay wouldn't make a bit of difference.

"Oh I can't do that." She sounded more than a bit like a Stepford wife even though Big Ed was at work. She couldn't go against what he had probably ordered her to do.

"Why not?" I said through gritted teeth.

"Henry, where are you? I can come and pick you up. We can work this out, son," she said, reminding me that I was speaking with denial royalty.

"I am where people take me at face value, where I am accepted for who I am and not looked down upon for what I want to be."

That's what I wanted to say in a perfect world, in a world where I wouldn't have to defend my choices, in a world where I wasn't stoned out of my gourd. And seeing as the seconds were passing like molasses because of my partaking of the green, the fact that I was talking to my mother again had become very surreal. And I realized that the longer the conversation went on, the more likely that I would return to an altogether different version of the Troy that I had left. Instead, I opted for a very mature response.

"Whatever," I all but grumbled into the phone before terminating the conversation, hanging up on a life I wanted to comprehend but didn't want to live again.

I wasn't so sure I liked the new identity and situations I had found myself in, but they seemed better than the alternatives I was presented with.

I glanced at the clock. It was just about eleven o'clock. I intuitively felt that I had about four hours. I rushed into the bathroom, not dealing with the anger that was surging through my veins or the tears that wanted to come. I had shed one too many tears today, and I did not feel a command performance was necessary.

Instead, I checked the ghetto blaster for batteries, hoping against hope that there were some already inside so that I wouldn't have to rummage through George's junk drawer only to find out what the face value of Duracells were or some other nasty surprise.

For plot convenience's sake in the story of my life, there were six C-sized batteries already residing inside, ready to fill the early afternoon with song.

I hurried back up to the roof, channeling my anger into my swift pace, taking the stairs two at a time until I reached the top. And when I did, my heart started pumping harder, the breath in my body forcing itself out faster at what my eyes were seeing.

Troy had decided the rooftop would be clothing optional; his black Speedo now hung on the chair that I had previously resided in. It wasn't a white flag, but I definitely took it as a sign of surrender, a letting down of guards. He stared at me intently; I thought I must be having another blond-induced hallucination. I blinked my eyes several times in quick succession, but the scene remained the same.

"Why don't you put some music on, and then you can come help me get those hard-to-reach places."

He had already started to apply the baby oil to most of his torso, so it wasn't hard to not get a visual on where those pesky crevices that required a helpful hand might be.

I did as I was told, choosing KISS FM as the musical interlude to our pre-afternoon delight. Setting the mood were the soothing strains of Sade's "Smooth Operator." I found it a very relatable little ditty as there was no need to ask—he's a smooth operator. I just wasn't sure if it was more apropos of Troy or me, but as I knelt down in front of him on the towel, I didn't really think it mattered.

I picked up the bottle of generic-brand baby oil, rubbed some into my hands, and began to travel all over Troy's body. Aside from Stephen and Angel, he was the only other guy I had been with that took good care of himself; he may be the closest thing to Danny that I would ever get.

With each swipe of my hand, I wiped away the residue of all of the older man lovin' that had been coming down the pike as of late. Now I had done the father, was about to reach down and start doing the son, and began to wonder when the Holy Ghost might happen my way.

I took Troy's already hard as a rock, bigger than his dad's shank portion into my hand. He leaned back his head and began to gently moan. The more my hand moved up and down, the louder the moans got. Sade gave way to USA for Africa's "We Are the World," the song that you could not escape that summer. I didn't know that giving a hand job to a song about the plight of starving Ethiopians verged on sacrilege, but I wasn't about to stop.

I was focused on Troy deriving pleasure from my touch, from the motion well-rehearsed on myself, but I kept waiting for him to start his portion of reciprocation. About the time that Bruce Springsteen is singing or, rather, sounds a tad constipated in the song, Troy let go with an explosive force of white ribbons that landed on the towel and all over my hand. So now I had baby batter mixed with baby lotion and still no reciprocation as I stood up, and Troy opened his eyes.

"Thanks, bro," he said, reaching out for his Speedos, covering his genitalia, and more than likely covering the memory of what he clearly didn't want in his immediate past. "Damn, I am really stoned."

So he was going to play it that way, I must have been really high because otherwise it wouldn't have happened. He was staring at my hand dripping its contents onto the towel, narrowly missing the almost-empty baggie of pot.

"You should go wash up," he said this and walked across to change the station to KROQ, which was playing "Love My Way" by the Psychedelic Furs.

"That's better, can't stand that faggot music," he muttered somewhere between a whisper and a bark.

I stood still, mouth agape. This would have been another one of those great moments in life if I had a script to read from for a snappy retort. Infuriated, I just sulked off, literally wanting to wash my hands of the whole mess.

Back in the palace I had an immediate sense of claustrophobia. Everything seemed to be tightening its hold on my staying there, and now I had the disillusioned heir apparent to deal with.

I stood in the living room on my way to the bathroom and looked back. I watched as all of the furniture seemed to move covertly sideways. The black leather couches became panthers waiting to strike in order to prevent my escape. The gold trim on the black lacquer coffee table unfurled itself into a python-like pose, affixing itself to a lamp, and the dining room table like some sort of mid-eighties version of barbed wire.

I was waiting for the women in the Patrick Nagel prints to leap down from their artistic poses and try to tackle me. Or maybe the clear white marbles and the opaque neighbors that resided in vases that sported faux orchids on either side of the leather couches would begin shooting themselves at me.

What I didn't predict was that all of this scene would be so vivid to me that it seemed to be actually happening or that Troy would be standing in the doorway, the shine from his baby oiled body all but blinding and giving him an other-worldly presence.

"You must be trippin' by now," he said.

"What was in that pot?" I queried. I knew something was up because if the Nagel prints had come to life, I would have hallucinated them into hunky men. And I didn't have the facilities to perform even my most rudimentary imaginary skills.

"Let's just say it's pot with something extra. Come on, let's get you cleaned up." Troy always seemed to be treading the decision to be or not to be. And that could be in relation to his sexual leanings or whether to be nice or not.

He led me into the bathroom. I was feeling incapacitated but not completely out of control. He turned on the water in the sink and stuck my hand under it. His slippery body pressed against mine was telling me that he had again changed courses on his emotional landscape.

A sudden eclipse came over my vision; my world was swirling down, like the water into the drain. The next thing I knew, all of my clothes were off, I was bent over the sink, and Troy was doing the bump and grind from behind.

"What are you doing?" I asked to his mirror image, like I didn't have a clue as to why it felt like there was a logjam happening in the back section.

"I am doing what you asked me to," he said this in a breathless way, each thrust into me punctuating each word.

Since I had momentarily blacked out and I did find Troy to be a visual ideal anyway, I decided to go with the flow. I knew the minute he was done, all bets were off that he could be the kind of savior I was looking for.

Well, it turned out to be more like the second he was done.

More white ribbons from my surprise party package. But the biggest surprise was when I saw that he hadn't been wearing a condom. I heard his father's voice ask, "You're sssafe, right?" But the words were coming out of my mouth, sans the leaky-tire routine.

"What do you think? I'm no faggot." He stood there sneering, a poor man's Billy Idol.

"Well, you certainly fuck like one," I said it calmly, and for once I had said it out loud. It didn't come to me hours later as what could have been the perfect comeback.

I braced myself for the verbal lashing that was sure to follow. What I hadn't expected was that Troy would be the one crying. He was doing his best "Glenn Close crying in the shower" impression from *The Big Chill*. But I knew that he couldn't be entirely gay because he was next to the shower on the floor and not in it. Had I been in complete bitch mode, I could have told him that he cried like a fag too.

Drawing from my own experiences, I didn't need to kick him when he was down. What I didn't know was if I should approach him to maybe let a sleeping dog lie or sexually confused guy cry.

"Hey, are you okay?" I asked this of him; although I could clearly see that he was not. I didn't know what else to say or do.

"No." He was breaking down into huge sobs that were racking his whole body. "I hate that I am like him."

And there you had it. Troy had unknowingly created a bond between the two of us with seven words. He looked at me with eyes even redder because of the laced joint we had smoked. This moment definitely had a *Family Ties* group hug moment written all over it. I was more than subscribed to see where Troy's heightened emotional state might land him. I really felt for him, maybe not so much in a Chaka Khan kind of way, but I could understand the conflict that he was verbalizing. I could see now why Troy was doing the whole push-pull routine, much more so than our sexual encounters had entailed.

Without another word, Troy perfected his Glenn Close by taking his tears into the shower; he closed the door behind him, shutting me off from any further disclosures.

I went into the den, feeling naked on the inside too. The room looked like a cyclone had hit it, the wreckage of Troy's hatred of his father clearly evident in the aftermath. I didn't know if I should clean it up or not; perhaps Troy wanted his father to confront him about it so that they could have it out.

"Just leave it," Troy said from the doorway; he was dripping wet from his marine shower.

I just nodded as I headed into the bathroom to take a shower for the second time today. I was feeling more cognizant of the true world around me and realized I needed to get motivated if I was to meet Angel at our designated time. I felt like I was starting my day all over again, hopefully with better results this time around.

I emerged from the shower feeling new and ready to get on with my day. I cruised into Angel's and now my bedroom, slipped on a pair of shorts and my favorite blue Nike tank top. My ensemble wasn't much of a hard choice. I had a pile of laundry I needed to do now that Angel wasn't expected to take care of that anymore.

The discarded pile of clothes encompassed so much history. There was a story in every garment, including what I had been wearing before Troy had stripped me and I had decided to leave on the bathroom floor.

The one item that caught my eye in particular was the muscle tee of Oingo Boingo that John had bought for me when it was deemed by my parents that I had been too young to attend the concert. I wished my brother, John, was here; he would protect me just as he had done when I got into scraps with bullies in my much younger years. He was crossing the Pacific, steering towards home, while my compass seemed to be pointing in all directions at once, leaving me unclear as which route would be the best for me.

Ever since I had seen the movie *Footloose* the year before, I had wished all of my life's problems could be solved with a kicky dance routine. But in the real world, there are betrayal, deceit, lies, and no stunt double to fill in for the arduous times.

I also took my money out of its new hiding place, an empty cassette tape of the Thompson Twins's *Into the Gap*. I didn't bother to count it, put it in my pocket, grabbed my Walkman for the bus ride into the big city, and headed out the door.

I sensed I was heading into something that may be bigger than I could possibly imagine, and after considering all of the options of what Angel may have to say, trepidation was running like a live wire through my body.

What I expected and what often occurred were such different entities; I almost never counted on the element of surprise.

Suffice it to say, I was a little nonplussed when Troy pulled up to the bus stop down the street from the palace and offered me a ride. I found it odd that Troy, who had allegedly driven in from Iowa or bumfuck Egypt, was tooling around in a very familiar-looking VW microbus with California plates and an abundance of surf stickers.

Chapter 12

I took in all of the familiar smells, the surfboard wax mixed with traces of stale pot smoke, in complete and utter disbelief. I did not know how to broach this subject to Troy because in doing so, if he was friends with Danny, I would blow my Billy Collins alias out of the water.

My worlds were colliding together. I was almost convinced that this was a leftover hallucination from the pot with something extra. Oh it wasn't. I felt like I was twelve all over again, sitting in the passenger's seat, not wanting to say anything that would give me away. I had to know how this was possible.

"Wow, I haven't been in one of these since I was a kid."

I figured using the word *kid* would annul any of Troy's suspicions that I had not been above board on telling him I was eighteen. The look he gave me was a chillingly familiar one; it was his father's "Oh pleassse, Mary," which was trotted out for those skeptical occasions.

I wanted to follow up with a line of questioning that began, "Is it yours? Where did you get it?" I didn't want to raise his ire nor his suspicions as to why I would be fascinated by a microbus that wasn't even in great condition.

But I was Billy Collins, and maybe he was fascinated by relics of yesteryear and could appreciate the true beauty of what it once was. That particular line of thinking would certainly be equivocal with the company I kept in the palace. What I was hoping for was that by casting out the fishing line that Troy might take the bait, and I could reel in the full story of how he might know my big one that got away.

"Oh yeah, it's kinda funky, huh? Very *Fast Times at Ridgemont High*," he said in high spirits. "'Dude, that's my skull, I'm so wasted.'"

Well, it was a nibble and a Sean Penn as Jeff Spicoli impression and a pretty good one at that. Despite myself, I laughed, and then I tried to remember the last time I had actually done so. I looked over at Troy; he was grinning, and I figured now was as good a time as any to hook my line again.

"Is it yours? Where did you get it?" I almost smacked myself in the forehead. Perchance Troy would mistake the urgency that was rampant in my voice for curiosity.

"It belongs to a friend of mine." He put a weird emphasis on the word *friend*, either meaning they were more than that or he really didn't like him.

Whatever the case was, I was surprised that he did not take his hands off the steering wheel to do rabbit-ear quotation marks.

"Oh," I said this, trying not to sound deflated, "is that where you are going right now, to see your friend?"

I struggled to make it come off as casual banter so that he wouldn't figure out the true reason I was inquiring. How could he, really? I also hoped that he didn't think I was one of those "We slept together once so we're married now" variety of gay guys I had heard George, Angel, and Nick talking about.

I was far from stewing in jealousy. I was steeping in confusion. So much had happened in the last day, and now it seemed that there was a new wrinkle happening at every turn.

"Well, if you must know, *Magnum, P.I.*, JR." He smirked as he said that, obviously pleased with his catchy turn of phrase. I was just glad he hadn't called me Nancy Drew. "And you have to keep this under your hat." He turned to look briefly in my direction when I had decided to answer with a nod. "He's my dealer, and since you and I smoked the last of what we like to call the Shit, I need to pick up some more so I can cope with the parental."

"Is it hard having a dad who's gay?" I asked this in all innocence until I remembered that he was cursing himself earlier for being like his father.

I mentally battened down the hatches, preparing for Hurricane Troy, when an unexpected shift in the course of the storm brought an answer onshore instead of nature's fury.

"Sometimes. But I think it's just because of the kind of person that he is in general. Obviously, I could care less about who he sleeps with," he answered with a faraway look in his eyes. "But I will say this about the old man, he does get some fine ones."

I thought for a moment he was going to feign engine trouble, pull over to the side of the freeway, close the microbus's curtains, and go for round two with the look of longing he gave me.

"And that's the problem. Dad likes 'em young, and I can't believe that motherfucker is still doing this shit when he promised me he would stop. He promised me after—"

A car cut in front of Troy right at that moment, and the encroaching storm was back on target.

A slew of obscenities that would have made Big Ed proud to call Troy his son came free flowing their way out of Troy's mouth and into the brownish haze of the Los Angeles sky, adding their own taint to the existing smog.

I held my breath, awaiting impact with the other car; I closed my eyes, listening to the horn blaring almost in time with the apropos song playing on the radio, "Relax" by Frankie Goes to Hollywood.

Surprisingly for a stoner, Troy had excellent reflexes, and he managed to not only steer us out of harm's way, but off the freeway altogether, exiting at a very convenient off-ramp.

He pulled into a Circle K parking lot, stopped the vehicle's engine, and reached over with his right hand precariously close to my crotch. He swerved effectively at this juncture, just as he had on the freeway, his fingers grasped on to the glove box and opened it. He removed a lone joint and its partner in crime, a lighter, and wasted no time in utilizing both to their fullest extents.

"In case of emergencies," he said this after holding in the smoke for close to a minute then handed me the joint.

After what had happened with the other joint earlier, I was more than a little bit skeptical, I didn't want to be hallucinating if I was really pulling my little-brother area of expertise, tagging along to see Danny. Deciding that a few tokes would help eradicate the shakiness I felt from being in close proximity to Troy and what had turned out better than most of the near-miss car collisions I had witnessed on *CHiPS*, I took a baby toke. We passed it back and forth at least two more times before I put up my hand to signal I was good.

Not sure of which way was best to pick up the dangling piece of information that had skidded off the conversation highway, I was about to go for the nonchalant route and ask him, "And you were saying?" He decided to beat me to the punch.

"Yeah, my dad, father of the year never will he be," Troy said in a very good Yoda impression, and the fact that he was doing imitations and being humorous seemed to be emanating from a galaxy far, far away.

"Well, maybe he has a hard time dealing with his tour in Vietnam," I said this, and as I did, I couldn't believe that I was practically sticking up for George.

Sometimes my mind had Tourette's syndrome that made me say the first thing that popped into my head. I was just looking for some excuse for George to be treating me the way that he was, and at the moment, being a shell-shocked war veteran held more validity than my own actions as to why George wanted to pimp me out.

"Dude, what are you talking about?" Troy took away his focus from the joint he was close to finishing off and was staring intently at me.

"You know, maybe he's traumatized from the accident in Vietnam? The one where he was almost blown up by a booby trap? It knocked his teeth out?" I said, everything as a question and as though I was addressing an adult who could only read a first-grade primer.

See Henry talk; see Troy listen.

Then I had a thought; maybe Troy didn't know about his father's troubles that stemmed from Vietnam. Did George only reserve that story for the young men that shared his bed for a pity value that parlayed itself into sex? I watched Troy's face for any signs of full-moon ferocity. What I saw instead sent a shiver down my spine. Troy broke into a smile and then started laughing, so hard in fact that he began coughing.

In between gasps for air, he was perfecting his Neanderthal monosyllabic vocabulary.

"Vietnam [cough]. Booby [cough]. Trap [cough]. Teeth [cough, cough]." He did this until he was red in the face and about to be red on his thumb and finger that were still holding the almost down to the nub joint.

He got it together for a minute, snuffed out the joint, and then started the process all over again, reacting like he had just been listening to Eddie Murphy recant the tale. He looked composed after another minute, was about to speak, and then coughed instead. This set him off on another minute before he could properly tell me why what I had said was deemed comedy gold.

"Jesus, he told you that? The closest my father ever got to Vietnam was taking me to see *Apocalypse Now*. The only booby trap he ever walked into was trying to be a married man and covering up the fact that he liked young men. My mother knocked his teeth out when she found out he was…"

Uh-oh, it looked like the comedy hour was going to be replaced by a drama midseason as Troy's face went expressionless. I was supposing the next sentence would be on par with what Craig had told me had happened between himself and his brother.

"Well, he was taking pictures of my friends." A distinct yet remote sadness overtook Troy's face. He left it at that, and I knew he wasn't talking about George footing the bill for a trip to Glamour Shots.

Apparently, George had evolved from Polaroids to videotapes when he moved to Los Angeles, Troy explained as he backed the microbus out of its momentary holding pattern, and back to the freeway we went.

Well, *moved* was a strong word. It was more like forced out of the community by angry parents after George's extracurricular photography activities were discovered, when one of his subjects had a Poloroid given to him as a keepsake discovered by a very non-plussed parent. As Troy was recanting this tale, I had visions of angry torch-wielding villagers running George out on a rail, sans teeth. Leaving town meant leaving his son behind. Troy told me he never could forgive his father for what he had done.

He had foolishly hoped that George had stopped luring in those who were easily preyed upon with his lies and deception and the promise of a fast buck. I could invoke that image all too easily in my mind's eye.

"It will be our sssecret, now here's a dollar," George said against a black backdrop.

That was why, against his mother's wishes, Troy had kept in touch with his father. His yearly visits were almost that of a parole officer checking up on George to make sure everything was above board. Well, he could see that sitting not two feet from his right was the most recent addition to the roster. And only a few hours ago, he had watched one of his friends who had missed the first draft picks but was fitted into the rotation at a later date.

Troy hit a snarl of traffic, slowing us to a crawl, but the backstory of his father was doing at least eighty miles per hour now.

A few years back Troy had come to visit, and it was Angel who had welcomed him to the palace. Since Angel was of age and seemed to be more of the roommate type, there was no reason for Troy to become alarmed that anything out of the ordinary was afoot.

Oh but there was. As we headed slowly south, it was if I had resumed my penchant for the invisible had been brought back for an encore; Troy seemed to be performing a stream of conscious dialogue, reenacting a scene from *King Lear*, but in this case, it would've been the more appropriately titled *King Queer*.

I only wished I had some popcorn, partly due to the way he was weaving the story and also because I had a slight case of the munchies. Then I remembered a long-ago summer when I had sat in this very seat and ate popcorn, the night of beasts about to strike, male frontal nudity, and being Danny's copilot.

This memory was firmly entrenched in the time before, when life was all about fantasies sustaining me, before reality smashed them into a million and one pieces. I wondered where Danny fit into all of this? I supposed if I quieted my mind for a moment, or three thousand, that answer would be revealed as Troy's performance continued.

Nick had also been present during that particular visit, and again, there was some sort of strange quality about Nick that went unspoken, a secret chemistry that lay in his bloodstream and lured you in.

He certainly wasn't a Tom Selleck knockoff; I had started seeing him more as Tennessee Tuxedo's sidekick, Chumley, with his big walrus-like moustache. He gave off such a sexual vibe that you couldn't help but be pulled into it. We were simply planets orbiting the radiance of his sun, forever stuck in his gravitational pull. Angel conveniently had things to do, people to see, or vice versa, people to do and things to see; George wouldn't be back from work for a while, and Troy wanted to find out what kind of man Nick really was.

Well, Nick was the type of man that knew about a secret in the palace's den closet. He was involved in a certain remodel he had helped George install, where they had spent two weeks setting up their very different version of *Candid Camera* in the closet.

They had gotten a two-way mirror from one of Nick's cop buddies, purchased the latest in video camera accessories, and decided to dabble in a little independent film enterprise that would cater to only a select few. That certainly explained the stockpiles of chicken titles and how there was one starring Troy and Nick. One summer, Troy was the star; the next it was his friend. The summer after that he brought a halt to production. Hollywood was a bitch mistress.

Troy had come to visit in the summer of '84. He arrived early, found the door unlocked and his father in a compromising position with a young prostitute friend of Angel's.

I wondered if it was Rocky or Pollo or some other wayward youth that I might be in cahoots with tomorrow night. Well, this "up-and-coming for the camera" actor didn't care if he was being filmed, so the camera was mounted on a tripod in the middle of the room while the young actor was mounted on George.

All of the hurt that Troy felt replaced the hope that he had that his father had changed his ways. He ran over to the camera, knocking it from its perch, as the young man hopped off Troy's pop. Troy saw that the closet door was open, exposing the secret chamber.

His cry of "What the fuck?" remained unanswered against his father's silence. Troy lost it. In a fury, he grabbed the toppled tripod and smashed out the mirror; he beat at it until George grabbed his arm, nearly getting bashed by the tripod himself.

The prostitute, figuring he was trespassing on Troy's man, gathered his clothes and slunk out of the room, only leaving father and son.

What was there that Troy could say?

For starters, he screeched at George, trying to make him see the error of his ways and to get a not-so-simple promise to stop out of the man, who had been vested in his "hobby" for 15 years now. The best he got was a bobbing up and down of George's head, a painful reminder of his own time in the secret spotlight with Nick. How could George explain his way out of this one? The simple deduction was that there was nothing either one could say as far as their actions went.

Troy stormed out of the palace vowing to never lighten his father's darkened doorstep, that one day all of his illicit actions would bite George squarely on his ass.

He went to Venice Beach rather than drive all the way back to Iowa. Troy realized he was not only beyond upset at his father but also at himself for not keeping closer tabs on George's illegal proceedings.

He was also perplexed that after all he had been through with his father that he could still care about him and not want to see him get into trouble with the law. He sat on the sand, a conundrum, trying to sort out his conflicting emotions.

It sounded like Troy was also a heavyweight champ when it came to beating himself up for his sexual proclivities. He had dabbled occasionally with guys, but at the onset of orgasm, another wave would rush over him, comparisons to his father providing the crest, guilt making up its crash.

Then right in the middle of his internal struggle, he watched as a lone surfer made his way towards him. As the surfer got closer, Troy drew in a sharp breath as their eyes locked and then traveled down the surfer's landscape, stopping at what was being transported inside the crotch of his wetsuit.

Without a word, the surfer plopped down his surfboard and knelt down, asking if Troy was all right. Troy had been so deeply entrenched in his emotions that he hadn't realized he'd been crying. Now, he was so mesmerized by the surfer that had grown up on my street, who had been my ideal, that he felt no guilt at taking Danny up on his offer for a place to crash after talking in code about why he had been crying, knowing that he wanted him and hating himself for it.

"But he was such a gentleman," Troy said. "And still is."

"And what was this gentleman's name?" I said, unconsciously paraphrasing dialogue from *Grease*. There could still be a chance it was all just some sort of coincidence, a fluke.

"Danny, Danny Woodson."

Way to go, Troy! You sank my battleship!

Troy explained that he and Danny clicked in a way he never thought possible, and I thought I might be the one to start crying. All of this time, I had expected Danny to be the one to save me from the plight I had fallen into and to stupidly be available for me when the time was right.

Now, it sounded like he and Troy were lovers up until the point when he explained that he couldn't handle the pressure, that his demons escaped from hell daily and no amount of brimstone and treacle inhaled through a pipe would quash them.

Alas, he and Danny became friends, much like the long-ago reading exploits of Frog and Toad that I devoured in first grade. Troy actually decided to stay in Los Angeles, not telling his father, so that he could perform his own brand of surveillance, one that didn't include constructing a secret nook. I tried to imagine the den and could not place a mirror near the closet, only a large painting that hung on the wall. Perhaps George had stopped his spying ways.

Yeah, but just because he wasn't filming anything did not mean that he still wasn't up to any good. I wasn't sure if Troy had discerned the palatable tension that hung in the air at the palace; even without George's presence, its aftereffects lingered in every corner. Troy had definitely brought his own brand of tension along with him, making a shambles of the *Chicken Hawk* signature series.

He had probably tapped into the wellspring of disparity that emanated in the palace, all but threatening visitors and residents alike with its negative wrath. I wasn't really sure why Troy had spilled his guts to me. Was it because I was a semi-impartial observer or that he just needed to get it off his chest, and I seemed like a sympathetic ear?

Whatever the case was, we were creeping nearer and nearer to Troy being privy to finding out my true identity. I was vacillating between wanting to and not wanting to see Danny. Sure, he might be able to rescue me from having to face George's ultimatum. Then again, he might see the trouble I had gotten myself into and put an end to my subterfuge with a well-placed phone call.

I watched the odometer click off another mile very slowly gone by and wondered again if the truth would set me free or if it would become a game of capture the fag.

I was at a crossroads in the middle of the freeway and wanted to choose wisely, to get on with life using the proper footing. How was I to do this? Every man that I had trusted to show me the ways of life had always been resigned to get me to a certain point with the building blocks of life and then, like a spoiled child, would knock down what had been constructed, leaving my foundation exposed to try to build again.

My eyes drifted to the traffic jam ahead, behind, and on all sides of me now. I knew that it was impossible to unclog the congestion that seemed to be impeding the direction of my young life too. What I needed to clearly see were the red brake lights blinking, signaling when it was safe to proceed, so that I did not end up another casualty on the highway of life.

What I wanted and what I needed were very fine lines to tread. I had learned that great distinction between the two early on. I wanted to be a semi-well-adjusted gay teenager. I needed to realize that there would be some enormous growing pains that went along with the process, which I obviously wasn't equipped with the sense of self that made the transition an easy one. I coveted the freedom I'd acquired but was so unsure as to the price that I would have to pay for it.

When I was six, my mother and I used to play a game called what-if. My mother had come up with this game to redirect my boat-load of questions about different aspects of things in this world. My endless questions that were of the "What if zebras had spots instead of stripes?" variety must be phrased as a question; otherwise, they went unheeded, just like they did it on *Jeopardy*.

My mother would play along until she realized she had created a monster for my unending curiosity, wordlessly chiding herself that she ever invented the game.

Well, what if I had been born first? What if I was the same age as Danny? Would I have been his boyfriend? I wanted to grow up so quickly, not realizing I could never reach back in time and reclaim my youth. I supposed that my days would always be like this—wishing I already knew the outcome of what was to be, still dreaming of what was to come, and regretting what had been.

I hoped that I would be a self-sufficient man, not relying on others to fit the pieces of the puzzle of himself forever. I wasn't setting up that version of life very well, now was I? In turn, I wanted so much and knew so little as to the best way to get what I needed. I wished I had an internal map that could show me the final destination of the roads I would be choosing to trek in life, even when I changed course.

Sometimes I felt very happy with my decision to uproot myself from the depths of the dark forest so that I might have a better chance to grow. It was only in the last day, which held so much upheaval, that I could feel the unease of fear drift in like a morning fog, causing temporary blindness.

Troy was noticeably quiet, not seeming to notice that I had claimed that land as mine. I wasn't sure if I should break the spell with a revelation of my own. I could see the exit for Sunset Boulevard fast—or slowly, really—approaching. Before we exited, I needed to decide how much I could really trust him. His character traits of hot sprinkled with very cold dictated a sense of defeat as to how he might react to the fact that I had known Danny first.

Troy took the off-ramp while I took a detour on the low road to jealousy. I looked over at him; he was as deep in thought as one could be while driving. I saw him stripped away of all of his pretenses; he was nothing more than a second-rate solution to the age-gap problem between Danny and myself.

I couldn't believe that Danny had been gullible enough to let Troy's game face trick him until the midnight hour, when Troy ripped off the facade, screaming, "Unmask, unmask!"

Leaving Danny with nothing more than conflict where he had hoped that love would emerge. Troy may very well have ruined my own chances with Danny. But what chance was there really? Danny had definitely categorized himself as a lesson learned in the world of fantasy versus reality. It wasn't like he had lived up to his potential, that he had accomplished the dizzying feat of becoming a soap hunk. No, he was nothing more than a porn star that had hit the skids in that venue, subsidizing his income by becoming a drug dealer. He was nothing more than damaged goods and light years away from the guy I had lusted after and pinned my dreams of salvation on.

A stop sign drifted in front of my mind, like the street signs that were alerting Troy that he was nearing his destination. I had so much uncharacteristic judgment directed at Danny. I had heard a saying once; most likely the source of its wisdom was from a soap opera character's mouth.

"When we look under a microscope, maybe we should be looking into a mirror instead."

It wasn't like I was a prize catch either. The stain of my actions, the retribution of karma were starting to undermine my bid at happiness, at true freedom, and put me in the same class as Danny. I had been willing to do whatever it took to escape the clutches of the town we grew up in, so why was it that when applied to Danny, it made him a lesser person? It was nothing more than a case of somebody got there before me.

Whenever things did not go my way, I would mutter under my breath about someday, even though I hated the word. Well, it felt as though someday was today as it encompassed all of the earmarks of a make-or-break quality.

And that time was now, according to Jon Parr's "Man in Motion."

Troy maneuvered the microbus into a Doris Day parking spot—a term picked up from George—in front of Danny's apartment building. Before the van had completed its flight and the crew aboard the makeshift time machine had a chance to thank me for choosing riding with them, I made my own choice. I bolted out of my seat, flung open the door, and ran away from seeing the new and maybe not-so-improved Danny.

This way was best, illusions should be preserved, and I could eventually fill in the cracks that the truth had threatened to expose.

Troy uttered something like a startled bark, bewildered in his stoned trance. But nothing was going to prevent my escape, as I proved all of the kids in my PE class wrong by running, well, like Greased Lighting. "Go, Greased Lighting, you're burning up the quarter mile," played in a loop in my head as my feet connected with the concrete. The wind at my back was pulling at me like an invisible hand trying to prevent my escape. It also carried a confused-sounding Troy, who was calling out my pseudonym; the volume of which made me look back to see if he had given chase. He was stationary near the van, so I slowed down just a little.

If I had kept looking back, I would have seen a familiar figure emerge from his upstairs apartment and down the stairs onto the brown patch badly in need of water that served as a lawn.

Troy's shouts had already driven Danny to his window; he was already en route to it upon hearing the recognizable din of his microbus that needed a new muffler. Seeing his former neighbor scram out of his on-loan mode of transportation was not what he expected as this life he was leading was not what he had expected either.

He could almost tap into his once-thought-of dream profession of acting and muster up a double take, looking at me then at the contents of the pipe he was smoking, shaking his head, and muttering, "I've gotta lay off the wacky tobacky."

Although he wasn't feeling like he had been making wise choices as of late and wasn't exactly sure if what he was seeing was real, Danny decided he could get a closer look, heading at a fast clip to his front door. Fine wisps of smoke escaped his mouth, a vaporous apparition that gave him a locomotive appearance as he made his way to chase down a ghost from his past.

Had I known that Danny had seen me, would I stop running away and instead begin running towards? Had I heard his banshee cry of my true identity which did not reach my ears, would it have mattered?

All I knew was that I had achieved a certain telemetry, and nothing was going to slow me down. I didn't stop running until I got to Oki Dog. I am sure that I had looked like the typical Southern California health nut out for a run in the blistering heat.

I had made the perfect choice in my Nike tank top that day, as if it was preordained that I would need to be athletic. I realized there was one jogging accessory that I was missing that would have made my ensemble complete, the Walkman that I had left behind in the microbus.

I silently cursed myself, the muttering probably looking to anyone who cared to notice like I was wheezing self-motivations to myself. It felt that ever since last night, an eternity of revelations, that I was involved in some sort of man-made video game. George represented a Donkey Kong–like figure meant to keep heroes at bay, squiring the reluctant beautiful ones in his clutches. Nick was akin to Star Castle, a game in which players tried to resist a gravitational pull shooting at the outer walls to get to the inside. Troy and Danny were like the ghosts in Pac-Man, giving chase and then becoming the pursued as I followed the dots in the maze, trying to reach my destination.

And I had finally done it. I had surmounted the obstacles of the day that, at just shy of two 'o clock, already felt twenty-four hours too long.

I stood at the entrance of Oki Dog, catching my breath as I had it taken away twofold. Navigating its way down the block at a slow clip was the microbus, and this time it was being helmed by its original captain, Danny.

The microbus was moving stealthily, a shark patrolling for its dinner, careful not to let its telltale signal of danger, its fin, break the surface. But this shark was an anomaly from times gone by standing out among the more colorful vehicles in sports-car form. Danny still didn't look like he had spotted me; I darted inside and ran smack-dab into George.

Chapter 13

George sat motionless, a mountain of a man that I had literally just bounced off of. I started to back away towards the door. George remained unmoving, but his stony glare never left me. I began to search for any signs that Angel may be present and accounted for. For all I knew, he could be hiding behind the monolith that George had become. For all intents and purposes, he may as well be serving as my obelisk; the hatred was seeping out of his pores.

I began to wonder if I was going to end my days on the patio at Oki Dog. I looked past him at the clock on the wall inside; I had arrived fifteen minutes earlier than I had anticipated, if the clock was to be trusted. I didn't know who to trust or what to believe in anymore.

It seemed that an impasse had been reached, and my choices were to stay and face George or to run out onto Santa Monica Boulevard and into Danny.

I was still waiting for George to speak, to spew forth his true intent, but he remained unchanged, a carbon copy of himself. Perhaps I could just edge my way to the patio entrance a little more. As I took another small step backwards, I could see that Angel was not hiding in the shadows that George was casting as the afternoon sun came streaming in the front door.

There was no sign of him anywhere as I looked around at the nearly deserted patio area. There was a businessman chowing down on a hot dog while a peroxided Depeche Mode wannabe stood up and crossed the patio. Perhaps he would be the one to save me from George since I could not seem to do it on my own. But I wasn't so sure a shirtless, parachute-pants-wearing synth-pop knockoff would not be able to succumb to George's wiles.

I was waiting for George to unearth himself from the spot he seemed unable to move from. However, George had focused his sole attention on me. I was hoping that it was just a coincidence that I had run into him here. But I knew that it couldn't be, not for *George of The Gourmet Jungle*. He was less apt to eat one of these greasy confections as he was to join a gym and transform himself into Mr. Universe.

"Ssso what have you been doing today, Billy?" He broke his self-imposed silent treatment; his mouth now forming words where a thin and tight line of defense once resided.

His eyes remained the same emotionless orbs as when he had adopted a new pose, standing between me and the door. I began to go over in my head as to how best answer him on a day that was never ending. Well, I had sex with your son, twice. I watched him smash videotapes. I heard him tell me about your troubles. I learned that he knows my first crush. So much had happened that I felt like I needed a scorecard or a cheat sheet to keep it all straight, for lack of a better word.

"Nothing. Are you here for lunch?" I answered him with a question, hoping that he had not picked up on the inflection of the poorly phrased first portion of it.

I also hoped that he did not notice that I was sweating profusely, and not from my impromptu run. I could only pray that I was diffusing the time bomb in George that was beginning to tick.

"Nothing? I see." As he said this, I caught an upgraded version of his "Oh please, Mary" look that was fraught with hatred.

I backed up even farther from the door. The blazing sun, a fireball in the sky, backlit George, giving him the ominous shadowing of a gunslinger. The mini eclipse gave the illusion that he was ready to draw his weapon and do battle.

I had to wonder what his weapon of choice would be. More treachery underneath his guise of the mild mannered would be the bullet in the gun that shot down the rest of my preconceived notions about him.

However this moment played itself out, it appeared there was going to be a showdown at the Oki Dog Corral; instead of reaching for his six-shooter, George swooped forward, pulling me close to him. I could smell traces of alcohol mixed with a pot chaser on his breath. Did this mean he had been at the palace? I had wanted to ask myself if he had been home, but I didn't know where that was for me. Had he seen the goings-on between Troy and me? More importantly, would he have had the capabilities to film it and, in turn, distribute the next installation in the now defunct *Chicken Hawk* series?

"What kind of game are you playing, Billy?" he said this through clenched teeth—I mean dentures.

Although I knew he was angry, I wanted to scream at him at the top of my lungs, "I'm playing the Game of Life, brought to you by the good folks at Milton Bradley, and my car is filled with little pink people!"

It was just esoteric or nonsensical enough for me to escape his mitts and resume my impromptu afternoon jog. More than likely, the THC in my system made it seem like a viable option. Then I thought maybe the Game of Life had been brought to the populace by the Parker Brothers. Then I realized that it didn't matter in the very least. There was a vein now pulsing hypnotically down the center of George's forehead, shattering the façade of his quiet calm last night. And that's when it hit me: maybe he was having a delayed reaction to last night's proceedings.

"Look," I said as his grip tightened on my right arm, "if this is about last night with Nick or with Angel…"

I let the thought trail off, realizing that it had come out sounding a tad on the slutty side.

"No," he said, trying to get a handle on himself and to speak with an inside voice outside as to not draw unwarranted attention to an apparent lovers' spat with a thirty-year age difference. But who would notice? The shirtless David Gahan disciple was now circling the businessman, awaiting final confirmation on a landing, sipping innocuously on the soda that he had ordered from the cashier, who was now engaging his coworkers with mindless banter.

All it would take was just one look or glance from his Brooks Brother opposite and Depeche Mode would lead him away to some alleyway to blow him. This might be me in a couple of hours, trying to use my male persuasions to make a few dollars in order to survive. I began to think about where it was that I thought I was running to when standing in front of me, in the closest of proximity, was George, the one I wanted to run away from.

"Thisss isss about today. It'sss about a certain matter of destruction of private property. I came home early to sssee if Troy had arrived. He hadn't. But it looksss like you went after my video collection with a baseball bat. Isss that how you choossse to thank me?" he inquired, his question punctuated with a tighter grip that was beginning to hurt rather than a question mark.

It only took me a moment to respond nonverbally. I kneed him squarely in the balls, David knocking down Goliath by hitting him in the stones more accurately than with them. George let out an *oof* noise, expelling the mixture of his poisonous breath into my face, before he let go of my arm and dropped to one knee in a horrible mockery of a marriage proposal.

Now I was off and running again, out of Oki Dog and away from the consequences of my actions. But when it really boiled down to it, it wasn't my actions I was defending. For some reason, I had decided to not rat Troy out. I knew that I felt a kinship with him in the "I hate my father" arena. Besides, wasn't it about time that some-one hit George where it would hurt him the most?

After all of Troy's dispelling of the myths that George sur-rounded himself with, I realized I was nothing to him, just a play-thing. I knew that my time in the palace was officially ended, but with one well-placed knee to groin action, I had solved the problem of what I was going to be doing with my night tomorrow. I wouldn't be forced into something I didn't want to do.

I didn't think that rang true for some reason. I had heard the term "Do what you love and the money will find you." Was this my career path? I did have a lot of expendable sex drive and not as much cash to match it right now. It seemed destined somehow and that I would somehow fulfill that prophecy when I had laid down the gauntlet with my curiosity that stemmed from the Hollywood versions I had seen of prostitution over the years.

But as always, I needed to focus on where I was coming from in order to get where I was going—in a very literal sense, as my feet pounded off the sidewalk and away from one possible future and to not be snared by the past that was patrolling the boulevard, looking for someone who didn't exist anymore.

I planned to keep running until a thought would cross my mind and take me in the direction that I needed to go. What I hadn't expected was for an arm to shoot out of an alleyway and pull me into the shadows.

Angel stood flush against the semidirty wall. I was half expecting Troy or Danny to be attached to the disembodied appendage or maybe even the Depeche Mode knockoff who liked my moxie and figured that would translate to a hot encounter. Even though I had been focused on George and what he may have in store for me, I did keep a compartment open in the back of my mind for Angel's whereabouts.

"Where were you?" I tried not to channel my mother, but since talking to her today, maybe some of the old Kate Dodge "You can't cross the street without looking both ways" tone crept into my query.

"I got to Oki Dog early and was waiting. Someone tapped me on the shoulder. Of course, it was George. He had been home and found the note I left you. And I guess you worked out your aggressions on his video collection."

"I didn't, it was Troy." As I said this, Angel shook his head a fraction and then stopped.

It was like Angel was programmed to be George's yes boy in the eventuality that there may be a slanderous remark made about him.

Angel was half hidden in the sparse shadows, looking as though he was trying to decide to remain on the dark side or not.

I didn't really know anything about Angel. I wasn't sure why he had wanted to meet me today or had suddenly thought a blow job was going to be an ends to a means last night. Perhaps he had been doing a preemptive strike, sensing that my tenure at the palace was his swan song there. I had inklings of ideas of what he was going to say to me at Oki Dog, just as I had inklings of the kind of life he led.

He seemed to live his life like an emotional vampire feeding off those that whispered into his ears that they would take care of him, driving a stake into interlopers' hearts if they tried to get to know him. He had a tough surface, as was exemplified by his hard-knock-life appearance, and a face that was aged by nights spent on the sidewalks of Santa Monica Boulevard, looking for a "date."

"George said Troy left him a message on his machine," Angel stated. "Something about having a flat tire and not making it into town until later."

As Angel reported his findings from the front, I could feel a chill overtake me. Troy was setting me up, and I had actually protected the bastard because I felt sorry for him! I had kneed his father in the family jewels just so I could be assured not to drag Troy into the picture, whose frame was broken and the glass was cracked, a mere shadow of the family portrait it once was and could never be again.

"Angel, you've got to believe me!" I pleaded.

"The problem is, I know all too well that you are telling nothing but the truth." As he said this, he smiled his most beauteous mouth-ful-of-haggard-teeth smile, a contradiction of terms.

Then surprisingly, he began to weep for those who had passed over the threshold of the palace and for one soul in particular, who had been a fixture for a while now—himself.

I watched his hard-boiled textures turn to putty in the wash of his tears, his face becoming a blank canvas. I could sense he was vacillating between sorrow for himself and anger towards George. I wanted to find out what he knew, compare it to what I had found out today, and then formulate a plan.

I just let him cry until he was reduced to hiccups, which made him laugh.

"Are you okay?" I asked this before I had time enough to figure out in my head that he probably was for the first time in years.

He nodded, wiped away the tears almost theatrically, signaling that what I had thought had been the truth.

"Yes, yes, I am." he said with an inflection that had Afterschool Special written all over it. "I believe you about Troy. Do you want to know why I believe this?"

As he asked this, he siphoned some of the snot that was clogging his nose down into his throat, a symbolic gesture that he was ready to clear the air with me. I positioned myself on the right side of him so that I could keep a lookout for either George or Danny and still maintain the illusion that I was hanging on every word.

I didn't answer him with anything, a vocalization that I understood he was going to tell me something important or a nod to silently signify that I got the gist. Angel was like any other palace dweller; he wore many masks at the masquerade. I wasn't quite sure what the outcome of what he had to tell me would be, but I knew I liked the mask that currently resided on his face. It was one of someone who had been trod upon, put down for too long, and was trying to help someone else from making the same mistakes he had. In a way, Angel would have proved to have been a better surrogate father once he got past the fact that the new baby always garners more attention.

"I have been with George for three years now. I have gone from bein' his bitch, to bein' his bitch and his maid," he began with just a hint of venom. "He took me in off the streets, you know? So I felt lucky to be in his casa. I seen him bring in new meat on his own and the new meat that he pays me a finder's fee to locate. I have decided that you are my last finder fee. I cannot stand to watch him use people anymore!

"I've let him use me for too long. I could have gotten out of what I have been doing for, you know, work a long time ago. But George always tells me I am lucky to be doing it, that anyone would even pay me. I'm not stupid, Billy. I can see the games he plays. He says that so I'll be out there even though I am getting tired of it, you know? So what does he do when I say I am tired of it? He starts giving me Tina. At first I like what it does for me. One line gets me going for a whole day, makes me even hornier than I would already be, you know? Helps me keep that fucking place cleaner too. But there's one thing George didn't count on. It also gives me more time to think, you know? It gives me time to go over things that are fucked up with me. Well, I knew that I couldn't do Tina anymore after this one time when I didn't sleep for almost a whole week, you know? So what I have been doing is taking the Tina that George gives me. I know this is wrong, but I don't know how else I can get away from him. I have been selling it on the streets, just like I sell myself."

Angel was quiet for a moment, taking a dramatic pause in his soliloquy for a tweaker. He rubbed his hands over his eyes as if trying to shut out memories or to block the sunlight that was managing to become his personal spotlight and was getting into his eyes.

I didn't know if I should use this intermission to answer the barrage of you knows when, in fact, I did not know what it was like to be Angel. I did not know what it was like to sell your body; it's not that I didn't think of my time with George as a form of subtle whoring, but it felt more like barter.

I did not know what it was like to be associated with Tina, but from what Angel had just told me, she was not a friend I would like to claim as my own. What I could relate to was what he had said about George and his manipulative ways. Maybe Angel and I could strike out on our own, start up a West Hollywood chapter of the We Hate George and All He Stands For Committee and find the lives we were looking to lead.

The suspicious part of my brain was rightfully thinking that Angel was laying a pity-me trap so that I would be unsuspecting and off guard when George popped into the alleyway for some retribution on his aching ball sack.

I started running down the options for escape in case this happened, and the only way out was straight ahead. All of Angel's dialogue could have been a clever way of keeping my attention while

George came to meet Angel with me in tow at a designated meeting spot, preordained in the wee hours of the morning.

Somehow I wanted to deem Angel's true confession as real as there was a very believable quality to it. I was about to tell Angel of my idea that we should become roommates when he picked up his monologue where last he left it.

"I am through with selling myself short. I used to want to be something, to be anything, you know?" he said with a pleading quality to his voice. "Now I'm hoping I can just be somebody. I don't want to be fake. I don't want to be like George."

At the mention of his name and even though I was at a vantage point where I would see him approaching, I almost thought that Angel was alerting me to George's presence. For all I knew, George could be cutting a stealth path down the street, very purposeful in his stride now that the throbbing in his balls had most likely subsided. I focused my attention back to Angel.

"I know exactly what you mean. Everybody that I've met here has some kind of secret or is playing some sort of game," I said, not unaware of my double-standard assessment. "I took off from home because I was tired of living a lie, because I knew that even after I told the truth, I would have to hide it somehow. I just don't get it, I really don't. I just want to find a place where I can belong. Sometimes I feel like I'll never find it no matter how long I look. Everything is always about someday. Well, I want that to be today. I want to know what my life is going to be about, that it's going to mean something."

Angel took up my silent nodding in agreement as easily as I had picked up on his monologue ways. This moment had group hug written all over it. I moved closer to Angel, and he put his hands up, as if warding off some demon from the seventh layer of hell, rebuking what he though was a sexual advance. All it was going to be was one person reaching out to another, but what it brought about was very unexpected.

"Umm, look, Billy, there was a reason I wanted to meet with you, you know? Now, don't freak out, honey. But how do I put this?"

He put his hands on his hips, just like he had the first night that I met him. But there was something about him that was different; he seemed softer, with less of an edge. What he told me was definitely hard to hear and cut me to the quick.

"Well," he said, looking down like the ground had the answer as to how best tell me the news, "I've noticed some, ummm, stains in your underwear. Do you know why you get them?"

I felt a flashback sensation, like I was talking to my mother and all of a sudden she might ask me about why there are funny stains on my sheets. I gulped, sensing that I was not about to hear a tirade about proper stain-removal techniques from Angel, who was now looking at me with a vulnerability that shattered his glass ceiling.

I didn't know what my face must look like, but I could invoke images of a Tex Avery wolf, and its jaw dropped to the ground, setting the scene for me to trip over my tongue. That wouldn't be a problem; it felt as though I would not be able to command myself to speak at will until Angel provided me with an answer to that proverbial question of why.

Angel most likely took my moment of reverie as me going over in my head the possible reasons why he couldn't Shout out those pesky stains. Assuming that I wouldn't get there as fast as he would, Angel cut me off at the mental pass, a desperado who knew all too well.

"George gave you gonorrhea, you know? I guess there's no other way to say it, sorry," he muttered.

"What are you talking about?" I knew that my voice seemed a bit shrill and that my question came out as incredulous sounding.

I remembered learning about STDs in my junior high health class, but I kept focusing on the fact that I couldn't get VD from a doorknob. No, but it seemed that I could get gonorrhea from a man that I was glad that I had kicked in the balls. Wasn't I supposed to have a burning sensation? I felt that I had one that did not emanate from my penis but was getting all fired up in my head.

"And the really sick part is, he knew you'd probably get it, you know? Didn't he ever give you his safety-measures speech?" Angel was talking rapidly again. Thinking he was going to break into another monologue, I interceded with my own brand of police interrogation.

"Oh he gave me the speech, all right. I can't believe he actually made me feel guilty about me being safe when that motherfucker was the one all along that…" I trailed off before I veered into a new line of questioning. "How long has he had it? Why wouldn't he tell me?"

Then a thought came into my head and, just as quickly, came flying out of my mouth.

"Did you know about this all along, Angel?"

I could feel the slow burn beginning to take hold of me. All of my mother's warnings came up from the night I told her I was gay, each one a stop sign, but they may as well have been a marker measuring what she presumed as the truth and what I was finding out could be my reality.

"I don't want you to get AIDS" seemed to be the one that came coming up over and over again.

If George hadn't bothered telling me about this, he could just as easily be keeping that huge secret in his back pocket. The climate around AIDS was fear based; it was an immediate death sentence. The air dancing around AIDS was also one of mystery, yet there was one piece of conclusive evidence that I had not adhered to with George. I didn't have safe sex with him because he told me I could trust him.

Now I was asking a question of one of his cohorts in the hopes that he would tell it true. But why should I bother waiting for an answer when I could do the usual take-flight methods I had practically honed down to a science? How could I be sure that Angel wasn't just yanking my chain as well? I was just about ready to run when he spoke.

"I was waiting for George to tell you, like he said he would." His voice was on the verge of something along the lines of tears mixed with rage and came out sounding like a very bad Kermit the Frog impression.

Then it hit me. This is what George and Angel must have been discussing when I was taking an ersatz nap that day. Angel had broached the subject with George only to be shut down by him.

Somehow I believed Angel, or I wanted to. I knew the night before I had asked George point-blank about the very topic of what was on his mind, but he had answered the question about what I was training for. But George had not answered the last part of Angel's inquiry that early evening, "When are you going to tell him about…"

Well, George hadn't gotten around to that, had he? But Angel seemed to be rotating 180 degrees. I remembered how hateful he had sounded on that particular night, assuring George that they could make a lot of money off me. I started to tap into the wellspring that comes with being manipulated, of being discarded at a moment's notice. And in that moment, I had a pretty good idea of what some of Angel's life was like.

"I'm sorry I didn't tell you sooner, you know? But George would have kicked me out. I wasn't really sure that I liked you until last night, that you weren't the enemy."

"Well, I kinda figured as much when your dick was in my mouth," I said this with just a fluid ounce of venom as it was all I could muster in my panic-stricken mind. What if George was not telling me other things, as he was the master purveyor of secrets. I would just go on the hope that Angel would tell me if things would get worse for me, if he knew.

I mean he and I had gone further in this alleyway conversation of unlocking the barriers that were keeping us prisoners at the palace. He was not quite a friend, more than an acquaintance, a brother in arms. Then I had a thought that really illustrated that I should have paid more attention in health class.

"You're not going to get this because of last night?"

"No, mijo, I will be okay. But we need to take care of you, you know? That's why I wanted to meet you, to take you to the clinic. I was just hoping that you would be okay with finding out, you know? Are you?"

"I guess so," I said this, feeling as though my world was slowing caving in, eroding at a frenetic pace the last twenty-four hours, ready to implode at its core.

And a lot of this collapse was due to one man, King George, as he was first introduced to me a millennium ago. I could not believe that a human being could have such little regard for anything or anyone beside himself. I felt another hot ember start to sear away at my heart at the thought of the substandard excuse for a man. He was the pantheon of selfishness, the antithesis of caring, and had only a modicum of what could be construed as human. He was also stepping into the alleyway, unknown to Angel, and I couldn't seem to find the words to warn him.

Chapter 14

There wasn't time to warn Angel. George was moving surprisingly quickly for someone of his size. He had a singleness of purpose, which was to get back at me at all costs. Somewhere in his mind he knew that he could always deal with Angel later; had George been privy to our conversation, he might have thought differently about his former right-hand-job man.

Whether he had been lying in wait or had developed telepathy, it was right at the millisecond I had that thought that had George become poised to clock Angel. I stood frozen, trying to muster up some sort of vocal early warning system, before George's nukes spelled Angel's *The Day After*.

With George just an inch away from clobbering him, Angel must have seen something in my eyes; realizing that, I was caught like a queer in the headlights. He swiftly kicked his right leg back, and for the second time that day, George went down for the count with a well-placed kick to the groin.

Working on the streets had instilled a sixth sense, a perception when danger was near for Angel. He was now reaching for my hand to lead me away from the man who was trying to keep us both down.

Well, he was the one that wasn't going to be able to walk away just yet. George appeared immobilized; his head was cradled in his arms, like we had stumbled upon him taking a catnap in the alley.

Well, if I had learned anything from the incalculable viewings of all of the *Halloweens* and *Friday the 13ths*, it was this: even when the killer (or in this case the man who was trying to kill my youthful innocence) looks like he is defeated, that is the time when he pops up, wholly resurrected and ready to claim more lives.

And stepping over him was a dicey prospect, as according to horror movie lore; a fraction of a second later, George's hand would spring up, trying to latch on to his fleeting youth by grabbing a hold of ours.

I reached out to Angel's hand and started pulling him back into the alleyway, trying the leader's role on like a new pair of pants. It felt ill fitting and needed some time for me to get used to it, and time was definitely of the essence.

After about a fifteen feet of hurried shuffling, I realized why I had been subscribed to the follower position my whole life. There was a brick wall and some trash cans that peppered the accompanying other two walls of white brick, all but sealing our fate and boxing us in.

If I didn't know any better and if there wasn't some graffiti and dark smudges against the whiteness, I would have sworn that we were at the entrance to heaven. Yet I supposed that we were trying to escape the devil incarnate himself.

I had a surging feeling in my brain; an override of déjà vu was stopping me dead in my tracks. Flashes of images crept into my mind, and all of them were of a sexual nature. I didn't think I was developing a fetish for dirty alleyways while danger was imminent.

Angel was speaking to me, but I did not hear what he was saying as an ocean's roar filled my head. It was drowning out any and all surrounding noises; everything in my head sounded like the television was on the fritz.

And that's when I realized why this place seemed familiar; I had seen it on television just last night.

This was the same alleyway where *Up Your Alley* was filmed! I was walking in the very alleyway where Danny had been nude, where he had shown me, via the magic of celluloid, that he was of this earth and dwelled among mere mortal men.

I thought it more than happenstance that I should run into Danny in a roundabout way today, but now I was residing on his movie set. There always seemed to be some magnetic field that was always binding us together, yet we were like polar opposites, only allowed to get so close before the gravitational pull became a push, sending us light years from each other.

"We're going the wrong way, mijo. Hurry up, you know!" Angel said with a strong dose of urgency.

I looked in George's direction; he was still in the "I played so hard today that I need an instantaneous nap" mode. I wanted to stay put, to never have to run again, to stand up and confront the man who had manipulated me at every turn.

But now I had Angel to think of. He had also tendered his resignation in the same fashion as I had. I guess with all of the coincidences today, I would have to coin a new version of an old phrase: All gay minds think alike or, more accurately, seemed to subside in the same microcosm.

It was one created by George. George begat Troy. George is friends with Nick, who had his way with Troy on film. Danny had made a porn right where I was standing. Troy had destroyed his father's homemade porn collection and pinned it on me. Danny and Troy knew each other. Everyone had a secret, only Nick knew mine, but I was sure that Danny would have to explain to Troy why he was hollering after Henry.

So many subplots, so many twists just in the last day alone, would be enough to make anyone's head not only swim but stand an above average chance of drowning. So where did that leave Angel and myself in the grand scheme?

We were both puppets, sex on a string for George to utilize only when he felt the need; and once the amusement factor died out for him, we were put back into our places. We boxed ourselves up and resided high upon unreachable shelves, waiting for the one that didn't play games. But that was never going to be George again; too much had occurred today for both Angel and me.

And we had both been relegated to acting out our frustrations by kicking him where it counted most for him. Now he had been put in his place and was very likely taking his own faux nap to see what information he could glean, just as I had done.

Well, I was wide awake now. My eyes were peeled to the truth behind George's caring pretense. He wasn't a savior or saint, an answer to all my prayers, but he was still blocking my way in discovering all of what gay life could really offer by his mere presence.

I spied down the short distance, which felt like miles, and took a gander at the human roadblock that was finally beginning to tire of his catatonic state and was stirring. While he was doing so, getting up on one knee and milking whatever thespian talents he may have had, it was Angel that appeared shaken, not stirred.

He had quite the stricken look on his face. I could see that he was rethinking his actions; the doubt of what he had done in the name of fast friendship and for his own sake was abundantly clear.

And I saw him again tap into the raw emotional nerve of how George had disposed of him, tossing him aside as easily as some of the trash that was strewn throughout the alley.

The next thing I knew, Angel was taking a cue from Billy Idol, and with a rebel yell, he made a flight of fury that was propelling him towards George at a ferocious clip. As he started to get up on one knee, milking his AARP card member in good-standing status, George caught sight of Angel. I thought he was going to pull the old duck-and-cover routine. Instead, he sprang up in a jack-in-the-box that's going to kill you impression, defying the fact that he was twenty years Angel's senior, had at least 150 pounds on him, and was not about to be thrice kicked in the balls.

I decided I should join the fracas that was about to be in progress. George almost constituted as two men due to his size and the anger of being manhandled in a way he wasn't at all pleased about.

Everything was slowed down to bionics, the running, the noise of the world around us, just like on *The Six Million Dollar Man* or in this case *The Bionic Woman*. Angel was just a stone's throw away from George; I was in hot pursuit when Danny's microbus came to a sudden halt on the street. The screeching of tires managed to garner George's attention away from the encroaching vehemence that was Angel and the ultimate in tagging-along accessories, me.

I was still planning on helping Angel out in venting our mutual frustrations with the man who would be king. But as both the driver's door and passenger's door opened, I realized we were going to be in good company. Troy had emerged, looking as riled up as Angel was.

Danny had not yet spotted me, but I could not take my eyes off him.

He was rushing to catch up with Troy, who was now in the process of trying to pull Angel off George. Well, it had appeared that Troy was going to help out his father, but with one swing of his right hook, it became crystal clear that wasn't going to be the case.

He was cocking his fist for another go at the man he had the misfortune of being related to by blood when Danny grasped his wrist so hard that Troy might have had the straightest wrist of any borderline gay man in all of the land. He was rendered unable to draw blood from the man whose own had given him life.

"Leave him alone, Troy! Just back off!" Danny said in a voice that belied his laid-back surfer persona.

This stopped Angel from attempting his own "fists of fury" manner; he immediately dropped his fists to his side and adopted a hangdog expression, like he had been caught with his hand in the cookie jar. Troy also succumbed to the same look, although there was anger still apparent in his eyes.

"Danny? Is that really you?" These words were not spoken by yours truly but by one unlikely to know whom Danny was, or so I thought.

Angel's question resounded back to me, echoing off the bricks, ricocheting its full impact into my brain. Angel knew Danny. How could this be? It looked as though Danny and Angel were going to hug, almost like they had been lovers in a previous life well before I had arrived to serve as the catalyst for the downfall of a king.

I felt the scorching heat of betrayal becoming prevalent, burning more onto the scene than was really occurring, conjuring up a cavalcade of imagery. In my mind's eye, I saw Danny clasp Angel's hand in his and, without even looking my way, headed off in the microbus for destinations that would remain unknown for me. Next, George would leave, then Troy faded from the picture, and I was left standing all alone, no one giving me a second glance, as if I did not exist or ever mattered to them.

My breathing was becoming labored as I tried to force-feed myself the jealousy that was being dished out and I was beginning to choke on. If I wasn't careful, I might need to have the Heimlich maneuver performed on me, but given this alley's past serving as a makeshift porn set, I was more apt to end up getting the hind-lick maneuver.

I didn't want any of the men present and accounted for to perform it for me. The disdain at the crafty way each and every one of them had manipulated me was enough to make me curl up in the fetal position.

Pretending to be my friend or that they really wanted to know me or love me, for that matter, was not on their agenda. I was just a toddler trying to advance from crawling to walking in this new world I had found. But it seemed that I was being tripped up in my attempts with every little step and falling flat on my face, which was opening up fresh wounds without the foresight of which was the best way to cover them up, allowing them to scab over. But knowing myself, there was apt to be some picking involved.

"Well, well, well," George managed in his best attempt of "Nothing's wrong" voice, "isssn't thisss jussst like old timesss?"

It seemed that two kicks to the groin had caused extra air leaks in his speech pattern. He was trying to reestablish his dominance after being laid so low, just as he had marked his territory by giving his boys the badge of dishonor, which I was thinking might garner more than just a swift kick to the coconuts. I started to emerge from the alleyway so that I could be in the line of fire and closer to the action.

"Hello, George," Danny answered, knowing that he was the long-lost boy and that he was talking to none other than Captain I'll Make a Hooker out of You.

"Well, Danny, thisss certainly isss a coincidence." His eyes roved back and forth between Danny and Troy. "How isss it that you two know each other?"

For a split second I thought he may have been addressing me. Even though I was close to the fray, I had inadvertently resumed my role as the invisible boy. Nobody was focused on me. All eyes were on George, and his voice had a hypnotic quality about it.

"C'mon, George, you know. You know?" Angel had obviously missed the eye targeting that George was exhibiting and answered the question without really answering it for those not in the know, you know.

"I wasssn't talking to you! I wasss talking to the blond book-ends!" George thundered, trying to counterbalance all of the hits he had taken today.

He wanted to appear strong while we all knew he was weak; it was only George that wanted to keep up the front that he was in command. A small part of me started to tremble. I was tapping into Big Ed's furious rants every time someone raised their voice. I mentally shut off the valve to my emotional connections to home, which was difficult when it was standing a few feet away from me. I froze up the pipes so that I could redirect the source of my own anger, but right now the course was proving to be a preponderance.

It was hard for me to decipher where to channel my anger, which was now tainted with jealousy over Angel and Danny and Danny and Troy and with my hatred of George. Now I supposed I was tainted too. And that was thanks to the man that was trying to reestablish his credibility amongst his minions, which now seemed to include Danny into the fold, thus causing a new wrinkle. Danny, who by his mere presence, created a soothing calm to those in close proximity.

Fortunately, I was the perpetual outsider, and I didn't need to "do it for Johnny," to paraphrase Matt Dillon from the movie that could've been called *Henry's Story*.

I needed to do something for myself, to take a bigger risk with better end results than having unprotected sex with George had garnered. Oh shit! My mind fired this off without a warning and the hazy memory from a few hours back. Troy hadn't used a condom either! More than likely someone was going to develop a case of the green trots, and it was all thanks to his own father, unintentionally.

I really did need to look into producing a line of anti-Hallmark cards to mark even the most audacious occasions. Rather than herald this dark day with a flowery rhyme, I knew the information would have to come from me. Suddenly the day seemed even hotter; there wasn't a sudden solar flare except for the one I was experiencing as far as my temper was concerned.

"Well, George, I knew you weren't talking to me because that is something that you don't like to do, is it?" I said with a ferocity that was not at all surprising to me.

But to the world at large, the only four people in the populace as far as I was concerned, all turned back and looked like they had heard the wail of a banshee.

When I was greeted with nothing but silence, even the background noise of traffic had seemed to vanish at the timber of my voice, and seeing the smug look on George's face, I continued.

"Is it?" I roared. "Or maybe I should speak a language you'll understand. Isss it?"

And there it was, not only had my anger released a lion, but it had freed the elephant that had been trapped in the living room. These are the next two things that I saw: one was that everyone, with the exception of George, replaced stricken looks with a look that conveyed "Oh no, he din't," as Angel had been apt to say on occasion. And secondly, George was rushing towards me. I was done running from him. I stood my ground; and as we stood toe to toe and face-to-face, I whispered something to him.

"Rosssesss are red, violetsss are blue," I cooed, "you gave me the clap, so now your ssson hasss it too."

All right, so I did address him with a flowery rhyme. But it did beautifully convey the message that I wanted to get across to George and not to Danny; that you shouldn't fuck with me was something I wanted to keep under wraps from Danny.

I am sure he still thought of me as the naive youngin', and I wanted to preserve that illusion even though my perceptions of him weren't up to snuff. They were more or less up to snuff film. He was still the unobtainable goal to be reached, the pantheon of my desires.

Before George got off a clever retort, Danny was pulling him away from me, most likely worried that I was going to be hurt by him. Or maybe, since he knew how my father could be when he was enraged, Danny was worried for George's sake. There was such a strange sense that I was treading between a parallel universe, and Henry and Billy would be the worlds that collide. I didn't want George to know who I really was when I wasn't really sure of who I wanted to be.

Could I truly be independent if I was relying on the not-so-kindness of certain strangers? Was I only the frustrated boy trying to be a man, the cock-assured Lothario taking names and breaking hearts all so mine wouldn't get broken itself, a mental smart-ass that was now vocalizing those quips as he gained more confidence? Or was I lashing out against the perceived and substantiated injustices I felt against others? I am sure that I encompassed all of these qualities.

What I felt myself gearing up to was like one of the movies that I had watched at George's one lazy afternoon, which certainly wasn't like today. And not to worry, this is before I discovered the *Chicken Hawk* series. I sat down mesmerized, not only by the fine reefer George had kindly left me, but by what I saw as the living embodiment of what I felt like playing out on the screen.

Rebel Without a Cause left me feeling as though I was James Dean and that I was being torn apart by others and they were now left to pick at the scraps of what was left of the carrion of my naivety.

I could see by George's face that he had clearly underestimated me. I could tell by the pounding of my heart that I was truly alive, or else I was just hyped up from the one-sided confrontation. I was again on the fringes; this time I was happy to be an observer, to see how the scene would play.

"Ssso... Well..." George began and stopped a "begins with the letter *S*" address to the troops, except he was more or less the captain of a sinking ship, and the rats had finally learned the capabilities that they had and were already manning the lifeboats.

"Well, before we were rudely interrupted," he hissed, shooting daggers in my vicinity, "I was jus—"

George's motorboat was starting to flounder, sputtering in the tides that were turning against him.

"How do you two know each other? Troy? Danny?"

"Oh, are you talking to us, the blond bookends?" Troy said in a bold and haughty manner. "Well, why should we tell you anyway? When have you ever been up front or even honest, for that matter? You've been lying to yourself all of your life, then you lied to Mom, to me. Do you even care about anything else but what you want? Do you know what it was like after you left? What an embarrassment you are to me? Still, I have tried to understand you so that I can understand myself. Maybe not so much to love you but just to find out why you are the way you are. That's why I have been living in LA the last year and haven't even told you. I have been keeping close tabs on you. I see that you haven't changed at all. In fact, you seem to have gotten worse.

"Danny's my roommate, but I also know that he is your dealer," he exclaimed. "I went with him one night on his rounds. Do you really think you can hold people hostage by making them drug addicts so that they have to depend on you to get what you want? Is that what you're doing to him? He's only sixteen! I'm sure that makes him even more desirable to you, you sick, twisted fuck! You just use people. Well, it's going to stop at Henry!"

He pointed in my direction and answered the question if Danny had divulged my true identity. Two out of the four heads swung in my direction, George's only for a brief moment, in case his son began pummeling him again.

Angel looked a tad on the hurt side, like I should have told him sooner. Well, up until last night I had thought he was an asshole. Should our conversation in the alleyway had not been interrupted, I am very sure that I would have told him.

I wanted to say something, not necessarily in my defense, but just to have a voice as Henry. I was about to get a word in edgewise when Troy finished his thought on his father's people skills.

"Because that's what you did to Angel. And before him, that's what you did to Danny!" he practically shrieked.

My ears were wide open, receiving every ounce of information that Troy had either rehearsed at great length or gleaned parts of from any given soap opera. However, the last part he had said, that couldn't have been something on a soap because it couldn't be possible.

Danny and George?

I didn't want to believe. I wanted to bury my face in Danny's Quicksilver shirt and have it become my own hunk-attached Kleenex. That's what the old Henry would have done because from the chrysalis of Billy had emerged someone different, someone stronger. I was now a hybrid.

I had really learned some invaluable insights into the nature of the beast during my stint in LA, and it looked like Danny did too. I looked at him with new eyes, not with the eyes of first crushes, but with the eagle eye of a sharp shooter at the ready to dispatch old perceptions. He was still very handsome, but something about his appearance made him look run-down. He had the look of someone who had hoped this wouldn't be the life he would be living but somehow couldn't avoid the pitfalls along the way.

The sheer magnitude of happenstance made it clear that the journey of a thousand miles does not begin with a single step; it begins with George. I really wanted to think that I had misunderstood what Troy had told his father.

Well, it did make sense as I began to think about it in a detached way. Danny was just seventeen when he left to pursue his long-hidden desire to become a Hollywood star. He kept his dreams to himself, especially the ones that might label him a fag amongst those who craved the waves.

I would usually hear reports that his mom told my mom, who then passed along the information to whomever was sitting at the dinner table contemplating what exactly was for dinner even though it was residing on the plate in front of them. More often than not, I was the one who received the news, especially after John joined the Navy.

Every time I heard some snippet of information about Danny, I began to fantasize about what it would be like to drop in unexpectedly on him in LA.

Well, I never imagined that it would end up in an alleyway where he had made a porno movie more than likely to pay for the drug habit he had already established back home and that had progressed to the more serious avenues of addiction thanks to George's help. I took myself out of my head, out of the past, out of my summations. I needed to answer "Present" in case the teacher demanded to know if I did, in fact, exist.

"But when you think about it, you are really no better than he is, now are you, Danny? You enable him to keep that allure of free drugs by supplying him. But nothing is ever free with my father. You pay with your soul, and when he's done with it, there aren't any refunds. So that makes you nothing more than a second-rate pimp. Do you want to tell Henry or Billy or whoever the fuck he is just why it is he happened onto my father's little enclave? How you sold him out after his mother called and said he had run away and that he was probably coming to see you. How you immediately called my father and told him to put Angel on alert just in case he didn't get to you first. Hell, you even took them a picture of him so that they wouldn't bring home the wrong blond! Oh wait a minute, guess you don't need to tell him, me and my big mouth," Troy recanted with more than a hint of bitterness.

Troy and his big mouth? Right now mine felt like it was about an inch off the trash-strewn pavement. There was a fear of overload, that I really and truly could not handle anymore revelations that would cut me to the quick. George was a universe unto himself, and I was not referring to his portliness; or to put it another way, he was a black hole snuffing out existence. And he had drawn not only myself, the newest member of his "use 'em and lose 'em" contingent, but also my childhood crush, who seemed more like a childhood pulverize now.

I wanted to feel empathy for Danny that he had sunk so low that he would even consider putting me in harm's way because he was so cash poor. I didn't know that I could. Danny had put me in the mix, fully knowing what his own outcome had been; or maybe he was so caught up in his addictions that it seemed like a great idea to make me a drug-addicted whore?

I may have been steering towards that darkened patch of deserted highway myself, but I certainly hadn't needed a helping hand. My brain was at odds trying to take a position on Danny. Scoundrel? Saint? Stud? It felt as though I had Jiffy Pop residing in my head, and at any moment, I was going to burst through the aluminum-foil top!

I was glad to be in the know, you know, which led me to Angel and Danny. The chance that he and Angel had been an item burned a line of jealousy from my head to my heart. Maybe they were just old friends. The thought seemed to quell the mental acid reflux. Whatever the answer was, they were linked by the barbed-wire togetherness that George's association provided. This time, George had incorporated the wrong element into the palace by bringing me on board. I needed to decide if it was fight or flight time.

"Back off, Troy!" Danny had adopted this as his mantra for some reason.

"Why should I? And don't take it out on me. When you should be taking it out on him," Troy exclaimed, pointing towards his father.

For a split second, I thought Troy was going to spit on his father; instead, he moved behind Danny. I did not think this was the appropriate time for Troy to try to get within the sight line and catch a glimpse of Danny's still-fine ass.

What Troy managed to do was to create a visual representation, a mosaic of a united front bearing down on the enemy. I decided it was my time to join the fag-rag team of resistance to George's dwindling reign. I stepped out of the alley and joined Angel's side. The moment felt solidified, that it took all four of us to come to an unspoken meeting of the minds for this to happen so that George could be banished no matter what had transpired between us.

I expected George to buckle, to fall to his knees for the third time today, in a way altogether unfamiliar to him and that he wouldn't derive any pleasure from. I was hoping that the sight of the four of us would prove to be that of the title of the new James Bond movie that I wanted to see, that it would be a view to a kill.

I didn't think that I wanted George to actually die, but I wanted him to pay some sort of retribution for his crimes against gay humanity. I was harboring a lot of anger towards him, especially since I knew that he had personally tarnished my own perception of my one-time angel, Danny.

In his case, a simple blackmail just would not do as it had with Steve. He needed to pay in other ways. I didn't know if I was going to be the one to make him ante up either. Apparently it wasn't up to me. Per his "No women and children first" motto of life, George removed the gun from his pants waistband that he had appropriately hidden underneath his sports coat resting above his ample ass.

He fired once, aiming for any one of us that were trying to man a lifeboat as the waters around him churned blood red.

Chapter 15

The first shot was a misguided warning one; it broke open a trash bag from the local eatery adjacent to the alleyway, spilling spaghetti sauce from its innards. I knew that trash bag could have been any one of the four of us that were held by the grip of fear.

I couldn't tell what kind of gun was pointing straight at me. I could discern that it wasn't of the Dirty Harry Magnum variety. It looked slightly more on cue with something that Loni Anderson and Lynda Carter had toted in their ill-fated television pairing on *Partners in Crime* as it could've fit into a lovely clutch purse.

In this case, it had been concealed underneath a sports jacket with little chance that anyone would detect it until the dramatic moment it was pulled out. Nonetheless, it was out, proud, and pointed directly at me and was proving to be scarier than Loni Anderson's big coiffed hair helmet. But that was last year, when Loni was teasing her hair so much that she could have possibly been charged with assault with a deadly weapon. In the now, there was only one deadly weapon I was concerned with, and it wasn't a big-haired actress who peaked on *WKRP in Cincinnati.*

My mind was designed to take in the terrifying, whether it was Big Ed's vocal blasts or, in this case, possible death, and give it a pop culture spin.

Not even my knowledge of all things trivia could eradicate the fear that was now registering in my brain. I was a frantic bride-to-be facing a shotgun wedding. I had my something borrowed in a new name; my something blue in my sweat-stained Nike tank top; something old, well, that was George; something new was my perception of Danny; and something screwed, which was the fact that I could be the one biting the bullet at any nanosecond.

There would be no church wedding for me, only a very probable trip to the morgue. I was staring down the barrel of the gun as it vacillated at George's insistence between the four of us. He seemed to be mentally deliberating as to who had wronged him the most. I knew that I could be facing the possibility of death. Ever since I had come out and announced that I was gay, it seemed that death was lurking around every corner. I had heard George and Nick sitting around the dinner table, sipping on beers, recanting what it was like in the good old days, in the time before AIDS.

I hoped that someday I would be able to experience what seemed like a chapter out of a history book now. It was easy enough for me to imagine the alleyway sprouting a satin lining on its two walls. All that was needed was a lid to enclose me in the darkness forever, as there were four pallbearers at the ready to escort me to the other side.

I may very well have been privy to a premonition of an early demise that felt very much at home with my recent viewing of *Rebel Without a Cause*. Live fast, die young, leave a pretty corpse.

Or the footwork that I had been doing to snuff out Henry Dodge's life was surely trying to materialize. I had been dying a slow death ever since I was a child, not wanting to be who I really was. Up until the very recent disclosure that I was not Billy Collins, I had thought that it was curtains for Henry Dodge. Right now, I was just hoping that George didn't think I was the worst offender in his line of fire, drawing a permanent cease-fire to either existence I had carved out for myself with a broken spork.

I was not planning on falling victim to my mother's warnings; in my rebelliousness, I wanted to prove her wrong, even if this was not exactly the scenario she had in mind that being gay equaled death. In a way I could see her reasoning. When I came out to her, the hope that she had that I would lead a so-called normal life passed away, giving credence to her thoughts that being gay would somehow be my death knell. I didn't want to die; my whole reason for coming to LA was to live in freedom.

All I had found so far were those who were intent in teaching me the harsh realities of what life, and not a gay existence, had to offer. It was like I was stuck in an Anita Bryant rally for all that was pro-hetero, that all of the rhetoric she had spouted on the newscast I had seen with Big Ed in the long ago was the gospel truth.

So far I had dealt with backstabbing, double crossings, incest, and pornography, all of the things that warranted gay life to be looked down upon. But wasn't that indicative of human nature and not just subscribed to being gay?

Everybody, regardless of their sexual leanings, has something to be shown by example in life. Sometimes there are hard lessons to learn. I was being shown these extreme cases, most likely, to dispel of my own uncertainties at sixteen of what being gay truly entailed. Where was the brotherhood, the camaraderie that I so badly needed to feel a part of? I knew it was out there because I wanted to believe in the good of others; that naivety was still a carryover from my past life. But there was a place for it in my new life as well, if I was afforded the opportunity to live.

It was hard to circumvent the fact that this could be the last internal dialogue I would be having with myself. But it had proved a valuable one-sided conversation. It reminded me that I had stood up to adversity before by declaring to myself and to my parents that I was gay; that was an act of bravery.

By tapping into the feelings that resonated from my mother's dire warnings, I was able to see that I should not be standing still, awaiting George to make my fate by his doing. I had to make my fate, whatever it would be. Sizing up the gun again and seeing a slight shake to George's hand, I decided to pull a *Charlie's Angel* move as it would prove far more effective than doing nothing. I moved in to give it my best shot before George had the chance to take his.

I waited a split second more until George had shifted his sights onto Angel. I then set about figuring out exactly where I would have to kick George in the hand to make the gun clatter to the sidewalk so that Danny, Angel, or Troy could pick up the gun and say something pithy like, "The jig's up, Georgie."

Then a convenient police car would just happen by, and justice would prevail. The imagery was so strong in my mind that I actually thought I heard the police approaching. Apparently, so did George and the rest of the gang. They all had their heads cocked like Pavlov's dog, but it was only George that seemed to be drooling at the sound of encroaching imprisonment. He gave us all a precursory nervous glance, trying to gauge the distance of the police car and their arrival versus which one of us would pay the piper right then and there.

When he took off running, everyone arrived at that answer at the same time, causing splinter groups, thus the enemy had been defeated by his own doing. I was just starting to ponder what it was about alleyways and cops that facilitated dramatic changes in my life when someone grabbed my hand.

It was Danny, and he was starting to pull me towards the van. Angel was already riding shotgun, resigning me to the backseat, a place I was not willing to sit anymore, especially with those who had violated my trust. But it was either that or be picked up by the cops, so I sulked as quickly as I could to the van. At this instance, I did not have any choice.

Danny jumped into the driver's seat and turned the engine over; it didn't take. Flashes of nine-sixteenth wrenches, metric sockets, and wasted hours helping Big Ed work on the car washed over me and of one time in particular when Danny had stopped by and stood above me. I remembered that I had seen a glimpse of his penis that day, and just last night, I had seen the whole kit and caboodle in action.

Even after what he had done to me, I still wanted him. I couldn't say that I necessarily loved him. After all of the circumstances that kept thrusting us together, I could only hope that was just a precursor.

Finally after two tries, the engine turned over. Danny gunned it and came to a complete stop a second later. He popped out of the driver's-side window and began yelling for Troy.

I looked down the street and saw that Troy had started chasing after George immediately because he was on top of his father, beating him with the butt of the gun. The sirens were getting closer, and people were beginning to react to the scuffle but stood back resigned to not getting too close to the fray.

Danny led by example, bolting over to where Troy was just about to strike his father again. Troy was a live wire, jerking every which way, trying to seek out George, his conduit of hatred, plugging into everything he perceived as being wrong with him due to his father's treachery.

Troy had worked George over, mostly hitting him on his torso; had Danny not reclaimed his superhero status, Troy may have rendered his father as unconscious as the motives that drove him to act the way he did. Troy had expounded earlier on the hurt that his father's dealings had caused; he was just getting in touch with his inner rage and channeling it in a not-so-healthy expression.

If he wanted to avoid assault charges, he better stop trying to shake free of Danny's grasp. And if we all wanted to avoid the police, one of us was going to have to take the driver's seat. I wanted to tell Angel this, but the little-brother voice in my head was saying he was closer.

Although I had known Danny ever since he and his family moved up the street from us, I didn't really know him as well as Angel, Troy, or even George did. I think he was starting to realize that he didn't know me at all. I wasn't so sure I recognized the face that was staring with concern in the rearview mirror. The illusion of the innocence that was once inherent upon my face had been vaporized in a puff of smoke, a magician's not so grand illusion, just like our chances for escape if somebody didn't do something quick.

Well, Angel did something. He got out of the passenger side of the van and ran over to help Danny like some haphazard version of a sidekick. He was forcing me from the usual backseat thinking I did and literally put me into the driver's seat.

Well, I knew how my last attempt at playing follow-the-wrong-leader went, Angel and I ended up at the opposite end of the alley. This was my chance to play the hero, the one who could save the day, and break my "Charlie Brown can't do anything right" image.

I had driven John's car a few times before, but he had a Mustang like what Kelly Garrett drove on *Charlie's Angels*. We had nicknamed it the Green Bomb. Danny's antiquated mode of transportation was a different type of animal, and much like everything about Danny, it was bigger.

I took my place behind the wheel. My right foot wasn't quite reaching the gas pedal. I needed to make some adjustments to the seat. Once I was about two inches from the wheel, I took a deep breath, steeling myself to the task that lay before me. I tried to turn the engine over. Where it took Danny two turns, it took me four to get the engine to roar to life and then die and gasp with a kitten's mew.

I looked out of the windshield as Angel arrived to try to subdue Troy and to make sure the sirens that were filling up the day with their urgency weren't right behind me. Troy was still resisting, causing the not quite a throng of four passersby to stop, look, and then briskly walk on by faster than the Dionne Warwick song of the same title sped up to 78 rpm.

If they hadn't thought there was any innate danger that they would be hit up for change and have to listen to the lunatic ravings of an obviously drugged-out street urchin, then the gun that Danny was wrestling from his grip was more than enough motivation for them to skedaddle.

I wasn't sure if George was unconscious or, again, was just waiting for the perfect moment to add an element of surprise to an already overloaded-with-surprises type of day.

I attempted the engine again. This time it took on the fifth try, and as I got it into gear, it actually seemed that it was going to take this time. But it didn't, and I was fiddling around with the ignition again when I thought I heard the engine backfire. That's funny, I thought to myself, I was under the distinct impression that the engine had to be running in order for a backfire to occur. I searched my memory banks, unlocking protected files about the fine-tuning of automobiles, and I did remember Big Ed yelling at John to shut the engine off on the station wagon when it started backfiring.

I looked up, and this is what I saw. George was up and stumbling; Troy was giving chase and already was closing in. Danny was knelt down before a bleeding Angel. The sirens were also sounding like they were taking a left turn inside of my head; they were that loud.

I felt like I was watching an episode of *T. J. Hooker* that had taken a frightfully wrong turn until I remembered this was real life, and I was the special guest star that could turn it all around.

I didn't want to buckle under the pressure and suddenly thought that Tina Turner didn't have the right idea in her theme song for *Mad Max: Beyond Thunderdome.* We did need another hero, and it was going to have to be me.

I turned the key in the ignition and caught the engine's attention on the second try, giving it a reason to live. I silently hoped that would be the case for Angel, but I could see that Danny's Quicksilver shirt was not a quicker picker-upper. It was sopping with freshly spilled blood.

I tried to remember everything I had learned in driver's ed, and all that came to me was the gruff voice of my chain-smoking teacher for both that class and PE barking out "SMOG" (signal, mirror, over the shoulder, go).

I skipped the first three and focused on the going part as it seemed to be a case when extreme measures called for the skirting of protocol.

It took me only three seconds to get to them; I had almost started to wonder if I should've made the attempt of playing hero at all. All of those doubts were replaced with dread upon Danny opening the side door to the microbus. Angel was barely conscious, bleeding all over his shirt that had once been tan and that was now a dark brown in the spot over his abdomen.

Danny had taken on the role of the frightened child; his face contorted to someone who had lost his favorite toy and had no idea of how to go about getting it back. He placed Angel gently down on the backseat, swiftly shut the door, and sailed around the passenger side to the driver side. He pulled open the door with such force that I thought he would tear it off at the hinges; instead it was my head that got torn off.

"Go sit back there with him!" he screamed at me. "Jesus Christ! Why is the seat so fucking close to the wheel?"

I tried to focus that he was under a great deal of duress as I made my way back to Angel. But that didn't stop the tears from beginning their fluid journey from my eyes. While I hadn't gotten the microbus to start and be driven for a slew of kudos and wasn't really expecting a thank-you, I guess I was expecting some acknowledgement, just like I had always been seeking. I was the perpetual puppy that had been saddled with a neglectful owner; all I needed was one scratch behind the ear to know that I mattered. It always seemed I got the reprimand instead.

Maybe I should just pull one of my patented disappearing acts and exit out the microbus's side door into the world where I could find someone, anyone, to acknowledge my subsistence, that I was solvent as a human being.

I took one look at Angel, and the source for my liquid display turned into tears of sorrow for him. How could I be so selfish when there was the very real possibility that Angel could be easing his way towards death moment by moment? Danny got the van moving, and I took my place where I knew I was needed.

I sat next to Angel, not focusing on the scarlet stain that was steadily spreading outwards or on the fact that I had been thinking only of myself, trying desperately to turn this experience into something altruistic. I was hoping that Angel's life wasn't fleeting away from him as we pulled away from the scene of the crime.

Danny's driving was jerky at best, lots of sudden stops and near misses punctuated by the blaring of his horn and peppered with profanities, not at the other drivers, most likely, but to the situation itself.

As we drove down Santa Monica Boulevard, we caught sight of George being tackled by Troy. The son tackled the father with such force that George's dentures came flying out of his mouth at a dangerous clip. If the window had been rolled down more on the passenger side, I was sure that I could have heard them clattering, taking bites at the concrete, until they came to their final and fitting resting place into the gutter.

Seconds later, the advancing sirens that had heightened the tension in the air materialized into two black and white police units. One of which came to a screeching halt, went up on the sidewalk in front of the Niles family's impromptu reunion, and came to rest on George's jettisoned dentures.

The other cop car pulled up behind Troy, all but boxing in the chances for an escape. Troy seemed oblivious to the cops at first; he was too busy trying to pound some sense into his father's head by pounding it into the sidewalk. He looked like he was concentrating very hard at exorcising the demons that possessed his chances at having a normal father-and-son experience. When the two officers in the car bringing up the rear grabbed Troy, he resisted momentarily and then crumpled like gossamer threads captured by the wind. His eyes never leaving his father, who was bleeding the same blood that flowed through his own veins, intertwining them, binding them together for all time despite the circumstances life threw their way.

We were past the danger zone. George and Troy were becoming smaller and smaller in the rearview mirror now. I looked down at Angel; red rivers were cutting a path down the sides of his shirt. His face seemed evocative of his name; he looked so peaceful that I began to think that he was dead.

I reached out with my finger, not sure if I should poke him or not. I suspected that if I wanted a finger that looked like it had been dipped in strawberry preserves that I had better try taking the pulse on his neck and just avoid the area that was most likely heralding his death. I gently laid my finger on the side of his neck. Too bad Danny had never been on *General Hospital*. Even artificial medical knowledge would have come in handy right about now.

"Motherfucker, it hurts!" Angel shrieked suddenly, jerking up like the former puppet on a string that he had been.

I jumped back, hitting my head against the window, seeing stars that lined the universe before me, realizing that Angel had pulled an

E.T.. I wasn't the only one that acted surprised by Angel's sudden resurrection. Danny swerved the microbus, nearly missing a rear-end collision with a Mercedes.

"What the fuck?" he raged for a moment and then caught sight of Angel.

He had a cross between a puppy that had barked at its master and "I just yelled at a dying man" look to his face. He gained his composure and returned his focus on the quickest route that would take us to the hospital.

Just as this whole summer had been steering me towards something, not necessarily something bigger than myself, but something that was supposed to show me the kind of person I could be and was geared towards being a clear cut destination point of where my life could go. As Angel resumed his suffering-in-silence routine and Danny was steadily nearing a destination, I came to one as well. Maybe Danny had sold me out as certainly as George would have on his own, but I needed that instance to happen. I needed it to happen so that I would be able to survive my final stages of growth from a teenager to a man.

These instances would be my measure, my jumping-off point, my extreme litmus for the rest of my life. I still had only one foot over the edge and waited for the final trajectory, a bigger push to get me going in the direction I needed to be heading. I was in a freeze-frame moment, and it seemed to me that too much had happened for me to retract the footing I was laying down on the ground of tomorrow. In the moment, there was another life at stake and time enough to learn of the whys behind the actions of others. I felt firmly planted in the belief that I needed to see this journey out to its end result.

"What happened back there?" I asked of Danny. I still did not know who had shot Angel.

"That's a very good question," Danny mused, probably relaying more into the question than had been meant.

What had happened to him? How was it that our paths were still crossing after all these years? Why had he become the person he was today? I could see the wheels turning in his mind as certainly as I felt them hugging the pavement below, guiding us to a safer place.

While I did not want to remove focus from the task at hand, I did want some resolution to the reserves of anger that were being misdirected in my mind.

"Well, when Angel came over and tried to help me get the gun away from Troy…" He stopped momentarily, choking on Troy's name, a splinter piece of a bone wedged in his throat. "It was like trying to take hold of a…well, something that had an incredible resistance, like a shark that won't drop its meal."

Leave it to a surfer to come up with that analogy, I thought bitterly, still trying to fight the urge to clock him in the head. There would be time enough for that after I found out from him why he did what he had done. First, I wanted to make sure Angel would be all right, then it was time to go for his jugular.

He began to speak again, his words no longer holding me at bay and instead made me immediately question if he was going to cover up for himself or Troy since Angel would not be a staunch defender of the truth.

"It was George. George did it. He jumped up and put his finger on the trigger. And he shot… And he shot…"

Danny could not continue this conversation without the risk of careening off the road and plowing into innocents just as he had mowed down any hopes that he had been the one to show me the true meaning of what I had hoped love could be. I decided to let him concentrate as I sat back and soaked up the reality that George had proved to be the triggerman after all.

My anger was starting to find the proper channel for its purpose of existing. I blamed Danny; if he had not set into motion all of this, then perhaps Angel would be riding shotgun rather than in the back with a gunshot wound. I decided to just stew in my anger, feeling it rise, slow bubbles of hatred growing and bursting.

We arrived at Cedar Sinai. Danny told me to move the van to a parking spot and stay put as he resembled once more the hero I had come to worship. He was also representing the taker of life; even though he had not pulled the trigger, he was just as responsible for Angel's condition as George was. Taking Angel into his arms carefully, he and his white Quicksilver shirt got another new decorative splash of crimson red.

After I found a spot and carefully pulled into it, I was left alone in the van, the proverbial little brother, not allowed to tag along this time. Now that I had all the time in the world to think and to catch my breath, I intended to do so.

In all of the brouhaha, I had almost forgotten why Angel had wanted to meet with me. Right now, my body was rife with a sexually transmitted disease while his was possibly leaving this earthly visage.

I checked my shorts pocket to make sure that I still had my ill-gotten gains. I closed my hand around the flattened semiwad of cash just as I closed my eyes, intending to do so for only a moment. The next thing I knew, someone was tapping on the window of the van, trying to awaken me.

Chapter 16

I was startled back into reality from the sleep of the damned, unsure momentarily of who I was, where I was at, and why it sounded like there was a woodpecker to my left doing his business.

I had been dreaming that I was in a forest, running on dead, dry pine needles with my bare feet. Each resounding crunch was thunderous, letting the one that was chasing me know the exact location of where I was headed when I didn't know where that was myself. I kept running, each step convincing me that I could outrun whatever was giving chase and emerge through the final thicket that stood between the light of knowing and the darkness of doubt. Every step closer also saw me losing an article of clothing until I was nothing but flesh. I had to take a running leap into the unknown. Just as I was about to soar into the air, the woodpecker began its repetitive song, thus bringing me back to whatever reality was constituting as these days.

I was sitting in the dark; diffused streams of light from a nearby streetlight provided me with a hint of my actual locale. I was sitting in the van, where Danny had left me in order to tend to Angel. I was Henry Dodge, and my head felt like it was full of sand, each grain slipping through the grasp of a mindful hourglass, careful not to divulge too much at once. But the hourglass shattered when I saw who was tapping at the window, the ever-diligent woodpecker that rousted me out of my much-needed slumber.

I saw only a body type, which was large and shadowed. I immediately thought that George had pulled the impossible and talked his way out of jail or had even escaped from the police. Somehow that image made me think of Benny Hill's high-speed chases and accompanying wacky music that he would do on his show; which would cause peals of laughter to escape from me and Big Ed, breaking the usual silence that was a mandatory part of television viewing with my father.

I couldn't fake-sleep my way out of this one. George was on to that act of mine. If it was George, what could he really do to me? After all, he had his dentures smashed by the wheels of justice, rendering his bark much worse than his bite.

I saw that whoever the shadowy figure was, his meaty glove of a hand was poised to take another attempt at awakening a sleeping beauty. A car driving towards the hospital caught him in the act of trying to do so. The headlights bounced off his glasses, headed south to his moustache, and gave me a fleeting glimpse of Nick before plunging me back into the dark again. I sat upright in an instant, as relieved to see Nick as I would have been to discover it was Rob Lowe trying to awaken me.

I was about to feel free to move about the cabin and unlock the doors, but I stopped myself while my suspicious nature took free range instead. The what-if game, established in the summer of 1975 by a mother tired of answering a barrage of endless questions from her inquisitive son, resumed itself ten summers later.

What if George had sent Nick to come and find me? What if Nick was going to pull a Mafioso move and eliminate weak branches of the makeshift family tree? Could I trust Nick?

This was the biggest question that needed answering. There was no way I could really detect malice or compassion on his face without getting up close and very personal. I knew the best way to get the answer I wanted was my idea of seduction skimmed from the frothy ponds of the soap opera world. I would surprise Nick with the very thing he may not have come here for but that I knew he couldn't refuse.

It would have been as simple as dropping trough, and being sixteen, the wind could have been blowing, and I would have achieved a hard-on in seconds flat. My inclination was towards the art of the seduction; the reality that I hadn't even had time to find out today if there was a disease riddling my body deflated that plan.

In all of the events of the day, in all of the madness that had ensued as revelation upon revelation was unleashed, there was a more-than-likely chance I had nothing to clap about, so to speak. If I had gone the seduction route, then I would have been making a U-turn near the corner of Danny and George Avenue.

It would have been easy not to let on that I may have a sexually transmitted disease to have gotten what I wanted and find out the information I needed at the same time. Realizing that tonight would have been the night that I was to be performing tricks on the boulevard without a safety net, all of my choices had been propelled by the deception behind that high-wire act, inching me out further and further until I had no choice but to proceed to the other side with a lackluster resolve.

I decided to go on instinct; Nick had proven himself more ally than foe. But I would have never thought that Danny would have initiated my journey down the River Sold either. Besides, if I could outrun George, I could certainly escape from his far reaches if that were the case. I went to the sliding side door, unlocked it without trepidation, and waited for Nick to come around and present himself in whichever incarnation he would be.

"Hey, Billy, I mean, Henry," Nick said, catching himself in my lie.

It was at that instant that I realized something. If Danny had put George and Angel on the alert that there was a new meat shipment coming into town, then that meant they had known all along that I was never a Billy and always a Henry. I had thought that I was so clever, that my believability factor would be rated very high.

All I was, all I was trying to be, it was nothing but a lie, making me no better than George or Danny.

But there were distinct differences. I was just trying to discover new avenues and to find people who I could consider neighbors that wanted to live as I did, rent-free of guilt for my sexual preference. Danny must have more to his story; otherwise, why would he have tried to sell me into a subtle form of white slavery?

If he had known George was the type of man to reel in a fresh catch of the day with baited promises of an easy life, then why had he put me on a hook he had already dangled from? I knew I needed to find out from the source, but he was keeping a death-watch vigil on Angel, and it was not the appropriate time. Appropriate or not, I wanted to know why.

I felt the anger on its slow ascent and decided that I would not take it out on Nick. I would find out what he wanted and then go and find out what I needed to hear from Danny.

"Hi, Nick, just in the neighborhood?" I gave it my best non-chalant Kathleen Turner in *Body Heat*, trying to verbally label myself as aloof so that Nick wouldn't want a repeat of yesterday's escapades; and I wouldn't have to say out loud why there wouldn't be any seconds tonight.

"Danny called me. He told me what happened." He pushed his glasses to the bridge of his nose unconsciously. I could see him taking the sight of me in, trying to gauge me. "How are you doing?"

That was the *$64,000 Question*. How was I doing? If you considered that I had run away from a homelife that wasn't conducive to growth along truthful lines, where I wasn't understood as surely as I was speaking a foreign language, then I was great. Considering that I had almost been sold into a form of white slavery by the man who had fueled my longing for escape and was somehow a drug dealer for a low-grade pimp, then everything was wonderful, couldn't be better, old chap.

I realized that everyone wore a mask and that could only be pried off in time, shattering to the ground, fine porcelain deceptions that unveiled the reality of what was hidden underneath. And it wasn't always pretty. Then strike up the band, I feel like dancing. But I felt as though I was never gonna dance again, guilty feet, they have no rhythm. No, guilty feet, they walk you in directions that may have gone untraveled and put their walkers on streets and avenues that they were ill prepared to traverse.

I was pretty sure that Wham! had not covered that in "Careless Whisper."

I was starting to take a walk down Lonely Street, destination Heartbreak Hotel, when I redirected myself. Sure, I was okay. I wasn't Angel; I wasn't laying on what could be my deathbed.

"Yeah, I'm okay," I said it with confidence, and it did not sound like I was repeating it as a question. And it also came out not sounding like a lie.

"I've been so worried about you." Nick gasped. "I went by George's this afternoon, and you weren't there. What happened? The place looked like a hurricane hit it!"

The streetlight I had parked under was dormant upon our arrival; it now spotlighted the genuine concern that was apparent on Nick's face. I remembered him mouthing something along the lines of "It will be fine" last night, a thousand sunsets ago. With all that I had been through today, I felt that I could trust him.

"It was Troy, he smashed all of the videotapes." As I spoke this, Nick's face became a question mark.

"I didn't see any videotapes," he said.

"In the den, all of the tapes you and George made, Troy smashed them all, even the one with you and him on it."

Before I knew if I should or shouldn't mention the tapes or not, I had.

Nick didn't answer me; in fact, he turned away and muttered "Son of a bitch" under his breath. He stepped into the shadows for a moment and away from the spotlight that was pinpointing his emotional state. I stood still, unaware of what I had divulged that had upset him. I had naturally assumed that Nick was aware of the *Chicken Hawk* series and, in particular, volume 2, of which he was a costar. I was feeling like it was my turn to ask Nick if he was doing okay, and just as my mouth unhinged itself to form the words, Nick stepped back into the frame into the scene that was being set.

"Did you actually see this movie?" he asked me with a tinge of sadness playing a symphony on his vocal chords.

"You mean did I watch it? No, but I saw the tape after it was smashed. It had a label on it that said *Chicken Hawk 2: Nick and Troy.*"

He turned around and did a full circle until he was facing me; he resembled a dog that was endlessly chasing its tail. I didn't know if this was meant to be symbolic, that somehow he felt the situations of the day were spinning out of control.

"That son of a bitch!" he practically screamed it until an ambulance reminded him of his location, and he took on a more somber tone. "I can't believe George would do that."

It's funny how people can be friends for years and still not seem to know anything at all about each other while people who meet in the short term find out more than they bargained for. My thoughts again turned to Danny and Angel. I really needed to know what was happening. I was hoping that Nick and I could continue this conversation inside the hospital.

"Hey, Nick," I said this in my best librarian-for-a-minute voice. "We should go find out how Angel is doing."

This seemed to quell the storm that was starting to rage inside of him. I knew from the look he gave me that there would be time to pick up this conversation later. It was Angel we needed to be thinking about. In silence and surprisingly without his head bowed in shame, Nick made his way to my side, and we proceeded across the parking lot to the hospital..

We found Danny in a waiting room, cradling his head in his hands; sadness was hanging in the air around him, a radius of dread clouding his usual sunshine demeanor. It was a balmy summer night, but Danny's personal forecast was for a flash flood warning to cleanse him of his misdoings that had ultimately ended up with his friend being shot. Danny seemed a perfect fit against a hospital backdrop. If he had been on *General Hospital*, he could have pulled off any number of roles from lovestruck hero to devious doctor. Right now the role he was settling into was causing him immense pain; reality had torn the doors off his subterfuge.

Nick and I joined him on the couch he was sitting on, flanking him on either side. I sat to the left of him, and when I did, he brought himself out of his haze of self-loathing long enough to see that his face was tear streaked.

His brown eyes were pools of warm mud after a hard rain; each tear delineated specific references to the misery of his life. He seemed to be grappling between being glad to see me and wanting to jump under the couch and hide from everything. I knew I did not impose a forbidding presence, but I got the sense that Danny was afraid of me. Nick remained utterly silent as Danny returned his focus to his hands, trying to trace his lifeline up close to see where it had veered off in the direction he was headed for.

I took for granted that since Nick knew George that Nick also knew Danny and vice versa, as that seemed to be the way things worked around here. But Nick just sat next to Danny, just looking at the two of us. They didn't address each other. I could tell why Danny wasn't but wasn't quite as sure about Nick until he spoke.

"Danny, you should go eat or get some fresh air, something," he said this with the love a father reserves for his most troubled offspring.

I didn't know this from firsthand experience, mind you, but I distinctly remembered a *Brady Bunch* or two where Mr. Brady's voice held the same intonation when Greg was on trial for manslaughter. Oh wait, he had only lost his father's designs when he went to work for Mr. B. on a one-episode story arch.

There was an underlying hint of anger that was prevalent, but it consisted mainly of care. I didn't know what that was like; my father was an extremist, usually drifting more towards the angry side. I looked at Nick very differently than I had the night before. It probably helped that he wasn't on his knees in front of me, allowing me to see time's cruel march as it had paraded hardest towards the back of his head, revealing a semibald spot.

Maybe Nick would be the one that would save me? I felt as though somebody had to, that I had branched out a little too far in my discovery of all things new and few things similar. Nick was sized just right for me to grab a hold of, hang on for dear life, and pray that he was the man to show me the way.

"Henry, why don't you accompany Danny?" As Nick said this, I looked away from Danny.

Nick had given me a look that conveyed, "Keep a watchful eye on him." After what I had found out today, that was not going to be an issue. We stood up. Danny seemed very robotic, and he was steadying himself like he was elderly, but I think the reality was that his foot had fallen asleep. And here I had thought that he only had poor circulation to his deceptive heart. I felt myself drifting back over to the place where all doubt dwells from, the land of spiteful. I knew that I had good reason to be just from the circumstantial evidence. I was hoping that Danny was going to play judge and jury on himself on our sojourn away from the possibility of death.

Nick approached the nurse's station, and I half expected to see him talking to Bobbi Spencer, nurse extraordinaire of *General Hospital*, to be giving him the statistics of Angel's chances of survival.

We made our way outside, the warm night at odds with the windchill factor between us. Neither one of us had said word one to the other, perchance if nothing was said, then there was no reason to explore the depths of deception. Each step we took, almost in perfect synchronicity, widened the canyon of silence between us. I didn't know how to broach the subject at hand of Danny to Danny. He seemed obviously distracted, until the moment he looked down at his T-shirt and cringed. The maroon had spread, drying in a haphazard splotch that Quicksilver had not designed.

"I need to get another shirt out of my van," he said this, clearly stating the obvious and avoiding its origins as well.

I remained silent, worried that the first words out of my mouth would be hateful, full of the anger I was harboring that he had allowed me into this situation. He hadn't gotten me into it, that was my doing, but he knew the kind of man that he had put on the fresh-meat alert.

I was also at odds about the timing of all of this. Danny had been keeping vigil for Angel, which showed a remarkable amount of compassion. I was hoping to have compassion myself, but with all that had happened in a twenty-four-hour span, I wasn't so sure I was up to the task.

Danny fumbled in his pockets for the keys; as he did, I couldn't help but notice that his pendulum was swinging to and fro. The stirring sensation of longing seemed out of place given the circumstances. But I couldn't help myself. I was sixteen, and it had been at least five hours since my last sexual encounter. Then I remembered why Angel had wanted to meet with me and wanted to raise my fists to the sky and denounce life's cruel ironies!

Danny was still scrounging around in his pockets, unaware that I was the one that held the key. I felt like making him squirm, laying the foundation of blame solely on him. I began forming a checklist in my head. As Danny realized that I had the keys, without a word spoken, I handed them over. It was probably safe to assume that had Danny not sold himself and, in turn, me out to a man who had very likely given me gonorrhea, then we could be releasing years of pent-up desires.

But as was the case, that would not be happening. I started mentally marking off points under the category of Life's Not Fair. I could feel the slow burn taking hold as I became a loaf of bread squashed at the bottom of a grocery bag.

Each new injustice that was catalogued bore the weight of the world, a thousand cans put on top of me by a careless bagger. If the day had gone as planned, I would have known if I had an STD or not. Then Danny and I could have had our way with each other; right now was a perfect example of why I wanted that to happen.

He had his back to me, bent over just slightly, rummaging around his backseat for a shirt that he knew he had left back there after surfing one day. All it would have taken, had circumstances prevailed, was for me to simply walk over, sidle up behind him, press my body next to his, and wait for the reaction I had been hoping for. Why was life so unjust?

Well, as Danny turned around, replacement shirt in hand, I got the visual to my pondering. There was scarlet deception caked on Danny's shirt. He peeled it off, not effortlessly; the blood had soaked through, clinging to his body like I wanted to. At least I had the luxury to bitch about life being unfair. What did Angel have—except a bullet inside of him deciding his fate? Here I was bemoaning the fact that I would not be partaking in something I was taking for granted, something that had gotten me into all of the day's events in the first place.

I wondered how the other members of our tight-knit dysfunctional family were fairing on this night, where the stars seemed to burn brighter with eyes that could truly see. I could imagine the king trying to reestablish his self-proclaimed reign in prison. He was either running the place by now with his blend of treachery that even the most hardened criminals had not experienced; or he was Spike's bitch, figuring out how he could manipulate a new pair of dentures out of his newfound friend—until the time when Spike would tire of him and probably stab him with a makeshift knife made out of sharpened Popsicle sticks. Cherry red stains already prevalent would mix with George's blood.

He needed to bleed for what he did to Angel. Chances were he would end up talking his way out of it somehow. Hell, maybe he had even convinced Troy that it was really his doing that Angel could potentially live up to his name. Maybe he was calculating a plan of revenge as all of us remained unaware.

But right now, in this twilight of opportunities both won and lost, it was just Danny and myself, just as I had always wanted it to be, yet fate had dictated very different circumstances. I could not take my eyes off Danny's torso. It was not because it was still chiseled from his rides on top of the waves. Partially, it was lust mixed with curiosity plus a dash of revulsion.

He looked a little gaunter than I remembered. Some of the California glow had eluded him as well, as he desperately tried to wash away Angel's blood with his own tears that were coming out of him at a rapid-fire clip. He sat inside the van, slumping up against the backseat; only his legs were visible from my vantage point. I needed to muster up any shred of resistance I may have to his vulnerability. I also needed to exercise restraint from hauling off and hitting a crying man. I steeled up the courage and forced myself over to him, unsure of the consequences.

I walked up to him warily, as if I was approaching a stranger. Somehow that is what we had become due to time spent and the places in our lives that we were at. Back home, it had only been a five-year age difference that had ever stopped us from taking it to the next level.

Now, I had traveled upon the same road as he had, seen some of what his life had really been like, and witnessed what had not been up for discussion between his mother and mine. I had started down the road on my own, and Danny had steered me in his direction, and I was very curious as to why he had done that.

He seemed miserable himself—so why subject another person to that? Was this some kind of trial by fire for the small-town set? I wanted to fire off a round of questions at him, but he was still doing his impersonation of a Rainbird sprinkler. The emotional pendulum inside me was swinging back and forth, performing lazy circles and loop-de-loops. Then I remembered his pendulum swinging to and fro inside of his pants, ticking down the moments until we acted upon our mutual admiration of each other. I became noticeably aroused. Was there ever going to be the right time, the proper setting, just the right fraction of moonlight caressing his flesh?

I went from wariness to horniness in less time than it took the Mustang convertible I wanted to own someday to go from zero to sixty. I walked right up to where he was, crumpled in shame, ready to show him there were no hard feelings. Well, maybe one.

I felt it was the only way I could show him the absolution of the moment. He raised his head aware of my presence, more aware than he had been of it in forever. He was looking me right in the eyes, unwavering. Tears floating in the marble brown were ceasing to exist; the radiance I had always wanted to bask in was returning, providing the proper lighting. There may never be a right time for Danny and myself, so I pushed all of the day's dramatic events into mental storage, somewhere between knowing how to program the family VCR and the care and feeding of goldfish.

I laid my hand upon his chest; it was taut and sinewy with just a dab of sweat to ease my hand for guidance. Danny had managed to get all of Angel's... No, I wasn't going to think of that right now. All

I wanted to focus on was taking us both on a voyage away from our minds, cast adrift on a sea of bliss, turning the tides on the existential diatribes that had been turning me in circles.

And only Danny could provide the course, freeing me somehow by acting on my first crush, of restoring innocence lost; by me charting the unfamiliar with him, all of the knowing looks over the years could now be drowned in the sea of doubts.

He took my hand in his; I had feared it would be a firm grip that signaled it was not the appropriate time. But he began guiding my hand all over his torso until we hit a spot that was still semi-sticky. I turned it around in my mind by thinking he had gotten some surfboard wax residue on himself. Nothing was going to halt this moment that had been building for so many years. "Out of sight, out of mind" was quickly becoming my new life philosophy. And there was something that could help us both become more forgetful.

"Do you have any pot?" I asked, my hand still intertwined in his, feeling so natural.

"I always have some, in case of emergencies," Danny replied as each word, each syllable was bringing back the Danny I remembered.

It also brought back a fleeting snippet of a memory that stuck its foot into the door from the past. Troy and I smoking the emergency joint earlier today was a hazy memory, something from another lifetime, and I already had two of those to contend with. Danny shut the sliding side door closed, snapping off the memory of why Troy and I had been smoking the emergency provisions.

The why of it would have brought me back to the roundabout of where I was, what I was doing, and how I had gotten here. I just wanted to focus on the art of seduction and nothing else, trying to shut my brain off, deciding that draping myself across the backseat would suspend the qualm of uneasiness that reality was trying to achieve.

I wanted to rationalize that taking our minds off what had happened would have been what Angel would have wanted. I was already putting him into the past tense, just like I was throwing myself into a past tense state of mind. By going back to a time before I had even gotten to Los Angeles, when Danny and I lived on the same street, deciding to act on our unrequited desires seemed like an act of desperation. But certain instances called for desperate measures, and the night was fraught with it.

I could hear Danny rooting around the glove box, like a raccoon seeking out its dinner in a trash can. He wasn't being particular in looking for a specific item; he was very noisy about it and had begun to mutter under his breath.

I figured feigning innocence in this case was probably for the best, and I cursed myself for stopping the love train as it sat at the station and was finally picking up steam. Now my yearning to shut my head off and up was causing Danny frustration.

"Hmmm, that's funny," he said this tersely, and I knew there wasn't going to be some witty aside that he was going to recant.

I sat with bated breath, waiting to see if he would explode or not. I didn't know if my silence was a dead giveaway or not; it probably was. I needed to say something, anything that would prove I had not partaken in his libations earlier.

"What choo talkin' 'bout, Willis?" I said it before I had the chance to stop myself.

I was already nervous enough, standing at the precipice of obtaining the unobtainable, and quoting Gary Coleman was not the way to go about procuring that side of beefcake I had been hungering after. But as Danny burst out laughing, I thought perhaps I had staked a claim to a comic gold mine. But when he continued laughing well after the soundtrack on *Diff'rent Strokes* would have stopped, I knew something else was causing him to guffaw.

"It wasn't that funny," I said; casting out a blanket statement line in hopes of reeling in an answer by not outright asking a point-blank question was quickly becoming second nature to me.

"I think Troy smoked something he shouldn't have. I had some laced joints for a cus—for a friend of mine. Troy must be trippin'," Danny said this, hiccupping with laughter.

Then his face turned into the mask of sorrow that I had seen him wearing at the hospital, announcing that his jovial masquerade had been cancelled.

He stopped looking for what wasn't there, knowing that he had spent so much of his life searching already, unsure of what he was really trying to find, always hiding who he really was.

That's what I gleaned from the volume of tears that escaped from him as he sat down in the driver's seat, unaware of what direction his life was heading. I didn't know what to do. Should I console him as a friend, a hopeful paramour, or as one who knew what it felt like to shed the same tears?

I was just about to go over and sit in the passenger seat when he started speaking.

"I keep wondering how I let myself get like this. Every time I go over it in my head, it all comes from the same place, the same starting point," he explained between sobs. "The mistakes I've made aren't anybody else's fault, really. I was the one that moved to LA without any money, thinking I could make it big. So of course, I landed flat on my ass. Then I met George, and things got better for a while. But I know now that my whole fucking life has been such a goddamned lie! I am a fuck up, and I'll never amount to anything or be anybody. All I can do is hurt people or use them. I'm worthless, absolutely worthless."

He stopped talking, sat back in the driver's seat, facing away from me, but he sounded like he was facing himself.

I went up to the driver's seat and knelt down next to him. For all of his faults, I still wanted to worship at his temple, and years of idolizing can make a lot of things forgivable. He reached down with his right hand and absently began stroking my face.

He placed two fingers under my chin and had me look him straight in the face. Even as an emotional wreck, he was what could only be termed as impossibly handsome.

My nervous meter shot up a notch, registering high on the self-doubt scale. There was no way I was good-looking enough to be with Danny; he was just being kind, giving me a mercy fuck for what he had done. I felt very self-conscious about my hygiene, that I had sweated so much today, that I probably smelled musky. Maybe my breath was rancid too. I could just imagine that I smelled like eggs that had gone rotten, that my breath would put Godzilla to shame.

When he bent down to kiss me, all thoughts, negative or otherwise, vanished from my head.

My brain shouted that this was it! This was the moment I had been dreaming about ever since Batman was the only predominant male presence that I thought would rescue me from the dangers of languishing in the obscurity of the unnoticed. Everything felt heightened; every one of my senses were in overdrive. I felt the heat of his body leaping to mine like a cinder propelled by a Santa Ana wind, igniting dry brush and catching everything in its path on fire.

The lingering smell of surfboard wax coupled with Danny's scent was something more than pheromones; it held the past, the present, maybe even a hint of the future.

Danny was a great kisser; there was no doubt about that. He didn't just jam his tongue down my throat like George had done. There was a dreamlike quality that I was actually kissing him, that any of this was actually happening. The touch of his hands moving under my tank top was almost more than I could stand. So it was a good thing that I was kneeling, stretching up towards the heavens that Danny provided. The sight of him always made my stomach knot up; the proverbial schoolgirl crush was now a reality.

He got out of the driver's seat, but I would let him remain in control. When he hunch-walked past me, a man on a precarious ledge of our confined space, I thought immediately that the dream was over.

But all he wanted to do was pull the curtains on the windows. I thought that was funny but kept the joke to myself, not wanting to spoil anything; if anyone happened by the van, I was sure the steamy windows might have been a tip-off to the activities inside.

It would have been easy enough to have had Danny drive us to his place, but somehow taking a poke at each other in the van felt like a homecoming and one that was long overdue. I could easily slip into the mind-set that this was that summer in 1981 at the drive-in, and this time Danny and I would act upon what had taken four years to understand.

Now it was Danny's turn at the art of seduction as he sat down and leaned back against the backseat. All it took was a beckoning motion of his head, and I was his, breaking a new world's record for the ten-second dash.

Half the battle was already won. Danny was shirtless, and as I grasped the sides of his shorts, he was pantsless in a heartbeat. I was gaining more confidence in my own abilities with each removal of clothing from Danny. His underpants fell around his ankles with abandon; I stared at them for a brief moment, secretly checking them for the green invaders.

Danny had most likely slept with George, so it seemed logical to assume that he may have had the same condition as I did. I didn't even know if what Angel had told me was true. It could have been another clever manipulation to keep me at bay at the palace. But it probably wasn't a clever ploy. I tried to slap back the hand of reality that was threatening to seize me in its clutches, dragging me back kicking and screaming to its world.

I raised my eyes away from the harbinger of telling the truth; the underpants left my sight line in a blur of white. I was just about to open my mouth to admit my true confession, but instead of words coming out, I put Danny's sleeping giant in my mouth to stop the words from forming.

My mom had always said it was impolite to talk with my mouth full, and I thought this was an odd time to heed that advice.

Soon enough my mouth was getting full, and I knew Danny was really starting to enjoy what I was doing. It was like everyone before him was just practice, that I had fine-tuned my skills with the others so that I could make a lasting impression on the one that I had wished would have been my first.

I had to close my eyes; the visualization of Danny's length was compacting the ache my jaw was starting to feel. I felt myself starting to stiffen, but didn't want that to happen because if it did, it could signal curtains on what was a one-man act as of right now.

I was happy to let Danny kick back while I did all the work, but I was thinking that his mouth stretcher was going to puncture through the back of my head via my throat. He was going so far back there that I was worried that I was not going to be able to accommodate him without the chance of barfing, and that would be a poor showing.

I decided to finish him off with a hand job, making sure to keep the focus on him. Not that I had tons of experience with the menfolk, but Danny made me realize something. Obviously, every man's penis is of a different size, shape, and/or variety. So the grip with which you give them a friendly tug varies. Wouldn't it be great if human hands incorporated the same function as the crescent wrench—at least I thought it was a crescent wrench, but I was tool illiterate, so what did I know? Any job, be it small or large, would have the perfect grip and save you from all of the headaches of figuring out which grip felt good, or not so much, on your sexual partner. It could be marketed as the Handy Dandy. I could see Lee Majors, former *Six Million Dollar Man*, and Mr. Farrah Fawcett as its pitchman. The tagline would read, "Get a grip!" I realized I was losing my own; I put the product-placement thinking aside and made my hand open wide and said, "Ahh."

Danny seemed lost inside his head, behind closed eyes, emitting a moan approximately every thirty seconds to let me know that what I was doing was a derivative of pleasure for him.

He was making things easy by not trying to reciprocate. Still his hands were roving all over me, but they seemed to be subscribed to upper-torso exploration. If he had reached down, he would have found me as hard as I had ever possibly been.

I realized something as my hand was feverishly jerking up and down: I was very all or nothing. What I had wanted to do was to take a ride on what I hoped wasn't going to be a one-trick pony (or horse, in this matter). I wanted Danny to fill me up to capacity, I wanted him to reciprocate, but then I would have to explain why he couldn't.

My glass wasn't half empty or half full; it was lying shattered on the ground, fragments of what it was.

I somehow suspected that Danny didn't carry an "in case of emergencies" stash of rubbers, like he did with the joint that Troy and I had smoked earlier. So that would have led to that conversation that I did not want to have in order to fulfill a fantasy. I had to be the low man on the totem pole and not in a good way.

If everything had a dreamlike hue attached to it, and I was clearly awake, then I was living a dream half realized. I did not reside in Danny's head. I spent way too much time in my own, but he didn't seem to mind that I was still in a full Southern California wardrobe. I was cursing myself for letting my long anticipated get-together with Danny be taking place now, of all times, of all nights.

I felt like I was carrying on a conversation with an elderly friend of my grandparents, making polite niceties, looking for an exit. I was here in the moment that had been pending for an eternity, and what was I doing? Well, I had invented the infomercial. More importantly, I was losing focus on what had seemed so important for so long. Danny seemed close to reaching his resolution; my hand was beginning to cramp, as surely as my brain would do at some point that night. I was a slave to my thought process, shackled to pop culture references and flights of fancy whenever the veracity of given situations became too apparent.

Someday I would emancipate myself. After the incredibly long day I had experienced, it would have to remain in that "I'll revisit this at a later date" file, which was already packed to capacity and seemed to be accruing more and more things for me to work on.

I had prayed for this moment to transpire, and in the thick of it, I couldn't allow myself to enjoy it. Danny, however, was not facing that dilemma. He grabbed a tight hold on a chest that was not yet developed, unlike most of the citizens of West Hollywood proper. He squeezed his eyes shut even tighter, breathing now like he was in labor, and soon enough produced a fine batch of baby batter. Most of which decided to swim upstream on rolling waves of the inhaling and exhaling tide of his stomach.

I realized I should reach my own conclusion and that if I didn't sound like I did, Danny would start a line of questioning as to why I didn't get off. So I hopped on an impromptu stage, ready to give an Academy Award performance, well, at least a Golden Globe nominated one for best faked male orgasm. I realized this would have to be a mostly audio category.

How could I visually fake an orgasm? It wasn't like I had a container of hot yogurt at the ready, and if I had, it would have been just my luck to have grabbed the kind that was fruit at the bottom. And that could bring up a whole mess of questions I did not want to delve into.

That's why I was faking it in the first place. I started by sticking my hand down my shorts, like it had been there all along, keeping a perfect synchronicity with Danny. I shut my eyes, opened my mouth, and let out a grunt-groan combo that would have fooled anyone, even George; although I shuddered to think of the possibility of having that experience again.

Upon opening my eyes, Danny was using his discarded, crusted-with-blood shirt as a cum rag. He was silent; I was worried I had strained my vocal chords after my rousing "jump to your feet and applaud" performance, so I remained a kindred spirit of the unspoken.

He offered me the shirt; I shook my head, indicating a negative as opposed to the positive that I needed it to clean up. There was no need to have that shirt in my hand, seeing as there was not such a pretty mess in my pants. Danny was taking the shirt back into his fold, staring at it then looking in the direction of the hospital, and focused on me.

The stricken look was returning; the weight of the world was coming back after he had fasted briefly on momentary pleasure. He had struggled and lost the battle, the constant lobbing back and forth of reality versus fantasy. I was way ahead of him. What had become of Angel? What would become of any of us? When Danny opened his mouth to speak, I thought he may have the answer I was hoping to hear. I would be sadly mistaken.

"I have to tell you something," he intoned. "And you have to promise not to get mad."

Chapter 17

Danny seemed as if he were sitting on a cactus instead of basking in the afterglow that could sometimes follow sex. For me, the glow was melting into a shadow, a faded sunset of what could have been. The pained expression on Danny's face did not parlay itself into an admission of eternal, never-dying love. It deeply reflected the troubled nature that was presenting itself, taking the place once more of my boyhood crush. I knew that any sentence that began with "I have something to tell you" and ended with "And you have to promise not to get mad" was never one that you wanted to hear, particularly, right after a dirty deed that was not dirt cheap.

I began to wonder if maybe Danny was harboring his own sexual secret. Was he going to tell me that he would be the first person I knew to be among those that were contracting a deadly virus only to be gone before his time? Or was it something less earth-shattering, more along the lines of a personal attack that I would have to defend myself against? Was there more to his deception that I had yet to learn about?

I was now getting used to the men in my life proving themselves to be major disappointments. The precursor was having a father that had set that standard, that protocol, for men so unlike himself converging the idea that all men were created equal in matters pertaining to Henry Dodge. My trust had been pulverized, the pieces so finely mashed that I did not know where to begin to put them back together.

I decided that by remaining in my present position, I would only further perpetuate the notion that I was to be trod upon. I got up off my knees, steeling my face against a crestfallen look, silently cursing myself for giving Danny the chance to redeem himself.

He obviously had more bad news at the ready. Just when I thought he would turn a corner back to his old self, he kept walking down the street I was unfamiliar with. Every inch of my body was starting to come alive with the beginning hum of anger's slow-rising tune, reminding me of the huge power lines I would throw rocks at as a child. The metallic clang was always overshadowed by the constant hum of a collective hive of bees with no stingers. My own stinger was poised, ready to take aim at Danny and puncture his mysteries. His body was still on display, acting as a semidistraction and one that I felt was conscious on his part. Or maybe the unconscious was prevailing, signaling that he was ready to be naked before me in the emotional sense.

"Okay," I said, trying to convey that I was deadly serious, a little bit pissed off, and not one to mess with, "spill it."

This was meant to remind him of the pleasure that had just resulted at my hand. I was hoping this would counterbalance the pain, most likely the end result of what he had to tell me.

"Well… No, never mind. You're going to get mad," he said, shaking his head back and forth to further illustrate the point of his indecision.

"Never mind? Oh okay, exit stage left, even!" I said this out loud. Did it sound as bitter as I thought it did?

I was wondering if there was an unchecked diagnosis of Tourette's syndrome that I needed to address. No, the only thing that needed to be brought to the table was what Danny was playing cat and mouse about telling me. I waited a beat before I would commence the countdown to my annoyance, watching as it launched off into the stratosphere.

He had not-so-deftly circumvented my anger at the unknown. The "Let's not tell Henry what's going on" syndrome was one that I had not really come to terms with. The exclusion I felt as a child, the years I spent hibernating, hoping my confusion about my sexuality would melt into certainty, that I would be just like everybody else had melted away as my spring awakening was making its presence known; icy waters ran in rivulets through the snow pack I had protected myself with for so many years. The wanting to be normal at all costs was being chipped away at, albeit slowly.

But I wasn't, and I was going to great lengths to be reveling in my difference instead of hiding from it. Now I had Danny reminding me that I still had miles to go in my trek of freedom when someone I supposed had been in the same boat was toying with me.

"So are you going to tell me or not?" I practically roared this at him in my head, but it came out of my mouth a lion's whisper. My patience had worn so very thin; it was as translucent as a discarded onion skin.

Danny appeared to be in preparation for the Hemming and Hawing Variety Hour to return from a commercial break. One look in my direction told him we were live in 5, 4, 3, 2, and pointing my finger as someone behind-the-scenes on a live TV show would do to indicate it was time to interrupt his regularly scheduled program of secretive behavior to broadcast his news report.

Danny looked right at me, hints of reservation surrounding the thing he needed to say. I felt ready to unhinge his jaw physically if need be. I was so tired of being treated like a little kid that needed to be protected. Part of me found solace in it, that someone would take the time to care if I got hurt or not, but the bigger part of me resented it. And that pretty much summed up the way I felt about Danny. I was at odds with memories versus the authenticity of who he had become. He was still silent, his face dejected, posture slumped, a man defeated by his own self.

"Hey," I said with soft intentions, but he looked like there was nothing but malice behind the three letters, "tell me something. How did you meet up with George?"

"Umm, well," Danny muttered, obviously thrown by the dime turning, spinning around, awaiting its final cue.

He shot me a look that conveyed that he didn't usually like surprises, but this would be a rare exception to that rule.

"I met him the same way that you did. Angel took me to him. I came here hoping to become somebody, but I didn't want to deal with who I was," he recounted. "I didn't have enough acting experience to make the cut most times. One place I did make a lasting impression was that fucking boulevard. They all loved me there. I was a star.

"It was easy to pretend I was acting there, acting like I didn't care what I was doing or what could happen to me. All I cared about was having enough money to buy myself my forget-me-lots, I used to call them. One night, I ran into Angel, he gave me some tweak for free, promised me there was more where that came from. Where that came from was George. And he took a big liking to me. I became one of his family of misfits, his rotation of boys to use and toss aside when he was done. I never paid for the drugs he gave me. But there are all kinds of ways to pay, aren't there?" He was sitting more upright, sitting towards the edge of the bench seat, his body language dictating a shift in his demeanor, as his story continued. "I paid a heavy price, far greater than I had intended. Once I wasn't George's boy anymore, the free trade dried up. I got into heavy debt with him. So I, well, I had to…"

Danny had begun to flounder in his recanting of actions taken that had turned him into an almost unrecognizable entity to me. He was actually eloquent; perhaps he had dropped his alter ego once he had adopted his true identity. His story had begun to unfold, and the more I heard of it, the greater the emotional current was pulling inside of me. If he knew George was like that, why knowingly put me in harm's way? This game of tug-of-war, the grappling between wanting to feel pity and just plain hating him, was seeing the white scarf creep ever closer to the hate side.

"So you had to make a porn movie?" I filled in the blanks of his life for him, not afraid of damaging his fragile nature.

"Yes, but that was only part of it." His eyes that had briefly stared at me when I revealed I knew about his starring role in a skin flick were now downcast. "To pay off my debt, George and I made a deal. I would become a recruiter for him. I would find him new talent when mine was no longer viable. You see, Henry, once I reached my twenties, George couldn't get me work in his movies. Every day, a newer, younger version of what I had become was popping his head inside of slowed-down cars, asking for a date. So I had to find others that had been like me, others that might get a longer run at it."

"You mean someone like me? How could you do that? Why would you do that?" Impartiality flew out the window, as words peppered with hatred catapulted from my lips.

I saw Danny as one of those tetra fighting fish that my brother John had kept as a pet when we were younger, swimming in solidarity, unable to socialize without the fear of harm coming to those it may encounter. But he had hurt people, and my heightened state of emotionality sprang from the comprehension that Danny had put a taint on my exploration. I was finding gay men to be filmed in 3-B: bitchy, backstabbing, and all bluster.

"I didn't want to do that to you, Henry. I thought that you were coming up here to see me, and I didn't want you to see what a fuck up I am," he said with a sigh. "Maybe you don't think it matters to me, that I would actually have feelings for you. There is something inside of you. I don't know what it is, but it shines. I saw you put up with so much with your dad, and it broke my heart. But I knew if I ever said anything to him, I might not get to see you. Because you are younger than me, I knew I could never act on any of this. Now, you seem like more of a man than I am. I really hate the way I am. I feel so stuck, that I will never stop being this way!"

Danny spat out the words he had been choking on for so long, performing a Heimlich maneuver on extracting the truth.

But I didn't think that was the "I have something to tell you" portion of—wait—did he say he had feelings for me?

"Danny, what are you trying to say? That you love me? Feel sorry for me, what? I think if you did feel anything, which I doubt you do, that you wouldn't have done what you have done. And you've done a lot. Question is, why are you doing it? You claim to feel one way, but your actions, well, they tell a very different story," I said all of this in almost one breath because I knew that if I didn't get it out, I could get swept up in the moment.

He had raised my bar on wariness while lowering my expectations on how men could really be. I supposed I could have gone the lovestruck route, swept his problems under the carpet, and reveled in the fact that he had finally professed his feelings for me.

There was a glint of self-awareness buried underneath the mire of self-loathing, capturing him, causing him to struggle in the traps he had laid for himself, unable to break free.

If I had learned anything from my parents' marriage, watching my mother decay in a dead union, was that there had to be more than one option. I felt robbed, stabbed, beaten within at least nine inches of my young life. This should have been cause for celebration, but I felt like the lone pallbearer at the funeral for my own perception of finding love, carrying the weight squarely on my shoulders, my balance off kilter as I struggled down an isolated road heading towards no-man's-land. He was supposed to be the one. Danny was my ideal. I bemoaned that fate had dictated otherwise.

"What I am saying, bro, is that I had to do what I did. I am sorry I did it, but it happened. There's nothing I could have done to stop it, dude! If I could take it back, I would, but I can't!"

He slipped back into the So Cal jargon as he became angrier. He also subconsciously put his shirt, crusted with Angel's blood, back over his crotch.

I was expecting him to start whistling. He was flushed with red against his tan skin, reminding me of the tea kettle my mother would put on in the morning once she switched from coffee to tea.

Even though the only snatch of light was dimmed by the drawn curtains, I was in such close proximity that I could see his temperature rising. I didn't know how to stop it from happening; maybe he needed a big outburst so that he could see the error of his ways.

A bigger part of me wanted to appendage myself to any part of his infrastructure, be it his brain, his eyes, his heart, so that he could learn it from someone else since he could not seem to grasp it on his own.

A malicious part of me wanted to keep digging at him until I buried any feelings I had for him. Danny was turning into a flickering image just outside of my peripheral vision: there one second and, as I would turn to face him, he would be no longer.

"Well, sometimes sorry just isn't good enough," I spoke the words that had been familiar to me from somewhere.

Oh yeah, it was from *The Brady Bunch*, where the kids all drive Alice away because they think she has been ratting on them. When they confess their unusually out-of-character cruelness, that is the line that Mrs. Brady says to them.

I must have subconsciously figured it was both appropriate and necessary to say to Danny. We were both reverting into our own holding patterns, waiting for a signal that it was safe to land. We knew where we came from; we just had no idea of where we were heading.

I thought Danny was going to be the one to break down and cry his eyes out for what could have been and might never be. I was wrong. Tears blurred Danny from my view, washing away any visual recognition that I was crying in front of him. I felt so alone, cursing myself for allowing this show of emotion when I had wanted to have the upper hand and be above it all.

A voice drifted into my head on lonely wisps of the fog bank of my clouded mind, "It's a lonely life." Maybe one by one all of my mother's dire warnings would come true. Was all of this seeking out an existence in a world that I belonged in for naught? Would I end up where Angel was now, awaiting death's freeing embrace from the confusion, torment, and anguish that seemed to surround what I had discovered about being gay so far?

Well, fuck that! I circumvented eloquence for a more rousing pseudo macho battle cry. My life didn't have to be lonely. I could certainly see to that. I didn't need anyone but myself—not even the man that was putting his arms around me, sheltering me from the slings and arrows that always seemed to be striking me in the heart. I wanted to struggle free, but I was tired of the mental tennis game. All of the back and forth was wearing me out. I just wanted to be sure of something, of anything that had validity, and right now Danny's arms around me represented that.

I was residing on strength that I had built up over the years; the immunity to life's cruelties was always, at best, a gay façade. Maybe I needed to adopt a theme song to help me rise above it all? "Walking on Sunshine" seemed a little bit too gay. "Eye of the Tiger" was very 1983. "One More Night" seemed a little too morose in light of the circumstances.

Then like the lightning bolt makeup that lead singer Patti Smyth sported in the video, the song came to me, "The Warrior!" Because when it all boiled down to it, I was shooting at the walls of heartache, bang, bang! I had been dealing with the disappointments that accompany heartbreak in its various incarnations for years. From my father apparently detecting a gay scent about me and leaving me to fend for myself, to the feeling that I never belonged anywhere, I was no stranger to heartbreak. Right now, I just wanted to bask in the warmth of Danny's embrace and not have to think about anything else just for a minute.

"Are you all right? " Danny inquired as my tears drying up provided an answer for him already.

"Yes," I murmured even though I was currently traveling along an uneven patch of road, swerving back and forth over the double yellow lines that were trying to get me to pick a side.

So once again, I had expected the worst-case scenario. But Danny's true confession was that he loved me; no, that was too compartmentalized. He had feelings for me.

"Well, there's never going to be a good time for me to say what I need to say," Danny said. "So what I wanted to tell you…"

I wanted to hold onto the fleeting bliss, so I cut him off at the pass.

"We can deal with everything later, we have time enough. Let's just enjoy this right now."

I sounded needy, the human equivalent of a clutch purse wanting to be held firmly and never let go. For all of the sidetracks to finally reach him, I felt as though we were finally connecting, our paths had reached the crossroads, and I wanted to pick the destination together.

I didn't want to talk about what could prove to be obstacles: our age difference, his drug problem, my alleged STD. What he told me next ruined any chance of that being a possibility.

"Well, that's just it, we can't," he said matter-of-factly. "I called your brother tonight. He's back from his West Pac and is on his way up here to take you home."

Chapter 18

I had been waiting for the other shoe to drop. This had felt more like it had plummeted out of the sky, a shoe meteor that smacked me, knocking me into the impact crater it created, trapping me in a hollow place, without being able to catch my breath and it made for a very shallow grave. I absentmindedly put my hand to my forehead, checking for an imprint of the Nike emblem. I didn't know how to respond, hoping desperately that Danny would follow up what he had said with "Psych." But I could tell from the look he was giving me that he was deadly serious.

He appeared to be both solemn about his admission, pensive to my reaction, and apprehensive to banish my existence back to its former misery. The last thought put it all into perspective for me. I would be relinquished back into the not-so-wild life I had been living. Danny had pulled a catch and release on me all in the span of a few moments time.

Well, just because I could be returned home did not mean that I had to stay there. As a matter of fact, I would not be staying there. I knew that Danny wouldn't want to wager any bets that Big Ed would not be accompanying John on the drive to reclaim me. In fact, he

288

must have been pretty subscribed to not having to deal with his children lately. Both were out of sight, very likely out of mind—that had to be somewhere on our family crest, the credo that enabled certain behaviors.

Each member of my family had always been blind to the other: my mother to my father's alcoholism and the way he neglected her, my father to his own neglect of everything not named Budweiser, and John thinking none of this affected him just because he could see far-off lands by escaping familiar terrain. But memories, they travel across landscapes of time to find you when you least expect it.

"So when is he supposed to be here?" I said this with an air of resignation that I was fully on board to be taken back to my native habitat that the big city life was not for me.

This tact would provide me with the information I needed without having to cramp my jaw. I was just hoping that I would find out if I had enough time to come up with an alternative strategy to anything resembling a homecoming. I had not found that place for me yet, and I knew that it was out there somewhere, and I was going to keep looking until I found it.

"Oh, Henry," Danny said, relief evident in his unconscious reference to the candy bar of the same name, "I'm so glad that you understand. Things are just too dangerous here, but I think you already know that, huh, pal?"

He was getting downright jovial for a moment until he uttered that last line and fully comprehended once more the complications brought on by his actions.

"Yeah," I said, "you are right about that."

For a moment I had halfheartedly believed that Danny possessed the power of mind reading and was referring to my mind as the place that had gotten too dangerous. And it had. I was going all over the board with where I stood with Danny.

Granted, he wasn't helping matters by sending the posse to take me back to Dodge City. Why couldn't he let me find my way? If he told me it was for my own good, I was going to haul off and punch him. He was making me feel volatile in his caginess and inability to answer my simple question. Was he stalling for time? Had our sexual encounter been a mere interlude to distract me? Somehow that made more sense to me, that the words he had spoken were made up of nothing and thusly represented the same. I felt a berating coming on and had to stabilize myself so that I did not indulge it.

"Well, your brother isn't actually on his way yet. He got home today, so he asked me to keep an eye on you until tomorrow morning," he said the last word as a separate entity from the rest of his sentence, giving it a much stronger impact.

And there in the rest of the sentence was the appalling truth that I did not matter in the scheme of my family. I could be put on the back burner, relegated to a mere chore that needed to be performed, like taking out the trash.

For the first time in, well, it seemed like forever, I thought about my secret sketchbook. This would not have been one of the scenarios that I had drawn; it seemed like one that I would rather erase from my memory. I had invented Billy Collins as my new moniker to quash any of the Dodge traits that were inherent within me; perhaps rumors of his demise had been greatly exaggerated.

"So no one else offered to come and get me? You didn't want to go out of your way to take me home yourself?" I asked in hopefulness that was fleeing.

I tried to lessen the spitefulness by adding a dash of pity, trying to concoct the perfect recipe which, once consumed, would find Danny unable to cast me aside. I asked these questions even though I already knew the answers. Did I really want my father or mother to be the ones to come and get me? No. Did I want to ride in awkward silence for the two plus hours south with Danny, each click of the odometer representing a silent resentment towards him? No. What I wanted was what I couldn't have, and what I couldn't have was Danny shaking his head in the negative affirmative that only John thought enough of my well-being.

It would by no means be Danny, probably not now, probably never. A huge sense of loss was creeping across my brain; slow and steady would win its race.

Why should I have expected Danny to keep me for himself when he had such a high disregard of himself? Even though the van was stationary at the moment and Danny was not the one taking me home against my will, I could already feel the miles between us, vast and endless.

Well, at least I had a time frame now, leaving me hours to plan an escape. The wheels immediately began turning, looking for something that I had never thought of as a means for my escape. I could always resume the night's original plan and strut my stuff down Santa Monica Boulevard and procure a new home that way.

But there was too much of a chance that if George did get out of jail at some point, he would be able to find me. Right now I wanted to remain lost. There had to be somebody, but I just couldn't think of who it was.

"Hey, we'd better get inside. Nick will be wondering what we've been up to," Danny said this unassumingly, providing me with the answer that should have been a cinch.

There had been so much buildup surrounding Danny; I needed a complete mental release, detoxifying all of the negative aftereffects of today from my rational radar.

"Fuck you!" I screamed this at the top of my lungs and from the bottom of my broken heart.

I was almost as surprised as Danny that I was letting out all of my pent-up frustrations with two words, granted I had forgone eloquence for a raw, emotional response to the day, the night, and my life.

I had dropped my own bomb but had no intention of hanging around to see its aftermath. I felt very evocative of the times I was residing in; the threat of a nuclear attack was always imminent with a question of when and a matter of time all brought on by provocation from two opposing forces.

Yup, that pretty much summed up my day; I had been bombarded.

The fallout from my outburst was nothing I had protected myself from with a radiation suit or by effectively using the duck-and-cover routine. I was exposed to the threat of having my skin melted from my frame, nerve endings uncovered, unable to protect my body from any further onslaughts.

I stood still for a moment longer, waiting to see how the shock wave would affect Danny. He reached out to grab me, to pull me into the comforting embrace I had been lulled into moments before. Well, I wasn't going to be cradled into a false sense of security by him. His arms were not welcoming. They didn't want to protect me; they wanted to hold me down and force me back to the places that I didn't want to go to. Back home and into believing he had genuine feelings for me seemed to be conceived from the same tapestry now, which was now threadbare and unraveling at an expeditious clip.

I wished he had been able to locate an "in case of emergency" stash of forget-me-lots vanquishing all of today from memory, if only temporarily.

A snowball began rolling itself downhill, gaining speed, escaping the flurry of reminiscences, becoming a white blur that gained in both speed and size with each passing second. Everything that was in its path became a part of it. Nothing was too big or small as it ingested so much that it was the size of a boulder, and its gentle forcefulness caused all that were in its way to flee. My memories were what propelled me, gaining insights with each passing year; but all I could see was the blinding white escaping from the monumental chill, trying desperately to find shelter, endless shuffling of my feet were taking me nowhere, save for dangerous places. In my mind my feet were affixed, but in actuality, I could take flight.

And that's exactly what mine were doing. I was moving away so suddenly that Danny was left in the lurch. I opted for the driver's-side door as it was closer to the street, to freedom. My foot kicked at something, almost tripping me up, therefore quashing my last dash away from Danny and a life I did not want to return to.

My Walkman, beloved savior of drowning out the outside world, filled my ears with siphoned through orange sponge symphonies, allowing a means to escape while I carefully dissected lyrics trying to figure out if there was any hidden gay messages within the songs I gravitated to.

I wish I could say that it was in one fell swoop that I scooped up my precious cargo, stealthily opened the door, feet connected with concrete, my battle cry of freedom filling up the night. I did scoop up the Walkman without any trouble whatsoever, but as my hand reached for the handle to open the door to the possibilities of never returning home, another one clamped down around my torso, dragging me back.

"Don't worry, I've got you. Where are you going to go, huh? Where are you going to go?" Danny asked me as he also made up my mind for me that I would not be going anywhere I wanted.

His voice had taken on a very soothing tone, vaporizing the F bomb that I had dropped on him, at him, and for him. He spoke gently into my ear, the soothing strains of a lover, but all my head was hearing was nothing sweet about his sweet nothings.

His naked body up against mine did not have the desired effect that he was hoping for; my mind was too busy thinking of ways to escape to want to take that familiar road of distraction. I wanted to believe I was safe in his arms, that nothing could do me any harm, except for the man that was holding me.

There was my conundrum; I did not believe I had the fortitude to convince Danny to hide me out, to make up a story to my brother, John, about my whereabouts. Even if I could convince him to hide me out, I was not so sure I wanted to stay with him. Conceivably, if this were a different time, a different place, and we were both different people, it might have worked.

"You're right." I half sighed as I said this, wanting him to believe he had the ability to convince me otherwise when an idea got stuck in my head.

Spending so much time in my mind had made me headstrong, running mental marathons, spinning an idea around and around in my mind before releasing it by action or regret, catapulting it like a shot put to its destination. I felt this was an instance where I needed to pole-vault over Danny's ill-conceived notions of who he thought he was dealing with. I could let the games begin too.

"Just stay with me, you're safer that way," Danny spoke like a Boy Scout, but I knew that it came out of the mouth of a barracuda. "And I want you to."

I could sense that I was giving myself over to him; there was an oddly calming effect that his voice, sans "Dude," had. But the last sentence broke the spell because if he wanted me to, then it must be wrong to do. Besides, I may be young, but I had a mind of my own to consider, and it was telling me to get away from him, not to trust him.

"Well, maybe I don't want to. Did you ever think about that?" Yup, I was definitely going to have to submit for a schizophrenia litmus test when I had a chance to see if I had the big G.

Vacillating back and forth in my own head was something altogether entirely different than actually vocalizing it. No wonder Danny wanted to pawn me off back to an existence that was conducive to this type of behavior.

"Hey, calm down, bro. I am just trying to help you."

Now I had done it, I had made Danny say *bro*.

As certainly as the shark in *Jaws* would appear following the first few strains of its theme music, then it could be counted on that Danny's utterance of *bro* usually signaled an element of frustration. It started out slow, rhythmic, "Bro, bro," then gained in impetus, "Bro, bro, bro, bro," finally reaching a crescendo of epic proportions, "Bro, bro, bro, bro, bro, bro, bro, bro, bro, bro!"

"You, help me? That's ridiculous! You can't even help yourself." I interspersed my laughter after each statement.

I wasn't intentionally trying to be cruel, but the truth was I did feel this way about him and thought it a bit absurd that he thought he could shield me from life's booby traps.

Maybe I should have been focusing on shielding myself as his fist rebounded off the side of my face; the cacophony of *bros* did not warrant this attack. Knowing that the best offense was a good defense or something along those lines, I brained him with my Walkman. In fact, I hit him so hard that he not only stumbled backwards, releasing me from his grasp, but the clocking turned on my portable cassette player. Appropriately enough, Culture Club's "I'll Tumble 4 Ya" was the song that was playing. Seeing as I was in the land of make believe, it seemed very surreal.

My face began to instantly throb, but the shock I was feeling from the assault seemed to be numbing it. I turned and gave him what I figured would be the customary smoldering last glance. What

I probably resembled was a deer caught in the headlights. Danny was practically on top of me in no time flat, pouncing from his vantage point a few yards away.

There was a feeling of disbelief that latched on to its counterpart fear as certainly I was affixing a death grip on my Walkman, my only line of defense. Danny raised his right fist once and let it connect with my torso this time while his left hand held me down. This did not mean that I was docile. I was squirming more and more as his right fist took on a pneumatic rhythm. After the first punch, I felt anesthetized to the subsequent few that he managed to get in before I was able to somehow kick him off me, giving me the ability to make my escape.

Everything was happening at a fast clip yet seemed to be mired in the molasses of slow motion. The fulcrum effect of me getting Danny off me had landed him squarely on his ass, where he began weeping like an unloved child, muttering, "Not again, oh my god, not again. So sorry."

He said it in a repeated succession so quickly that it sounded like a prayer used to ward off evil demons. And maybe it was. He just may have very well been talking to himself as my Walkman softly crooned to an audience of one—boys that cross the street, you never know who you might meet, who's in disguise indeed.

I would not be tumbling for Danny; in fact, it was taking all of my strength to not go to him and console him. In my fragile state, I would have been hard-pressed not to waver between pity and the pain that I felt; opting for the pain, slipping the wires of the headphones around his neck in a game of turnabout is fair play. Why should I lower myself to the gutters that he swam in? He was a scavenger feeding off others, using the human suffering he felt to create the same for those around him.

I wondered if he had convinced my brother to pay a bounty for babysitting me tonight. Well, he was going to have a lot of explaining to do. Because this time I was gone for good, I looked at him sitting there, crying, muttering, and realized there was nothing that I could say to him that would make him feel worse than he already did about himself. But I wasn't going to let that stop me;

besides, he looked too broken up about what he had just done to me to try it again.

My adrenaline had skyrocketed; if it came to it, I could take him on. So I lit the fuse on my smart-ass dynamite, boarded up my heart, declaring it unsafe, hoping that what I would say would cause Danny to cave in.

"Goodbye," I said it with such finality that I was sure it would be more effective to devastate him than any zinger I could produce.

And I was right. He was hanging his head in shame, and I was trying to keep mine out of memory lane and to fortify my resolve that I would never see him again. I could feel myself already making up excuses for the bruises I would most likely have tomorrow, covering up for what he had done.

The art of the underscore was one that I was so familiar with, that a terrible situation like this would suddenly have a shiny gloss of justification to help make it easier to swallow. I looked at Danny wallowing in self-loathing at everything wrong he had ever done. He reminded me of a neighborhood dog that went by the name of Chipper, a Scottish terrier who seemed to live up to his name very easily, always wagging his tail, looking very happy to see you.

But as soon as you went to pet him, Chipper's ears went back against his head; his low, resonant growl grew in intensity if you were brave enough to continue the charade of "Who's a good boy? Yes, Chipper's a good boy!" Teeth were bared, ready to shred every ounce of flesh from your body, and if you stayed in his vicinity long enough, Chipper would chase you away. That was Danny, all right; he came off as friendly but could bare his teeth in an instant and make you move away from him.

Eventually, I learned to not even approach Chipper, and I needed to apply that lesson to Danny. His face, when not buried in his hands as it was now, seemed to convey that he was a caring person; but he hid behind his ferocity, tethered to the absolute resolve that he would always be a mess. I shut the door behind me; it made a hollow thud because I had practically slammed it and not even realized it. For a minute I thought it was the sound of my heart breaking into unrecoverable pieces.

As soon as I was across the street and around the corner, I dropped my brave front on the concrete that I sat upon. Each glistening tear was shed for a different frailty, injustice, and slight. I was mourning the loss of hope, of dreaming big, getting what I wanted, of ever finding happiness.

I had very much reached a literal watershed moment, and I didn't think the tears from fears would ever stop their journey. As for mine, I knew that I could very easily go inside the hospital and find Nick and appoint him my newfound liberator. But I was done with the palace gang and any offshoot factions of it.

Did I really need another abject lesson in the way people use one another from Nick? Should I put all of my trust in him only to have it manipulated into something that would benefit him? I had spent so much of my time here putting all of my eggs into different baskets with the same effect; the eggs came back smashed and left me feeling scrambled and hard boiled.

If I sat still, bemoaning my luck, one of thirty things were going to happen, and they all seemed to be derivative from my brother's impending arrival. I could sit here boohooing and let other people dictate my life, or I could tap into my own propulsion that had landed me among the angels and devils in the first place.

My need to discover had to now outweigh my desire to want to hold on to old ideals, such as Danny is a great guy. He may have been at one time, but he was just a war-torn vet in the battles that he waged on himself. But did this mean I would also be marching off, hiding in the foxholes he had previously occupied? I just had to be careful not to snare myself on the barbed wire that would render me unrecognizable.

Hitting the boulevard did seem the likeliest of choices for me to make a quick buck or two before going off to the great unknown. I did not want to stay in LA any longer; all that it represented to me now was not what I thought it would be.

I was beginning to realize very few things in life often are.

Like the first time I had sex, I thought I would be striding down the hallways at school, purposeful in my stride, cock of the walk. Nope. It just gave me more just cause to hide among the shadows.

I still had a bit of the currency more or less stemming from that first encounter that I had parlayed into seed money to fund my expedition. It would be easy enough to hit the bus station now. I felt like the walking cliché of the small-town boy beaten by the big ole bad city, I needed to pick a destination that was affordable and would leave me some funds to eke out an existence that I had been dreaming about, an existence that saw me surrounded by people who cared about me and I didn't have to pretend around them.

Such a place seemed completely fanciful, a figment of my imagination, yet completely tangible given the light of recent circumstances.

I walked away into the night.

Chapter 19

I wasn't bounding towards the boulevard. I was dragged along by its still magnetic pull. It felt necessary, like I needed to say goodbye to it and all it represented now. The street was even more alive than ever, a multitude of rainbow flags overtaking buildings. I spied with my little eye a banner that wished everyone a happy Gay Pride, which seemed like a very big oxymoron to me.

The streets were starting to accommodate bar patrons, whether it was those still in their cars looking for the elusive Doris Day parking or even a lesser parking space not too far away, a Sandra Dee spot.

Those who were fortunate to find parking already were bee-lining it to their favorite haunts. I had nowhere to haunt, but the ghosts that resided in me were starting to rattle their chains, clamoring for attention. I didn't want to pay them any mind, my brain was exhausted from walking around the spook house once too often today, trapped in the cobwebs of indecision.

I didn't look anyone in the eye as I walked against the tide of bodies. I felt like a castaway, lost in the sea of people that were walking by me. Most of them were fit and tanned, looking for their doppelgangers.

Every step I took seemed hindered with the weight of trepidation. Why was I being drawn towards this particular flame? The omnipresence of George and Danny hovered over my left shoulder, the vaporous visage of my parents over the right. Neither one really represented pure good nor pure evil to me as each had to embody some kind of humanity that I was unable to detect. Certainly their actions did not dictate this assumption.

I was certain that I looked worse for wear but did not care if any of these pretty boys wanted to try me on for size. A part of me, small and seeking, wished I did fit in, that I could partake in the joviality that seemed to be prevalent this Friday night. But if I had been a part of the crowd, and I was standing in the middle of the throng, and I screamed, no one would hear me.

I decided it was time to shut my brain off without the drugs that I did not have and to shut off my heart to the sting it was feeling and my body to the pain it had incurred at the hand of Danny.

I slipped on my Walkman's earphones and pressed the cassette player's play button. My hand came back a tad sticky as Culture Club gave way to Bronski Beat's apropos "Small Town Boy." There was a hint of blood on the play button from when I had tried to stop Danny; the memory of him pummeling me with his fists was made even fresher with this discovery. I hit the mental rewind button on his assault on me, playing it like an unfamiliar tune over and over in my head until its lyrics were easily relatable as a "somebody done me very wrong" song.

I secretly wished that there was a way that I could slip into the bar nonchalantly, sidle up to the bar, request something strong from the barkeep, not be asked for ID or any questions whatsoever. If just for a minute, to lock up my brain and throw away the key to remembering would be very welcoming. But I knew the minute the key went skittering away and hung precariously over the dark edge of forever that I would want it back.

I always seemed to want the unobtainable, whether it was the seemingly nice guy that turned out to be damaged, or to find my place in the happiness spectrum. I felt like I was on a quest of sorts. But I kept vacillating between being the knight in shining armor, or was I a damsel that needed saving? I kept my feet moving, almost as fast as my mind, eyes unfocused, which resulted into me ricocheting off people intermittently.

I couldn't hear if they were telling me off or asking if I was all right. "All that was filling my head was, "Run away, turn away, run away." Had I been paying less attention to a song that seemed to encapsulate my present existence and more to my surroundings, I would have noticed a familiar face in the crowd.

He was hanging back so that he wouldn't scare me off at the sight of him. His good looks were commanding quite a bit of attention from the crowd, as was his manner of dress code; had I seen him, I would have gone running into the night. He may as well been sporting Jason's hockey mask from *Friday the 13th*, Freddy's razor glove from *Nightmare on Elm Street*, and carrying Michael Meyers's butcher knife from *Halloween*. The sight of him could have induced an instantaneous heart attack in me.

He gradually started making his way to me, closing the distance between us until he was just a breath or two away from me. He was almost to me when he was corralled by two faux cowboys making their way in from 1980 apparently, when the *Urban Cowboy* craze had been in full swing.

But this was a town of to each his own, and lookin' for love in all the wrong places in too many faces was still applicable, even though it was now a loaded proposition. I mean, where else was my brother, in his Navy uniform, going to start false rumors of a possible Village People reunion but in West Hollywood?

"Hey, stud, you lookin' for a little fun tonight?" one of the two Randy Jones knockoffs inquired.

"Um, well," John stammered, dreading the fact that he had not thought to change into something a little more casual Friday, that had less of an effect of fulfilling some guy's errant fantasy of you sank your battleship into my ass.

"Don't worry, honey. It would be twice as nice with us," Randy Jones #2 cooed, practically salivating at the proposal that was less on the table than it was in the gutter.

John was trying to think of a polite yet effective way to bow out of the conversation while keeping his sights on me, and Randy Jones #1 followed his gaze.

"Oh come on, Terrence, he likes chicken. Pity," Randy Jones #1, also known as Percy, said as he started pulling his companion similar in chapeaus by the hand.

"Why have chicken when you could have a nice pork?" said the ever-persistent Terrence, thinking he could wear my brother down with a food-based sexual entendre.

Well, if John lost sight of me because of these two, it was likely they would be eating a knuckle sandwich. John didn't have anything against gay people. He was in the Navy, after all, and had been approached on more than one occasion. But he didn't want his little brother to be enveloped by the night, falling victim to the predatory set.

How was he to know that I had been residing in a nest of vipers during my Los Angeles sojourn? When he had gotten the call from Danny, they had formulated a plan to keep me unaware that John would be coming to get me. Yet they had not discussed why I would have come to see Danny and what fascination I would find with accidentally happening upon Santa Monica Boulevard.

John had been away from home for a while; he had not born witness to the changes I had gone through. He was probably just seeing me as the same little tagalong begging for attention. Well, having this group of people eyeing his little brother was not the kind of attention he thought I wanted. Boy, had he thought wrong, and at that precise moment, he had also thought a little bit right.

"Thanks, but no thanks, guys." Well, it was polite but not quite effective.

Terrence thought his actions would speak louder than words. As Percy took him by his left hand, he brushed his right against the crotch of John's uniform, gave him a wink, and got no reaction from John. Percy sighed in exasperation. Even though the two were visiting from Texas for the first time, they had been down this boulevard before.

"The boy doesn't want to play," he said this quietly in conspiracy tones.

He did not want to unnecessarily provoke John, who was only standing at attention in his posture. The recent rash of hate crimes towards gays had rewritten the rules of feeling safe within the bubble.

"I am sure I can persuade him." Terrence leaned in closer to John, expelling a mouthful of whiskey breath strong enough to knock over King Kong.

John turned his head to the left momentarily to escape the pungency of Terrence's breath. When he turned back a fraction of a moment later, he had lost sight of me in the crowd. He pushed Terrance away from him, not caring about how he'd be perceived by anyone on the street, not fearing implications; he rushed down the street to locate me, deathly worried that I had been abducted by the Terrences of the world.

His impression and mine of what the gay world was like were starting to mesh. The big difference was I had been holding out for the hope that things were not as they seemed and that I had just been viewing everything with tunnel vision.

I was too busy trotting off to even notice that my past had caught up to me and then was running past the alleyway where I had stopped to relieve myself. I was over my quota of alleyways by about one today. At least this one didn't harbor any of the connotations that the other one had.

I wouldn't be surprised to see Danny show up in this one, scouting locations for his next magnum opus. It was more than likely that I was going to be seeing my name up in lights tonight. Henry Dodge Is Billy Collins, the marquee would proclaim and in smaller letters, For One Night Only. Let Danny or anyone who wanted to stop me show up unexpectedly; I was starting to feel impervious.

Then I put my left hand up to my face and almost pissed all over my tennis shoes. My face was stinging, but my penis wasn't, which made me believe that George would have sent me to one of his associates posing as a doctor, who would slip me some type of mind control in caplet form.

As I finished up, making doubly sure I didn't cross my own stream, I tried to banish any further conspiracy theories from entering my domain. It was hard to think that I was some sort of pawn in a much bigger game. But it was time that I played the game by my rules again, setting up the board for a game of Risk that Big Ed and John wouldn't have thought to play. I could only hope that my aspirations wouldn't get upended, signaling an end to playtime.

I started emerging from an alleyway for the second time in a day. The subtle difference was that this time I wasn't facing down the barrel of a gun, fearing for my life. I stopped momentarily on the cusp of rejoining gay society, and my thoughts turned to Angel. He had struggled so hard to break away from the restraints that held him down by selling himself in the dark of the night. Now he was what? He was probably going to die, and that seemed puritanical, righteously unfair.

He was making strides to get his life on track, and faster than a speeding bullet, more powerful than a locomotive, along came George to remind Angel of his subservient role that he had portrayed for endless, sleepless nights, one melting into the next in a blending of complacency. In the short time that I had known—knew— Angel. Oh shit, I had put him in the past tense, already assuming the worst, for I did not know that Angel was a fighter.

I cued the Angel montage, all remembered in slow motion, so I could hang on to him. He was strutting like a peacock the night I met him, trying to take my inventory and determine my resale value, the momentary puppy-dog look of needing to be appreciated hidden behind his snarling comments.. The night that he practiced his routine for *Puttin' on the Hits*, a show where contestants lip-synched to their favorite songs and were judged on performance, originality, and appearance, I was not so sure the Saturday morning set was ready for Angel in a pair of his high-end satiny hooker shorts, no shirt, mouthing the words to the Mary Jane Girls's "In My House" accompanied by very suggestive choreography.

I gave him kudos for his performance, secretly delighted he had called a truce long enough to ask my opinion. I had told him it was good; almost as soon as I did, his face adopted a dejected look, and he had said, "Oh yeah? What do you know?" He huffed out of the room, not talking to me for days on end. Had I known that his pre-audition for an audience of one was just one of the ways he was trying to earn an honest buck, I would have given him a standing ovation.

But I didn't know that then, I surmised. It was parallel with just starting to know Angel, even like him and not see him as my rival, his newfound silent treatment from the bullet of a gun could make that situation permanent. There was a distinct possibility that he may never utter a single word again, that his life would be cut unexpectedly short, all because of the company he kept.

I wouldn't know because I was running away again; it was like running away squared. Was this the way I would always be? Things don't go my way, so I'm outta here? That didn't sound like a very good mantra to adhere to. One of these days, and I knew it wouldn't be soon somehow, I would have to stop the marathon of "You're not good enough" that ran the ten-yard dash in two seconds flat, crossing the finish line of my mind.

I needed to believe in myself, but doubt, fear, and uncertainty were all running a distant second behind the winner and still champion, low self-esteem. The way that my two very different lives of before and after coming out had intersected, had brought me to this moment of decision; yet I did not think I could be decisive. I needed some kind of signal, a sign to know that I was doing the right thing.

I looked out into the vast darkness, feeling it mirrored my life perfectly, endless with no direction. There were no neon signs or streetlights lighting the way, allowing me to stumble along blindly, calling out "Marco! Polo!" hoping that someone would heed my call. I wasn't treading water, only trying to navigate the cavernous, shadowy hole where my heart should be and the sharp, stabbing pain of hesitation that had replaced it.

I wanted to be resilient, the epitome of being above it all, but I was wedged into a world of hurt with no idea of how to get myself unstuck. I knew I could travel the familiar routes, distract myself from the pain that encompassed every fiber of my being in any variety of methods. But I did not feel like sitting through *Desperately*

Seeking Susan for the fifth time would do the trick. I really wanted to see *St. Elmo's Fire* but couldn't go without a parent or legal guardian attending with me. The irony of my life was that I was living an R-rated existence, doing the things that characters were doing up on the silver screen, but I was still only thought of as PG-13 material. I knew that scoring high on Galaga wouldn't prove to be anything to me right now; that's how anesthetized I was to the world at large.

I actually didn't feel like feeling. I wanted to further numb myself somehow, but there was no way to do anything but face up to reality. I was about to remove myself from the shadows of my cocoon, reemerging more confident that I was doing the right thing. I made a motion to step from the alleyway a new man, from Clark Kent to Superman, but it felt like somebody was stepping on my cape holding me back.

My eyes caught sight of something that made me realize that I at least should rethink my positioning in plain view. My brother, it seemed, had arrived early. He was scouring the boulevard with his eyes, trying to catch sight of me, moving his head back and forth robotically. Sarah Connor?

Those two words immediately leapt into my head because John was here to terminate any strategy I had about altering the course of my future tonight. I couldn't believe he was here; his arriving early showed that the hometown crowd still had the propensity to care. But why exactly had he come to Santa Monica Boulevard and begun ferreting for me here?

Well, there could be only one reason with two possible answers. Either he had figured out on his own the true nature of my trip or Danny had tipped him off, pinpointing all of the little clues over the years that John had chosen not to notice, bringing about the logical conclusion, his brother's a fag. Elementary, my queer Watson! If I was James Bond's martini, I would be shaken in a cement mixer. I ducked back into the alleyway, not ready to change back into Clark Kent yet.

The little brother in me wanted to run over to him and have him clean the clocks of all of the bullies that had done me wrong. He was dressed like Popeye, so maybe I should acquire a can of spinach first before I had him give 'em the old one-two. But I knew the minute I drew his attention, it would spell the end of any further exploits that Billy Collins could concoct.

It would mean I would be forcibly removed from a Wonderland that had left me with as many questions as I had answers to upon my arrival. Instinctively, I felt close to unearthing the true nature of my visit, to the something that had brought me here. Sure, it was easy enough to say it had just been Danny, but there was something deeper than that.

If it had been just Danny, then I would not have fallen in with George and company. Even though I now knew that had been preordained, I still had to be a willing participant to go off with Angel in the first place. I had been compelled to come here, drawn in by something, an otherworldly force, so that I could emerge more man than boy. If I had to go back home at this juncture, I needed more than some gold-plated souvenir purchased from a vendor on Hollywood Boulevard that would eventually chip, flakes of faux gold dust falling to a beautiful death.

I was not ready to go, not yet; there was more footwork that I had to do, a kind of homework that my mother could not help me with or that my father would be too busy for.

No, this required field research into the hows, whys, and wheres of homosexuality, and I had to find it by striking out on my own, not dependent on anyone or anything but myself. It was time to utilize what I had learned during my time here. I had gotten a glimpse of how to spot my own kind from George, able to place suspect queers on sister patrol, as he used to call our journeys into West Hollywood.

One way to denote a could-be from an isn't was which ear his earring was in. I thought it was a weird standard by which to measure one's potential gayness as I thought the wearing of jewelry was, in and of itself, pretty gay.

It did make me think back to the not so long ago but very far-removed days of reading, writing, and arithmetic. There were a lot of New Wave types that sported earrings, had girlfriends, but listened to a lot of the Smiths and the Cure at my school. Hmmm, highly suspect in retrospect. While I couldn't remember if the ear that held the adornment was in the gay ear or not, which was the right one, it was nothing but wrong in the eyes of many in that town. Now that I thought back on it, my high school had probably been teeming with gay life. But like me, nothing could be said for fear of implication.

I stopped, shook the memories of high school, of oppression, of life back home out of my head.

But there was one memory that was flesh and blood patrolling the streets for me, looking to place me right back into my least-desired living situation. Problem was, as much as I hated my homelife, of not being understood, I was tempted to run up to John and ask him to take me home.

I was standing at a great divide, struggling within as to what to do. If I didn't take this chance and continue searching until I found what I was looking for, I may never build up the courage to do it again. There was always time enough to return home at some point, or maybe never.

The fact that my brother had come up here to find me, it was messing with my head, for lack of a better term. I had built titanium steel defense mechanisms to propel me further along in the last few months that John had been away. One of those being that no one in my family cared about me, and the proof against that wasn't necessarily in the pudding but on the boulevard.

I knew the longer I waited, there was the chance that a few things could transpire One, he could give up and seek out Danny, leaving me to patrol the night scape. Two, he could walk over this way, find me deep in thought, and capture my flag—just like our long-ago games of Stratego. Or three, I could remain in this alleyway, inside of my head until winter came, playing another childhood favorite game, hide-and-go-seek.

I figured the longer I stayed hidden, the more of a chance that my brother wouldn't be mentally sizing me up for a right-hand earring. If he didn't call out "Ollie ollie oxen free," there was less of a chance that he would see with his own two eyes that Danny had told him the truth. I wasn't ready for John to see me differently.

For some reason, for him to know that I was gay was a much bigger deal than my parents knowing. In some ways, John had been like a surrogate father to me, including me into his world, and I didn't want to be left out of it now; but I didn't want a return to it either.

With conundrums abound in my head, my feet doing the hokey pokey, I turned the volume almost all of the way up on my Walkman, trying to drown out the white noise of doubt that plagued me. I closed my eyes, trying to vanquish everything that was bothering me, while Frankie Goes to Hollywood told me to relax at full blast. I only wished I could heed their advice, but so much seemed at stake.

Realizing that I could be there a while, I opened my eyes again, hoping that I would see the world anew. But alas, I was subscribed to utilizing them in their very perfunctory manner. I peeked around the corner; John was still scouting for me, standing on the corner. Great, leave it to my brother to show me up on my newfound turf and to have a gimmick to boot! "Hey, sailor, new in town?" And wouldn't you know it, a vehicle approached him, slowing down to a crawl. Rather than looking for some man on man in the back of his van, the driver was asking John if there was any sign of me. I was beginning to wonder that as well. Danny unlocked the passenger door; John got in, much to the chagrin of some onlookers too nervous to approach John.

If I had learned anything today, and there was a lot to take in, it was that alleyways lingered in for too long equaled trouble. My impetus was dictating to stay with my original plan and head 'em up, move 'em out. Now I had to find a roundabout way to my destination with John and Danny teaming up to track me down. The last person on earth I wanted to see was Danny. The anger that I had been trying to desensitize was back, fingers creeping up the back of my skull, reaching in and grabbing a hold of my brain, giving it a forceful squeeze.

I tried my best to blend into the crowd, as I had always tried to do. But now I was on the lam, and I didn't want to get caught. I was *The Fagative.* Almost as soon as I stepped out of the alleyway, a vehicle approached at the top speed that the boulevard could allow on a Friday night, which was a bit faster than a tortoise. With lights flashing on and off, its horn honking intermittently, the car moved in my direction. Not waiting to find out who it was, thinking that it was most likely Danny and John, I started running, as I was so very apt to do.

Chapter 20

My feet were slapping off the sidewalk, but I could not hear them. Don Henley was telling me that his love would still be strong after the boys of summer were gone. I thought he would be the only one loving me, and had I known that the song was about baseball—and not a man-on-man kinship—as I liked to think of it as, I may have stopped dead in my tracks right then and there.

I needed to keep moving, never stopping until I arrived at whatever destination I was supposed to reach. Like so much of my life, I did not know where I was running to, only from. The headlights that were flashing a hair shy of synchronicity with the song filling my head were starting to get closer by the moment.

I clutched the Walkman in my hand tightly, not wanting to have my saving grace shatter upon the sidewalk, leaving me to face the dark recesses without a soundtrack of distraction to accompany me.

I wished it was tomorrow morning; the dark skies of doubt would give way to endless blue, the infinite azure of resolution. I wanted to keep running until I reached the horizons of certainty that were remaining elusive. Everything would make more sense. I would make more sense.

As I was evading my pursuer, watching the faces of curious onlookers blur into one conglomerated entity, the unanswered-questions marathon in my head caught up with the one-man parade I was at that moment, feet and head moving at a quick pace.

Here were the questions I thought needed immediate addressing. Primarily, how did I go about dodging what people must have thought was a rehash of the scene in *Risky Business* between Tom Cruise and Guido, the killer pimp? But more importantly was that eternal question of, where was my place in the scheme of things?

There was a greater division between coming out and proclaiming your sexual proclivities than I had even bothered to fathom. Because I was this way, did it mean that I could not like people that were that way? Was I now only supposed to run with those in my own pack? Was there a set percentage of straight friends I could have? Would I have to say one day, if this did occur, "Sorry, Tammy, I am full up on my straight-gal-pal quota, try back in six months."

Not that having that problem for me would be an issue, I was sure, but I just wanted to know the parameters. I did not understand how to make it all fit together, all questions coexisting with tangible answers and peace of mind. My mind was currently winning the race over my feet, thought processes slowing down what I hoped was an agile stab at athleticism that would not see me falter, tripping over myself.

I wasn't even sure if I would have the opportunity to broach these subjects if this was Danny and John hot on my tail in an entirely different manner than I was used to with men chasing me or being hot on my tail, for that matter.

"Thank you, I might be here all week. Try the veal."

I chanced a look behind me. The car had edged forward slightly, and I could see a shadow of a driver waving at me. The headlights were lower than what would have been on the microbus, so it couldn't have been Danny and John; and it appeared to be too long to be George's VW Rabbit, which always skated very close to looking like a clown car due to George's size but without the humor and merriment that was associated with that image. I slowed down both paces I was keeping, trying to see who the shadowy figure was.

Then, inexplicably, I stopped running altogether, my feet firmly planted, my mind ready to see what I had been running from in vehicle form, knowing that I could take up my stab at track minus the field if I didn't like the outcome. I even turned off my Walkman and slid the headphones around my neck, alerting the stranger that I was present and accounted for. I took in all of the street noise, feeling fearless, not caring what anyone might think of my peculiar behavior until I heard someone say something about it.

"What's her problem?" stage-whispered a muscle-bound man of Asian descent to his equally in-shape audience of one, a Caucasian bottle blond.

"Just say no comes to mind," Ms. Clairol 5 replied, his slight traveled in stereo as they walked past me, off to what the night had to offer.

I was about to shoot off a pithy retort, but nothing sprang to mind except "Whatever."

Besides, they weren't really that far off the mark. Granted, it had been a few hours since my last partaking of saying yes, but I didn't think I looked the part. I was still relatively innocent, well, looking anyway. I stood 5' 9", a little on the in between. Weightwise, I was not scrawny nor buff; so I did not feel I was the least bit imposing or held the telltale markings of a drug abuser as seen on TV.

My childhood freckles had seemed to all melded into some-thing that belied my English/Irish lineage and now resembled a tan. The dark brown marbles that took in the world at less than face value had now become hazel, sometimes green, depending on my mood. I could only imagine that right now they were dark as coal, stoking the fires of confusion that raged inside of me.

Right now, they were temporarily blinded, not able to see myself clearly, not able to see my surroundings in a luminous flash, as the car pulled up curbside. It could be the devil himself pulling up adjacent to me, and at this fraction of a second, if he could offer me anything but bewilderment, I didn't know that I would have the fortitude to resist his offers of an easy ride at a high price.

But as luck would have it, I would not have to broach that dilemma. Nick unlocked the passenger side of his 1978 Cadillac Eldorado; its brown elongated body was reduced to a rust color underneath the halogen streetlights.

I had sworn off the palace and its contingency of guards protecting the many secrets behind its flaking gilded walls. I was just about to politely walk away, casually sauntering at a reasonable clip, maybe whistling a little tune, the modicum of nonchalance. It could've gone that way until Nick rolled down the windows with the flip of a button.

"Get in, Bil—Hen—just get in the car, now!" he boomed, throwing out his verbal grenade, splintering his usual casual demeanor; the shrapnel of moist spittle lodged itself into his moustache.

The intonation alone was enough to get me into the car. If I had also glanced in the direction he was looking in, his eyes vacillating between me and something beyond, I would have not hesitated to get in the car in the first place.

The microbus was coming towards us, moving at a molasses pace, followed in not-so-quick succession by George's VW Rabbit. It looked like a funeral procession led by the Volkswagen set. I was still too wrapped up in my head to see it or to ask Nick what the rush was all about.

I knew enough to get in the car, feeling the malaise of twenty-four hours catch up with me in one fell swoop. I sank low into the seat, wishing I had fastened my seat belt a minute later as Nick shot out into traffic, nearly avoiding a collision. If he wasn't careful, I would next see him where I had left him, at the hospital.

A thought struck me with the impact that had been reserved for two cars a moment ago had Nick not embodied a human variation of his cartoon counterpart Speed Racer; come to think of it, he was more like Pops Racer.

Anyway, it was Angel. Something really bad must have happened to Angel! Well, outside of him getting shot, the only thing worse than that was death. My mind flashed the Angel montage, this time including him cleaning the house in nothing but his daisy dukes, singing along with Patti Labelle's "New Attitude."

But a new dress, a new hat, a brand-new idea, as a matter of fact, could not change the irrevocable damage that had been done to Angel or any of us. On a personal level, I wasn't feeling good from my head to my shoes, knew where I was going, or what to do. Perhaps I needed to tidy up my point of view, get a new attitude?

I closed my eyes briefly, unable to shut off the images of Angel; I looked out the window at everything blurring as Nick picked up speed. The scenery blended into the montage now appearing on the window, memories of a certain drive-in movie experience that was now sullied forever, tarnished by the truth and scratched by perception.

As I saw the montage playing itself out reflected in the passenger window, some distant cousin of the cheesy special effect incorporated in music videos to tie in a song from a soundtrack by having the singer interacting with clips from the movie, I happened to glance into the mirror that was hanging on for dear life on the side of the door.

What I saw made me suck in my breath. The microbus was not necessarily closing in on us, but its driver was doing his best to keep up with Nick's impromptu stunt-car driving. Nick was able to move through the traffic due to the pride weekend while chartering his land yacht; actively avoiding Danny was another perplexity that I would be mum about until we were out of harm's way.

Suddenly the microbus gave birth to a smaller Volkswagen, George's Rabbit, as it appeared from out of nowhere on the right hand side, making harm's way seem very far off in the distance.

My hand gripped the seat belt strap, yet it wanted to be on the door handle. I was vacillating between wanting to get strapped in or to take a flying leap out of the whole scenario. Not knowing why this particular chase was on made me opt for the former and not the latter. Besides, knowing my luck, I would eject myself from the safety of Nick's boat on wheels and most likely end up underneath the tires of the microbus. Then Danny could finish the job of pulverizing me, crushing my physical being further along with whatever hope I had held on to.

I took my hand off the seat belt, felt the knot that was growing on my face fueled in growth by the red-hot shame behind its origins. It was nothing unusual for a teenager to be sporting redness on a face, but the case for that was usually clogged pores. No, this came from the clogged mind of Danny. "Not again, oh my god, not again," registered in my brain, and I realized its impact, striking a blow as strong as Danny's fist had. He had done it before, but to who? Why did he do it to me?

Nick dared a look at me briefly; it is at the precise moment that I have not so absently touched the spot where Danny has raised welts of mistrust.

"What happened to you?"

Nick's question penetrated my brain, registering with its point-blank approach.

"Everything. Nothing."

This was the best way I could summarize all that his question meant in its bull's-eye hit and all of the around-the-fringe meanings as well.

I turned away from Nick, hiding my face in the shadows, much like I have spent so much of my life, shadow dancing. I want to zone out, forget everything that has happened to me, is happening to me, and will happen to me. I stare out the window anesthetized, Angel's montage a distant memory.

The stars seem closer tonight, tangible, within just enough reach. I could pluck one out of the sky, put it in my pocket, stockpiling endless wishes, countless possibilities. Alas, I suppose the moment that I reached out, the stars would wink out, leaving an infinite blackness where light once shone. The all-consuming darkness would envelop me; there would be no stars aligning, each one connected to each other, creating a map in the sky. I could not discern any shapes, Milky Way or otherwise, that could be pointed to, clearly solvent.

This was indicative of the events of this particular never-ending day. There were hints that all that had transpired were, in fact, part of a bigger galaxy. Yet I remained a star voyager, hopelessly lost in space. There was more than met what my eyes were not seeing, fine filaments of deception were blindfolding me.

There were forces at work, clearly beyond my comprehension, rendering me semiconscious and a partial human being. To become flesh and blood, I would have to see beyond myself, tear the blindfold off, sunlight burning my retinas.

Nick was doing his best to keep my past from catching up with me via the VW incarnations. Right now, I have to regain a measure of trust—trusting in myself and in Nick, but that was getting to be a more congested road than the one we were fleeing on.

The road I was traveling was potholed with the mysteries I needed to unravel, the center divider of adversity blocking it. My path to freedom had disparity, conflict, and vagueness preventing me from making any exits. There was no green background with white lettering signs proclaiming any semblance of detouring what was the best way to go. For that matter, there were no other signs alerting me what or who was slippery when wet either.

I was trying to make a go of it with a map that held no clear-cut final destination point, only a line that ran upwards on the page where it branched off into several different options. My options resembled fingers that caressed the knowledge that it held in its grasp. If only I could get a firm grasp on myself.

Nick's choice of radio station was playing what I would term a school bus song, "Slip Slidin' Away" by Paul Simon, as it would play on the tinny speakers on early morning journeys to higher education. It seemed that all of the songs I was hearing tonight were indicative of what was transpiring in my life at the precise moment I needed to hear them. "You know the nearer your destination, the more you're slip slidin' away," the diminutive crooner perfectly captured the moment I can feel myself detaching, slipping through the fingers into everything but mostly the nothingness that encapsulated my day, my life. Was it possible to have a midlife crisis at sixteen? I felt I could be the poster boy for the possibility.

Every side street taken, each streetlight that punctured the night with its luminescence made me edgy. Was I doing the right thing by going with Nick? Was he to be trusted? I turned to watch him; his face passed in and out of the shadows. The lights of oncoming traffic reflected off his glasses, giving him a spectral quality, a film-negative image of himself, a hint of a man. I tried again to blend in with the shadows with the efficiency of a chameleon who had more than a fleeting knowledge of a life harbored in the gloom. I thought I had accomplished this task until Nick addressed me.

"You all right over there, kid? I think we lost 'em," Nick asked and informed, trying to dispel the fear that must have been evident on my face.

I checked the rearview mirror for signs of any recognizable forms of transportation. Not seeing any, I let out a breath that would have shamed Godzilla in its intensity.

"Angel, how's Angel?" I randomly asked, his visage in the window miles back.

I wanted to deter any further questioning about how I was when I did not have a concrete answer for that. I only had the weight of the cement holding me still, incapacitating any movement.

"He's in surgery. But it looks good. Wish I could say the same for your beauty mark. I ain't no Angela Lansbury, but let me try to guess who committed that crime. Danny, right?"

My smart-ass proclivities kicked into overdrive; instead I silently nodded, confirming his suspicions. But my mind barked, "Of course it was Danny!" I didn't think some random stranger would do this to me. But I also hadn't figured on Danny providing this particular chink in his knightly armor. He was supposed to rescue me, yet he threw me into the dragon's lair unarmed, and he himself was the dragon.

The big jackpot question in the game show of my life was, why? I would have made a shitty cub reporter, as this was the only question that I could never ask aloud but forever pondered on the inside. I circumvented the who, what, where, and how, always stuck on the why.

"That son of a bitch! When he did that to..." He trailed off, catching himself a little too late, despite his name, not in the nick of time.

He returned to the task at hand of maneuvering through side streets, just in case, our destination unknown to me.

"Not again, oh my god, not again" followed by the "So sorry" symphony were nothing but a broken record to Danny, a familiar tune that had been taken out of rotation temporarily and put back on the playlist for yours truly. How very special I felt, almost as great as if Danny had phoned a certain popular Top 40 countdown DJ for a request. "Casey, I'd like to dedicate this one to a certain, well, a special friend. Can you please play 'Hit Me with Your Best Shot' by Pat Benatar?"

Why, scratch that, how come Danny had sought fit to do that to me? Did I really deserve to be a punching bag, an invisible Everlast tattooed on my forehead, for him to take his frustrations out on?

I felt as though I had walked into a movie at the halfway mark so as to have missed crucial foreshadowing into the true nature of the characters. I closed my eyes, slumped even further into the seat, as I would have had the movie I walked in on been *Out of Africa* and not *The Henry Dodge Story*.

Behind closed eyes, the cavalcade of questions burned themselves into my brain, the synapses firing off embers that just as quickly burned out, smothered by the uncertainty of what the truth may hold. Overload was imminent; my mind knew it should be piecing the puzzle together, each section a question directed at Nick.

But I could not; part of me wanted to remain blissfully ignorant, a West Hollywood idiot savant. Somehow, and I wasn't certain how long it was, sleep overpowered me. I was left at Nick's mercy; hopefully his sense of direction was better than mine was. I had not an inkling of what the new dawn held in its pink-hued horizon.

Chapter 21

Diffused sunlight, soft yet still holding the power of the summer heat that was to come, hit me in the eye, and I awoke with a jolt, sitting bolt upright. Where was I, and why was I naked?

There was a gentleness comforting my body that I would not have associated with sleeping the night away in Nick's car. It would have been from the mattress that was cradling my sleep-riddled body; its counterpart, the pillow, still held the impression of my head in its snowy clasp. Levelor blinds were providing the fragments of slanted light that were now cutting patterns into the unfamiliar room; swirls of small particles of dust danced majestically nearest the light source. I detected a very strong smell; it was that of stale cigarette smoke infused with the lingering odor of last night's dinner, something with seafood. Obviously, I was in Nick's apartment.

I felt like I was in a cave, spelunking new depths without as much as a match to light the way. I saw there was a crevice left by my bedmate. After a moment's time, my eyes adjusted to my surroundings as did my ears. Nick was in the shower from the sounds that were emanating to my left and had gone on a wicker-furniture shopping spree, from the looks of things, as my eyes completely viewed the room.

There was a wicker chair with a blue cushion in the corner that was acting as the catchall for a mixture of Nick and my clothes next to the closed bathroom door. The haphazard way they were strewn on the chair led me to believe they were taken off in a hurry. A wicker dresser that housed a pack of cigarettes, a lighter purchased at an ampm, the requisite ashtray that still housed a smoldering cigarette sat off to the left of its wicker sitting companion, apparently Nick wasn't worried about the chance of a fire.

A mirror was nailed to a wall above the dresser. The suspicious part of me was not yet rousted from slumber; otherwise, I would have gone over and checked it to make sure I was not being filmed. My image stared back at me through the smoky-hued reflection. I saw something that startled me on my right in the real world, on the left in the mirror.

On the white wicker night table sat a jar of Vaseline, alongside it a washcloth still dripping water. Even more disturbing to me was the fact that Nick's two fake teeth were lying nearby underneath a dormant lamp. Not that I was an expert in all things Nick, but he had caused me to believe that he only parted with his teeth when he was sexually preoccupied.

A drop of water from the washcloth dripped from a corner of white, picking up fragments of light that set off the one in my brain. "Oh shit" was immediately followed by "Oh fuck" when I realized what this little diorama of a one-night stand could represent. I checked my backside for any signs of entry by the perp while I slept, feeling less *Cagney & Lacy*, more *T. J. Hooker*, and nothing but confused. I didn't detect any residue from the Vaseline, and there wasn't any fresh sheen from a recently wash clothed ass.

A nagging sensation deeply rooted in the soil of the unknown sprouted from seedling to sap in seconds flat. Much like the book that I had given Kelley in lieu of the Andy Gibb shirt for a present in the long ago, I was having a haunting from *The Green Ghost*. I still didn't know what my medical condition was, and if Nick had slipped me a hot beef injection, then he had put himself at risk. The fact that I had been asleep at the time apparently wasn't an issue for Nick.

I scooted closer to Nick's side of the bed, becoming more awake by the moment, crawling across a white-sheeted desert, to the oasis of the washcloth. Water, water, everywhere and nowhere, dripping from the cloth, but now the shower had stopped.

I assumed Nick had to at least comb his hair or his moustache, leaving me a few more moments to inspect the scene of the alleged crime. Not factoring in that he had two less teeth to brush may have been my undoing. I was in midslide, putting my left hand out in front of my right when it happened. The sound bubble in a cartoon would have read something like "Splatch!" My hand came in contact with some remnants of Nick's folly right at the instant that Nick opened the bathroom door.

"Good morning. Thomebody's got a cath of the hornieth. Don't let me thop you." He crossed the room, came within a few inches proximity of me with a hand sopping up cum, picked up his teeth, giving them a cursory dice throwing. "Need theth."

He retreated to the bathroom, a song in his heart, a certain buoyancy in his step that all but cemented my fear that we had done the deed. Why I was blissfully unaware of it seemed peculiar, but I felt like I had slept the good part of a month away, so it was possible that I was comatose through it.

I got a momentary chill, like ants running relay across my spine, that was just plain creepy. I was not even awake for five minutes, and Nick had planted a new line of questioning in my head. I supposed I could have outright asked him if we had done it, but I didn't want to cause him undue stress. Cause him undue stress?

The stress of not knowing what could be taking over my body as effectively as a pod laid unknown to me by the side of my bed ala *Invasion of the Body Snatchers* had a tidal effect. It flowed out when the other proceedings of the past day overwhelmed me but ebbed back in sooner or later and was taken out to sea to drift. The broaching of the subject may not come to be if I could further substantiate my case, which left me feeling defenseless.

I grabbed at the washcloth, figuring I could further investigate it, while ridding my hand of Nick's residue. I was also hoping against hope that a condom wrapper would be hidden, trapped underneath an avalanche of white, awaiting discovery. I picked up the washcloth in my right hand, trying to balance on my left one, hoping that I wouldn't conk myself out on the wicker surface of the nightstand so that Nick wouldn't have an opportunity to take a stab at unconscious lovin' round two.

Realizing that being on my knees could prove beneficial in a whole different way, I found my balance. Plucking the semiwet washcloth up, peeking underneath, resembling a nervous newlywed lifting the lid and checking the consistency of a dish she whipped up, I looked.

Finding nothing but a sigh emanating from the deepest part of my being, I placed the washcloth down.

I retreated back to my side of bed. Defeat was present; disclosure was imminent. Then a thought came across the threshold: the wrapper could have fallen below, on the side, or behind the bed. My peace of mind was slipping behind the obsession of finding that wrapper! I was determined to find it so as not to have to broach the subject of the why behind it. I got off the bed naked as the day I was born, crawling like a newborn in seconds flat. There was no sign that the Trojan War had been fought, no giant wooden horse acting as a consolation prize for my panicked brain.

"Lose something?" Nick asked with his full mouth of teeth, real or otherwise.

I wanted to answer with, "Only hope."

Instead, I got out of the current position I was in, not wanting Nick to think that my ass being up in the air equated an invitation. I had never thought of myself as a big crybaby, but the waterworks were the only response I could muster through all of the frustration. I slumped against the wicker nightstand so hard that I threatened to topple it; felled was the mighty washcloth and all of its hidden connotations. It landed next to me with a splat on the beige carpet; droplets of water hit my leg and tumbled from my eyes.

"Hey, hey, hey," Nick said with a Fat Albert catchphrase not lost on me.

I could feel the disease grow more resolute with each breath I drew. Any moment now it would pop out of my chest like the infamous scene in the movie *Alien*—unless I provided the springboard and let the information burst forth from me, flowing as freely as the tears I shed. Nick laid his hand on my shoulder, a fatherly, comforting gesture that I wouldn't know from Adam. Rather than elicit more tears, it dried them up in a heartbeat.

Compassion and a friendly touch reminded me of the reason I would need to receive them in the first place. In the shadows of the room, in the mirrored reflection, smoke caressing my image, I had forgotten the bruise that I had received from Danny's anger.

The cycle was beginning, the mere thought of his anger and outburst was begetting anger within me. Stronger than a cup of pitch-black coffee, the sense memory of his betrayal halted the weakness he must have sensed in me to perform such a heinous act. I calmly removed Nick's hand from my shoulder, stood up straight as an arrow, looked him square in the eye, and asked him what was on my mind.

"So what exactly did we do this morning?" I inquired, feeling my heartbeat increase tenfold.

I wanted to give the appearance of being in control, steady as a rock, unwavering in my conviction. Knowing this was not a time for tears or the like, I marveled at my stoicism. I could have pulled the ultimate soap opera move, been facing away from Nick, waiting to hear his answer. Then, once I had pirouetted, my hair flying and exposing a shattered look upon my face to combat any truths I didn't want to hear. But I stood facing him, facing myself.

"Well," he began, "we didn't do anything."

"Then, what's with the…"

I nodded down so as to fully encompass both the Vaseline jar on the nightstand and its companion that I had knocked to the floor, not wanting to give voice to their proper names so as to further disassociate myself from the possibilities that they encompassed.

"Oh, that." A slight blush spread across already ruddy cheeks, an impressionist painting of embarrassment. "I, ah, had some business I needed to take care of. I haven't had someone as good-looking as you in my bed in quite some time."

His eyes momentarily glazed over. I thought I might have to defend myself from a pouncing, but he seemed deep in thought for a moment. Nick slightly shook his head to snap himself out of whatever reverie he was experiencing.

I was relieved that nothing had transpired that would require a lengthy explanation, just a tad freaked out that he had been watching me sleep while he jerked off. Was he whistling "Mr. Sandman" through the gap where his teeth were? Now there was a visual! There was something about Nick that had set him apart from the other palace dwellers, something I couldn't quite put my finger on. He seemed very trustworthy, but there was an underlying creepiness about him. I decided to go on what passed for instinct with me and confided in him anyway.

"Nick, I need to tell you something," I started until the ghost of Danny saw fit to haunt my house; rather than clanking chains or such, his voice floated into my mind, "And you have to promise not to get mad."

The very thought of Danny was enough to stop me from producing the flow of words and achieve some kind of absolution.

"All right, what is it, pal?" he asked, filling in the gap caused by a pesky poltergeist.

"Well, I don't know how to say it," I said in one fell swoop, discarding any semblance of being cool, calm, and or collected. But the truth of the matter, I had never crossed this certain moss-covered bridge before; one misstep could send me over the edge. I assumed a fair dose of tact and decorum was called for.

"George gave me the green trots!" I barked this out before I had a chance to edit myself.

I could tell a few things immediately from the look on Nick's face. First, he was trying to suppress a case of the church giggles. Then I saw him controlling the muscles of his face, not allowing any laughter to escape. His fight for supremacy of his vacillating reaction had given him what appeared to be rictus whenever he attempted to speak. I, on the other hand, must have adopted a look that stated I was clearly not amused because Nick coughed once into his hand, and there was a return to his concerned parental visage.

"You don't have a thing to worry about, kid," Nick's answer was fraught with sincerity and only added to the confusion that was my constant companion.

A multitude of responses bounced around inside my brain, pin-balling, threatening to tilt me. The only one that summed everything up was just one, and its intent wiped the surly look off my face.

"Huh?" I asked.

Nick looked to be on the verge of his "Dr. Helpful and Mr. Snide" routine again, but he managed to rein it in. And that lasted all of ten seconds before he let out a smoker's enhanced donkey bray. His laughter burst into a fit of coughing, resonant and deep. I thought I may have to search out his inhaler.

"Sorry," he said in all earnestness, catching his breath with each syllable, "I am not laughing at you at all. I can't believe that George is still running that scam. It's his way of establishing control in a very sick, diluted way, guy. But that's George."

The stopper was pulled back again, letting loose another barrage of metallic pinballs, all designed to ricochet off bumpers, making bells whistle, lights flash, disabling the flippers allowing entryway into the dark abyss. Each time the ball neared the flippers, I lost any question that I had to ask Nick; my propensity to string along complete sentences seemed to have left me as well.

"Huh?" I inquired again in less than thirty seconds time.

If Nick had a concern about it, he was probably chalking it up to me just waking up. If this was any indication of how the day was to proceed, then it was back into bed, covers up over my head, and count one thousand tomorrows until all of the confusion was resolved. Now, there was another added element to the true nature of the people I had met; with everyone's hidden behaviors flourishing in the summer heat, there was a jungle of deception that lay before me to traverse.

"Well, Henry, it's like this, kid. George is a sick fuck, that's the short of it. The long of it, well, that is another matter entirely. I have known George for a very long time, and since the beginning of our friendship, there were certain proclivities that he has displayed towards the younger set.

"When there is a threat that they might abandon him—God, he would kill me for telling someone this—he would make it appear as though the hapless kid had the green trots, as you so eloquently put it. I am not sure what he used, but he would wipe whatever the concoction was in their underwear, send them off to a doctor friend of his, and voila, he would tell them that they had given it to him and that they now owed him somehow. When he was done with them, he sent them packing, no harm, no foul. Guess he still wanted you around for a little while, eh, kid?"

The freedom of Nick's sentences all strung together with a musical quality that sung the sweet chorus of redemption. Each note, light yet powerful, lifted my soul causing it to dance uninhibited. I had one less thing to worry about; the relief was palatable. I felt a sense of weightlessness followed by the inevitable brick drop of reality plunging me back into the ice-cold waters of doubt. Barometric pressure came forcing its way upon me from all sides trapped fathoms down.

George had lied to me, trying to keep me in check, and had all but lined the exit signs with Post-its. Danny had betrayed me. The only person I thought I could possibly trust was going to be going under the knife; a team of surgeons would extract a nugget of duplicity from him. Why should I trust Nick? Why should I trust anyone?

The bigger question that begged asking was, could I trust myself? By putting my life into other people's hands I left myself open to be an easy target. A target made me think of hunting, hunting made me think of a gun, and a gun made me think of what happened to Angel. If Angel hadn't been coming to meet me, he wouldn't have been shot. It was my atypical logic, starting at point A, skipping the midpoint discovery that would lead to point B. I had glossed over the fact that George was the one that pulled the trigger, not me. My imagination was set afire; self-imposed drama was rife with possibilities.

"Henry, you all right over there?" Nick's voice dripped with a genuine concern.

"Yeah, I guess so." It was the best answer I could come up with as uncertainty once again coursed through my veins.

Would I ever achieve peace of mind? Not with the way my brain had a way of jumping to conclusions while crawling low to the ground, underscoring at every turn. I didn't know if it was possible to proclaim it a national holiday because I didn't have gonorrhea, but I would have thought the elation could have lasted longer than a microsecond.

I wouldn't be Henry Dodge if it was, I supposed. My Billy Collins stronger façade was chipping away, exposing me to the elements.

The need to fill my life with some type of distraction was the fuel for the fire. Any joy derived from it was purely coincidental and soon after became snuffed out by reality. The smoldering embers remained hot briefly, flickered out, ashes scattered on the wind, blowing me any which way. The need to discover had landed me here, hoping that the ash would enrich the soil, causing tremendous growth in the sapling I was. The environment was inhospitable to such growth, all of the soil was becoming bone-dry, and the vultures that were perched on my branches, waiting to feed on my defeat, were capable of breaking them.

In this desert I was an anomaly, a hopeful mighty oak uprooted, transplanted, left to fend for itself.

But isn't that what I wanted, to be on my own, free to make the mistakes that come from forcing myself to become a man too soon? Yes, it was, but I didn't think it would turn out this way. How could I have known that there would be this many fault lines ready to rumble and swallow me whole into the ground? I didn't know that I needed to watch my step so carefully. Now that I did, there was no turning back; it was only a matter of forward motion to get me to be who I was.

"Hey, how about some breakfast, junior?" Nick had crossed the room to the wicker dresser, lit a cigarette, and it was his mirror image that was asking me, plumes of smoke framing his reversed image.

Not remembering the last time I had eaten, I was subscribed to not find it amusing if Nick happened to cook green eggs and ham to celebrate my being disease-free. Not so inexplicably, since both the sun was up and I was breathing, another appetite was pushing itself to the forefront.

My parents should have named me Randy, as that is how I acted. Seeing as I had held back with him, the man of my dreams that was a walking nightmare once known as Danny, I felt that I was overdue for some lovin'. Although I was able to touch his flesh as I had always dreamt of, it was his actions that had gotten under my skin. He was my first abject lesson in heartbreak and would forever be my go-to for all of the failings that men could represent.

"I'm more in the mood to celebrate," I said offhandedly, looking to the right-hand side of the room, then caught his gaze in the mirror, hoping he would catch my drift.

A snubbed out cigarette had its fire put out, Nick's back was present in the mirror moving further away from it, until I had him in my sights and gave him my most seductive look that could have relit his dead cigarette. Objects did appear closer than they would in the mirror as his moustache brushed against my lips, a scratchy and soft sensation.

His small dash from the dresser to the bed cemented the fact that he got me. So I let him have me. My mind-set was dictating the misnomer that there was collusion between love and sex. I was more than willing to forgo the former in pursuit of the latter.

I would become a machine, never stopping, never resting, unable to reprogram the intricate wiring that one brutal touch had wrought defective. There must have been something wrong with me to make Danny do what he had done. Well, fuck him and his McDLT philosophy of living—always keeping the hot side hot and the cool side cool.

I didn't need to second-guess Danny's lack of emotional state. I didn't need anyone or anything. Just as it had always been, I needed myself.

It's a lonely life drifted up from the ethers. I'll give my ghosts credit; they were always applicable. I kissed Nick hard, and we tum-

bled back onto the bed, where we spent the next hour pawing, groping, and the like, wearing ourselves out and catnapping until 11:00
a.m.

I was free, unshackled to the idea that men could offer me any
more than that. At sixteen years old, I was on the fast track to becoming bitter. Should I really hold all men accountable for just one man's
misdeed? I knew only time would tell. Where hours, minutes, and
seconds had once seemed fleeting and random, there now seemed to
be a sense of urgency surrounding them; or so seemed the case when
Nick all but bolted out of bed faster than he had gotten into it.

"Dammit, I'm late!" Tension was evident in his voice, as were
the remnants of a little prenooner that had left him looking like the
pair of paint-splattered jeans that were sitting in front of his closet
door.

He looked down at himself, started with the washcloth, and
realized that he would need another shower to get himself present-
able. I saw my own yesterday's ensemble in the wicker chair, a patch
of blue cloth reminding me that I had left all of my things at the
palace. Well, not everything. I still had the dwindled wad of cash that
had funded this expedition residing in my shorts pocket.

I wondered if all of this had happened to me because of the
way I had acquired the bounty. I deserved all of the negative ions
circling around me, pummeling me with their energy. Nick bounded
into the bathroom, and I laid my head back against the pillow. I
envied Sleeping Beauty for falling asleep for one hundred years; upon
reawakening, she was still as fresh as a daisy and none the worse for
wear. Bitch! I felt as though I had aged myself somehow in the last
few months, but it wasn't in the physical sense, and there was no
Prince Charming awaiting to sweep me off my feet.

The shower started then stopped five times in quick succession,
as if there was operator error on the part of Nick, or he had become
post coital discombobulated. When he sprang out of the bathroom
mere seconds later, I knew it was because the sands of the hourglass
had slipped by faster than Nick had been aware of.

"Are you going to be all right here by yourself?" Nick asked as he
raided his underwear drawer. "I should only be a while."

He emphasized the point with a waistband snap of his tighty-whities. He fished out a pair of socks, hopped on one foot to get the left one on, and repeated the process for the right foot. A white T-shirt of the Big Ed variety was pulled over hair that would remain slightly disheveled, patted down with both hands, in lieu of a comb that was in the bathroom. The paint-splattered pants were thrown on in the same manner as the socks had been. His glasses that had been discarded during the sexual melee were now being placed on the bridge of his nose and behind each ear.

I hadn't really thought about what my next move was. I guess the interim at Nick's would be sufficient. As the sun had moved across the sky towards its sinking point in the west yesterday, my options had become fewer.

"I don't have any clean clothes," I said, not an answer but a non sequitur that seemed of utmost importance.

"Well"—he sighed heavily, looking for his car keys—"I guess we could stop by George's and get your things. I have a key. In the meantime, see if any of my stuff will fit. Or just stay naked, kiddo." He smiled, winked, plucked his car keys up off the floor, where the jeans he was wearing had been hiding them. "I'll see you in a bit. Try and get some sleep and make yourself at home."

His exit line seemed a bit old hat, a tad game show hosty in its delivery—like I had won an all-expense-paid trip to Mazatlán on "The Dating Game"—and reserved for those special tricks that got to sleep over.

I appreciated the genuine concern that seemed authentic. Too bad I had the seed of an idea that was firmly taking root inside of my head, digging itself in deep, and would not react to the Weed b Gon notion that I should extract it from my mind. I turned my head on the pillow, hoping that the thought would exit through my ears. Instead, the tendrils of the imagined roots punctured the down softness of the pillow through the harder fibers of the mattress and into the carpeted floor. I was unable to move my head; there was only one thing I could do to release myself from it. And that was to poke around Nick's apartment.

Chapter 22

If there was at least one thing I had gleaned from my time at the palace, it was know your surroundings. At least that's what I was telling myself as I casually ferreted through Nick's belongings. I had an overwhelmingly strong sensation that I should be doing this for my own protection, just to make sure Nick was on the up-and-up regarding his apparent regard for me. First, I found my clothes piled in the chair, my shoes standing guard at its base. I put them on just in case I discovered something that required a quick escape. The clothes held the taint of deception on them but nothing Nick had would even come close to fitting me.

I checked behind the two mirrors, the one that was in the bedroom and the other one I found in the living room. I was careful not to catch my reflection. I did not want to see if there was an homage to Prince's "Raspberry Beret" resting upon my cheek, or I would walk in through the out door, out door.

There was nothing except another explosion of wicker in the living room. Damn, that must have been some sale! There was a wicker coffee table that had a glass top; a smattering of magazines lay on its surface. I spied an identical twin to the bedroom-bound wicker chair–blue pillow combo, and no room would be complete without a semiflimsy-looking wicker entertainment center.

I looked at the entertainment center with more than a mild curiosity. The television itself must have been only a ten-incher while the VCR seemed gargantuan by comparison and was years older than others I had seen. Well, if the amount of dust that lay across its casing, a fine lunar sand, was any indication of its age, then it was old as fuck.

It was a top-loading kind, similar to a cassette player, with the play, rewind, fast-forward, and stop buttons resplendent with four different colors to indicate what button performed each particular function. It was a good thing for the owner but not for an inquisitive guest as all indications of which one was which had been sandpapered with the passing of time.

I could see that there was a tape in the machine but could not discern what type of movie it was, well, at least not by just looking down upon the black casing of the videotape that bore no markings. Making myself at home had taken on a different connotation than Nick had probably meant for it to have. I turned on the television, it hummed for a moment, the picture tube finally kicked in, and there was light or, in this case, Christmas in June, as snow had overtaken Nick's viewing pleasures. I tried changing the channels, but the weather prevailed on each station I tried. Nick didn't even have basic cable; it was more like he had nonexistent wiring.

Growing up in a household that was slow to grasp new technology's hand, holding it in friendship, rather than rebuking its advances, I at least knew how to work a VCR. The irony of that was that Big Ed was a mechanical engineer by trade and couldn't even set the clock on the VCR.

So number two son was in charge of taping the epic miniseries of the day, like *The Winds of War*. Too bad it happened to coincide with another war, the one between alcoholic father and the brooding son; and oops, wouldn't you know it, the last ten minutes weren't taped. Now, how did that happen? Well, to paraphrase a childhood saying, that's for me to know and Big Ed not to find out.

Finding out seemed to be the theme for today, as I hit the power button on the VCR, set the channel on the television to 3, pressed the green-means-go button, and got an assault to my senses.

All it took was a mere five seconds of footage to have me scrambling to shut off the images emblazoned across my field of vision. The last thing that I had wanted to see today, to be reminded of, was Danny. And there he was, having his way with some other not so innocent on top of a trash can. I felt like I had presented the porn academy with just a sample of the range that Danny encompassed in *Up Your Alley*, submitting it for their approval. Well, it still didn't meet with mine.

After what had happened, I felt like taking the tape from the VCR, ripping a nursing child feeding from its mother, and pulling a Troy by smashing the tape to bits. I wanted to tear the strands of tape from the guts of its devastated body, each yard bringing solitude that there would be no physical evidence of what I had been a witness to; it was the mental residue that I was worried about, that the scene would play over and over on a loop in my mind for eternity.

I left the tape safe as houses, turned off the television, as it would offer me no distraction today. I sat down in a wicker doppelganger, thinking my little scavenger hunt was over. I had discovered something I didn't want to see, which seemed to encapsulate my time in wonderland. I felt that I was constantly tripping over myself, falling endlessly down the rabbit hole. A thought entered my mind from an unlocked back door. Maybe I should go home. Instead of finding anything tangible, I was ensnared in tangled webs of deception. What hold did Los Angeles have over me now with its big-city draw, promising everything and giving nothing in return?

I knew I could stay with Nick, but that was contingent on a couple of things. One, his offer to make myself at home included him picking up my room and board and, secondly, and of far greater importance, that the snow I saw on the television melt away to the spring freshness of cable.

I didn't know if that would be possible from the looks of things. Nick's apartment was not George's palace; it was more like a guest cottage for the servants. In the time and space where beggars can't be choosers, I knew it would make do.

It was atypical of me to not only leave my fate up to the whims of a stranger, but to let television mold the unformed clay of my decision-making process. Ever since I was a child, television had cast a spell over me. Enchantment came from constant viewing; addiction blossomed innocently at first, tender blooms on a small upstart. Visits to *Sesame Street*, *The Electric Company*, and *Mister Rogers's Neighborhood* had sent me in the right direction, while boyhood crushes on almost anything older male had made me cross the street to the other side.

Television raised the bar of believability high, far out of reach of anything resembling reality, which made it the one I ran to for solace. It had also shown me my first ephemeral glimpses into gay life, lasting long after the television set was shut off; the faded pinpoint would reopen in my mind's eye, replaying what I had seen and replacing it with questions that still went unanswered, begging for answers.

Most of the people that I had met since coming out were just like the stereotypical caricatures I had seen as played by on television for years now, and that bothered me a little. Perhaps I was drawn to them, a moth to a television tube; because they reminded me of images I had seen on the airwaves. I wanted to know if there was more complexity to gay life than I had been exposed to, as I certainly knew there was more drama attached to it. I halted my thought process on that one statement; an orange-hued corona surrounded it, giving off a light show, illuminating the shadows. Was that a true proclamation?

When you really boiled everything down, stripping the meat off the bones, didn't everybody huddle under the umbrella of drama, running between the raindrops? It wasn't only the gay community that had the corner market on crisis mode. I had been witness to plenty throughout my life. I had seen enough of it in my homelife; any family sitcom gave me more than the fleeting knowledge that my family was not all it was cracked up to be.

There was that thought again, home, nagging, insistent, complicated. Should I return to my regularly scheduled program that I had sidetracked with my own spin-off? Hell, if it was good enough for Joanie and Chachi, then maybe I could tuck what passed for a tail between my legs and slink on home.

But what was a home?

A place to sleep, eat, providing shelter from the elements in the most general of terms. But shouldn't it also be a place to grow big enough within and leave? An image jumped into my mind of my head sticking out through the chimney, arms sticking out of stuccoed walls, legs knocking down the front door; a home should be a place to outgrow at an appropriate time and not a place to escape from. I could just imagine my return, the never-prodigal son forced into some sort of indentured-servant scenario. Or I could stay in LA and live off the lay of the land, so to speak. It seemed that with freedom there came sacrifice, with sacrifice there came choices, with choices there came growth, and with growth came pain. Who was I channeling, Yoda? Confused was I.

I was thinking of the pain that came from adversity, not of the variety that crept upon you in the middle of the night, stealing from you—like the kind Danny had inflicted upon me. I had to see what it looked like, this physical evidence left at the scene of the crime. Danny had broken and entered my heart; now I was left with nothing, robbed of hope. My hand tenderly rubbed my bruised cheek, treating it with kid gloves, whereas Danny had felt the need to go bantam. I made my way to the mirror that I had actively avoided a short four hundred thoughts ago. I saw the bruise; it felt bigger on my face than it actually appeared. It was like a sigh of relief and a kick in the gut both at the same time. For all that had transpired, I didn't look that much worse for wear on the outside; it was my insides that were feeling the aftereffects of so much upheaval.

Everything seemed to be internal. My exoskeleton was collapsing in on itself, leaving any trace that I ever existed to be open to speculation, just like all that had happened and hadn't been fully explored yet. I stood looking at myself, not seeing anything, only a blank slate, a fragment of something corporeal. I wouldn't feel whole until the irksome questions I had parading around in my head took a detour.

I imagined a marching band leader, baton in hand, making an errant decision, turning left, and plummeting over a cliff. I would have no such luck. Even though I had detoured myself from the task of securing the premises, I couldn't shake the nagging sensation that I was overlooking something. Knowing me, the answer could be staring me in the face while I remained oblivious. I decided it was time to return to my role as *Fagnum, P.I.*, and the answers may come to me.

Approximately twenty minutes later, after rooting through the kitchen and part of the living room, I headed into the bedroom. I wasn't going to take a catnap, but I felt as keyed up as a feline on a catnip-dipped mouse hunt. I was convinced there was something, a shred of wrongdoing that would link all of the happenstances together. Why I thought it resided here, I did not know.

Call it an intuition, a gut feeling, or just a way to pass the time without television. The more my head had cleared itself of yesterday's residue, the shinier all of the relationships would become, almost as shiny as the key that I found in the medicine cabinet in the bathroom. It was hidden behind an old tube of Brylcreem but didn't appear to be as ancient as Nick's need to keep his hair in place.

Now I was getting somewhere. And it only took me a moment to realize that there was only one door that I had not checked as of yet; I crossed a sea of beige, hacking through the dense wicker jungle. The closet door was indeed locked. A bland painting of a seascape hung to its left, belying no malice.

Nick's apartment was almost the antithesis of George's. Everything was oldfangled rather than new. There was no sparkle, only dullness. Even the key that I held in my hand was semi-new but was accruing a little hint of rust from its time in the bathroom climate. It fit into the lock of the door with little effort, but upon trying to turn it in either direction, it put up a fight. Then with a stubborn cork pop, the lock gave way.

There wasn't a light switch, just a lightbulb with a cord to pull for instant illumination. But to turn it on, I had to enter the closet. As I had already broken into it, I had half of my B and E completed. I wasn't sure why the troublesome feeling was residing in my head that Nick wasn't all he was cracked up to be. The simple answer was that I needed to check his good-guy credentials and not be taking people at face value after Danny.

Somehow, a locked door of any variety was a sure sign that there was something to hide. I knew all about hiding and its implications, and had I realized the irony of entering a closet to find the answers rather than emerging from one to do so, I would have busted a gut rather than do what I did.

I walked right into that closet, pulled hard on the light's cord, almost ripping it from the ceiling. And then there was light. I was hoping that the alleged smoking gun would be out in plain sight. The only thing my eyes could see were this: clothes of the late-seventies variety hanging off to the right-hand side. Boxes on the left hand side of the rather large walk-in closet were what my eyes focused on at first.

I walked over to the clothes, handling them as if they were on sale at Chess King, inspecting them with both vision and touch. A pair of gold lamé pants told me that this was both an everything-must-go sale and that Nick had apparently tried out as a Solid Gold Dancer. It was very difficult to imagine that these clothes had actually been worn by Nick at one time, even harder to fathom them fitting him.

There was nothing I could discern from the clothes, except gratitude I hadn't been forced to Saran Wrap my ass in tight seventies couture. I moved onto the boxes. There were ten boxes, five stacked atop each other and five more randomly distributed against the left wall. None of the boxes were marked, and I wasn't sure if I felt like playing Nancy Drew and the Case of the Heavy Lifting.

There was one box that was closest to the door with what appeared to be a scrap of paper hanging out from it. As I got closer, I could see that the paper had a familiar-looking sheen to it. It was glossy, it was a bird, it was a plane, it was porn! I was more than intimate with its look, the velvety texture when caressed between thumb and finger was like pinching a slicing heaven. What I was not expecting was the feeling of disinterest, the clinical nature of search and not necessarily destroy. I may have been down on both knees, but it was only to get a better look at the box and not to get my rocks off.

I pulled it forward with a hearty tug; the box fell over on its side, and the top popped open like a jack-in-the-box. Suddenly, I was assaulted with a seemingly endless stream of nudity. I muttered curses under my breath, mumbled something about being a klutz, and then stopped vocalizing altogether.

As I piled the mass of pages into one complete entity, I noticed all of the images were of the same person. At first, his blondness caused an immediate knee-jerk reaction in my stomach. But as I inspected the immense stockpile of images, I saw that it was not Danny.

Butterfly wings, magnificent constructs of yellow turned flame red, crashing and burning into the pit of my stomach then, like the mighty phoenix of lore, resurrected themselves, taking flight once again. It might not have been him, but it was one of his costars, the one with the penchant for trash can lids.

I hadn't really been paying as much attention to him as I had his costar, but I must have stored his face in my memory. Although I was looking at a magazine layout, I could have been looking into a mirror. There was an eerie similarity between us, right down to our choice of bedmates or, in his case, an alley mate. It was like seeing someone out of the corner of your eye, uncertainty making you turn your head quickly, and then, upon closer inspection, you see that it was not who you thought it was. This perfectly summarized Los Angeles to me so far.

I was staring into the face of what could have been and still might be. There wasn't anything written in the stars dictating a particular route to take. I began the task of putting the multitude of imagery away piece by piece, like I was retracing his career visually. Some of the photos were of him solo; many of them, I would say more than half, featured him and Danny.

These were the pages that I flipped through fastest, as if flames were licking my fingertips, tossing them into the box so that I wouldn't be compelled to rip them up. I finally put a faux name to his familiar-looking face. Corey Adams was his moniker, and I could only assume it was his stage name.

Maybe he had picked his name listening to "Sunglasses at Night" followed in quick succession by "Cuts Like a Knife." Either one of these songs would be very event appropriate for knowing Danny. Just how well, aside from biblically, did they know each other? That son of a bitch! When he did that to…when mixed with not again, oh my god, not again provided the missing person reference that Nick had censored himself on.

I must have born more than just a resemblance to Corey; maybe he had gotten lippy with Danny too. There had to be more to all of this. Switches were slowly being flipped, but the lightbulb wasn't using its full wattage as of yet.

I wasn't sure if this was a pertinent discovery, what I had unearthed from the borders of cardboard, but I pulled one page aside and tucked it away in my shorts pocket. But that was the only thing that was in my pocket. My money was gone! I guess in my frenzy for undercover work, I hadn't thought to check, and my mind was so preoccupied that I hadn't even noticed its weight was not being distributed in my pocket. Maybe Nick hadn't absconded it from me; so far, his apartment had checked out. The cash could have fallen out of my pocket, I supposed. Although I still had a good portion of the cash, my pockets weren't that deep. I needed to retrace my steps.

Rather than retrace them, they stopped dead as I heard the door to Nick's apartment open. I was in my constant state of uncertainty. Should I go balls to the walls and confront Nick about the money when I wasn't completely sure that he had taken it? If he hadn't, then I would feel ridiculous that I had let another man's misdoings alter the landscape of trust.

If I went along as nothing had happened, secretly harboring resentments against Nick then using him, wouldn't that make me just like Danny? It was bad enough that I looked enough like his costar that we could have passed as brothers, so now I would always have that on my mind too. Like there wasn't enough on it already, my brain was a crowded subway car on a Friday after 4:00 p.m.: packed, everyone jamming everyone's space and wanting the solitude of the weekend.

I guessed the best approach was the direct route, as my life had become mired in sidetracks lately. I was just about to step out into his bedroom when I heard a voice that could ignite fire through words spoken.

"Ssso thisss isss your placcce?" he semi-whispered, adding minimal spark to a prevalent flame. "Iss he here?"

"Hang on, buddy, I'll check it out."

His footsteps approaching, I quickly shut the closet door as quietly as possible, moved to the lightbulb's chain with more than a sense of urgency. Before I reached it, my feet almost gave way on the avalanche of porn threatening to upend me. As I balanced myself out, I saw something that reminded me of a *Sesame Street* song, "Which of these things is not the others, which of these things are kinda the same." I spied a piece of paper, not glossy, no nudity, no photo was its calling card, just a headline followed by a story.

I put the newspaper clipping alongside the pictorial of Corey. I managed to get to the light switch and turn it off just as I heard the unmistakable loping gait of Nick. I could visualize him entering and surveying the room, reminiscent of the shaky Bigfoot footage that Ray Patterson had filmed in the sixties. Each footfall clearly delineated Nick's presence as the legendary mysterious monster's heavy steps had marked him.

Pitch-black enveloped me. Dark shadows caressed every inch of me. Fragments of light tore from underneath the door at the sudden eclipse. My mind was alight with an inferno of perplexity; George was here with Nick, why?

From my viewings of the Ewings on *Dallas*, a person jailed for attempted murder could be released on bail. At least that's what happened to Pam's sister, Katherine Wentworth, when she had shot Bobby. But why had Nick bailed him out? Did his loyalty run deeper for George than I had realized? It must have because from the sounds of things, Nick had also procured a new set of choppers for George too.

"He must've taken off. He'll be back. Where's he gonna go?" Nick asked backwards to the living room and George, indirectly asking the question I had been pondering now that I was trapped in the closet.

But it went beyond that moment of solitary hide-and-go-seek. Where was I going? If I had known that, I wouldn't be hiding out in Nick's closet. Could I really forget all of the pieces that equaled up to a lot of nothing right now but seemed geared towards a something? Didn't I want to figure out what was going on? Or was it time to start running again, the ambiguity I would leave behind fueling my trek to escape? Didn't I owe it to Angel to pull all of the pieces into a cohesive picture, instead of leaving it like a discarded puzzle, a sliver of the real picture?

I felt that I did, maybe not as much for Angel as it was for myself. I only wished it was light enough to read by so I could see what the newspaper clipping said. I detected a faint musty odor that hadn't been discernable when the door was open. The air was beginning to thicken, invisible agents placing nonexistent hands around my neck. I had never known myself to be claustrophobic before, but the walls that I could not see were starting to close in on me—but not as much as the conversation that ensued between George and Nick.

"Maybe he went to your place to get a fresh change of clothes," Nick asked away from the closet door, indicating that George had entered the room. I was flabbergasted that there weren't any tremors preceding his arrival.

"Well, he would be in for a little sssurprissse then. When you were waiting in the car, I gave hisss clothesss to a homelesss man. That will teach that little bitch to ssside againssst me."

"I don't understand why you are being so hard on the kid. I really don't think he knows anything," Nick said, protecting my best interest and his.

I wanted to break down the closet door, battering it with my body for added dramatic effect, and scratch George's eyes out. All of my clothes were gone, given away and never to be retrieved. I could just imagine the homeless man sporting my first concert T-shirt, my Oingo Boingo *Good for Your Soul* muscle tee, not understanding the meaning the shirt held for me. Why did George hate me so much? Sure, I had slept with everyone that had crossed the threshold at the palace, but his loathing of me was as surprisingly profound as his allegiance with Nick.

"Oh get off it, Nick!" George fired out with the ferocity of a spitting cobra. "He'sss in on it with thossse little bassstardsss. They sssent him in like sssome sssort of ssspy to sssee if I knew what they were trying to do to me. Why else wasss he there? That'sss why Danny sssent him in."

"Speaking of Danny, he, umm, took out some frustration on the kid." As Nick uttered the turn of phrase "Took out some frustration," I could visualize rabbit ears adhering themselves to the expression.

Even a cute and fuzzy animal reference couldn't hide the ugliness of what Nick had said and Danny had done. But something that George said overshadowed Nick's recanting. George had pluralized *bastard* to *bastards* and had distinctly used the word *they*.

My mind flashed immediately to Angel. Was that what he had really wanted to tell me but didn't have the chance to do so before George had shot him? Was Angel the link between the goings-on at the palace, reporting back to Danny on the sly, and just what form of gratitude did Danny show Angel? They did seem pretty familiar with each other. A twinge of jealousy, like an intrusive back spasm, bit at my brain, threatening to take a huge gulp, swallowing my resolve to hate Danny whole. I didn't let it nor could I. I was caged without bars, ensnared in this makeshift prison because of whatever Danny was doing.

"Oh really? Jussst like with Corey? I knew it wasss only a matter of time before Danny sssnapped again. That'll teach 'em both." George let fly his unsympathetic nature in sentence form.

"George, you do understand the gravity of what is going down here, don't you? It's us! Not them, us! Even without their interference or maybe in spite of it, we are going to lose everything! You shot

Angel! What the fuck were you thinking? They are going to nail you for that. If they put you away…"

Nick began to sob recklessly, a child wailing for its mother or a boyfriend afraid of a future without his partner and a relationship that few knew about.

"Hey, come here. Don't you worry about a thing. We've been through worssse. How about the missusss finding usss in bed and chasssing usss around with a frying pan and knocking our teeth out, huh? Come on, sssmile. For sssome reasson, that always makesss you laugh. You have been with me through the worsssst timesss in my life. We'll get through thisss. Besssidesss, we have an ace in the hole—Corey."

There was the unmistakable sound of the bed groaning underneath their collective weight, teeth being disposed of on the nightstand, followed by slurping noises. Even with a door between us, I still managed to get a mental picture of the clash of those titans, rolling back and forth on the bed, lip-locked, and resembling a pair of mating sea lions.

It was a good thing I was both sitting down and hadn't eaten breakfast as I was having a moment of shock and eww. I was being overly critical of them since I had just dabbled with one this morning and the other not too long ago.

It was my way of assimilating to the information that had literally leaked out of George. My ears were burning, not from what they had said about me, but that the two of them had been secret lovers from way back. Did that mean they were just picking up where they left off from before, or had they gone long term, never telling anyone? So Nick had been run out of town on a rail with George. Why had Troy edited that part of the story?

I sat in the closet with nothing to do but remain silent and ponder. It was a good thing I was now familiar with the name Corey. He seemed to hold the key. Jesus, the key! I had left it in the lock!

Chapter 23

I sat in the dark, like the key sat in the lock, unsure of which way to turn. I could certainly use Nick and George's love fest as a means for escape, seeing as the assorted "Oh yessses'" and "That'th good, babys" were still at a fever pitch, signaling preoccupation.

But what of the afterglow?

I was 99.9 percent certain that George's resonating impression of a buzz saw would cut through the afternoon heat. Nick could go either way, based on the two experiences with him. He could also fall asleep, convenient in its own right, but he could also head off to shower. If Nick happened to spy the key, he might investigate. If he investigated, that could go either way too. He seemed to have some compassion towards me, but would it turn to disgust once he found me in my present location, a location that still felt too confined and was growing hotter by the second, perhaps from summer, perhaps from the passion radiating off the lovebirds?

It was starting to feel tropical, my very own Club Dread. I wished I could see, if only a little bit, and had some paper and pencil. Most of the artists I had studied in art class and on my own seemed to thrive in adverse conditions. Hello, Vincent Van Gogh. I wasn't sure that sitting in an increasingly uncomfortable closet constituted as torturous, but it was boring as all get-out. By latching on to something that was a word I was increasingly starting to hate, *normal*, perhaps I could quell the recent deluge of information.

What exactly was Danny trying to achieve? If George and Nick were so in love with each other, why hide it? Why was I thrown into this mix? None of it made any sense to me whatsoever. I was having the blondest of a blond moment that was neither from lack of intelligence or street smarts, but it was appropriate that I was sitting in the dark.

I was utterly perplexed by the goings-on and certainly didn't know where my allegiances could be found or if I even wanted them to be. It would be very easy to go tearing out of the closet, scamper through the wicker labyrinth in the living room, bolt through the front door, and taste the sweet air of freedom.

But the air outside was cloyingly deceptive, laden with misguided notions that I could just walk away from all of this. Maybe it was because Curious George was my favorite kid-lit character or, more likely, that I felt there were too many perpetual unanswered questions; but I needed to stay and find out what was going on. Now all I needed was a man in a yellow hat to show me the way. Or maybe, just maybe, it was time to do this on my own.

Every time I turned to someone for guidance, it was like touching a hot stove, my hand retracting from the searing heat, and I would slink off and nurse my wounds. Maybe it was about time I started adding some fuel to the fire, stoking the embers of confusion into the inferno of knowledge.

Better yet, I should wear a warning label, something along the lines of "Contents under pressure are combustible." Figuring there was only so much more I could handle before I was an arrow pinpointing visually to the emotional equivalent of you are here.

All of my life I hated being excluded and just got used to it after a while. Whether it was all of the regular boys' non reinqueer games or just slipping naturally into my role of the invisible boy, I had a compelling need to know what was going on, to not feel left out, but never say anything about it.

There was somebody that had always included me, and that person was my brother, John. He had even come up here to help me. Was he still driving around looking for me? He and Danny in some parallel universe of the good ole days of driving around trying to scam on chicks? Now Danny was trolling for man meat, and John was hoping to take me back to my former existence.

I was now living in some grade-B sci-fi schlock fest from the fifties. It seemed that Los Angeles had been overtaken by one enormous mosquito tapping into my inner fears then sucking the life right out of me.

Well, it was time I excavated my natural resources, exposing them to the outside world, unafraid of the consequences, and shunning the pain that could follow. I wanted to beat down the closet door, not that I was locked in or anything, but to show George that I meant business and was nobody's pawn. How dare he give away the few worldly possessions I deemed appropriate to abscond from a life that hadn't fit me anymore. And what of Nick? Why had he taken my money, all but stranding me or forcing me to seek out my brother to save me? I wanted to jump out the closet and clang both of their skulls together. But I could wait. I had the element of surprise on my side, that was for sure. But would I use it to the best of my ability?

A fragment of a song gone by came to me, "I feel so lonely in the belly of the whale." The group, Burning Sensations, that recorded it may have been off the pop chart map now, but that one line from the only hit they ever had clearly defined this moment. I was all alone. The door that kept me in, the walls that should cushion the blows of hurt that had multiplied tenfold, were failing to keep the wolves at bay.

I was left with the facts that I had been too busy, too blind, or too naive to notice. Hindsight was a bitch, foresight a near-to-impossible foe, and both of them seemed to be collaborating in tandem to keep me down. My edification process began as a way to shed some light on my current situation and to diffuse the noises from the squeaking bedsprings, soft moans, and other assorted sounds of the outside world.

I set my mind to remember, willing it to come up with some-thing, anything I had missed before. At first, all of the visuals were as snowy as Nick's TV reception, then I picked up a signal being broadcast from Mars.

For some reason, the first lock in I got was on Nick's reaction to me being only sixteen, his eyes ablaze, like he was seeing me for the first time. Seeing me for the first time and not seeing who? That's where my mind muddled, until I got a mental picture fixed in my brain plus a math problem I could easily solve: Corey on the trash can in the pages of a magazine and my resemblance to him equaled one plus one not being two but one in Nick's mind.

The sheer volume of mementos of Corey's porn-star life, the tape in the VCR, a box full of pictorials, Nick's going out of his way to rescue me—it all had to mean something.

Another song du jour came floating in on the airwaves of my mind, "Obsession" by Animotion. Was Nick helping me because I looked like Corey? Another thought interrupted my regularly sched-uled programming of afternoon Top 40. I did not have my Walkman to shut out the world at large with a steady stream of constantly flow-ing waters, calming as a soak in the Jacuzzi. Wait a second. Soaking in the Jacuzzi was my euphemism for seeking out my secret stash of "borrowed" (I hated to think of myself as a thief) materials for self-gratification. My mind leaped to the logical conclusion that Nick had locked away his fondness for Corey, hiding it from prying eyes.

I thought my time spent in solitary would magically provide answers for the multitude of questions. Instead, it had increased their numbers, like the weeds that would pop up again if you did not pull them up roots and all. It was no use second-guessing, grasping at straws that were inflexible, unwilling to snap my memory, causing an all-seeing, all-knowing epiphany.

Right now I would have settled for the opposite, a nice mind-numbing joint of the variety that Troy had supplied yesterday. My head was starting to hurt, not quite as bad as Nick's from the banging that both he and his noggin were receiving from George and the headboard respectively. It sounded like they were going to either splinter the wicker headboard into oblivion or George was going to be adding on a room to Nick's apartment by knocking his partner through the wall.

He just might have too, with what Nick muttered upon climaxing.

"Oh yeth, oh yeth, oh, Corey," Nick said as a boxful of pins dropped on the carpet. Or that's what must have happened because the silence was sudden and deafening in its own right.

"Excussse me? Corey, isss it?" George sounded more than perturbed and addressed Nick as though he had forgotten his name and was trying to connect it to a face.

But George knew Corey, just not as well as Nick did from the sounds of things.

"Huh? What are you talking about?" Nick said, his voice thick with postcoital bliss that was drifting into a malaise.

"You called out Corey'sss name. Hisss name, why? What kind of game are you playing, Nick?" George inquired, his voice sounding much closer to the closet, indicating he had gotten off the bed. "You know how much I detessst even hearing hisss name, let alone talking about him. Are you trying to hurt me on purpossse?"

I scooted myself closer to the closet door, wishing I had some popcorn to munch on, as this was building up to be quite the drama unfolding.

"I did? Thorry, honey," his explanation was short and sweet. "Come over here, leth finith you off."

I could hear Nick patting the bed just as George's fist banged on the closet door, a booming reminder of his temper and eerily reminiscent of a gunshot.

"Godammit, Nick, you can't jussst glosss over this one! Corey'sss gone, and it'sss all your fault!" He punctuated his sentence with another fisticuffs against wood. And this time there was a knockout.

A small pinhole of sunlight hit me in the eye as the key fell from grace with the lock. My heart immediately began thumping harder. There was always the slight chance that the fallen key would go unnoticed.

"What the…" George began asking as the key hit his bare foot. "You do have a key for that clossset after all!"

"Oh yeah, umm, didn't I tell you? The landlord found the key about a month or tho ago, must have slippth my mind. Now, leave that thilly thing alone and come back to bed." Nick feigned nonchalance very well, even cranking it up a notch with a promise of sex that permeated the air.

I didn't know what the big deal about the key was between George and Nick except that it had unlocked some sort of dissension. What I did know was that I had better make use of the dark recesses of the closet just in case. I chose my left and George's right, a plundering pirate hiding among gold treasures better left buried.

If George did enter the closet, I could certainly put on some of the clothes hanging in it and give him the fright of his life. The ghost of Solid Gold past and present merging into one phantasm that would hopefully be heart-attack inducing felling the mighty Kong of a man.

"Was it the airplanes that got him?" Someone would ask.

To which I would answer, "No, 'Twas bad fashion that killed the beast!"

My only regret was that we were not atop the Empire State Building so that I had the pleasure of watching him plummet to his death. I was harboring an equal mixture of loathing and fear regarding George, and as the closet door opened, fear became the dominant force.

"I think you have sssomething to hide, Nick. Aha, what do we have here?" he bellowed, sounding very "Fee-fi-fo-fum" in his delivery.

I gave myself a heart transplant as my heart jumped up into my throat, lodging itself there to restrict the flow of heavy breathing—or any breathing, for that matter. It was as if time was standing still. There were no seconds ticking by, only a reoccurring loop of assorted gunfire going off in my head to remind me of what George was truly capable of.

"What the hell?" George asked not necessarily to Nick, but to the air in general. I thought he had caught a glimpse of me hiding

among the gold relics, but his next turn of phrase put that fear to
rest. "Oh will you look at thisss? It looksss as though sssomeone wasss
thoughtful enough to ssstart collecting picturesss for a sssscrapbook
on…well, well, well, on Corey."

I could hear the pictorials being rifled through; the frequency
in which George was plowing through them intensified with his
breathing.

Nick defied the law of gravity, sprinting from the bed to the
closet in seconds flat.

"You keep your goddamn handth off of him, off of thoth!"
Nick's face was both determined and crestfallen, a half-baked cake
not sure if it wanted to rise up to meet a challenge. He realized that
he had made a slip up by referring to the pictures now haphazardly
scattered on the closet floor.

"Why ssshould I? It's obviousss you never could! Do you think
I am blind? How about ssstupid? Huh? Ansssswer me!" George was
livid, teetering on the edge of dangerous, terrain he was all too familiar with.

So would it seem that Nick was too; he stood stiffly, bracing
himself for the inevitable hurricane of accusations and unanswerable
questions that would only add bluster to the storm. I was very accustomed to that environment myself, having traded in an actual father
for a father figure that walked the same path. Although George's
behavior was more like an idyllic stroll at first, a nice idea on a lazy
Sunday afternoon, until you hit the steep incline and realized what
type of hike you were in for.

"You knew?" Nick whispered.

"Oh yesss, dear. It wasssn't too hard to figure out. You would
practically ssswoon whenever he wasss around. It wasss very hurtful.
I know the bessst yearsss have passed me by. How could I compete
with that? I ssshouldn't have to." George went from zero to sixty on
turning his anger into pity.

I felt myself feeling a little bit sorry for him, but something told
me it was a ploy. Call it a gut feeling or a tender wound on my face,
which was dictating me to not be as trustful.

All it had taken was just one act to completely and irrevocably shatter my trust in anyone, even myself. It was very easy to imagine that I was viewing this scene, not so straight out of *Masterpiece Theatre*, on television and not through a discrete hiding place complete with gold lamé curtains flanking my field of vision. I knew this was just the first act for George; soon act 2 would begin with his irascible nature feeding him lines.

"You knew?" Nick asked again, sounding hollow, vacant. "You knew!"

He said this less as a question and more of a statement. Something was clicking in Nick's mind, which must have been the mental equivalent of a cookie-sneaking child, single-minded in its dogged pursuit, but not quite tall enough to grasp its ill-begotten booty.

"Of courssse I knew. How could I have not? It was ssso obviousss. Pity that he jussst up and took off. Did he ever call, drop a note, anything?" George waited a moment to gauge a reaction from Nick and mentally tightened the strings on his violin so that his instrument could play a more streamlined pity anthem before he continued. "What did you expect him to do, Nick? Really now, did you think you and he would play houssse—here?"

The last word was said with such disdain that I was surprised that George didn't have a hazmat suit on. That would have seemed to be more conducive to his reaction to Nick's quarters.

"I mean, come on, get ssserious, Nick." George chuckled. "What would a hot young thing like that really want from you? At leassst with mine, I get what I want from them, they get what they need from me, and then I am done with them, no illusssions whatsssoever. What you did with Corey violated a trussst that I had in you. I'll admit I am no ang—sssaint. But we had an undersssstanding. You can look, you can touch, but you can't fall in love."

George tilted his head downward, eyeing the floor. Was he looking for dirt? The reality was he was awaiting a reaction from his lover and was clearly ashamed of his outburst that had vacillated between hurt and his atypical accusatory nature.

"The whole reason I invited you into my busssinesss wasss to prevent what hasss happened," George continued. "I thought I could trussst you, Nick."

"What did you do to him?" Nick whispered a fraction above what was the audible counterpart of conversing with a flea.

"WHAT DID YOU DO TO HIM?" he roared with such ferocity that every hair on my arms was left standing on end.

I was certain Nick's next move would be to clobber George, pulverizing him to ground round. But he stood still, shaking like a jacaranda tree in a strong wind; a flurry of soft petals cascaded then plunged, purple bombs of sorrow exploding upon the cracked side-walks of George's lies.

While Nick had decided to take a stand, George sat on the floor naked as the day he was born, hatched, or sent from the bowels of hell. His perplexed look was priceless, like he had played a game of chicken with a semitruck and lost, but it did not lessen the anger that was raging within.

"George, look at me! Anther the quethtion!" Some of the bite may have gone out of Nick's voice, but he was still firing point-blank, targeting the truth.

"I did what I had to do becaussse I love you. Can't you sssee that? He wasss getting in the way of our happinesss, of our life together. He wasss trying to tear down what we had built," George replied in a noncommittal way, almost devoid of emotion, an automaton reciting a script that was programmed into his brain.

"No, I can't thee it, George. I have been blind to the real you for tho long that I juth can't pretend anymore. You uth people, that'th not mutual, ith a one-way street. I juth bailed your ath out of jail for thooting Angel. I should have let you rot! Why should I trusth you or believe that you didn't do the thame to Corey? I know he wouldn't have juth left without thaying good-bye. You killed him, oh Jethuth Chrith, you killed him!"

He said the last sentence in a raised voice loud enough for George to lunge up and clamp his hand forcefully over Nick's mouth. He had quashed what could have been an argument between Cindy Brady and, well, Cindy Brady.

"Lisssten to me, Nick, and lisssten good, you had better ssshut your fucking mouth, okay? Jussst ssshut it! You know what they are trying to do, to take away from me, from usss. I didn't mean to do what I did. I can't sssay that it wasss an accident, jussst…necesssary," he said this thoughtfully, choosing just the right words.

He truly believed in his own best intentions, but what else should one expect from a self-proclaimed king? He pulled Nick down to the floor, cradling him in his lap, a 250-pound, plus-size baby.

There was spittle flying from George's mouth as he said this, a cobra's deadly venom that had seemed to paralyze Nick. He wasn't moving or trying to fight back. His eyes were wide and unwavering, fixed as a doll's vacant stare. George must have figured that he had lulled Nick into submission, but I had seen this look before. George had induced an asthma attack on Nick with their war of words. George's face became a billboard of concern as a frown furrowed itself deep into his brow, trying to penetrate his thick skull.

"Yes, George, Nick is not breathing!" my mind screamed it even though my mouth had yet to give away my hiding place since the truth, veiled and still somewhat mysterious, was flying as fast and furious as George's spittle. Should I face the reality that George scared me so much more now that I couldn't even speak up?

Nick had begun clawing at the air. George's forehead ceased to crease. You could almost hear the audible click of the lightbulb coming alive in George's mind as to what he was going to do.

As I was plunged into darkness, I realized it had been the sound of George turning off the closet light, and as the door closed behind him, the darkness became all-consuming once again. I popped out of my hiding place, a groundhog unable to see its own shadow or anything at all. The darkness signaled nothing short of a nuclear winter that stretched into infinity. I certainly didn't see Nick's body slumped on the ground, unmoving, silent, as I tripped over and fell upon it.

"Sweet dreams, my prince," I heard the king mutter through the door.

Chapter 24

My head was resting on Nick's chest, and we looked like two lovers drifting off into slumber, snuggled up and keeping the world at bay. The exception being that one lover was wide awake, and the other one was possibly sinking into a permanent rest, from which no alarm clock could ever rouse him. I was just hoping that I could act as a makeshift alarm clock, each prodding I gave him acting as incessant as the annoying beeping. The only sound I could hear was Nick's heartbeat, growing distant, a train exiting a station.

I had to do something, but the fear that I felt surrounding George was rearing its ugly head. I was so brave in my mind; it was my actions that needed better follow through. I felt justified in my apprehension, leaving little room for heroics. He had left Nick to die and had been under the same illusion that an Angel-free world was a better place as well. What would stop him from harming me?

I did not know if George was lurking in the apartment. I had not heard the front door open and close, but then again, I hadn't really been listening out for that. But I did hear something now. It was the sound of my life taking precedent over a possible dying man, an empty opera house featuring a stuttering one man show, "I, I, I, me, me, me!" I was playing to the capacity of one, and my brain held the reverberations of selfish echoes. If I didn't do anything for Nick, I was as guilty as George of…of murder.

I shook off the fear physically; a convulsion-like shiver rattled my cage, opening the door. I acted now with the urgency I should have had before. My Nikes sprouted wings, and I flew like a freed bird and proceeded to bounce off the closet door. I didn't fall down or land on my ass or, worse yet, on Nick, so I resumed my flight pattern.

I put my hand on the knob, and while it moved, the door was proving to be quite the opposite. It wouldn't open! Panic gripped my mind as both of my hands now were wrestling the door. I was pulling with all of my might. Sweat reclaimed its territory on my upper torso, sneaking across the border onto my tank top, and was welcomed as a familiar interloper. My hands became conduits for moisture, causing the knob to slip out of them; even after I would wipe off the sweat, an immediate film would replace the previous one. I needed to get out of this closet, and I was hoping that the results would be different this time than the last closet exit I had made. I needed to hurry, and my own body was working against me, but not like Nick's was working against him.

A voice drifted up, and at first I thought Nick was talking to me, then I realized it was a ghost from television-viewing past, a creature from the boob tube lagoon. This is the worst mess I've ever gotten myself into, the worst! Marcia Brady had dolloped her candy-coated dilemma of two dates for the same night with just a smidge of drama. That girl, and I don't mean Marlo Thomas, did not know the meaning of the word *dilemma*. I felt my brain slipping into the familiarity of diffusing a situation with television references, and I needed to take a break for these commercial messages.

If I didn't focus and figure out why the knob would turn and the door wouldn't open even though it didn't appear that George had locked it, I would find out all about worse messes.

"Oh come on! Come on!" I could hear my voice breaking.

If I was more mechanically inclined, I could figure out how to open the door. If I was a stronger person, I would have kicked

George again. If I didn't hurry up, I could be stuck in the closet with a dead man. It was always about the ifs in my life: if I had done this, if I had said that. I wanted to know about the whens. When would life not be so complicated to figure out? When would this fucking door open?

"You need to puth," the voice, low and reedy, said, some distant cousin of Kermit the Frog.

This time it hadn't come from a snatch of dialogue from the wellspring of arcane television knowledge. Nick had said this. He was alive! The relief was palatable, the sweat was drying up instantly in reversed torrents, and my mind traveled the landscape of pop culture for a brief sojourn.

There was a *Far Side* cartoon where a fat kid in glasses was pushing and not pulling open a door leading to the School for the Gifted. Yet I was still standing in front of a closed door, a fitting analogy of my life. I pushed with all of my might, the door swung open, and light blinded me temporarily.

"I need my rethpirator. In the bathroom. Medithine cabinet. Thecond thelf," Nick said this innocently, trying to maintain his breathing with each snippet of information.

I took it as I needed exact instructions since I couldn't even open a door correctly. I couldn't really blame him. There was time enough to wallow in the shallow recesses of self-pity later; right now, I had to climb a ladder and get over myself.

I dashed more agile, more adept than I ever was in gym class, free to move about without my every slip up documented by the watchful eyes that I was sure were always on me.

I reached the cabinet in no time flat. It helped knowing my way around. I opened it so hard that I thought I was going to tear the door off by the hinges. Something in that closet had transformed me or, in the very least, had given me some sort of sense of the transitory nature of life. I had always heard the expression that life was short, but I never expected to see an example of it firsthand. Mine had always seemed too long, and it was all just a waiting game. I was waiting on other people to show me the meaning of life, waiting for just the right moment to be who I wanted to be.

If I sat by and waited like that, my whole life could pass by, snuffing out the candle I kept in my window, drawing nothing but dead moths. I had it in me to charter my destiny. My intentions had been solid in trying to discover more about gay life, but I had gotten way more than I had bargained for. There had been so much underfoot, secret allegiances, double crossings, and me stuck right in the middle of it all. As always, I seemed to be the odd man out. But I wasn't afraid to step up to the plate and ask the hard questions. It was cards on the table time, and everything would have to beat a queen.

It was a hopeful thought as I closed the medicine cabinet and saw George behind me, hiding in the shower stall, well, his silhouette anyway, and cue the *Alfred Hitchcock Presents* theme. I was waiting for George to spring from his sitting position and ease back the shower door as he must have heard me while trying to remain silent in his measures to remain undetected.

I thought it was a trick of the light coming in from the window above the shower that was casting George's head at a downward angle, giving the impression of sleep overtaking him.

Convinced it was another one of his tricks and remembering the reason why I had come into the bathroom was facing the threat of being shattered in my death grip, I scurried off to the closet. I was torn. While I hated confrontations, I knew one with George was inevitable. But Nick needed me more, and until I was assured he was all right, I would keep it mum that George was here. It sounded logical. It sounded reasonable. It sounded chickenshit.

"Here you go, Nick. There, that's better." I placed the inhaler in his mouth, cooing like a new mother while vacillating my view between him and the bathroom door.

In no time he was breathing normally, the wind whistling through the gaps where teeth should have been, eerily reminiscent of a spectral keening. I noticed my own breathing, rapid and shallow, like I was afraid to let out too much air and, in turn, take any in.

There was only one thing I was afraid of, and it was truly a case of fear itself. But in this instance, fear had a rotund body, a penchant for the younger set, bloodlust coursing through his veins, and went by the name of George. Maybe he was hiding out to see if he was 0–2 in the nearly killed someone category. Or he was hoping to increase his odds by playing a wait-and-see game, making sure he got it right this time.

But he had to know it was me rooting around in the medicine cabinet, didn't he? Was he chalking up Nick's dramatic shadowy weight loss to nothing more than a trick of the light? If I didn't go and investigate, all that would happen was a floodgate of questions would fly open with increased frequency. The only way to find out was the most obvious one, go take a look and try not to emit a scream, go flying out of the room with my skirt over my head. Eek, a rat!

"Did you hear that?" I quietly asked Nick so as not to give his lungs another chance to betray him.

He craned his neck towards the door, taking a more posing for my first nude photo shoot look of trepidation and wonder. He shook his head, preserving and regaining the strength that was returning to him. He resembled a baby bird that had fallen from its nest, not sure if it had really flown or just landed with a thud.

I placed my finger to my lips, indicating it was quiet time, and maybe he should just wait for me to bring him some animal crackers to his mat to assure a sounder sleep. Then it was my impression of the Supremes. I held my hand up, palm exposed, not telling Nick to stop in the name of love but to stay put. I backed out of the closet to further illustrate my point that I was in charge. I would find out what else was going on.

I retraced my steps on the beige carpet, intersecting footprints showing where I had been. They were now being covered over by where I was going. I stepped into the bathroom to a realization. I had not grabbed any type of weapon.

Then again, I did not think that the closet had been an armory, only a treasure trove of days gone by. I looked around the bathroom for something to help me defend myself. While a plunger may prove effective in the disgusting arena, I sincerely doubted that it would provide ample protection if push comes to shove or bitch comes to slap. An open box of razor blades on the counter gleamed in the mellow beams of sunlight that afforded shadows and answers. I hadn't remembered seeing those when I went on my version of a home inspection earlier, and they must have been all but undetectable moments earlier. My mind had been Nick-focused until I spied the long shadow that George cast.

I took a razor blade in my right hand and looked at the frosted shower door. The shadow appeared stationary, unchanging, much like I assumed my life and all of my perceptions would remain. By now George must have known I was a witness to all that had transpired. Or was he pulling a "like father, like son" and having his very own Glenn Close in *The Big Chill* shower moment?

After all, it was a lot of hard work, the art of deception. What with two attempted murders, a catnap in the shower stall was most likely warranted. There was only one way to find out. I steeled myself for the element of surprise that George had become synonymous with. I conjured up images of masculinity to help me cope with whatever was going to be coming my way.

But a cowboy riding off into the distance, a horse between his legs, the sunset at his back, just reminded me of the sketchbook I had thrown away eons ago. I only hoped that strength would not leave me the second I opened the shower door, flooding out of me like water down the drain. I opened the door, weapon in hand, but what defense is needed against a dead man?

George lay silent, nude, dead. George was dead. Some synapse in my brain registered that fact, but I didn't comprehend it. Rivulets of blood were running from his wrists, forming streams on either side of his motionless body, which was the only liquid in the bathtub; he had slashed his wrists without softening them underneath the water. My now discarded razor blade joined his, clanking off the porcelain coffin of George's making.

My mind was viewing the ghoulish scene as if I was one of the many television cops and/or detectives I had watched over the years. This seemed surreal to me. It couldn't be happening.

Something in me was silently snapping, assuredly as a leaf that cannot steel itself against gale-force winds. An Irwin Allen disaster of epic proportions loomed right in front of me. I had always wondered, if placed in a crisis situation, what type of person would I be? The brave hero, a fearless warrior cutting a path to safety? The constantly-needs-to-be-rescued person, like Carol Lynley's Nonnie in *The Poseidon Adventure*? Well, I didn't have the reassurances of Red Buttons whispering that everything would be all right. I wasn't wearing hot pants, but I still didn't know how there would be a morning after the day that was unfolding. I hadn't even had time to brace myself for this sudden turning over of the emotional tide as a wave of sorrow sank me to the bottom of its icy depths.

I collapsed to the floor, my butt striking the hard linoleum; I faced away from the scene of the crime. I didn't feel like crying or breaking into a chorus of "Ding Dong! The Witch Is Dead." The point was I didn't know what to feel. Grief? Shame? Sorrow? Hate? I felt a fraction of the first three and a bigger piece of the fourth emotion. What, had George hoped to achieve forgiveness by this act? He had slunk off to take his own life after leaving Nick to die.

But Nick was very much alive and stood staring in the doorway. His face was unreadable, a blank slate wiped clean. His waxy complexion was either from his own brush with death or George's. I was surrounded by death. It was behind me, in front of me, in the air, and a sign of the times.

Nick slowly entered the bathroom, using the sink area for support, until he spied the razor blades. He swept them to the floor with a grand gesture of his left hand, scattering them like a nervous gathering of birds sensing an approaching canine intrusion, taking chaotic flight. They fell, silent, unassumingly beautiful as the light refracted off their shiny silver bodies clattering on the ground. Their noise of final descent was mixing with what sounded like something strangely akin to a cat in heat.

Nick was uttering a half-mewling, half-sobbing sound that together added up to one whole of sorrow. He crossed the room, more or less in a shuffle, and was resting on one knee, a grotesque version of a marriage proposal.

Under other circumstances, maybe beneath the light of a full corn moon or in the same setting with the light pushing through the window just so, this would have been a magical moment.

As it stood, there was nothing but heartbreak orchestrated to hurt those left behind. Nick was frantically trying to detect a pulse while steering clear of the blood streaming from George. This was an act of love in the highest order. Did Nick develop amnesia from his lack of breathing? Why was he subscribed to helping this man that had been more than willing to let Nick's life flow out of him as effortlessly as water down the drain?

Despite all that had transpired, at his core, Nick loved George.

I did not understand the intricacies of love, certainly nothing near this version of it. I only wanted to experience the kind captured on celluloid and not the variety I had been exposed to all of my life, the dysfunctional kind.

Someone always had the upper hand, nobody wins in the end, and love looked like an exercise in misery.

These thoughts were becoming synonymous, intrinsic in my belief that the same fate would befall me should I ever let my guard down. I needed to make a stand, or at the very least, I needed to stand up and move away from this particular scene of the undying and the dying.

It all felt so intrusive, like walking in on someone you knew having sex. But I didn't know either one of these naked gentleman as they had never bared their souls to me, only the fleshy parts. I rose to my feet, which afforded me a bird's-eye view of the stage that George had set and the drama he had created, a wordsmith without a voice.

"Ssstop touching me, leave me alone." George's voice was onion-skin thin, but the annoyance in it was reminiscent of the nights in bed we had shared together.

After the lovin' and a requisite shower, if I deigned to try to rouse another go-round, that would be the standard response I would receive more often than not. "You can't keep a good man down" was a phrase I had heard over the years, and it always spoke to me of the resilience of the human spirit. How did it factor in for George? In less than a day, he had tried to take three lives, including his own, and his knowledge of Corey's whereabouts seemed indicative that the third time was not the charm.

I was silently cursing myself for every road that led to this moment, as if each backward step I was taking could erase my present location. "It had really seemed like a good idea at the time" was resounding inside the confines of my head. But it wasn't, no, sir, not at all. I wouldn't apply the term *dream vacation* to my days in LA, good old-fashioned *nightmare fuel* seemed more appropriate.

Nothing had turned out as it was supposed to. Fuck, that was an understatement, if there ever was one! How did I think coming here would be better than living at home until I could be sprung by the sands of time slipping through the hourglass that encased me at age eighteen? Like the sands through the hourglass, so are the *Gays of Our Lives*. I was on the verge of getting whiny—okay, whinier—when I was pulled out of my mental state.

"Henry, don't juth stand there. Find thomething to stop him from...from..." He punctuated each *from* with a hit of his inhaler.

I wished it was full of pot for me to smoke and take me on a mental break, but as it was, I would not be using the term, "Hey, don't bogart that inhaler."

I assumed the "From...from" was referring to George bleeding to death. There were no towels hanging in the bathroom, must have caught Nick on laundry day. I didn't want to ask him for suggestions as he was trying to still the fidgety George.

I made my way out into the bedroom, trying to quash the thought of bolting through that door and never looking back. Nick had helped me out, or so it would seem, and had always been kind, reassuring, trustworthy, like a grown-up version of a Boy Scout. Even if I was helping Nick save George, it didn't mean I was suddenly pro George. I guess it showed I had some compassion towards others when most of the time I didn't feel any towards myself. It was like I keep leaving myself off the checklist, remembering that I counted too.

I didn't think that sheets that were now postcoital two times over made for very sanitary lifesavers. I was starting to feel like the even younger version of myself, dashing around the garage to find needle-nose pliers for my father only to discover they were of the regular variety.

The pressure I had always felt to do the right thing, to be the right kind of person, resurfaced, a mud-soaked creature climbing up an embankment, trying to recapture its footing in my mind.

I had been so concerned with escaping my past life experience that I had forgotten to be an older version of the child that was "a good boy." Maybe all of the bad things that had happened to me recently were a direct result of instant karma coming back to bite me in the ass, give or take a few weeks' time. If I had never blackmailed or, as I liked to think of it, talked Steve into forced method of payment, maybe this whole series of events would have never transpired.

I drew the line straight down the middle, sanctioning my thinking to one side or the other. An example, Madonna's recently discovered nude pictures, her reaction was "So what!" I think that's "good" for her, potentially "bad" for her impending marriage to actor Sean Penn. The whole sordid situation could have signaled career suicide. Oh shit, I let my mind wander again!

I knew I was taking my sweet-ass time, distracting myself that George could be dying in a waterless tub, his body providing the liquid with currents of red that were still flowing because I was dawdling, ever the daydreamer.

A small part of me was incensed that George was resurrected. Nick had said it best: he should have let him rot. Each breath he took was an affront, the fact that Nick wanted to save him, appalling.

But I had never been in love, and I did not see myself willing to compromise in the ways I had seen people do so. There was a whole world for me to explore. The age of innocence had hit its peak; now it was truly to be an age of discovery. I wasn't feeling conducive in discovering anything presently, and when Nick asked from the other room, "What's the holdup?" I knew I had to start moving in a new direction.

Nothing seemed to fit the criteria for saving a life that might not be worth saving, which made me immediately think of the cache of yesteryear wear that Nick was holding on to.

Somewhere between a saunter and a trot, I made my way into the closet, retrieved the brightest piece of lamé, the color of a pirate's plundered gold. It was a shirt, but on Nick it could have only looked like a much-stretched-out washcloth.

I heard the crinkle of a certain type of paper, not of the variety on which to draw but the kind I most associated with hiding away.

I had almost forgotten the other forms of paper that had replaced the kind known as currency. When I had some downtime, I needed to read that article; but I didn't see that happening anytime in the immediate future.

I walked into the bathroom; there was immediacy in the air, a frenetic surging of ions mingling with the afternoon heat threatening to overtake every cell in my body. I wanted to fight it, to be the antithesis of anxious, the calm one. One look into that bathtub and all bets were off. The amount of blood had gone from a trickle to a stream to an ocean's worth. I felt faint, nauseated, and firmly grounded in reality. I had no reference point from any television show for this one. Shaking, I handed Nick the shirt, trying to take my eyes off the bathtub; but by turning my head, I had a parallel worldview. I saw Nick spring up. His face appeared in front of my eyes, blocking out his mirrored visage, an eclipse that was contorted in a facial display of rage.

"Wath there really nothing elth you could find? Why did you—" Nick stopped himself, removed himself from my personal space, and attended to George.

There was no further questioning of my reconnaissance skills. I exited the room, unwilling to play nursemaid and more subscribed to play detective for just a bit longer. I completely removed myself from the scene in the bathroom, the bedroom, and found an untainted quality about the living room. Sitting down on the wicker couch, I pulled out the pieces of paper.

Of course, I scanned the nude pictorial first; perhaps there was some kind of clue to be found among the fleshy skin tones on display. Nothing on the first page, just a broad smile that conveyed both knowledge and vulnerability, all linked to his sexuality.

If I glanced at the page in small increments, I could swear that I was looking into a small and very glossy mirror, save for the wrinkles from folding the paper. I didn't think the answer I was looking for was to be found in the pages of *Inches*, so I picked up the newspaper article. I had thought it was going to be something tied to what I heard Nick and George kibitzing about earlier, the untimely disappearance of one Corey Adams, porn star.

The headline from the *Sacramento Bee* read, LOCAL BOY TAKES SPELLING BEE. Huh? My curiosity was equal parts peaked and disinterested. I thought I was going to learn something earth-shattering, something of relevance, not something about a spelling bee. No, I was expecting scandal, the missing piece of the puzzle, not how—

My eyes scanned the page for the lad's name. "Adam Cornelius wowed the crowd with his spelling of *Zoroastrianism*." Wait a second! Besides not even knowing what a Zoroastrianism was, or did, I was more concerned with the name spelled out on the page. Adam Cornelius, it didn't take a lot of fancy footwork to figure out that Corey Adams had just switched his real name around and shortened it for his porn name. I knew a thing or two about false monikers.

I put the paper down and picked up the pictorial, trying to detect anything else that might have shown in Corey's eyes. I noticed they resembled a nightmare, vivid and haunting. There was a distinct sadness to them that no amount of a toothsome smile could extinguish. I saw something in the left-hand corner of the shot, something that didn't get cropped out.

"Henry, come here, quick!"

The urgency in Nick's voice was not beckoning me to come and see some amazing discovery. It could only mean that George was taking his final bow on the stage of life.

Chapter 25

I knew that this time Nick really meant for me to hurry, so that's exactly what I did. Exigency replaced discovery, and the need to study the picture more closely was no longer an issue.

I now knew something I wasn't supposed to have figured out. What I had seen couldn't have been a fluke. I was still unsure of why I had been tangled up in the network of deceit, momentarily brushing aside the webbed residue, seeing with a keener eye.

Upon entering the bathroom, I struggled to maintain a modicum of nonchalance, I felt that whistling would have appeared too uncaring and would have given away the fact that my suspicions were now pointed at Nick.

My mind flashed briefly on the pictorial, on a crumpled pair of clothes off in the distance. Yet one of the garments was very up close and personal right now, skewing my sight line, allowing me to focus only on it now. I wanted to look away from the makeshift tourniquet that Nick had fashioned, but it was if I was compelled to stare as it screamed into my mind, "Look at it!"

There could be no mistaking that what I had seen in the picture and what my eyes were looking at now, minus the blood soaking into the material, were one and the same. I was sure the queasy look on my face passed as natural, given the situation.

But when Nick looked directly at me, I felt as if he knew I had figured something out. The easy thing was for me to play dumb, as I didn't know the full scope of what was going on, per usual. The hard part was not allowing my mind to play its tricks on me; I needed to be running at full capacity and could not afford any stopovers in television land. Okay, maybe one, seeing as it constituted as a trip to movieland anyway.

In *The Wizard of Oz*, Dorothy's arrival to the magical land was heralded with a thud, as her farmhouse landed right on top of the Wicked Witch of the East. This visual kept playing in a loop in my head until I had the feeling I would be picking out splinters for days if I saw it one more time. The house served as a metaphor about what I had discovered about Nick's alleged behavior in Corey's disappearance. Finally, a clue had landed right on top of me, making it all but impossible to ignore.

I wouldn't trust anything until I heard a true confession; even then, I may not believe it. Why should I? What the hell was I still doing here? I wished that I had chosen wisely. But that's what life boiled down to, wishes and choices—wishing to be someone else entirely and choosing to either make that happen or languish in the quicksand of self-doubt and loathing, sinking ever deeper away from dreams with every step.

I felt equally stuck in my decision to be above board and help both of these men when both of them were criminals. I felt there was just one more piece to complete the puzzle I had stumbled upon, and I was curious by nature.

"Bil—Cor—Henry, whatever the hell your name ith, snap out of it! I need your help," Nick said with a tone that was very much on par with being capable of murder.

He had stumbled over my name with one moniker I had chosen for myself to rid the world of Henry Dodge and one that he associated with someone he had taken from this world. With that slip of the tongue, I knew that I had finally fingered the right man. Regretfully, I had done more than show him my private dick. The world didn't revolve around sex, but somehow, it made things spin a little faster for me.

I followed directives, stepping closer to the scene of the crime; every nerve was alive, jangling and kicking themselves into high gear. A fresh sheen of sweat came over me instantaneously, giving me a just-add-water look. I wanted to bolt from the room, not to be drawn closer to not one but two bad men. I thought that the mantra of the eighties of playing it safe was the best route to travel. If I ran, as was my proclivity, I could end up as bachelor victim number 3, and I had a feeling that a fabulous weekend in sunny Puerto Vallarta was not in the cards.

"What should I do?" It was an innocent enough question, but it held so much more in its implication.

"Do you know how to drive? Jethuth, do you even have a learner'th permit?" Nick asked a question and hurled an insult in one fell swoop.

He had a right to be upset, but I didn't appreciate the fact that he was taking it out on me. I could relate with the unmitigated stress. I wanted to lash out, strike back, but I felt helpless. There was nothing I could do, nothing I could say that would be of any use. So I did what I always did when cornered, hurled a smart-ass comment.

"Yes," I answered in a semi-snappy tone, "I can drive."

Granted, this was a shade shy of an all-out true statement. Sure, I was a wiz at Pole Position and Turbo, but those were video games; and yes, I had passed driver's ed. Hell, I had even test-driven John's Mustang II, not feeling very Kelly Garrett, but exhilarated that my brother entrusted me enough to get behind the wheel at age fourteen. The fact that he had called me a natural-born driver and had taken the time to show me how to do something meant a lot to me. It meant more than the world, the universe, or even the entire solar system.

Whereas my father had chosen to not bother with me anymore, John had picked up the slack. Then he joined the Navy, and I was left to flounder and explore new avenues. It looked like I had picked the wrong street to travel, but I had stopped myself from relying on a certain boulevard to act as a stomping grounds. I had proven that I could drive, at least a few feet, when Angel was shot.

There were so many loose ends, and I wasn't talking about the contingency of bottoms that resided in West Hollywood I'd oft over-heard a near dead man and a killer converse about. Everything seemed so up in the air. I should never have gone with Nick. Somehow, he always seemed the lesser of all evils. I wondered how Angel was, where Troy was, what John was thinking about all of this, and why Danny was, well, why Danny was like he was.

The laundry list of concerns showed that I was not someone who learned right off the bat. I was a firm believer that practice makes perfect or, at the very least, practice makes a new experience less fearful. Speaking of practice, it seemed as though my stomach was trying out as a cheerleader, doing cartwheels, somersaults, and a series of high kicks all geared to catch my attention.

"Well then, that'h good newth. My keth are on the kitchen counter. I need you to get the car ath far ath you can to the front door. I don't want any neighborth to see, goddamn nothybodyth, they'll ask too many quethtionth. I can't have that again. Anyway, most of them are probably at Gay Pride. Think you can handle it?" he inquired, disseminating a few more kernels of the truth in his directions.

There was a hardness to Nick's features that hadn't been there before. His eyes looked beadier, his features more porcine-like. The sweat matting his "shoulder length yet balding on top" hair only added to the juxtaposition it truly was, and the moustache now had a villainous overtone to it. Perhaps unknowing eyes had not seen any of this before and had slowly been opened. My naivety seemed like something that I had become unshackled from, breaking free of its constraints, allowing me to stumble from the darkness.

I walked out of the room with nary an utterance, smart-assed or otherwise.

I had wanted to yell in his face, "Put your teeth in or get an interpreter!" Yet I knew I should have been frightened, perhaps terri-fied, of this state of affairs.

I felt nothing but numb, coldly indifferent to what the palace redux and its bargain-basement politics had meant. The king was slowly dying, the dynasty was unraveling, and another killer was poised to usurp his throne. After this favor, I was done, out, kaput, riding off into some distant horizon on a horse with no name as my destination had not been charted.

There was a great deal of trepidation upon walking forth into the kitchen and spying the keys. Should I take them or languish in my head with a rousing pastime known as mental masturbation, going back and forth until the obvious conclusion was reached?

I wanted to be sure, deliberate in all future actions, since my keen senses had failed me up until this point. Something inside of me told me the inclination should be towards going out the door, if only for a break in scenery and perhaps to toil more of the "what to dos" of life.

I grabbed the keys from the counter and was just about to leave the kitchen when a shocking image affronted me in the reflection of the getting-to-be-a-relic stove from the seventies.

I looked distorted in the smoky mirrored glass of what appeared to be a microwave complete with orange, brown, and yellow paneling and metal push buttons. There was no digital display to let Nick know when it was time to take out his chicken pot pie.

My no showering for close to twenty-four hours together with the purple marking of Danny's duplicity stopped me dead in my tracks; Nick wasn't the only one with a newly acquired hard-edged look. I looked changed, older, and like a refugee from Billy Idol's "Dancing with Myself" video. While I didn't expect myself to win any beauty pageants, I also didn't think I would have looked like I got the short and, apparently, gnarled end of the ugly stick either.

My mouth felt like I had swallowed an entire field of cotton, and I was just on the border of smelling ripe. A cold indifference settled over me, icy fingertips tugging at a learning heart. But what had I learned really? That life could be cruel and unforgiving at this space and time did not serve me. I was deeply disturbed by all that had been going on, all that had enmeshed the falsities of an existence that I was not equipped to handle.

I was trying to draw upon reserves of strength that were nonexistent, tempering them with false hope and diversion. I would never see the world as a hopeful place awaiting my arrival. What point was there in fooling myself any longer? I had gotten exactly what I deserved; that was the second blast of arctic chill that blew in from the east, riding on the doubts of uncertainty, gaining momentum, leaving no time to prepare for the encroaching storm—a storm that was favoring low digits in the negative, sudden in its assault, weakening any type of defense I had. I was an Eskimo building an igloo in Fiji, ill prepared by the sudden shift in climate, location, and reality.

I had spent my whole life hiding from the truth of who I was, where I could go, and what I could do. This was so abundantly clear, this epiphany, and so goddamn real that I wanted to revert back to something I could never be again—naive. My eyes had been peeled open further than I had expected, allowing all that I had ever done to appear as a misty apparition, an unreal life lived by someone else. I had always wanted to be somebody, to have a voice, to come off better than I actually was.

And now, I couldn't pull that off. I probably never did and certainly could never pretend to again. Things were happening at a rapid-fire pace. All of the pretext of what I needed to glean about myself, they didn't mean anything at all. The men I had encountered weren't lessons-learned material; they were examples of what not to do. Why I felt any kind of responsibility to any one of them was beyond me. They'd no sooner sell me out in every sense of the word, trying to keep me in my place, then they would genuinely care about me.

Well, I wouldn't let them get to me. I would be damned if I would let them have that kind of power over me. It was time I took matters into my own hands, not idly sitting on the sidelines for things to work themselves out. It was up to me to, maybe not as much right a wrong, but to just have some dignity and walk like the man I had always intended to be, the man who was still becoming, always afraid of shadows.

I resumed whatever destiny had in store for me and walked out the front door into the blinding light and blazing heat of summer. Unfortunately, I had forgotten to put on my shoes and could feel the

371

pavement beneath me reaching up with a searing heat, burning holes in my socks. Each step I took away from Nick's was marked with a footprint of fire.

At least that's how it felt as I made my way in a half-run/half-hopscotch way across the parking lot. I didn't want to enter Nick's apartment, not even to reclaim footwear or my Walkman. I didn't need distractions right now. I only wanted to focus on how I was going to pull the land yacht out of the slip and get it close enough to Nick's apartment while remaining mild mannered.

With the keys in my right hand jingling with every hot step I took, I was surprised that I didn't warrant any attention from any neighborhood children who may have mistaken me for a pathetic version of the ice cream man. I was just being paranoid that my every move was being scrutinized; much like Rockwell, I always felt like somebody was watching me. From the look of Nick's apartment building and his accurate accounting of his neighbors' whereabouts, it appeared as though I had nothing to worry about. That was until I tripped, and the keys went clattering underneath Nick's behemoth of a vehicle.

The last thing I wanted to do was slip underneath the car on slightly cooler pavement that was currently causing my feet to feel aflame. Luckily, the keys had not gone that far beneath but still far enough to cause me to bubble like pizza topping if I got on my hands and knees to retrieve them.

With an ingenuity that was more or less a byproduct of flexibility, I grabbed on to the driver's side handle, positioning myself just so. My legs and feet were now swapping places with my arms and hands, a self-contained trapeze act. I could hear the keys scraping along, felt the grooves that unlocked doors and kept secrets between my toes, and saw a familiar microbus pulling into the apartment complex parking lot.

I was almost done, almost out of here. Why did Danny have to show up with his impeccable timing? The proverbial "If you were the last man on earth" coming to join the fray. I took the quickest of glances around. There was somewhat ample parking, yet there was a space next to Nick's car, and something told me that was where

Danny would park. I unlatched my hand from the door, signaling that the show was indeed over. I pulled something akin to Dick Van Dyke's advice on what to do in case of a fire PSAs of my childhood, and stopped, dropped, and rolled, Dick, rolled.

At least that's the part of me that found the keys. The pain lasted a moment, nothing was punctured, and I wasn't incinerated on the spot. The ground was much cooler than I had anticipated, but therein laid the problem. My penchant was for supposing how things were going to be, a predisposed assessment of how situations would play themselves out that were drastically different from what transpired. Wasn't that what had gotten me into this more than a mess? Hell, I would need one big ass roll of Bounty to clean up all of the messes that had spilled around me, and even then, its super absorbency would be hard-pressed to meet the challenge.

Danny, as predicted, pulled into the space next to Nick's Cadillac. He was barely in park when his door banged open, and I spied his tanned legs as though I was peering through a mail slot. Then the view became 3-D as my brother's shoes were suddenly less than a foot away from me, yet I had never felt farther removed from my family in my whole life.

They were starting to take residence in some compartment near the back of my brain, boxed in mental storage, awaiting a firm piece of masking tape to seal them up. I couldn't believe that John hadn't just up and gone back home, writing me off as a hopeless case.

I was surprised at the speed in which the shoes were gone, taking their owners with them at a furious pace, leaving me in the dust of a conundrum. The Clash had musically summed it up best when I was in eighth grade, "Should I stay or should I go?"

If I left now, I would miss all of the fireworks. A smaller part of me wanted to see some retribution paid by anyone, whether it was George, maybe not with his life, then with jail time. Danny could get the short end of a fist from anyone, and Nick could bunk with his clandestine lover in cell block H, for all I cared.

Besides the fact that it would be harder to walk away without any shoes or the small loan Nick had procured without asking for. But who needed shoes when you could drive or at least attempt to drive? It seemed a viable alternative, although a little voice popped up and said that maybe it wasn't such a good idea.

My emotions were twisted more than a double helix, and their juxtapositions were equal in weighing out my options. The first step was to get out from under the car. I did this in no time flat, still careful not to be seen, the story of my life.

I was feeling even more disheveled now. I ran my tongue over my teeth in an attempt to appear deep in thought instead of coming away with a precise answer; all I took away from the experience was a "moss has grown onto my teeth" feeling.

I was a mess, pure and simple and in every context of the word.

I had to at least get closer to the heat because the Power Station had been telling me all summer long, via MTV and KISS FM, that "Some Like It Hot." Maybe I didn't have to stand directly on the burner, but I could see or, rather hear, what I could find out by partaking in a favorite pastime, eavesdropping. I had never learned anything I needed to know by confrontation, so why not go with what I knew?

A few quick hops, skips, and jumps later, I was positioned between Nick's bedroom window and a cloyingly sweet-smelling jasmine on a trellis, withering on the vine, neglected; I felt an instant kinship with that plant. Nick had actually left his window open what could only be described as a tad, and I could already hear voices being raised but semi-muffled, as if being spoken into a cloth.

"What the fuck are you doing in here? Do you not underthand the conthept of knocking? Get out, Danny, and take your trick with you!"

He was vacillating between an authoritarian, outraged teenaged girl, and a spiteful ex-lover. From the sound of his voice, he was not in the bathroom and was pretty near the window. I drew back to the left so as not to be detected.

"Where is he?" I heard John ask, just short of barking out an order.

I could now pinpoint Nick's position as the white curtain pulled back, revealing him facing away from John and Danny, signaling that the show was about to begin. His white cotton T-shirt had caught some of the brunt of George's "accident." There was no mistaking two things: one was that they had not caught Nick in the middle of a spaghetti lunch, droplets of tomato sauce delicately and treacherously soaking into his J. C. Penny white tee, and secondly was that it was a good thing that I had stepped back. I was still close enough to hear him whistle through his nonexistent front teeth. The sound was hauntingly familiar to a train on a smaller scale.

"He's dead," Nick all but whispered for Danny and John, but his message was loud and clear to me.

"You son of a bitch!" John yelled then rushed him, from the sound of quick footfalls I heard.

The next thing I heard was Nick's body shaking the window frame so hard that the screen fell out, clattering softly to the grass-covered ground. His arm was poking through the divide between window and open air, the last wave of a drowning man, before it was retracted back inside. I did not think it was of his own volition. I could hear someone delivering a series of punches to Nick that sounded like bags of wet sand being pummeled.

"Danny, get off him! You're gonna kill him!" my brother said, vacillating between true concern for Nick and an outright sense of fear that his childhood friend was a madman.

"You killed him! You killed him, just like you killed Corey! I knew it wasn't George." Danny interspersed each word with a punch.

I moved myself closer to the window, squatting down so as not to be seen. And this is what I saw. Nick was protecting his body with the palms of his hands acting as defensive shields, but he looked like a slower version of Wonder Woman ricocheting bullets off her bracelets. Each time he went to defend himself, Danny was on to a new spot.

John stood dazed. The look on his face clearly looked like the equivalent of "What am I going to tell the folks?" His face was the essence of pain; I wanted to shout out to him, "Here I am!" But Danny's response was still in progress and had created a huge knee-jerk reaction in me. I knew what it was like to be on the receiving end of his fury, and I could see I had gotten away lucky. Even though it was not me on the floor, pitifully trying to defend myself from the antithesis of the laid-back surfer, each blow directed to Nick pained me nonetheless. John snapped out of his haze of sorrow momentarily and saw fit to restrain Danny from unleashing any more pain.

Nick immediately got to his feet; he looked infuriated, and that was replacing any hurt, physical or mental, that he may be feeling. Anger was coursing through his body, spreading out in red patterns from his face down to his neck, adrenaline acting as the catalyst, sending its soldiers off to fight the battle.

"What do you know about George, you little thit? All he wath to you wath a meal ticket! Look at you, thill hungry after all this time," he said in a raspy and belabored voice. "And how were you going to pay him back? By trying to take his buthineth, poithon his thon, Angel, anyone who would lithen to a nothing like you. Do you really think that he didn't know whath been going on? You're the one that thould have died, you tharted all of thith, your betrayal coth George hith life!'"

I was surprised there was no residual smoke from his endless chain-smoking piping through his ears, and his well source of nick-namery had fallen by the wayside as well.

Nick turned his back on my brother, and a man who would be king reached for his pack of Marlboro Lights, and looked in my general vicinity while putting his ampm lighter to use. He exhaled deeply, his eyes far off, unfocused, lost in the clouds of smoke surrounding his head.

My head felt a touch in the ethers as well. Taking over a business hardly seemed Danny's style, especially one that sounded as boring as accounting did. The only number Danny needed to be concerned with was one and how it could equal destruction when multiplied by the root of pie singular. Again math, not my strong suit.

Toxicity radiated from him, striking down those within close proximity. Nick was right in using the term *poison* in association with Danny because that's all he had to offer this world.

Well, if a lifetime of dreams hadn't recently been shattered and cooler heads had prevailed, I am sure that I would have seen his more obvious qualities. The bitter part of me screamed, "There aren't any! Move along, nothing to see here." He only had one thing to offer the world at large, and he had demonstrated that with Corey in an alley. Washed up at twenty-one was a sad state of affairs made only sadder that he had thought he could overthrow the king.

Hey, wait a minute! Danny wasn't looking to procure George's cushy number-crunching office; he wanted to usurp him as Studio City's answer to Hugh Hefner for the we-swing-this-way male set. I must have forgotten to feed the squirrels that ran around inside of my head, collecting bits of information to process in a timely fashion. Now, they were kicking it into high gear, making a connect-the-dots pattern, an outline of supposition.

I could only imagine some of what Nick had accused Danny of as not being the rantings of a grieving secret lover, which brought me to wonder, was George dead? I hadn't been gone but, what, five minutes tops? Had the good fight been fought and lost by one bad man? Seemed a little more than suspicious to me, now that the squirrels were back on their regular route of curiosity equals knowledge. Also suspicious was the scene playing out before me.

Rather than throttle Nick some more, Danny slunk to the floor; apparently he was in good practice for sinking low. Danny had tried to overthrow a kingdom without a shred of nobility running through his veins. But it appeared there wasn't ice running through them either. Danny's sobs silently racked his body; he looked as though he had a very bad case of the hiccups. I would have been more than happy to put a scare into him to make them stop. I knew Danny had brought me into the fold, but why?

"Where is my brother? Where is he?" John implored of Nick, but he was looking at Danny, clearly disgusted by the goings-on and wondering like I was, "What had I gotten myself into?"

"He took off," he answered nonchalantly and with a puff of smoke, indifferent to the fact that John and I shared any kind of lineage. He looked directly at me, knowing that I could speak up and say, "No, I didn't."

But he was counting on me to not show any backbone, just as I had exhibited so many times before. I watched from the sidelines, a director getting a feel for a scene before interjecting with a cry of "Cut!' But this scene had not been scripted. Nick had something up his sleeve, and I wanted to observe how it would play out before I determined where to edit myself in.

"When did he leave?" John asked, giving no room for doubt that he disbelieved Nick. Why should he? I was born to run.

"You juth mithed him. Now if you don't mind, I want to be alone, so get the fuck out of here. Go find your precious cargo, Danny. Go find your replathment for Corey." Nick absently stroked his moustache, not quite as effective as a Snidely Whiplash moustache twirling, but his dissemination of information, the eye contact, it was all meant to finally fill me in. I was a porn pawn, a pinch hitter that didn't want to be up to bat.

"What are you talking about? Who told you that?" Danny looked up with a tear-stained face.

"Oh, Danny, thertainly you know that dead men tell no taleth. Pleath leave, now!" Nick roared, threatening to shatter all windows within a three-mile radius. So much for keeping a low profile.

Without a word, my brother John exited the room. I heard the opening and closing of the few doors that were in the apartment. Nick raced out of the room, a mother bear protecting her cub. Danny was left alone in the room. The way the sunlight was playing off the tears on his face, the inherent sadness from within springing forth onto the surface of his face, actually made me feel sorry for him for a moment.

And just as quickly, the moment passed.

So he had sent me in George's direction to make me a fallen star even before I had the chance to light up the night sky. He wanted to reclaim his glory days by tapping me to replace Corey. Unbelievable yet so true to form for the man that Danny had become, extinguishing any of the boy he had been, the one I had my first crush on.

"Danny, get in here and call off your dogth!" an agitated Nick commanded from the other room.

Danny, proving that he was no better than an unreliable mutt, slunk off to the kitchen in accordance with Nick's wish only to be ready to bite at the first chance he got.

The bedroom stood empty, silent, and ready to receive visitors and fulfill its duty as a welcoming center for any that crossed its threshold. I didn't know if climbing in through a window counted as a threshold, but right now, I felt safe that whatever protocol I was taking would be just fine and/or dandy. I slid my arm into the space between the window and air, minding the gap and taking great pains to not let one iota of noise be heard. That would not be an issue, as Danny, Nick, and John just started their own version of *The Bickersons.*

"I know that he's here! Henry? Henry!" John called out, a mile shy of calm, cool, and collected. I wanted to respond in kind, but I was performing a death-defying stunt not to be tried at home: climbing through the window with the greatest of ease.

"You both need to leave, juth get out of here!" Nick was closer to pleading than I had heard since we had done the deed.

"Not without my brother! You tell me where he is, or so help me, I will have the cops over here so fast—"

John would have finished his sentence, but Nick pivoted on point and clocked John hard and fast across the temple. I didn't think Nick had acquired superhuman powers able to render much younger and stronger men unconscious, but he felled John.

I was worried for a fraction of a second as I made my way to where my shoes had been. John had always shown an inner strength that I wished would have been passed on to me instead. He doesn't like taking drugs, so he stopped. He didn't like our homelife; he joined the Navy. But wasn't I more than similar to my brother? In fact, wasn't this whole crazy scheme just a larger sign that I had what it takes to make of my life what I will? I showed some sort of tenacity in coming out to my parents, of actually proclaiming, "This is me, this is who I am."

Hell, neither one of my parents could fess up to who they had become: my father, nothing better than an abusive drunk, my mother some faint offshoot of an upstart suffragette wanting to make a change in her life, unsure of how best to proceed, so she withdraws back into her hermit crab shell.

If I was a combination of these two people, where did that leave me? I could ponder the complexities of interfamily relations all day, seeing as I was exercising avoidance, breaking and entering, and nothing short of cowardice.

I wanted to help John, but what could I do? I was afraid Danny's pendulum mood swings would be akin to the hypnotic quality of his penis, undulating seductively, capturing me in its spell. I knew that I had to get out of here. I was feeling very self-possessed in my endeavors to remain undetected.

If anyone caught sight of me, it was curtains for my one-man act of self-seeking. I wanted to just make a clean break, no fuss, no muss, be on my merry little way. It may be proving more than a difficult task at hand as I could hear calamity approaching. Those with a penchant for hiding in the shadows know what to do in cases of emergency, so I scampered under the bed as fast as I could.

"You touch me again, I'll rip your fucking arm out of the socket, fat ass!" John's entrance line left little for the imagination. "And you"—I could tell from the anger intrinsic to its wellspring of annoyance at Danny who John was addressing—"stop your bawl-babying and help me find Henry. You're the one who got him into this."

There it was, the Dodge family credo: someone else was to blame. Nobody in my family could have ever penned Howard Jones's "No One Is to Blame" because somebody outside of the family had to be at fault. I wasn't about to correct my brother. I was just waiting for them to leave so I could follow suit.

Then a thought hit me as clearly as my ears picked up the unmistakable sound of John restarting his search by opening the closet door: whatever happened to the fourth grader with the Andy Gibb shirt, the boy who had taken a stand? There wasn't any more room in my brain to ponder. I was on overload, dangerously close to a meltdown, especially when John's shoes came into view, stopping inches from my hiding place.

He was going to look under the bed and see me, and he was going to see me like he never had before. A deep part of me, unfathomable in depth, wished that my brother had never been privy to any of this. I scooted as silently and as best I could towards the other side of the bed until something dug itself into my side.

I reached down and felt a familiar body. It was my Walkman, and lying next to that were my shoes. Now, if only the money Nick took from me was somewhere to be found among the dust bunnies, I would be all set.

"Get out of my houth! Get out!" Nick could have been channeling the demon that had haunted *The Amityville Horror*, but I knew that he had met his quota of unannounced houseguests, especially those of a suspicious nature.

I watched John's shoes move away from the bed, over to the closed bathroom door.

"What do we have behind door number three? Oh Jesus!" John was pumped full of adrenaline from his fight with Nick and felt that all rush out of him upon viewing George's body.

Nick raced to where John was, struggling with him to close the door, playing the ultimate game of forestalling the inevitable that George's death would have to be dealt with. What they should have been more concerned with was the barely audible gasping for breath sounds that George's not yet a corpse body was besieged with. John won the war, but Nick put up quite a battle to shut out the allied assault on his home front.

All I could see were feet shuffling to and fro, bodiless entities engaged in ill-conceived choreography. But my ears did not fail me when I heard John say that George was still alive and that an ambulance was going to be called.

While Nick and John resumed their homage to the *Footloose* opening credits sequence, taking their show on the road from bathroom to living room, I took that as my cue to vacate the premises. I shuffled out from under the bed, a crab making a sideways trek.

With my Walkman in my right hand, my shoes dangling precariously between my thumb and index finger, I crept back to my entrance that would now serve the dual purpose of becoming my exit, dropped my shoes and Walkman out of the window, and followed in that pursuit.

I was just about to finish swinging my right leg over the windowsill when a voice loud as a clap of thunder threatened to knock me into the yard.

"Open the door! Police!"

Chapter 26

The sound reverberated in my ears. Ten thousand pots and pans dropped from the heavens, clanging down the sides of skyscrapers on their quick descent, adding to the cacophony. I didn't need a rain shower of cookware to strike me in the head to realize that the arrival of the police heralded the quickest route back home. The best thing to do was to just get away, as far as I could, never looking back.

I didn't care what happened to anyone. I was just a momentary blip on the radar in these people's lives, there one moment, gone the next, a phantom apparition. I felt a momentary pang of guilt for my brother's involvement in this, but I had an inclination that he would never look at me the same way again. I would always be lumped into some faction of societal outcast, and his being thrust into the world I had discovered did me more of a disservice that I would be able to lead a happy and, dare I say it, normal existence.

Wasn't that what this sojourn had been all about in the first place, being accepted? Flash-forward to a few months later and I was still no closer to finding that elusive creature, still tracking it through the underbrush. I supposed somewhere in a hushed corner of my mind, Leonard Nimoy was resurrecting one of my favorite seventies

TV shows, *In Search Of,* narrating it in secretive tones, using stock-piled memories as file footage.

The only thing I was close to being was back on the ground as I swung my leg over the window's ledge. But in my rush to evacuate the scene of many a crime, I miscalculated my dismount and landed with a resounding thud. I could not breathe; all of the air had been knocked out of me. I felt paralyzed, unable to even crawl away at a snail's pace. The longer I remained pinned to the ground, the sooner I would be discovered. And as two hands grabbed me around my waist and hauled me up, I saw the curtains in Nick's apartment appropriately close behind me in the just-starting-to-stir breeze.

Why hadn't the police added in their unwelcome greeting, "We have the place surrounded?" That would have been pertinent information to have known. But now, I could only guess that the jig was up as the two hands, entities in their own right, pulled me up and backwards. I was rendered speechless, having been given the Miranda rights by countless television cops over the years; I knew I had the right to remain silent.

"Don't say a word," a familiar voice whispered into my ear; the faint odor of a pot-laden breath drifted in my general vicinity.

The arms dragging me back were suddenly familiar, as was the sensation of déjà vu. I had been in the same position with this person before, albeit we had been nude in his father's guest bathroom. I turned my head slightly to make sure I hadn't suffered a concussion and was hallucinating this. Troy's handsome face, backlit by the midafternoon sun, all but resembled a mythical god of sorts, his blond hair a corona of fire, yellow radiance.

Any and all rights I may or may not have been privy to went out the window, albeit a lot more adeptly than I just had. All of this time, Troy had been the dark horse to bet on. It made sense in hindsight; we both had pretty severe father issues to work through. Maybe we could do that together?

And there it was, the thought process that always got me into trouble. The supposition that the other person would want or even consider what I wanted as being one and the same.

I was the epitome of the little brother, surviving on scraps of hope, scouring for any semblance of nourishment on which to feed, forever pulling on shirttails, all but pleading to be included. But when the answer was yes, my feet did nothing short of a happy dance, my feet flailing wildly, something akin to a human counterpart of Snoopy when it was suppertime.

After all of the double crossings, I was still willing to take Troy at face value, no questions asked. I had thought naiveté a thing of the past, yet here it was, The Ghost of Christmas Present. Inertia of the mind compelled me, had dictated to just choose the alleged lesser of all evils.

I really couldn't take much more, but right now the only snapping that I heard were Troy's tennis shoes traveling over fallen twigs. His dragging of me backwards was very forceful, and I assumed that he was thinking the same thought; our brain naturally in a mind meld of synchronicity, time was of the essence, on our side, and a clock of the heart.

I wanted to halt the process, walk on my own, but I figured that would break whatever enchantment had been put into place to have blinded me from Troy's irresistible charms that had been previously undetected. Besides, if I couldn't strike back at Danny physically, dating his best friend would deliver the effect of any sucker punch—quick, instantaneous, knocking him for a loop.

When we were near the parking lot, Troy swung me around, backing me up against the building. I was hoping for a star-crossed lovers' kiss, music swelling, with the audiences' imagination left to ponder, "Why can't I find a love like that?" Instead, Troy's face left nothing to the imagination whatsoever; he was enraged.

"You tell me and you tell me now! What the hell is going on in there?" he asked this through gritted teeth.

His voice was free of the playful nuances I had experienced when he was stoned before. There was nothing evident of that, only the fury that he had displayed more often than not.

"Is my father in there?" he asked an inch from my face.

I looked off to my left. The microbus and George's VW Rabbit were sandwiching Nick's Eldorado. It had been Troy and not George that had been tailing Danny, tailing Nick and myself last night. It made sense. George had still been in jail, singing the jailbird blues, and his son had charmed his way out somehow. Now he was following another Danny behavior, taking out his anger on an innocent.

Crestfallen is the word that best describes the immediate sensation that overtook my very essence. He wasn't dragging me off to his lair, some modern-day version of a caveman, but his Neanderthal qualities were immediately remembered as being tempestuous. I was straddling the very fine line between fear and outright panic. Or it was as complicatedly simple as post-traumatic stress.

For I was shell-shocked, a thin reed blowing in the wind, ready to snap. I didn't have the strength to create words, form a logical thought, or remove myself from the immediate danger lurking around every corner.

I stood still in my self-imposed game of freeze tag, feeling as though every circuit that gave me the sustenance to live had blown, fizzled, then exploded, leaving nothing but darkness. Words were betraying me, my mind playing tricks on me. Troy's head was replaced with that of Danny, but the voice loudly roaring at point-blank range was none other than Big Ed.

"Answer me!" he semi-bellowed, looking back at the partially opened window.

Everything here had been half full or half empty, and I had expected more, wanted no less than perfection, and had gotten nothing in return. My brain could fire off snippets of full-fledged thoughts pared down to mere shadows of their origins. I wanted to answer, speak the words that would quash his anger, water added to a raging firestorm. I could only provide nothing more than gasoline, stoking the flames higher until they licked the skies, blocking out the sun on my darkest day, the light from a funeral pyre my only illumination. And if I didn't speak now, there would be no forever holding of my peace. Either way, there was going to be a showdown, even though it was well past high noon.

I opted for my now-patented nodding without speaking. It felt like there was a ten-point degree of difficulty involved in performing this feat of Olympiad strength. Troy's fist unfurled itself out of its knuckle-dragging position and found the space between the end of the building and my head.

I was not the object of his affections nor his anger. I was just there at the ready to take on everyone else's pain and suffering, all the while stuffing my own. Troy wasn't moving backwards, only forward with his rage. But I heard a clear, distinct snap. It did not come from the outside world, only from the inside one, the place I had found so much solace in.

The snap intensified in volume, a crescendo of sounds that could only be identified as worlds colliding, mixing, and dissolving. The one around me vanished in the blink of an eye as I imploded the inner one. Everything I had never wanted to think about myself became as crystal clear as a winterscape, yet I was no longer snow-blind.

I had always thought of myself as a loner, but in truth, that was a falsity. Fear had been a constant companion, unwavering in its belief in me, only daunted when I chose to believe in myself.

When I stood up to challenges, it let go of my hand and head long enough for me to realize what a shallow kinship we had formed since—since always. My life had always been mired in dread. The what-if game invented innocently enough was in actuality a byproduct of fear, most likely stemming from the anxiety I always held deep inside of me. What if someone found out my secrets? What if I wasn't truly loved, only an inconvenience of a human being? What if? What if? I had spent my entire life constructing how life should appear, breaking ground on a shaky foundation, only concerned with the exterior.

It was time to bring in the demolition crew, wrecking ball, explosives, whatever it would take to knock down these years' old conceptions of myself.

I hated being at the mercy of others, yet I thrived on it; satisfaction was derived from being juxtaposed. I opened my eyes, perhaps seeing for the first time in years, and this was the first visual to confront my retinas: anger and rage contorting Troy's face into a death mask.

A dissonance was clearly reaching my ears, but I was unable to decipher the message it carried in its hateful song. The only sounds were of a heartbeat, gradually picking up steam, causing the blood to flow at record speeds, drowning out any other living thing in my ears, and creating a red hue in my field of vision.

There were no more distractions, only reality, which had taken possession of every part of me, no pop culture references to fall back on. I was live without a net and ready to take the plunge. I removed myself from the wall, a spider descending upon an unsuspecting snack. Troy was too busy moving his mouth, so I acted on an impulse and shut it for him with a well-placed punch.

I was hitting at injustices, both real and imagined, striking out at the world. Each time I landed a blow, I didn't care if it was inflicting damage or not. Then suddenly, I did. I was lashing out at Troy, a mere conduit to take my aggressions out on. He had triggered something primordial in me, Troy had unknowingly become an archetype for those who had angered me and was receiving the brunt of that wrath. I had knocked him to the ground; the element of surprise was the greatest weapon in my arsenal.

He was covering his head, fetal in his position, on grass that should have been cut weeks ago; its long, green stalks were surrounding him. I stopped my fist at the juncture of thought versus action, halting its swift descent. My fist unfolded, a lotus blossom opening, my fingers a divining rod seeking out the cool waters of forgiveness. I touched Troy tentatively, softly, as if I were stroking the fur of a dog I had just kicked.

His reaction dictated that he had just been prodded with an electrical jab. But he remained stationary. Troy didn't stand bolt upright in no time flat, looking like a live wire seeking a place to most effectively dump its unbridled power source. No, he looked fragile and haunted, remaining in the position that was most associated with awaiting birth.

"Oh shit," I said, "he got to you too."

Troy uncovered his eyes; tears had burned sad canyons from his eyes to his cheeks. He was taking a page out of the book of Henry Dodge. He silently nodded as more rivulets traced Danny's trickery. There was no mistaking that certain terms fit Danny; *blight* sprang immediately to mind. A scourge upon humanity ran a close second.

His kind of love was akin to a swarm of locusts come harvest time. He was hungry to give love a chance at first then able to decimate hope, cutting through it cleanly, effectively and devouring whatever feelings had been there in the first place. His appetite was proving to be voracious in its destructive nature. All that was left was a fragment of what the person had been. And in this moment, I was feeling no better than what he encompassed: a piece of shit with a brain but no heart.

The anger that I had misdirected at Troy rerouted itself with only one person in mind. I stalked off as fast as I could, moving from the slightly ticklish without anything being funny greenery to the slightly cooler hard concrete. My shoes and Walkman remained on the ground, commemorating the exact spot where I had taken a mighty leap into the great unknown. I didn't care that the police's announcement had been the momentum on which I had sought escape. In fact, it was lucky for Danny that they were present; he was going to need them.

The door to Nick's apartment stood open, not wide, not a crack; it fell somewhere between the two. I could hear slightly muted voices that weren't coming from directly behind the door but from another room.

The door creaked in my hand upon opening it ever so slightly. I was feeling very keyed up; every synapse was firing off in a rapid, hypnotic way that was lulling my brain into thinking this was a good idea. My sweating issues had returned, serving a different purpose on this go-round. It felt cleansing, almost like bathing in the waters of a rebirth. Salvation was at hand, hallelujah.

I had exited this apartment scared of what life had in store for me. I was returning fearless, ready to face up to any challenge. Even if that challenge wore a badge and carried a gun, I would remain undeterred in seeking out the one who caused so much pain, force-feed him retribution. He could choke on it for all I cared.

I followed the sound of the voices, alien in their pitch and frequency through the saturation of blood pumping inside of my ears, an ocean's mighty roar. There was no one in my immediate sight, which meant only one thing: my focus was to be the room I had made a not-so-stealthy escape from only moments ago.

I crept through the wicker graveyard, surrounded on all sides by it, each piece of furniture an obelisk marking the path to where the dead awaited. The slightest tremor of trepidation rang a hushed bell in my mind. Something was not right.

Somewhere in my mind a switch was flipped, and my "alien to English, English to alien" translator brought me again into the fold audibly.

"Are you sure he's out?" a voice from the bedroom inquired, drifting in on nonexistent wind and sense memory.

There was a familiar quality to it, something heard in a dream yet not entirely recognizable in the realm of the awake. A small bolt that was holding my bravery together unscrewed itself from my brain, followed in quick succession by several more. Fear was being ratcheted into the place where the bolts were vacating. Something wasn't right and became abundantly clear when I peered through the crack between the wall and the door, which afforded a minimal view that spoke volumes.

John was lying spread eagle on the floor, unconscious, dreaming the dreams of the uninhibited, when the voice from shadowy corners of my mind spoke again.

"Jesus, I guess I must've hit him harder than I thought."

The owner of the voice only filled up a quarter of the room without a view from my vantage point.

His back was to me, and his body language was dictating a rigidity that conveyed both a concern for my brother and for himself. His arms encircled one another, hands reaching out around the sides of a slight frame, straining to find an ounce of self-love via his attempt to hug and protect himself. His shock of white blond hair move into frame, begging to be noticed. He was no cop, that was for sure.

"You're not a cop, are you?"

I received my final confirmation on who it was with that snatch of dialogue that exploded into my brain. It was Rocky, he of the boulevard set, counterpart to Pollo, keepers of the gate but not necessarily the faith. They were more apt to run from the cops than to lend a helping hand in catching a thief when they were in fact stealing from themselves, trading in on looks that would someday be gone, youth that would be borrowed heavily against.

"It's okay, he'll live," said the voice loudly behind me that belonged to Troy, a sonic boom of a statement.

It wasn't happenstance that he had arrived on scene at just the right moment. His tears had all dried up, and he wore, pardon the expression, a queer look on his face. He grabbed me by the two straps of my tank top, guiding me into the bedroom.

Rocky took a quick step back, dancing away from my brother with no musical score to accompany him. He was not keeping to the beat of a drummer. No, it seemed that he had received his marching orders from Troy. As always, the biggest question I had was why?

"So, Henry, are you on the bandwagon to dethrone my father? Well, get in line! There's quite a succession of people in front of you. Why, there's Nick." His right arm shot past the side of my head, pointing to the chair in the corner that had housed all of my worldly possessions not so long ago.

Nick appeared to be catnapping; somehow I figured that he and my brother were in a forced state of sleep. He was also strapped to the chair with the remnants of Corey's gold lamé pants bound at the wrists and ankles.

"And Danny, now where is he? Oh yes, that's right! He's returned to the closet. He's so at home there."

I was shocked at the 180-degree turn in both directions that Troy had taken.

Suddenly, and as if on cue from Troy's narrative, Danny began pounding on the closet door. With a nod of Troy's head, Rocky approached the closet and gave the door a hard knock of his own.

"Keep it down in there unless you want something to happen to your little friends."

Rocky, dumb as dirt, looked at Troy with an "I did good, boss" look fixed upon his face; he was then giving me one that said, "I am so much better than you."

At that same moment, he went to hit the door again and struck his hand hard against the doorknob. He sputtered like a motorboat for a few seconds, latching on to one curse word and then another in a rapid stringing together of them all as one. Big Ed would be proud to call him a son. Troy didn't pay him any attention, indifferent to the core. He had all of the earmarks of a self-proclaimed dictator, a regular chip off the old block. Obviously, nobody had bothered checking the bathroom yet. Rocky's veiled threat seemed to quiet Danny down for the moment.

Standing here in the middle of it all, I began to feel the reserves of strength dissipate, running out of my body in the form of sweat. Fear, my intimate partner, grasped my hand, and within that grip was a welcome familiarity, an instant reconnection that told me it would always be there for me.

I didn't want its kinship. I was taking a liking to the new and improved Henry Dodge, now with flavor crystals, a chorus in the back of my mind bellowed. The pop culture references were trying to reclaim their territory, climbing up an icy slope, establishing their foothold, soon to plant the flag that would indicate the province as theirs. I knew inside there could never be any going back, any pretending that I would ever be the same from any of this. I was in the viper's den with men out for glory, forsaking all others in the process.

My comprehension of the word *man* had taken on many other meanings that I had not signed up for. Treacherous, manipulative, yet ultimately shattered creatures were the men that I had fallen into favor with. They fed off each other's frailties, undone by jealousy, lashed out like piranhas, seeking out a weaker creature that happened upon their part of the river, reducing it to nothing more than bones in a matter of seconds.

I couldn't let them get away with any of it, for Angel, for Corey, for myself. The arrival of Troy heralded something closer to what the truth had to offer. I allowed only one pop culture reference in, as it was deemed appropriate. Perhaps Troy, like any good Bond villain, would inform of his intentions and then flee the scene, assuming he had the upper hand.

Mayhap, I had to extract the information from him, carefully mining the darkened depths of his perfidious heart until I could tap a vein that would equal informational gold. My mind whirled a mile a minute, trying to latch on to anything resembling a plan of action. Troy released me from his stronghold.

"Hey, Rocky, keep an eye on the troops. Gotta go drain the flying squirrel," Troy informed in his best Bullwinkle voice.

So now he was back to doing his voices, an obvious chink in his tarnished armor; but how to exploit that weakness? While I was still looking for a possible solution, Troy let out a horrified gasp upon spying his father barely clinging to life. With the audible shock wave came the answer I was seeking. Rocky rushed to Troy's side, ever the faithful lapdog always hoping to curry his favor.

He turned back from the room almost the instant he reached it, looking like a bottle blond version of Anthony Perkins in *Psycho* upon discovering Marion Crane's body and his mother's handiwork. Another pop culture reference drifted in on what I hoped would be the winds of change.

I realized I was experiencing my own armor chinks, my defenses were depleting, and I needed to act before I lost the gumption to do so. I strode across the room, sidestepping my brother's still unconscious body. I could have untied Nick, let Danny out of the closet, but I needed to take this stand on my own.

Mentally, I affixed a pair of roller skates on my shoeless feet, and replacing my blue tank top was the toothsome visage of one Andrew Gibb. While that particular impasse circumvented my usual pleasant demeanor and the outcome may not have been what I was hoping for, it did serve a valuable lesson over the course of six years. I could remain complacent, or I could do something to change the way my life was going. I passed by Rocky, standing within whispering distance of Troy.

"He did it because of you." I let that statement hang in the air, invisible particles dancing in the late-afternoon sun.

He turned to look at me. There wasn't any anger prevalent upon his face, no red-hot temper causing solar flare-ups, only the cool blue awareness of what might possibly be true. He glanced back to his father, motionless in the bathtub, his lifeblood starting to dry and harden upon the white heavens of porcelain.

I braced myself for any answer from him, desperate not to let down my defense of a lie. Fields of cotton, billowy and plentiful, resided in my mouth, clenched teeth acting as a barrier, sturdy white soldiers guarding the fort. My jaw was locked up tighter than a snare drum, the music of my voice inhibited, tuneless. Errant streams of sweat made the familiar trek down the side of me, all marching to the increased palpitations of my heartbeat. My eyes flitted back and forth between father and son, disengaged, certain that the pulses emanating from the veins on either side of my neck are going to give me away.

Troy opened his mouth, a fish out of water, looked away from his father, and directly at me.

"You're right. He did." His speech pattern was fast and choppy, put into a blender and set for puree. "Oh my god, what have I done? What am I doing?" His eyes were far away, unfocused, as if he was remembering the specific instance that had brought him to this place in his life.

He crumpled to the floor, a paper man with his head in his hands. The little boy in me wanted to yell out, happy that I hadn't cracked under self-imposed pressure. But that would destroy the image I was trying to uphold. And I was right in keeping up appearances.

Apparently, Troy's show of emotion went against the grain of whatever hold he had over Rocky. He bolted from the room, the apartment, the negative vortex I had happened upon, making me realize he was smarter than I gave him credit for. At least he knew when it was time to go. I felt as though I had overstayed my welcome in Los Angeles a few moments shy of forever.

Troy was a broken man, and I had hit the right button that shattered him, just like a Rock 'Em Sock 'Em robot from days past. He looked up at me. There was no emotional output on his face, and it had the eerie pallor of a chalkboard that had been wiped clean; there were traces of him amidst the blank.

"What did I do? What did I do?" With his left leg tucked underneath his straight-ahead right one, chin resting on left knee,

Troy proceeded to rock back and forth, seesawing between to tell the truth or not.

"What did you do, Troy? What are you talking about?" I figured I was on a roll with the direct approach, might as well utilize it before it all dissipated.

"Corey."

Chapter 27

I took in a huge amount of air, let it out as a very audible gasp. Troy was behind the mystery of Corey. I saw him begin the fish *o*'s with his mouth and knew that soon enough I would learn the answers. I heard him begin to explain, starting with a single word, *umm*, then halting it, looking backwards towards his father. He turned his face upwards to look at me, all of his ferociousness washing away from the duress of both his secret and of grief. I wanted to prod him, every word an electrical charge that would get the truth out of him faster. I was done talking; it was his turn.

And from when he began to the time he finished, I remained enraptured, as if I were being told the most amazing tale that had ever been recanted. And it was, all of it as fascinating as being told by your mother about the first time you spoke or walked.

As he began telling it, first John then Nick drifted into the doorway and finally Danny; each one had helped the other out of their temporary prisons. I didn't even notice, so caught up in the yarn that was spun from the truth. I was the one locked up and unconscious to anything not being verbalized by Troy.

Upon his arrival in Los Angeles, Troy had taken a particular liking to Nick for purely selfish and warranted motives. Then they became altruistic in nature. Troy could confide in Nick in a way that he couldn't with his father. Nick could be listened to, something that George had stopped doing. Soon, that kinship became a cornerstone for a mutual attraction neither could deny. And they acted on it one afternoon in an all-too-familiar setting: George's den.

Unbeknownst to them, George had sensed a kinship between the two and had left his camera rolling day after day, hoping to mine the caverns of deception he thought both his lover and his son were capable of. Thus was born, *Chicken Hawk 2*, making Troy both a very unwilling participant and a great discovery in George's underground porn ring. George was not only an accountant, his little side projects were netting him quite the financial bonanza, selling as quickly as they were created and always leaving patrons clamoring for more.

All the while, neither of his sequel film stars knew that their exploits were making the circuits until a man cautiously stopped Troy on the street one day to tell him how much he enjoyed his work. Troy brushed it aside, not thinking much about it, until it happened for three days in a row. Finally, with the third man, Troy feigned a sexual interest in the bald-pated gentleman in his fifties. After arriving at the man's apartment, only interested in fact-finding in his mind and letting his body language dictate otherwise, the man, Lester, held up his coveted copy of said sequel.

The box itself was of a semi-professional nature, something that might catch your eye at the local video store, but with one exception. There was no picture, no title to make you say, "Hey, that seems like a fun way to spend my Saturday night!" But from the look on Lester's face, a half leer, half look of amazement plastered and held together by crow's feet, Troy knew this was more than his Saturday-night thing.

Troy went in for what, judging by the sudden occurrence of the erection in his pants, Lester was hoping for: his close-up with his porn star du jour. Troy knew that the only way to find the answers was to view this must-see film. Somehow he didn't think he was going to be blown away; but he suspected that's what Lester had in mind.

As of that moment, Troy had nothing to go on, only a three days in a row coincidence. What harm was there in indulging this man's fantasy when, in fact, he didn't know what the fantasy was about? Rather than out and out ask the man, "Can I see what's on the tape?" Troy would rely on using his male wiles. He drew himself in closer.

"It would be hot to watch the tape while we're doing it," Troy observed casually.

Without another word spoken and as if he were partaking in a private race, Lester rushed to the VCR; utilizing the adeptness that any chronic masturbator knows, well, like the back of his hand, Lester had the movie on in a matter of seconds.

There, not in glorious Technicolor, were he and Nick killing a particular rainy afternoon exploring each other's bodies. There was no awkwardness displayed on screen, just a natural ease: the same kind that Troy had taken to with Nick, far outweighing the timid experimentation he had previously dabbled in. He hadn't wanted to give in to the revelation that he was indeed his father's son. But he was, and here was the living proof, muted but speaking volumes.

"So where did you get this?" Troy nonchalantly inquired as Lester resumed his close proximity.

"Ah come on"—Lester adopted conspiracy tones—"you know."

The temper that was always bubbling just under the surface struck Troy with its voraciousness, a white-hot fireball. The point was, he didn't know and felt that Lester was mocking him with his whispered cadence. He had his suspicions, and they were pointing at Nick, just as the protractor in Lester's pants was pinpointing due north.

Lester exhibited all of the earmarks of a love-starved puppy, and Troy knew it was not in his makeup to fulfill that hunger. He reached out with his right hand. Lester closed his eyes, awaiting nirvana. Instead, he received the rough end of a shove, knocking him back, landing his slightly ample portions on the carpet. Troy strode to the VCR, hell-bent in his intentions; Lester called out from behind him.

"I like it rough, Sonny," he cooed.

"What did you call me?" The fireball exploded into a million pieces, each one of them burning with the intensity reserved for a supernova.

"Umm, Sonny?" Lester would have excelled at *Jeopardy!* as he answered in the form of a question.

Troy couldn't hear anything after that, just the dull thud of his heart being supplanted to his throat, blocking out his surroundings. Jesus Christ, that was his childhood nickname given to him by his father!

"Sonny, take out the trash."

"Sonny, help your mother with the groceries."

"Sonny, I have to leave, don't cry."

The last time his father had ever called him by the nickname was the same night that he had been banished from the Niles household. The last time his father had ever called him that, all of his original teeth had been intact. A mere moment later, his mother, hysterical and fearing the well-being of her son, had made sure his father left knowing exactly how much damage he had inflicted upon her, upon him.

Somewhere in his heart, in the part he liked to keep protected, Troy realized that his father had suffered too. So it surprised him that he had started to travel along the same path as his father had, keeping his sexual proclivities to himself, being especially sure not to divulge any hint of his true nature to his mother, forever reeling from the betrayal. And now, he had betrayed his father, and his father had upped the ante.

Not needing to acknowledge Lester's presence or his pleading, Troy headed first to the VCR then to the door and over to his father's apartment. Finding no one at home and not wanting to, Troy slipped inside. He made it to the VCR, the tape held so tightly in his right grip that the edges were leaving indentations.

The tape he popped out of the VCR was inconsequential; all that mattered was the tape in his hand. He stood in front of the TV watching the ghosts of familiar strangers; a shadow reflected on the screen. Of course, it didn't take Troy long to figure out the angle from which the film was shot. The eyes, covered by a pair of Ray-Ban sunglasses of one of Nagel's models, probably stared at him. The slight smirk she wore, usually construed as sexually enticing, was nothing short of mocking.

He had never noticed before that the artwork held an "I've got a secret, and it's yours" quality about it; perhaps that is what compelled his father to choose it. At least he could theorize as to why his father had acted a certain way in that instance. On other subjects, Troy could not even fathom the why behind his father's actions.

Troy took the picture down, and like much of his father's life, it was nothing more than a façade. Somehow, George had constructed a one-way see-through glass. The Nagel print was nothing more than an etching; strategic spots allowed for different camera angles. Where the picture had hung, denoted by scuff marks on the white wall, was the mirror he had mentioned as we had made our way through traffic…yesterday?

He tried to peer in and only succeeded in seeing himself; although he was up close, he felt detached. He wanted to lash out, to take it out on his father's apartment, at every goddamn thing that had ever been wrong with his life. But he played the tape through in his head, realized that would solve nothing, and he stopped the tape in the VCR. The next time his father went to watch a taped-off cable copy of *9 to 5*, he would be in for a surprise. He would know that either Nick or himself had discovered the videotape and would be on pins and needles awaiting retribution. It was a subtle form of revenge, yes, but one that he knew would drive his father crazy.

The only one it ate away at was Troy. His father never asked him why, either directly or through Nick, and it had been a month since he had taken what he believed to be the high road. That was an accurate analogy as Troy detailed his ever-growing dependence on marijuana to numb the pain of what his father had done to him. No matter how hard he tried, his mind could not let go of the injustice, and he began to dwell further and further on certain key points. Like for instance, his father was reaping whatever rewards that were to be made from the sale of his and Nick's filmed exploits.

Flash forward to Troy answering an ad in a local gay rag for models wanted. Flashes, lightning strikes before his eyes with each click of the camera, with his goal to capitalize on his newfound notoriety was in very sharp focus. One huge difference was, this time he signed a model-release form and could now profit from his foray. The word of mouth on Troy was excellent, so much so that the next photographer he worked with recommended him to a friend, someone Troy was very well acquainted with.

Nick answered the door, camera in hand, almost dropping it upon seeing Troy. His scheduled appointment was with one Sonny West, and never seeing him in a magazine, Nick was unsure how to respond. Was Troy merely stopping by for a social call? Nick was just about to tell Troy he was indisposed at the moment.

It would have been impossible, as Troy held up the piece of paper with his address written down in his friend Jack's handwriting, a cross between chicken scratch and ancient Sanskrit, making it completely recognizable.

"Mr. West, I presume?" Nick asked in a faux British accent.

Troy did not utter a word, only allowing his face and the look of bewilderment upon it to speak for him. Regardless, he crossed the threshold of Nick's apartment, entering a makeshift photo studio in the living room. White sheets backed by fans fluttered in the manmade breeze; a strobe light intermittently flickered, wavering like Troy's resolve to be standing in Nick's apartment.

"Funny way to learn about my little hobby, eh?" Nick said and did a little fake laugh for no added effect.

"Even funnier how I became a model," Troy responded, adding his own impression of Nick's fake laugh.

"So you know Jack?" Nick answered, uncertain of the shift in Troy.

"Well, I do and I don't, if we're talking about jack shit, that is."

"I am not sure I follow you, Troy." Nick attempted a half of a fake laugh but stopped midway through when he saw the look of contempt that Troy was throwing his way.

"Oh I think you do, Nick. My father's little side projects have made us both a little"—he paused for dramatic flourish—"infamous."

"You know about that?" Nick looked truly panicked.

"I know everything." Troy put a heavy emphasis on the last word.

"Oh shit, I went along with it because your dad said he would leave me if I didn't."

"Nick," Troy inquired, "what the hell are you talking about?"

"Umm, that your dad found out about us and told me the only way I could stay in his life was to keep filming what we were doing. That's what you meant by everything, right?" Nick grimaced like he had just made an accident in his underpants.

"Well, Nick, not exactly. I knew that dear old Dad was behind this. I didn't know you were. Is that why you put us on hold? Got enough footage to make a movie, did ya?" Troy felt the familiar surge of rage pushing itself to the forefront of his mind.

"Oh," Nick muttered, "shit."

"Oh shit is right. I'm outta here. I'd say take this job and shove it right up your ass, but I know how much you'd enjoy it. Just know this, you'll never enjoy it with me again."

Troy was visibly shaking, but it wasn't from the fans blowing inside of the room; it was from the midnight frost that had surrounded his heart that afternoon. He made his exit; another word was not uttered by himself or Nick.

And none was spoken until a winter's day some six months later. Troy had sworn never to speak to either his father or Nick again. But his career in modeling had become compromised by his ever-increasing temper tantrums. Soon, the jobs all but dried up, as did Troy's patience with Los Angeles. He could give a lick about his father, but he felt that he needed to set things right with Nick.

Really, they were both suffering the consequences of his father's disgust in their own actions, who had merely acted based upon the betrayal at hand. It was not a peccadillo, the way they had all fed off each other. Troy had done a lot of soul searching and realized that a constant reminder of the negative actions he immediately connected with Los Angeles needed to be a thing of the past.

His fist was poised to knock; his mind was telling him to just leave it, that it didn't matter. For his own peace of mind, he needed some resolve. Being in touch with his feelings was just one of the painful-at-best offshoots of his time in Los Angeles, of his time in the cracked spotlight. But now he wanted to hide himself from the sunlight, crawl into a cave somewhere, hibernate for the next five years, unshackle himself from the bear traps he had laid for himself.

He swallowed, knocked, could hear movement inside, swallowed harder, waited. Just at the juncture when it was between knocking again or just saying "Forget it," the door opened a crack.

Peering out was a younger-than-Troy almost-exact replica of Troy. It never occurred to him that Nick might have moved and he had disturbed the newest tenant. No, he knew this kid was here for one reason and one reason only. For Nick and his father to capitalize on his youth, to prey on the blood flowing in his veins, was akin to vampires feeding off the life of others to stay eternally youthful. All of the work he had done on himself in the last six months vanished in two breaths, which were taken in quick succession.

"Where's Nick?" No pleasantries, no "Hi, how are yous" were issued; just a rather clipped question fell out of his mouth deliberately.

Troy knew if he didn't create a strong impression, then the plan of action that popped in his head seconds ago would not work.

"Uh, he went out for a little bit." The young man didn't elaborate or offer to take a message. He only stared, realizing the resemblance between himself and a stranger was uncanny.

"Then I'll just wait for him. It's important that I talk to him." It took every ounce in his being not to pat the kid's head but to merely insert himself inside of Nick's apartment, no questions asked.

"Well, I guess so," the Troy redux answered.

Troy felt at that instant that the plans he was bouncing around in the confines of his head would work. There was no resistance on the kid's part to inquire into just who the hell this stranger to him may be. The kid was so green, he was practically a poster child for photosynthesis.

"Can I get you a drink?" he asked in all innocence and cemented the plan with that simple gesture.

"Nah," Troy replied, "I'm good." Upon saying that, he made his way to the couch, draped his arms along its back to denote a relaxed confidence. "So where's Nick?"

"He had to run out." Corey waited a beat before adding, "To pick something up."

"Oh I see." To clearly illustrate that point, Troy craned his neck to the left, peering into the bedroom, spying one leg of a tripod. "Looks like you guys are doing a photo shoot."

Corey just eyed Troy, unsure of how to answer. His mouth attempted to move then would stop itself.

"Hey, it's cool. Let's just say that I am one of Nick's former protégés. I thought I would just stop by, say hi."

"Wait a minute, you're Sonny West, right? You are, aren't you?" Corey's voice took on the timber and intonation of a fourteen-year-old girl. "I thought you looked familiar when I opened the door."

Troy had thought the same thing. It was if he was looking at himself years before all of the messes of his life needed to be cleaned up.

"Guilty." Troy held up his hand, palm flat, as if pleading the fifth.

"Wow, I really…uh…admire your work." A blush, fire-engine red, lit up Corey's face, as did the sheepish smile he was sporting.

"Thanks, always nice to meet a fan," Troy said, feeling every inch the celebrity. But inside he knew he needed to downplay it. "Actually, I came by to say goodbye to Nick. I am done with this town, this business, all of it."

"Really? Why?" Troy inquired.

"It's just not worth it anymore. What are you, kid, eighteen?"

"Actually"—Corey looked from left to right, as if making sure no one was eavesdropping in an empty room—"I'll be nineteen in a few weeks. Nick thinks I'm, uh, younger."

"Well, you're putting an expiration date on yourself," Troy stated, leaning forward, "especially with the company you're keeping."

"Nick's a very nice guy," Corey instantly defended Nick's honor, and Troy noticed that the weird mojo of Nick's had struck again.

"I agree, it's George you have to look out for. He'll chew you up, spit you back out, and still want seconds. That man is evil. He's why I am leaving town."

"Why? What's he done to you?" Corey asked.

"How much time have you got?" Troy asked without expecting an answer and proceeded to plow through a diatribe about how much damage his father had done. When he was finished, Corey was stunned.

"I had no idea. George seems so nice."

"That's my point, looks can be deceiving. And unless you can figure that out for yourself, then you'll never make it here. Well, I've said my piece. I only hope that what I've said has made sense to you." Troy had omitted Nick's involvement in his sudden shot to stardom; let the kid think there were some good people here, for chrissakes.

Hell, he needed to believe that too. Nick resembled Santa Claus enough for him, sans the snowy down of a beard, to envision that he was indeed a saint that helped bring joy to people's lives.

Corey didn't answer him vocally, just gave a slight nod with a faraway look in his eyes as he processed the information. Troy felt an unfamiliar feeling creep into him; it was joy, plain, simple, unfiltered. He had done the right thing by having tried to steer Corey out of the rough waters he was heading into.

"Hey, I've got to get going. Need a ride anywhere?" Troy asked.

"No, and thank you." Corey stepped forward and pecked Troy on the cheek, like he was kissing an elder or perhaps someone he respected. Troy actually felt himself blushing by the tempered show of emotion.

"You are welcome. You seem like such a sweet kid, Corey. I only wish the best to you, for your future."

Troy exited the room, next Los Angeles, then his father's life until recently, and his yarn-telling abilities. But what of Corey? I'd like to say he took Troy's advice and was now a well-rounded member of society, holding down a bank teller position. But there was a certain other position, one in which he was perched upon a metal trash can, and the one he placed himself in by falling for his hotheaded costar, Danny.

I comprehended that I had heard Nick accuse George of killing Corey. I was going to throw my two cents into it when Danny spoke up.

"Corey, he didn't make it home," he said through choked strains.

Nick's head snapped at attention to where Danny stood behind him, an angry dog on a short leash.

"Shut up, Danny," he practically hissed, and this was with all of his teeth in his mouth.

I watched with deep rapture as they verbally exchanged threats with nothing but their eyes, establishing a new language.

"No, Nick, I won't. I need to say this," Danny countered angrily. "I know what happened to Corey."

For a moment, Nick didn't react. Then he turned around and slapped Danny hard across the face.

"I will not have you disrespect a man that did so much for you, a man that is dead!" Nick looked at George then directly into Danny's eyes to make sure he was receiving the message loud and clear in their new lexicon.

"You need to let go of that, Nick. You need to stop lying to yourself. George didn't kill Corey, you didn't kill Corey. I did." He paused and looked at everyone else in the room. I felt my brother sidle up next to me, always at the ready to protect me from the bullies of life.

"It was an accident, a stupid accident. We were just goofing around, and he fell and hit his head on the…on the edge of my coffee table. He wouldn't wake up, he didn't wake up. Why wouldn't he wake up?" Danny looked as though he were living the event presently. "I panicked and called Nick."

"Well, Danny, If I 'need to let go' of my lie, then you need to let go of yours. Goofing around, was it? More like you taking out your aggressions on Corey and it got out of hand," Nick scoffed. "Fell and hit his head, eh? How about pushed backwards at full force into a glass coffee table? You killed him, it was no accident. I loved him, and you took him away from me forever."

Nick turned to face Danny, who stood immobile soaking in that his long-kept secret was revealed, and started pushing him backwards. Rather than help his childhood friend, John drew me closer to his side and navigated us out of the way. He clearly understood that we had stumbled into something that was beyond our comprehension, something that Nick and Danny needed to get out of their systems.

I only hoped that there wouldn't be any more death associated with this day. I was starting to think I was jinxed in the area of men. One lay dead in the bathtub, one had killed somebody, another was in the hospital, and the other—hey, where was Troy? My Los Angeles scorecard wouldn't be complete without him, but he was presently engaged in a conversation with a 911 operator.

Nick pushed Danny out into the bedroom; the curtains stirred in the breeze as the shadows crept along the lawn beyond the still-open window. Danny put his hand up; every tendon in his arm was taut, forcing Nick to remain stationary.

"Why are we doing this, Nick? Hurting each other like we are, it's not going to bring the dead back to life. We have both made such huge mistakes, catastrophes of everything we touch. You and me, dude, we are both the same."

"Maybe we are, but there's a huge difference. I didn't kill anyone, you did!" Nick shouted so hard at Danny that all of the blond was almost knocked out of his hair.

"You're an accessory then!" He turned to face me and John, peering out through the bathroom door, playing to the cheap seats of an unofficial jury. "He helped me cover it up. In fact, he wanted to set up George so he could take over his business."

He moved away just in time to avoid another slap from Nick. But he wasn't calculating how to move out of harm's way. He was moving towards the closet, where he had just been sprung from not so long ago. He went in and came out in mere seconds later, his two hands filled with familiar items.

But to my brother and Troy, who now was semiblocking entry into the living room, it was nothing but a fashion faux pas and some crumpled paper. I expected Danny to say that he wanted to submit this into evidence.

"These are his clothes, his belongings, all that's left of him. We were going to plant it at George's, place an anonymous call to the police. But that never happened, did it? You couldn't fuck over your beloved George after he had fucked you over so many times. Why, Nick? I just want to know why! Why would you do that?" Each question brought a red hue to his face. "Do you even know what I had to do to make ends meet? Do you have any idea? If it wasn't for Troy, I'd still be out selling myself any way I could."

Rather than respond, Nick started clapping, mouthing the word *bravo.*

"Save it for the cameras. Oh wait, they don't want you anymore. You're just a good-for-nothing has-been that never was!" Nick replied. "As for what you had to do, that was your choice. Nobody made you do anything. I felt sorry for you, Danny. I still do because you need to face the consequences of what you have done. I tried to help you, and you turned around and are trying to take away the thing that belongs to me."

He slightly paused and pointed at Troy.

"It's not your birthright," he said with a barking shout then moved his stubby index finger onto Danny. "And it is not owed to you." And then his finger moved onto a lifeless body in the bathtub. In the simple act of just pointing with his finger, Troy was able to avert his father's body from his view "He knew exactly what the two of you were up to, trying to take his business out from under him. Well, about two weeks ago, he transferred ownership over to me. So go find someone else's coattails to ride on, boys."

Troy and Danny both stood stunned, their scheme gone awry, leaving them with nothing to show for the effort except heartache. Allegiances were no longer viable in the "every man for himself" world I had been exposed to. Troy bolted from the room, giving a very pained look back in the bathroom at his father's porcelain sarcophagus. Danny pounced on Nick, trying to pound his head into submission on the carpet.

Well, that encapsulated Danny to a tee—cause the maximum amount of damage allotted without thinking it through. John looked at me; I looked at him. Without a word uttered, it was clear what the other was thinking. "I'm outta here" sprang to mind.

We were both done with everything that embodied deception; I was feeling somewhat numb with all that had transpired in the last day. I had a better and severe understanding about the downside of human nature. But I still felt a compelling need to dispel the mental image of Anita Bryant that was telling me that this is how all gay people were.

We made it out to the back of the apartment building as I gathered up my belongings. As we made our way to the parking lot, I spied George's, and now presumably Troy's, VW Rabbit becoming a pinpoint down the street.

Taking its vacated spot behind the Caddy were two police cars that pulled into the parking lot. No sooner than the cars were in park, then two sets of officers come bounding out of the vehicles. God, the last thing I wanted my brother to have to go through was a police interrogation. It couldn't be good for his Navy career, as he might be filtered right out of the possibilities that he was striving for in his life.

"There's something going on in apartment 4. It sounds like they're killing each other! You'd better hurry!" I placed a great deal of urgency in my voice, a smidge of panic, but nothing resembling any connection with the occupants of a certain wicker-furniture-strewn apartment.

"Thanks, son," one of the beefier officers who was trailing behind responded.

The same "We're outta here" look crossed over the Dodge brothers' faces in unison as we flew down the street. Once on the main fairway of Santa Monica Boulevard, as the day dwindled into the encroaching night, I stopped in my tracks.

Filling the streets were throngs of people, all of them just like me. I still craved finding out the answers that I had pushed to the back burner, the flames reignited in my mind's eye. I was among my people, and one or more of them could hold the answer. I hated to do this to my brother as he had come all of this way to get me and had been through so much in doing so.

But I ran straight ahead, a sea of people enveloping me, making it near to impossible for my brother to pick me out in the gayest of lineups. I could hear his voice behind and to the right of me, "Henry, where are you going?"

"There's something I need to find out," I called back as the tide of people carried me along in its familiar seas.

Chapter 28

At some point, I felt like I was drowning and desperately needed to surface for air. I tried zigging to my left then zagging to my right, but the riptide effect of the crowd was omnipresent.

Then as Moses had done in the Bible, I somehow managed to part not so much Red Sea as a pink one. I made it to the shore of a sidewalk, my breathing labored, not from the attempt to disperse from the crowd. I was, in essence, shell-shocked, the walking dead.

By any stretch of the imagination, I should not be walking but crawling through primordial sludge, my skin turned inside out, every nerve ending exposed to the elements, completely susceptible. I was quite simply numb. I had been so mired in the negative, I wanted—no, scratch that—needed to feed off some positive outlets.

So of course my mind leaped into mental-scrapbook mode. I was thinking of everything that had transpired, not just in the last twenty four hours, but a whole lifetime of instances.

I was seeing my life flashing before my eyes, snippets of an existence that I only partially understood. I could see how point A led to point B, but at what juncture did point C veer so far off course? Or was this the course that I was supposed to take to get to the unobtainable point Z? I blocked out the crowd, walking, pirouetting, stumbling on a Saturday night; each one had a reason to celebrate the unity that was observed on Gay Pride. As always, I felt alone, on the outside looking in, a mere observer, when really I could be a participant.

Nothing but trouble had been gleaned here in Los Angeles, and I might have swept the experience, save for some points. One, I would have continued my boyish crush on Danny forever if his true side hadn't been revealed. Two, my brother seemed to accept me or at least had the capacity to try to understand me. Three, I had some deep reserve of strength to draw upon that I never knew was there before.

This brought a small tear to my eye and, for some reason, made me think of Angel lying in a hospital bed, unaware of the events of the day. He hadn't appeared on my radar for a while, and it made me wonder if he had fallen victim to the collusive outcome of many a palace denizen.

I tried to map out where the hospital was, but all I got in return was a mental picture of Danny. I knew that I was fortunate for not having experienced the full extent of his self-proclaimed horseplay.

I shuddered, a violent racking of my back, neck, and finally, my head. I could feel the tectonic vibration make its way inside my brain, trying desperately to jar loose that shattered glass keepsake. Pulling me from the internal struggle was an outside presence, a hand reaching out from the crowd.

Immediately my mind jumped to the conclusion that it was John or some spectral force determined to stop me before I reached my intended destination. It was nothing more than a very libation riddled reveler trying to cop a feel. Speaking of cops, I wondered what happened to the remaining resident and visitor at apartment 4, and what had happened to Danny?

I didn't want to allow my mind full access down that lonely stretch of highway; I needed a detour sign to be posted at all times where he was concerned. I may be forever trying to recover my heart that was pinned underneath the tires of an eighteen-wheeler, always at the ready to traverse the rutted road of heartbreak, squashing my heart underneath its tires, finishing off the job that Danny had started. I put up the mental roadblocks successfully and they were momentarily causing any and all thoughts of Danny to be stopped dead in their tracks.

I needed to focus, I had become sidetracked by Da...by Ni... by Tr...well, outside elements, I'll call them for the sake of nonargument. I knew what I needed to do, could only hope I would see what I wanted to see. Undulating masses passed by, all celebrating the freedom that came with living a life without restraint; two leather men in harnesses wandered by, throwing a wrench into that analogy.

I wanted so badly to be a part of this revelry, yet I still felt like I was waiting to be picked last for sports.

All I could think to do was to bury my face in my hands and let go with an agonized cry. I wouldn't give anyone that satisfaction; I was stronger than that, wasn't I? The jukebox in my head put the needle down on the song "Mental Hopscotch" by Missing Persons.

Immediately I was filled with a great deal of dread and self-loathing. I screamed in my inside voice, "Of course you are strong!" Adding to that for good measure and to placate my ever-present dichotomy was, "You stupid fuck."

And that was me to a tee, understanding and underscoring myself in the same breath.

"To hell with that," I said unwittingly in my outside voice.

It did not draw attention from anyone. I was playing to an audience of one, trying to find my mark on the stage set before me. Enough with learning my lines; it was "lights, camera, action" time. First, I had some business to attend to.

I stood at the urinal at a gas station I had found a few blocks over. I had locked the door to the bathroom behind me, not wanting any interruptions at this particular juncture. I studied my face in the mirror; frightful didn't even begin to cover the way I looked. With hair that was practically standing on end, as a direct result of all of the day's doings, and of it being unattended to, my gaze traveled downward to the purple tinge underneath one eye.

If you threw a Hefty trash bag over my present ensemble, I could have joined A Flock of Seagulls.

I turned on the water on from the faucet smudged with finger-prints, and it cascaded into the "I assumed and hoped it was just rust in the sink." It was ice cold, all the better to freeze and exfoliate the little bits of motherfuckery that were living under my skin.

First, I splashed it on my face, careful not to touch the spot. I lathered up some grainy-as-sand soap from a dispenser on the wall; it felt as gritty as I did. Soon enough, I began to feel clean, the entire day washing down the sink in a spiraling effect. There was little more I could do with my hair than to wash and go, sans the Pert Plus, with what was available to me.

I got every place I felt might be offensive to the night at large. I attempted to use my finger as a toothbrush and some hand soap as toothpaste, which lasted all of two seconds, as it was spat from my mouth. I took a final look in the mirror. Something about me had changed; perhaps everything about me was different.

I looked older, a little worse for wear; the look in my eyes conveyed confidence and a haunted quality.

I emerged from the restroom feeling more or less human and definitely not feeling like a majestic butterfly emerging from a chrysalis. I was good enough to pass, to infiltrate the night, and to puncture the heart of my journey.

There was one tendril of my past shooting out of the black of night that I needed to address. The pay phone stood like it was mocking me by connecting me with the past, which I would now have to kill in my mind after tonight.

I strode over to it, purposeful, confident, and forgetful. I had not one iota of money on me. I was what my spirit and bad grammar combined would equal, broke. Even though the money I had black-mailed Steve for had probably cast a dark shadow over my expedition, it still would have been nice to have some remains of it.

Ni—someone had seen fit to have taken it from me. All that I had left was my trusty Walkman. I took it from its hiding place in my front pocket of my shorts. I had to gaze upon it, covet it, finding solitude in the fact that it was still mine when so much was not. The door that allowed the entryway of music into my life was ajar. In place of my cherished mix tape, there was money!

I knew my brain had been besieged with all of the goings-on, but I am damn sure that I did not put the money there. Then I remembered that Nick had placed all of my clothes and my Walkman on the chair that resided in the corner of his room. Perhaps he had detected the approaching firestorm, knew that too many sparks had flown to not constitute an all-out inferno.

He had been looking out for me after all.

I didn't hear the rattle associated with coins. So I would need to go inside the gas station and obtain the requisite quarter that my mother always warned me against leaving home without. She was a regular Karl Malden, that Kate Dodge. My mind immediately began to ponder what might be transpiring at home. Did John place a frantic call to my parents? He was most likely still patrolling the streets, avoiding the gay fray as best he could, not ready to give up on me.

Upon entering the convenience store portion of the gas station, which was nothing but a glorified pantry with fluorescent lighting, I realized I was hungry. I snatched up a bag of pretzels, a can of Pepsi, and gum to ensure the fresh breath that hand soap couldn't possibly provide.

I slipped a twenty out of my impromptu wallet before arriving at the register so as to remain as innocuous as possible. I quietly asked for one dollar's worth of quarters, averted eye contact, peering out into the night as if it were whispering my name, ready to tell me its secrets. I already had my fill of secrets, thank you very much. I walked out into its warm embrace, ready for the night to erase the day away with its deepening hours, each passing one of which took me further away from the events of the day.

I stood before the pay phone nervously debating dropping the quarter in the slot. I had to check in on the forgotten, needed to reach out and just say hi to the fallen. I had already looked up the hospital phone number, committed it to memory in one of those weird quirks I had discovered about myself. I was terrible in math, but I could remember phone numbers by rote. The phone rang; upon the third ring, a cheery female voice answered.

"I need to speak with a patient. His name is Angel. He was shot yesterday and was in surgery too," I said, satiated that all the details were covered.

"Do you know his last name, sir?" she inquired happily.

I looked behind me to see if Big Ed was present. Sir? Yes, at this occasion, that title should be bequeathed to my father. Well, Switchboard Perky had certainly thrown the proverbial wrench in the works, now hadn't she?

"Sir? Are you there?" Oh yes, she thought she was very clever indeed.

"Uh, I don't actually," I responded, sounding hollow.

I supposed I could schlep myself over to the hospital; somehow I thought that would just provide another chance encounter with people best left in my past. But who was left, really?

"So I take it you're not a relative then?" She adopted a slightly sharper tone in her stating of the obvious.

"No, just a friend. Maybe the only one he has left," I answered honestly, hoping that something would chip, tug, or melt away at her heart. "I'm really worried about him. Can you please help me?"

"I'm not really supposed to do this, but…" She trailed off with a sigh and then came back on the line a moment later. "Let me connect you now."

"Thank you very much," I said as my heart began beating faster.

"Certainly, sir," she replied, sounding every inch the vocal doppelganger of Jenny, the Time Life operator from the TV commercial. I mentally envisioned her with a severe brown berry tan, bad perm, and headset eternally fastened to her head.

The phone rang, then again, and one more time for the sake of tension. It was between ring 3 and ring 4 that I began to doubt my reason for calling. If ring 5 had not produced a groggy-sounding Angel answering, I would have hung up, chalking it up to yet another bad idea.

"Angel, it's me," I said, hoping the resonance of my voice would alert him to just who me was.

"Hey," he said a hair above a whisper, "Henry."

Yes, he did know me as Henry. Somebody had even given him a picture to make sure I was wrangled to that place. Why didn't I just leave with my brother when I had the chance? I knew what was prolonging my trip, but ever since I had come out to my parents, everything that should have been simple had become a series of sidetracks.

"How are you? I've been so worried." I trailed off, letting him think it was he that had all of the concern attached to his plight.

"I've been better, you know." And that simple statement spoke volumes about the human spirit.

Angel was only a fraction of the man he was before the shooting, but he still managed to throw in his signature "You know" to show me that he was going to be fine.

"I'm glad to hear that." As I said this, I could feel the tears begin to well up.

There was so much loss associated with this day. Thank God that Angel didn't have to be added to the final tally of casualties. "I know," two words, nothing more, yet there seemed to be something supplementary to that short statement. "I know everything."

He expanded a small statement and threw a huge net around his wealth of knowledge. But I knew that was no reason to play coy.

"How?" The perpetual little brother adapted the perennial sidekick lexicon of Tonto.

"Troy came by." As he said this, I could hear him slipping back towards sleep. "I'm sorry, Henry. Sorry you had to be involved. You should go home and forget about all of this, you know. "

Then there was a click, and the phone went dead. I had gotten some sort of absolution, but somehow it wasn't enough. And now Angel had replanted the seed that would flourish into a garden of confusion. What was I going to do? Where could I go from here? I hung up the phone gently, as if the receiver was a conduit to the fractured man I had been speaking to. I overrode the doubt and strode off into the night purposeful, confident, eager to leave fear behind with every step.

If I had been in Angel's hospital room instead of phoning in my condolences, I might have been privy to the secret he had been keeping. I may have walked in on a faceless man sitting in the chair next to Angel's bed.

As he hung up the phone, Troy put down the copy of *People* magazine he was not really vested in. The crack of a grin broke the surface of his face then spread itself into an all-out smile. Angel looked at him with puppy-dog eyes, sad brown entities that conveyed both a deep, abiding sorrow and a relief to be alive.

"It worked! We pulled it off! There's nobody standing in the way. Danny's going to jail, and Nick, who knows, and really, who cares about him. Everything we've dreamed about, everything that has been denied us will finally be ours, you and me, my love," Troy spoke this to the air as Angel had slipped back into slumber.

With the bouquet of flowers in his hand being squeezed so hard that they may turn into potpourri at any second, Nick stepped back from the doorway of Angel's room. He had been let go by the police, exceedingly speedy by both Danny's sole admittance of the crime and having a friend in high places within the department—the same one who had supplied him with a two-way mirror that had led to this whole sordid mess.

Now, it would have been better if he had been locked up behind bars because he could now feel a menace-to-society moniker being attached firmly in his mind. Troy was right in a sense; Nick no longer had someone to care about him.

Oh, but he knew all about self-preservation and how to take care of anyone that might stand in his way. He walked away from Angel, from Troy, from treachery, from memories.

But not from the hatred that was on a slow burn in the pit of his stomach. He should show them, he would show them all, and there was nothing that would stand in the way of that. He needed some time to lick his wounds, retreat until the time was right to execute the rumblings of a plan that were already hatching in his mind.

He gave the flowers to the oldest nurse on duty at the nurses' station, wanting to make her feel special that a stranger would give her flowers out of the blue, that she was still viable—something that he was not feeling at that particular instance.

I was not the proverbial fly on the wall, nor did I want to be again. I was trying to decide which bar had the shortest line and, of that choice, which one would buy that I was twenty-one. Granted, I felt these last few weeks and today in particular had aged me beyond comprehension. I was sure that, in and of itself, would not equate entrance.

I assumed that I must have cleaned up nicely as eyes roved over me, up and down, side to side. I stopped in front of what was arguably the busiest bar of the night and the one that had a name I was gravitating towards, Rage.

I was just about to move along and find a less crowded venue for my search and recovery of perceiving gay life when…

"Look at that little cutie," I heard someone near the front of the line say in a voice already saturated with enough alcohol to give anyone within twenty feet a contact high. "Hey, you, hey, blondie."

Knowing that I was in the land of the golden hair and not thinking of myself as particularly cute, I ignored the drunken catcall. I scanned the crowd, looking for someone, anyone that could, pardon the pun, set me straight about what it meant to be gay.

Everyone seemed to be focused on getting inside or completely oblivious to anything outside of their social circle. An interloper within my own community, I was ready to cut through the barbed wire and trespass into unknown territory, a land known as acceptance. It may provide greener pastures, but I would still be grazing outside of the herd, forever branded an outcast.

Suddenly there was a hand on my arm. Just as I was going to find a way into this new world, something about me had alerted the silent signal, tripping the wire. I half believed again that it was my brother, John, spotting me out of the throng of people, ready to escort me back home. Or maybe it was the bar's bouncer, ferreting out my true age and ready to prevent me from entering. There was that factor to deal with; I just prayed I would blend in with the crowd. I believed that I could gain admittance if age was gauged beyond years.

The hand on my arm was caressing it too much to belong to anything threatening. I looked to my right and was up close and personal with Mr. Party Pants himself.

"Hi," he slurred, "was yur name?"

The man with what could only be described as a slight frame wearing enough cologne to choke a horse equally matched by an alcohol-content breath assured to spell DUI asked me this with a dopey look on his face. He pulled himself in closer, put his arm around my shoulder, his hand absently caressing me like we were two long-lost chums instead of imperfect strangers.

"Henry," I said rather quietly, turning my head slightly to the right to avoid being fumigated.

If I had turned my head to the left towards the street and focused on something other than being pawed, I might have seen Nick en route to pack up his possessions. But as the case was, I was trying to figure out how to wiggle away from Mr. Gropey McFeely.

"Hi, Henry, I'm Doug, and my frens over there"—he paused to point rather dramatically at three other slight-of-frame gents— "Manny, Moe, and Jack, they're the three best friends your car ever had!"

He stopped and doubled over laughing, catching deep gulps of air in his mouth and expelled them with a snort.

"Sorry, sorry. What I meant to say was"—he furrowed his brow trying to recapture his lost thought—"oh yeah, you're cute. Wanna hang out with us?"

He put on what could only be described as a shit-eating grin. I was disarmed by how charming it was to see someone unabashedly happy, even if it was due to an altered state.

"Sure," I said then quickly added, "I forgot my ID though."

"No worries, cutie. I know the guy at the door, his name's Joe? Jim? Jason? Shit, well, it's something with a *J*." He rolled his eyes comically and stuck the tip of his tongue out of his mouth at a jaunty tilt.

He didn't question the validity of me not looking anywhere near the neighborhood of twenty-one. Then again, he was down the street from being sober, driving on alcohol fumes and hoping to park in me for the night.

"Okie dokie then," I said as we made our way back to Doug's friends, also known as the Pep Boys.

I felt electric, charged to the gills and ready to shoot off sparks. Suddenly I was flooded in light. For one brief moment, I thought it was emanating from me. It was a local news crew filming the celebration wrapped around this day of gaiety to give the naysayers more ammunition that we were nothing but heathens.

I retraced the last sentence that had formed in my head. I had said *we* and not *me*, meaning I was feeling accepted into the fold. All it was going to take was a single guiding hand, not the several that had threatened to pull me apart before.

I was so glad that Doug had noticed me, was drawing me into the inner circle, a moth to a flame. His guiding hand was now located on my lower back and started making a steady pilgrimage down and underneath my shorts. He gave me the equivalent of the trendy Hollywood two-cheek air kiss, squeezing each cheek once and then uttering something akin to a grunt.

I hadn't thought this through, and for the first time, well, for the first time in forever, I didn't want to barter my entrance into this existence with sex. I just assumed Doug had been consumed with the brotherhood of the day, had sensed my loneliness and confusion, and wanted to help.

The longer his hand absently massaged my right buttock, the clearer my mistake became. There was always a price to be paid somehow. We had reached his friends. I gave each one a nod as their names were read off the roll call, but all I heard was Manny, Moe, and Jack. I didn't pay attention. I was focusing on how long we had to stand in line, which may only be a few moments but seemed light years away. Doug had managed to take his hand out of my shorts long enough to perform a flourish of his hand that coincided with each friend's name.

I didn't want to appear to be ungrateful, but I was feeling done with Bartertown and all of the "two men enter, one man leave" symmetry that I saw on screen in *Mad Max: Beyond Thunderdome*.

I was just about to walk away, not only from Doug and company, but from the hope of finding any trace of redemption in a community that I wanted to call home. I would have too, and maybe my night would have ended up differently, even my life, for that matter; but the local news was back again to capture on film what most people would consider nothing short of a freak show.

The reporter, a blonde version of Sheena Easton with a mannish short haircut and wearing enough pancake makeup to make Aunt Jemima take notice, thrust the microphone into my face.

"What does Gay Pride mean to you?" she asked unwaveringly and most likely for the billionth time that night.

"Umm, well." My mind went reeling. I didn't know what it meant to me.

"Oh he's shy," Doug explained and observed. Not wanting the spotlight to swing away from him and his friends, he acted as my interpreter. "Gay Pride is a day of…of unity. It's a time to celebrate old friendships and make new ones."

He said this, and of course, his hand ended up on my ass to further accentuate his point.

"To show the world that we are fierce, fabulous, and not the freaks they say we are," he concluded with drunken enthusiasm.

"Thank you," Sheena-lite replied, as pleased with Doug's obviously rehearsed statement as he was.

She and I hadn't been privy to Doug's bathroom that morning as he preened and practiced what he would say if he happened upon the situation. He even wrote *fierce* and *fabulous* in streaky letters on his fogged-up bathroom mirror.

"Oh don't go yet," Doug pleaded slightly, motioning for his trio of friends to gather round. "We have something to show you. Ready, girls?"

He included me into that fold as I was flanked by Manny and Moe and Jack, who took their positions alongside of Doug. Two sets of hands were on either side of my back; the one that momentarily dipped down and gave me a squeeze was easily identifiable. I didn't know what was going on. Were we supposed to drop trou in tandem for the cameras? Get it while it's hot, fresh pound cake!

Doug began chanting a "dah dah dah dah dah dah dah dah" sound, and four sets of legs started a series of high kicks that would shame the Rockettes, working in tandem, a finely lubed machine. It took me a scant second to realize that I should instinctively know how to hot step it like a showgirl, shouldn't I?

And here came those nagging questions again as I tried to keep in step with my contemporaries. Did I have to act like this, kick? Was this expected of me, high kick? Did Doug and company think they had stumbled upon a roving correspondent for *Star Search*?

Apparently not, since Ed McMahon did not come out of the crowd to announce the judges' decision. He didn't materialize to tell me I was on *TV's Bloopers and Practical Jokes* for the last day.

"We're the Fuchsia Debs! Catch us Saturday nights at…" Doug informed the at home viewers and any other audience he could capture.

But the lights, camera, action swung away from us, roving the street for more "priceless footage," which was the term that Ms. Easton had used as she made her way through the throng.

We did finish to a round of applause from some and a smoldering, hateful glare from a strikingly tall black woman with a pink wig and matching pink lipstick and eye shadow. Doug was coming up from a bow when he locked eyes with her.

"Well, looky who's here," he said to his gang of fellow drag performers who had opted not to see the world tonight through false eyelashes. The rest of the Fuchsia Debs craned their necks.

"What's she doing here?" Manny asked.

"Bitch better step off," Moe stated.

"If her skirt was any higher, you could see her bra!" Jack observed.

"She ain't nothin' but a mess in a dress," Doug slurred, hissing loud enough to garner another ice-cold stare from the subject at hand.

A few other people in line looked in our general vicinity, dismissing Doug as an obnoxious drunk. I wasn't so sure how to take him; obviously there was some negative backstory with Ms. Pink Pussy Willow Wig. I felt like I was walking right into the flames that I had just managed to put out.

The pink lady was making her way into the bar, passing through customs without so much as any questions asked or quandaries into what she may be bringing into the new territory I was about to enter. I was traveling with my fair share of baggage, and it was nothing I was ready to declare as mine. I was fully subscribed to stow it away in a mental overhead compartment, but some of the contents had shifted watching Doug and the Debs lash out. I decided to let it go, figuring it was none of my business.

Again, and I didn't know why, I had seen the deconstruction that seemed to occur within the community. I just chalked it up to the slings and arrows that were trying to prevent my entrance as we gained the coveted spot at the main entrance. I knew I should be filled with dread or, at the very least, anticipation. But the combination of a certain sense of world weariness from the last day plus the last-minute sniping of the Debs had robbed me of that.

"Hi, umm, Joe, how are you tonight, doll?" Doug asked as we stood at the precipice, a threshold to the unknown for me and just another Saturday for the group I had fallen in with.

"Busier than jumper cables at a Puerto Rican picnic. The name's Dan, remember?" said the swarthy muscular gent with the New York accent who held one of many keys for me to turn.

A snippet of dialogue from last year's unanimous comedy blockbuster, *Ghostbusters*, drifted up from the reinstated ethers of pop culture, "Are you the gatekeeper?"

"Right. Have a good one," Doug said, walking forward followed by Manny, Moe, me, and then Jack.

Not a sideways look or asking of identification followed. I had done it. I had gained admittance. Wonderland lay ahead of me in its entire spectacle, obviously like nothing I had ever seen before.

Before me was a fantastic rendering of men, all shadows and light; any one of them could unlock the answer to my queries. Dazzling lights, all keeping time with the music of voices and song created quite the surreal moment that I was trying to absorb, a sponge in every sense of the word. The bar smelled of smoke, which intermingled with the fog machine that had just gone off on the dance floor; ghosts joined for the dance. I tried not to let any haunt my house, pushing poltergeists away from the forefront of my mind. It was as if nothing had transpired at all today, that this mecca was all I was supposed to experience in Los Angeles.

Dead or Alive came on over the sound system reminding me that there was "Something In My House." I had almost tuned out Doug and company. I wanted to thank him profusely then realized that would be a dead giveaway to my real age. I re-entered the group mentally, making sure my mouth was not opened too wide so as not to show my inexperience. I strained against the din of conversation married to music to hear what Doug and his friends were in cahoots about.

"I just can't believe she's here!" Jack said.

"Oh she's got some nerve." Manny concurred.

"Why do you guys hate her so much?" I asked in all innocence.

"Well, Harry, I mean, it's Harry, right?" Doug asked, diffusing the question to nothing more than drunken petulance. "What was yer name again?"

A cloud of alcohol fumes all but threatened to knock me over as he asked me this.

"It doesn't matter."

His total disregard of me, the lack of caring on his part, crawled under my skin, burrowing itself in deep.

"Anyhoo that black bitch stole my boyfriend," he droned on. "Now she's tryin' to compete with our act! I mean, really now, who does she think she is?"

He left me to ponder this question as he joined the shortest line of people awaiting alcohol consumption. I followed suit, wanting to know how, if we are all in the same boat, was there such a demand to push people overboard with nary an iceberg in sight.

"Your act?" I asked, sidling up to his right ear.

Okay, I'll admit it. It came off as a bit sexual. I didn't have many defense mechanisms for coping with unruly men, save for that one. Doug caught the inflection with a coy smile crinkling up the skin around his emerald green eyes.

"Yes, indeed. Bes drag show in town, bes hair, bes makeup, bes choreography, bes dresses. We're the Fuchsia Debs, for chrissakes.

Legends, stars, all-around entertainers." He was counting repeatedly on one finger as he slurred off the par excellence of the Fuchsia Debs, preaching to his own choir.

I thought of the high kicks we had done for the news, the practiced ease of it all. I was in the company of men who dressed as women who were dressed as men tonight. It all had a faint *Victor/ Victoria* ring to it.

And the only ironic reason I knew that was because my dad had made me watch it. In fact, Big Ed seemed to fit more of the time-honored perception of gay male. He liked Judy Garland, watched musicals, had also rented and enjoyed *Lust in the Dust* with John Waters's staple, Divine.

This thought set the wheels in motion again and, within their cogs, a pang of regret for stranding John.

There was a fleeting moment of "I never should have left home in the first place." I shuddered at the very essence of its reality, knowing the implications of never venturing out even though the results had been close to deadly. I pushed any reference to either of my pasts, the one as Henry before or Billy during, to the smallest compartment in my mind and slammed the door.

"So how come you guys, I…err…mean ladies aren't dressed up tonight?" I asked, not sure of the protocol of him versus her in these matters.

"Well"—his mind was searching for my name behind eyes that had seen sights mine never would—"doll, is like Halloween for us, today, that is. We dress up all year long as other people, ladies, if you will. So tonight we thought…" He lost his train of thought as we edged closer to the bar. "Oh yeah, why not jus be our own fabulous selves?"

He let out a slight burp then hiccuped, and he smiled as only really drunken people do: looking at you but seeing nothing, smiling regardless, oblivious to his surroundings. Then his face contorted into unadulterated rage and hate as he regained his focus long enough to see his nemesis.

"Tonight was suppos to be fun. And that bitch had to ruin everything." His voice raised steadily with each word as did his finger, which became an accusatory instrument, a shaky divining rod of ill will.

Doug left his place in line, walked over to Pinky Lee, and did his best Joan Collins slap. A collective *ooh* sound rose above the din as patrons stopped to see what the hullabaloo was about.

Fittingly, Frankie Goes to Hollywood had just begun singing about what happens when two tribes go to war. I was watching first-hand as I slunk back into the woodwork, not wanting to be singled out as being in cahoots with a rabble-rouser.

I still had not gotten a satisfactory answer, and I only had a few hours until last call to figure out the meaning of gay life. I did not want to be tossed out on my ear before that could happen.

A bartender left his post and stepped in between the two, Doug trying his drunken best to snatch his archrival's wig off. There was a calm refinement about his opponent. She hadn't struck back, and there was no wriggling to free herself from the bartender's grip. In fact, he looked as if he was consoling her, which raised Doug's dander something fierce. Doug started hitting the bartender with his clenched fist.

If he had his drag accoutrement, the purse, he would have resembled an old lady fending off a mugger, visions of Ruth Buzzi on *Laugh-In* danced through my head. There was nothing comedic about the look on Doug's face; bloodlust was running rampant on his features.

The rest of the Debs rushed to his side, pulling him away and into the night. This time I did not mind being ignored. I appreciated the fact they had gotten me in and watched in rapt wonder as the bar activities commenced. Two men directly in front of me resumed making out, the bartender manned his station, and I watched Doug's victimized enemy slink over to a darkened corner of the bar.

Maybe it was the luminescent quality of her wig, but something about her was drawing me in. I approached, enraptured, compelled, fearful. I was a few inches away, her back to me, when I heard her say something.

"Listen, I don't want no trouble," she said. "I've had more than enough from your friend lately."

"He's not my friend. I just met him outside. I wanted to see—to make sure you were fine," I said, wanting to qualify my remark with a *ma'am*.

Again, I was unsure if that was appropriate drag-queen etiquette but felt that it would be more respectful than *sir* or *miss*. I was moved closer to this majestic creature as a gaggle of party people nudged me aside to get to the dance floor, a gauntlet of strange hands straying on my ass and then gone.

"I am, and it's sweet of you to ask, hon," she said.

I could say she now without any hang-ups because up close and personal, you could tell she was all woman, even if that was partly true. She exuded the quiet grace, the elegance that I most associated with women and had seen through her dealings with Doug and the world at large.

There was something about her, something that can only be described as ubiquitous, like her soul had been freshly scrubbed with Mr. Clean. She was such a stark contrast to the stains of dark humanity I had been associating with.

"I'm Candy," she said, holding out her right hand with Lee press-ons limply, as if expecting it to be kissed.

I shook it awkwardly and took in the sight of her.

She certainly lived up to her name. Aside from the radiant pink wig, she had matching eye shadow and lipstick. Her blue dress was slit thigh high; parked around her right shoulder was what she called Das Purse, due to its enormity.

Anchoring her pink theme together was a pair of hot pink stilettos. Tina Turner had nothing on Candy. For starters, even under the plethora of makeup, I could tell she was fairly new to the bar scene herself but wore a weathered nonchalance about the experience. In my mind, that put her somewhere in the neighborhood of early twenties. I realized I was still staring and hadn't offered up my name to her yet.

"I'm Henry," I said, figuring it was fine to not present my hand as hers had just unclasped it nanoseconds prior.

"Well, that's certainly the name of a gentleman if ever I heard one." She smiled. There was nothing mocking in it; it was strictly organic. "Can I buy you a drink?"

"Sure, thanks. That would be great," I said in clipped reverence, coming off very William Shatner at that moment.

Had I been a more experienced bar patron or just less of a shell-shocked person, I would have offered her the drink. She had beat me to the punch, but that did not mean I couldn't reciprocate.

I would have to sneak away to the bathroom first and just take some money out of my makeshift wallet. The weight of my trusty Walkman kept threatening to pull my pants down, forcing me to give 'em a good hiking every few minutes. After viewing the goings-on here, I was sure that if I let them fall to the ground, I wouldn't have been the first guy with his pants around his ankles in here.

As we made our way through the crowded bar, I noticed I was making quite the impression. I was picking up a lot of stares, all directed first at my face then my pseudo crotch, and a new word was added to my gay vernacular.

"Goddamn size queens," she said, following the vicinity of their stares. "I'd say go on, boy, beat 'em off with a stick. That's all these jackals care about, gettin' some. Shit."

Her comment didn't come off as bitchy; rather it was endearing, protective. Perhaps Candy could see me for me, and I was glad to return the favor.

"What's your poison, doll?" she asked as we began the process of waiting in line.

Fortunately for us, the DJ had given a shout out to the pending marriage of Madonna to Sean Penn and then began spinning "Like a Virgin." Where there were once people waiting in line for drinks, now there weren't. That was the magic of putting Madonna on in a gay club; if you play her, they will dance.

"Uh," I stammered, assuming they didn't have pot for sale, and having only sampled beer, I wasn't sure how to answer, "whatever you are having."

"Two rums and Cokes it is then."

Two to three minutes of small talk followed as we waited to place the drink order, mostly surrounding music and our mutual love of all things Material Girl.

"I want to find out where her wedding is and see if she'd let me be a bridesmaid," Candy said wistfully; her voice took on a musical lilt, keeping perfect time with the backbeat.

We stepped up to the bar, and she ordered. I stood with my back to the bartender, still waiting for someone to end my charade, shattering my older gay farce with a battle cry of "We're on to you!"

I listened to the lyrics pouring out of the speakers, "I made it through the wilderness, somehow I made it through." I realized that I had wandered far from the wilderness of innocence, unsure if I could ever return to it again. I would never want something so badly; there was only disappointment waiting, disaster eminent. I scanned the room with a starting to tear eagle eye, a stranger in a strange land.

I was really amazed at the conglomerate of fellowship that surrounded me. People were jovial, gay even, and did not resemble the persecuted souls I had oft associated with being gay.

A good number of men would catch my eye, theirs roving up and down my body and then it was a beeline right for my crotch. I was really feeling self-conscious about this. I knew the night was fraught with party favors of every kind and couldn't fathom that any man, sober or not, would mistake my Walkman for my johnson.

Then again, some of them might be familiar with Danny's work.

And like that, it came out of left and right field, converging on my unsuspecting mind at the same time. A single thought, powerful in its entrance, dutiful in eliciting total surprise, subscribed to overstaying its welcome. Even if I shook my head for hours, in essence saying no repeatedly to the phantom thought, it was drilling into my cerebellum. I could physically feel it threatening to split my head, like so much casaba melon.

"Where's the bathroom?" I asked, abruptly cutting Candy's supposition on celebrity wedding crashing in two.

"Over there," she answered this with a look that said, "Lost another one."

She pointed and almost poked the returned-with-our-drinks-bartender in the eye with her Lee press-ons.

I rushed through the crowd, which is to say, molasses-like, given its volume. I made it to the bathroom; somehow I made it through that particular wilderness of men and was confronted with another line.

There was so much waiting in the gay world: waiting for the right time to come out, waiting to feel comfortable in gay skin, waiting, waiting, waiting! I tried the singsong route of distracting my brain from Danny, but the weight of all that had happened was starting to sink in further. I had spent years pining for Danny and what was it all for? Nothing but heartache, disappointment, devastation. I knew I was on the verge of crying, and I would not, could not give in.

Nor could I comprehend standing in line when I did not need to relieve myself; the only relief I had wanted was one not derived of sorrow. So I went against the mass of people seeking out the facilities, their faces blurring together, every one of them wearing a Danny mask; any one of them could be just like him.

I almost exited altogether, but one face caught my eye. Candy was delicately sipping her rum and Coke waiting for my return but more than likely not expecting that to happen.

I stood still for a moment, deciding what to do, until I knew what I had to. I relegated any further thought, discussion, mention of the one to be known as him to be banished. I was certain that willpower and the passing of time could see me through this endeavor.

I went back to where I had started, both in my mind with a fleeting sense of innocence regained and being in the presence of Candy. She had procured a small table, more like a tablette really. She was perched upon a black upholstered stool, the queen of all she surveyed.

"Hiya, toots, all better?" she asked with equal amounts of sass and motherly concern.

"Yes, much better actually." I reached for the concoction she held out for me, taking the tiniest sip through a black straw.

Well, I was better. Now, I wasn't so sure as the strong laced soft drink burned its way down my throat. I was sure I was going to cough it back up all over Candy's slinky blue dress. I managed a swallow, hard and fast, trying to put up airs that I was an old pro.

"So, hon, can I ask you something?" Candy looked at me dead-on.

All I could do was nod. I was choked up on the alcohol and of what Candy might ask of me. Surely my noticeable nonexpertise in downing a drink would lead her to ask me how old I was.

"Are you stuffing your drawers?" She leaned over, a co-conspirator in the fine art of deception.

I responded in laughter, not the mocking kind, but one that illustrated I was in on the joke. When I pulled the Walkman out of my front pocket, Candy did a spit take laudable of any comedienne worth her salt.

I stopped laughing long enough to take a bigger sip, then another, and another until my throat didn't burn and my senses were starting to deaden. Soon, I was just sucking air through the straw, which brought more guffaws out of Candy. I laughed too, albeit briefly, as a banished emotion tried to trespass, reclaim its territory.

My defenses were weakened by the alcohol, triggering melancholy immediately. I couldn't keep it from happening as assuredly as I couldn't reverse the tears that were now springing from my eyes.

One thought prevailed. Nothing will ever be the same, which was fueling the barrage of emotions in a public venue. Candy pulled a tissue out of her purse. There was something so motherly about her at that moment that I started crying harder.

"Oh, honey, what's the matter? Is it because of that shiner you got?" she asked.

And when she asked that, the tears stopped flowing as I put my emotions on hold.

"You really want to know?" I asked. "Can you get us a couple of drinks first? Please?"

"Sure, of course," she said, scurrying off to the bar and back in record time. She scooted herself onto the stool, moved it closer to me, like she wanted a better vantage point for some type of sporting event.

She sat leaning in for over a half an hour, only stopping long enough to sip her drink, as I detailed recent events. I couldn't tell from her face if she was enraptured, judgmental, bored, or what. Her face was a blank slate; occasionally, she nodded.

I pressed on with my story, feeling like I should be using cocktail napkins as scorecards to all of the dishonesty, liquid courage propelling me along in the pursuit of recanting. When I was finished, I took a deep breath. I was glad to say it out loud, to get it out of the hamster wheel of my mind, where it had been chasing itself in endless circles.

"Jesus," she remarked, "that's quite a story." I felt that she put too great an emphasis on the word *story*.

"I'm not making it up, you know," I said voice raised, immediately on the offense or the defense or whichever tact the alcohol flowing in my veins was taking as the night drained into a new day.

"Calm down, junior. Save the drama for *One Life to Live*, okay? I'm just trying to soak it all in."

"I feel like I have lost so much," I said, fighting back another bombardment of waterworks.

"Maybe you've gained some things too. Did you ever think of it that way, hon? You came out to your parents at sixteen." She practically whispered my true age, looking around as she did so. "You struck out on your own. No matter what the results are, that's an act of bravery."

"Thank God I only have to do that once, right?" I replied, taking in what she said. I had never thought of what I had done as being born of guts.

It always felt like a necessity, the thing that kept me at bay, to be uncovered and used against me.

"I wish. Oh, baby, oh fuck." She had gotten a case of the drunk-in-church giggles, guffawing into her hand. "I'm not laughing at you, really, I'm not."

These were the moments where the aura of feminine mystique vanished, and Candy might as well have been Chuck. But then she would compose herself, all chic once more.

"Coming out, well, it's an ongoing thing. The parents are a big one, and congrats on that, again. But there will always be opportunity to…inform people of who you really are." She smiled benignly, pleased with her analysis.

"That's my problem. I'm not sure who I am. I mean, I know for the most part. I guess what's tripping me up is…"

I made a wide circular movement with my hand to indicate "Within gay society" and ended up illustrating what happens when drinks are spilled at a bar. Even over the racket of a crowded, music-blaring environment, the bartender could hear the shattering of glass.

He immediately sent over a barback to see to the cleanup on aisle 5. I was more than slightly embarrassed until the barback winked and said, "Don't worry about it, hot stuff."

He was gone in the wink of an eye too but returned lickety split with two replacement drinks.

"Compliments of the house. Happy Pride."

And he was off again, in all of his Latino cuteness. But the message he was conveying couldn't have been louder. Even without a Mr. Microphone, I surmised that he was essentially saying, "Hey, good-looking, be back for you later."

"Close ya mouth, junior. You'll attract more than flies in this place doing that. That was nice of him, yes?" She looked piercingly into my eyes until I nodded. "Yes, it was. But you don't want to go home with him. Boys that work in bars get more action than a Sylvester Stallone movie."

"See, I don't know that. I don't know anything."

"Not with that attitude, you don't," Candy said with a sharp edge that softened with the next sentence. "Listen, I will help you as best I can. But a lot of this, it's up to you. Just consider me your fairy godmo—fairy god-slightly-older-sister."

And boom, it hit me! I was Pinocchio on a quest to become a real boy, and Candy was the blue fairy or maybe in this case a pink one. I was supposed to be here with her at this very time; it was fate. I was trying to steer clear of any thoughts on karma as I felt mine may be a bit off at the moment. In the black was more like it.

"God, I have so much to ask you. Ooh, I love this song!" I switched gears as Animotion's "Obsession" took hold of me with its infectious synthesized groove, and the alcohol-induced scattered focus ramped up.

Before when I had heard the song, I immediately equated it to sex. Now, I was finding new meaning in "I will have, I will have you, yes, I will find a way, and I will have you." It was a personal statement on acquiring the knowledge about what it meant to be a part of a community, my community. I refocused on Candy.

"Ask away," she said armed with a sincere grin.

If she had a booth with a sign that read Psychiatry 5¢, then she would have fulfilled the destiny of my long-ago nickname of Charlie Brown. He was always the outcast too, never fitting in. I wanted to aim higher than that, not receiving rocks in my trick-or-treat bag. I knew I had to ask concisely and listen precisely; otherwise, her answers would be as meaningless as one of Charlie Brown's teacher trumpet speak, "Wah wah wah wah."

"Okay, the big question I have is, if we are all in the same boat, why do we have to tear each other down?" I began. "What's being gay really all about? I only know what I have seen on TV and now what I have been through. I still don't get it."

"Honey, that's more than one question." She smiled demurely, sipped on the gratis drink.

Candy was silent for a moment, searching her mind for the answers, until she came up with more questions than I had asked her.

"And those are the million-dollar questions, aren't they? What's it all about? Why am I here? Who am I? Only you can answer a lot of those questions for yourself, and only time can provide most of the answers, hon. I do have one bit of advice though."

"What's that?" I asked, feeling severely deflated, increasingly buzzed, perpetually hopeless.

"Being gay, well, that should just be one part of your life. You are putting so much emphasis on it being your everything. It's just one piece of the pie." I saw her eyes scanning the room, looking for an example. "You see the rainbow flag? Right there on the wall! Little more to your left, hon. Bingo!"

She guided my head with her left hand until I had the flag in sight.

"Now, look at it, really look at it and tell me what you think of it," she instructed, more den mother than drill sergeant.

I studied the flag feeling like school was back in session, not understanding the assignment, unsure of what I was supposed to be seeing. I counted six different colors, red, orange, yellow, green, blue, and purple. I stared intently, looking for some hidden code sewn into the body of the flag.

All that kept jumping into my head was the first line of the "Rainbow Connection" by the incomparable Kermit the Frog, "Why are there so many songs about rainbows, and what's on the other side?" I studied the flag more intently, my growing buzz fueling nostalgic waxing of seeing *The Muppet Movie* with John as a child. "Someday we'll find it, the rainbow connection, the lovers, the dreamers, and me."

I thought more about the last line and how the first two elements equated the latter. That was it, that was all that my mind could figure out, and it was nothing.

"I'm not sure," I barely uttered, already feeling like a failure and not wanting to attract more attention to that fact.

"Don't worry, Auntie Candy will tell you." She paused, not as much for dramatic effect, but to replenish her fluids.

I was growing a tad resentful of being ill prepared for this pop quiz. I was almost at the decision to leave before she explained, to take my chances elsewhere. But where would that be? I hadn't looked beyond today, to the future, or any concept of it.

I suddenly envisioned Luke Skywalker training with Yoda in *The Empire Strikes Back* and Yoda's plea for Luke to be patient. Knowing that Luke could have veered off his path and been felled by the Dark Side, I decided to sit still and hear her out.

"Okay, I'm ready," I said, more to myself than to Candy.

"You will notice that the flag has six different colors. Each of those colors is unique in its own statement, while the flag as a whole represents the diversity of our community, hon. So if you really think about it, it takes more than one color to make up any one part of us. We are unified, yet we are different," she said.

I expected her to bow. If I would have come up with that analogy, I would have.

"Wow, you're wise, like Yoda," I said, feeling somewhat relieved and veering more towards drunk town.

"And you are cut off, love," she said, taking my glass that was half empty, or was it half full? She stowed it well out of sight behind Das Purse. "And I know you weren't calling me old. Yoda? Shit. Well, if there's nothin' else I can impart to you, it's this."

"What?" I leaned forward, waiting for some divine wisdom to be delivered upon me.

"It's never too soon to start moisturizing." She broke into a simultaneous laugh and smile.

Instead of feeling let down, I laughed too. I had a better picture within to sketch my existence, its borders more prominent, the pencil gripped hard in my hand and my hand alone. But there would always be those that could provide outlines for me to fill in.

"I don't suppose you feel like dancing?" she asked.

"As a matter of fact, I do." Her words of wisdom still resounding, the alcohol producing a separate, happy feeling, all equated happy feet; and happy feet, well, they needed to dance.

We made our way to the dance floor, me with my Walkman bulge and she with her cargo-holding purse. As soon as we joined the throng of revelers, the vocal thunder of Patti LaBelle shook the speakers. Then "New Attitude" melted into "Holiday" as the midnight hour drew nigh. I did the best I could to utilize my body in the confined dance zone, memories harkening back to Kelley and the days of disco.

Now, I was a pop boy dancing with a pink lady. I was surrounded by men making the most of the dark, some holding up little amber-colored bottles to their noses, the multicolored lights refracting off it, creating mini rainbows. It added to the surrealism inherent in seeing an oasis of men who weren't giving dancing together a second thought.

"What are those guys doing? What is that?" I whispered into Candy's ear, the synthetic texture of her wig catching my nose and tickling it.

"That would be poppers. They make you kind of high, then they give you a headache," she half yelled above the musical din. "Supposed to enhance the relations. But they ain't nothin' but a big waste of time."

Satisfied with that explanation, I resumed dancing, whooping along with the crowd when "You Spin Me Round" came bounding out of the speakers and onto the dance floor. The song was halfway over when Candy leaned hard against me, pressing one hand on me, the other one on her foot.

"Oww," Candy screeched. "Can we stop? These pumps were not made for dancin'. How Tina does it, I'll never know."

"Sure." I wasn't nearly done, but I didn't want to be rude. She didn't have to take the time to try to help me. Who was I to make her feet blister?

"Candy, I want to thank you so much," I said.

"Ain't nothin', Henry. I love me some dancing."

"No, thank you for talking to me." I was really fascinated by her duality, not only in her gender role, but in the way she spoke. "You are so smart, so, so smart."

"Thank you, sweets. And I think I need to take you out of here. You're a little tipped. I don't want you gettin' into any more trouble."

I didn't know if I really wanted to leave, but when it came to advice, Candy knew best. That's the funny thing about fast friendships: you learn a lot about the other person at a furious pace, leaving little room for doubt. I had no intention of being as trusting as I had before, but in a lot of respects, Candy was different. Then again, I was different too. I could feel it, like a long painful splinter had been removed from my brain.

We walked out into the night. I felt alive, glowing, practically radioactive.

"So, Henry, where are you going to go?"

"He's coming home with me," John said from behind us.

"John." The name hung there as my mouth followed suit.

"This is your brother. Oh good. I am glad you found him," Candy said, holding out her hand, ladylike. "I'm Candy."

"Hey," John said, I could see him trying to detect Candy's femininity. He shook her hand gently.

"I'm sorry I took off, John. Really, really sorry. And I'm sorry for you having to see me up here, for everything I put you through. You're probably mad at me, huh? I'd be pissed. So sorry. Sorry, sorry, sorry."

I meant to come off as heartfelt but ended up sounding like Otis, the town drunk of Mayberry.

"Dude, you're my brother. And I love you no matter what. I'm just glad you're okay, a little bit shitty, but okay," he said with relief pouring over his features and turned to Candy. "Thank you for looking out for him."

"It was my pleasure." She turned to me. "You're going to be all right, junior. I know you will be. I have faith in that. I have faith in you."

I didn't say anything. I didn't know how to respond to something as simple as human kindness. I let my body language dictate my appreciation as I gave her one of the biggest hugs I could muster. She responded in kind then slipped out from under the hug and walked off.

She turned back once, the streetlight catching her wig just so, and I swear I had never seen anything more beautiful.

"Come on, let's go home," John said.

All I could do was bob my head in affirmation. There was no place like home, no place like home. At least I would have a modicum of understanding from my brother. In time, the rest of the world would come around; in time, I would come around. We walked over to Danny's silent apartment complex. There was wasn't a sign of life to be found at his place—there never had been anyway, just a dead soul that was the stuff of legends now. I looked away from his darkened window, focusing on the Green Bomb parked at the curb. I was doubtful John would offer to let me drive, and I was fine with that. I was suddenly exhausted.

Heading south, heading home, heading towards uncertainty with a head full of rocks, I let sleep overtake me, waking up precisely as we turned onto Arroyo Street and parked in front of the house of secrets.

A single light shone in the living room window as we exited the vehicle, then the silhouette that drew back the curtains became my mother. She rushed away from the window, out the front door, down the four concrete stairs that I thought I would never walk up again. My mother embraced me as fiercely as I had embraced Candy some two hours and a lifetime ago.

"I was so worried about you," she said as we crossed the threshold, the three of us, a family. In his chambers, the king of this castle slumbered, helped along with his favorite sleep aid, Budweiser, blissfully unaware that the prodigal had returned.

I half expected everything to look different, smaller, unfamiliar. Nothing did yet everything did. Things have a way of seeming different on the outside, but it's what occurs on the inside that matters most; I knew I was forever changed by the events of the past few months.

I wouldn't exist today if it weren't for those plans that I made for myself, secretly plotting my great escape that I knew would bring with it greater changes. Although the road I had chosen was lined with glass shards, it was the ripping of my skin, causing me to bleed, that had unearthed what was hidden underneath, taking me closer to who I was supposed to be.

I was sad for the boy I used to be, hopeful for the man I might turn out to be. I believed Candy when she said time would shape these instances, molding me into the person I would become, separating me from who I once was.

But that's another story.

About the Author

Ever since the age of five, Tim Parks knew that writing was in his blood, and began writing short stories, one of which was published when he was 12 in a children's magazine.

Fast forward to now and Parks has amassed over 300 celebrity interviews, including Janet Jackson, Kylie Minogue, John Waters, Olivia Newton-John, Margaret Cho and Chelsea Handler to name a few. He relishes in the fact that he has gotten to thank the people who have populated his pop culture landscape over the years.

His 15 year freelance writer credits also include numerous other arts and entertainment pieces, including being a columnist that lampoons all things Hollywood. He has written for The Gay & Lesbian Times, The Rage Monthly and Gay San Diego in his hometown of San Diego; and has also contributed to reFRESH Magazine and the websites Digital Spy in the U.K. and afterelton, which is owned by MTV and Logo.

Even though his first novel, The Scheme of Things, is fiction; Parks likes to consider it a work of faction, as many of the events in the book are based on actual events in his life. He lives in San Diego, California and is currently working on the follow-up.